"An intricately plotted, compulsively readable novel that explores not only fascinating crimes, but also the mysteries of anxiety, the creative process, contemporary fame, and so much else." —John Green, author of *The Fault in Our Stars* and *Turtles All the Way Down*

"Maureen Johnson has a totally original mind, a passionate set of moral convictions, an extraordinary sense of bravery and ridiculousness, and she writes pretty sentences. Read whatever she writes." —E. Lockhart, author of *We Were Liars* and *Genuine Fraud*

"This read is perfect for those who enjoy twisty, turny plots and a high-stakes mystery." —Buzzfeed

"So much to love in this book! The dueling mysteries, present and past. The incredible mansion/school setting. The smart, diverse, and quirky characters. This mystery had us fooled at every turn! And the best news? It's the first in a series." —*Justine* magazine

Truly
DEVIOUS

MAUREEN JOHNSON

KATHERINE TEGEN BOOKS
An Imprint of HarperCollins Publishers

Katherine Tegen Books is an imprint of HarperCollins Publishers.

Truly Devious
Copyright © 2018 by HarperCollins Publishers
All rights reserved. Printed in the United States of America.
No part of this book may be used or reproduced in any manner whatsoever without written permission except in the case of brief quotations embodied in critical
articles and reviews. For information address HarperCollins Children's Books, a
division of HarperCollins Publishers, 195 Broadway, New York, NY 10007.
www.epicreads.com

Library of Congress Control Number: 2017951264
ISBN 978-0-06-233806-8

Typography by Carla Weise
18 19 20 21 22   PC/LSCH   10 9 8 7 6 5 4 3 2 1
❖
First paperback edition, 2018

For anyone who has ever dreamed
of finding a body in the library

ELLINGHAM ACADEMY

FOUNDED 1935

1. WORKSHOP
2. ASTERIA
3. GENIUS
4. ARTEMIS
5. APOLLO
6. DIONYSUS
7. DEMETER

8. GREAT HOUSE
9. MINERVA
10. EUNOMIA
11. CYBELE
12. JUPITER
13. VESTA
14. JUNO

NORTH

CATS KNOW BEST

FEDERAL BUREAU OF INVESTIGATION
Photographic image of letter received at the Ellingham
residence on April 8, 1936.

Look! a Riddle!
TiME FoR FUN!

ShoULd WE uSE
a RoPE oR GUN?

KNiVEs aRE shaRp
aNd GLEAM so pREtTY

PoisoN's sLoW,
Which is a piTY

FiRE is fEStiVE,
dRoWNiNG's sLoW

HaNGiNG's a
RoPY WAY To Go

a bRoKEN hEAd,
a NasTY FaLL

A CAR COLLIDING
WITH A WALL

BOMBS MAKE A
VERY JOLLY NOISE

SUCH WAYS TO
PUNISH NAUGHTY BOYS!

WHAT SHALL WE USE?
WE CAN'T DECIDE.

JUST LIKE YOU CANNOT
RUN OR HIDE.

HA HA.

TRULY,
DEVIOUS

April 13, 1936, 6:00 p.m.
You know I can't let you leave. . . .

FATE CAME FOR DOTTIE EPSTEIN A YEAR EARLIER, IN THE FORM OF A call to the principal's office.

It was not her first time there.

Dolores Epstein wasn't sent for any of the normal reasons—fighting, cheating, failing, absence. Dottie would get called down for more complicated matters: designing her own chemistry experiments, questioning her teacher's understanding of non-euclidian geometry, or reading books in class because there was nothing new to be learned, so the time might as well be spent doing something useful.

"Dolores," the principal would say. "You can't go around acting like you're smarter than everyone else."

"But I am," she would reply. Not out of arrogance, but because it was true.

This time, Dottie wasn't sure what she had done. She had broken into the library to look for a book, but she was pretty sure no one knew about that. Dottie had been in every corner of this school, had worked out every lock and peered in all the cupboards and closets and nooks. There was no

1

t. It was usually to find something or just to
be done.

e reached the office, Mr. Phillips, the princi-
ng at his massive desk. There was someone else
ell—a man with salt-and-pepper hair and a marvelous gray suit. He sat off to the side, bathed in a striped
beam of sunlight from the window blinds. He was just like
someone from the movies. He actually *was* someone from
the movies, in a way.

"Dolores," Mr. Phillips said. "This is Mr. Albert Ellingham. Do you know who Mr. Ellingham is?"

Of course she did. Everyone did. Albert Ellingham
owned American Steel, the *New York Evening Star*, and Fan-
tastic Pictures. He was rich beyond measure. He was the
kind of person you might imagine would actually *be on money*.

"Mr. Ellingham has something wonderful to tell you.
You are a very lucky girl."

"Come sit down, Dolores," Mr. Ellingham said, using an
open hand to indicate the empty chair in front of Mr. Phillips's desk.

Dottie sat, and the famous Mr. Ellingham leaned forward, resting his elbows on his knees and bringing his large,
suntanned hands together in a knot. Dottie had never seen
anyone with a suntan in March before. This, more than anything, was the most powerful sign of Mr. Ellingham's wealth.
He could have the sun itself.

"I've heard a lot about you, Dolores," he said. "Mr.

Phillips has told me how very bright you are. Fourteen years old and in eleventh grade. You've taught yourself Latin and Greek? I understand you do translations?"

Dottie nodded shyly.

"Do you sometimes get bored here in school?" he asked.

Dottie looked at the principal nervously, but he smiled and nodded encouragement.

"Sometimes," Dottie said. "But it's not the school's fault."

Both men chuckled at this, and Dottie relaxed a little. Not much, but a little.

"I've started a school, Dolores," Mr. Ellingham went on. "A new school where special people like you can learn at their own pace, in their own way, in whatever manner suits them. I believe learning is a game, a wonderful game."

Mr. Phillips looked down at his desk blotter for a moment. Most principals probably didn't think of learning as a game, but no one would contradict the great Albert Ellingham. If he said learning was a game, it was a game. If he'd said learning was a roller-skating elephant in a green dress, they would go along with that too. When you have enough power and money, you can dictate the meanings of words.

"I've chosen thirty students from a variety of backgrounds to join the school, and I'd like you to be one of them," Mr. Ellingham went on. "You'll have no restrictions to your learning and access to whatever you need. Wouldn't you like that?"

Dottie liked that idea very much. But she saw an immediate and inescapable problem.

"My parents don't have any money," she said plainly.

"Money should never stand in the way of learning," Mr. Ellingham said kindly. "My school is free. You are there as my guest, if you'll accept."

It sounded too good to be real—but it was true. Albert Ellingham sent her a train ticket and fifty dollars in pocket money. A few months later, Dottie Epstein, who had never been out of New York her entire life, was on her way to the mountains of Vermont and surrounded by more trees than she had ever seen.

The school had a grand fountain that reminded her of the one in Central Park. The brick and stone buildings were like something from a story. Her room in Minerva House was large but cozy, with a fireplace (it was *cold* up here). There were books, so many fine books, and you could take out as many as you liked and read whatever you wanted, with no library fines. The teachers were kind. They had a proper science lab. They learned botany in the greenhouse. They learned dance from a woman named Madame Scottie, who ran around in a leotard and scarves and had giant bangles up and down her arms.

Mr. Ellingham lived on the campus with his wife, Iris, and his three-year-old daughter, Alice. Sometimes, fancy cars came up the drive on weekends and people in marvelous clothes stepped out. Dottie recognized at least two movie stars, a politician, and a famous singer. On those weekends, bands came in from Burlington and New York and music came out of the Great House until all hours of the night. Sometimes Mr. Ellingham's guests would walk the grounds, the beads on their dresses winking in the moonlight. Even in New York, Dottie had never been so close to celebrity.

The staff was careful to tidy up, but the grounds were vast and full of hiding places, so they left traces everywhere. A champagne glass here, a satin shoe there. Endless crushed cigarettes, feathers, beads, and other detritus of the rich and wonderful. Dottie liked to collect these strange things she found and keep them in what she called her museum. The best thing Dottie found was a silver lighter. She flicked it on and off and was pleased by its smooth motion. She was definitely going to turn the lighter in—she just wanted to hold on to it for a while.

Since Ellingham gave its students freedom to work and study and wander, Dottie spent a lot of her time on her own. Vermont was a different sort of place—this wasn't like climbing down fire escapes or up water pipes. Dottie acclimated herself to the woods, to poking around the edges of the campus. That's how she found the tunnel on one of her first outings after she arrived at Ellingham in the fall. She was exploring the woods. Dottie had never experienced anything like this thick canopy of leaves and this deep quiet except for the occasional rustling noise. Then she heard something familiar—the sound of something thin and metal underfoot. She knew the drumlike sound immediately. It sounded exactly like the sound a sidewalk hatch made when you stepped on it.

Dottie opened the hatch and saw a set of clean concrete steps leading down into the ground. She found herself in a dark brick tunnel, one that was dry and well maintained. Her curiosity was piqued. She used the silver lighter to guide her down to a thick door with a sliding panel at eye level. She knew this sort of thing at once—they were all over the city. It was a speakeasy door.

The door was unlocked. Nothing about this tunnel seemed very secure; it was just there to be explored. So she explored. The door opened to a room about eight foot square, with a high ceiling. The walls were covered in shelving and those shelves were full of bottles of wine and liquor of every description. Dottie examined the ornate labels on the colored glass, labels in French, German, Russian, Spanish, Greek . . . an entire library of alcohol.

There was a ladder built into one wall. Dottie climbed it and opened the hatch at the top. She found herself inside a small domed structure with a glass roof. The floor was covered in fur rugs and cushions, several ashtrays, and a few errant champagne glasses. She stood on the bench seating that ran around the rim of the room and realized she was on a small island in the middle of the ornamental lake behind the Ellingham Great House.

A secret nook! The most perfect secret nook in all the world. This would be her reading spot, she decided. Dottie Epstein spent a lot of her time there, curled up in a fur rug, a pile of books by her side. No one had ever caught her there, and she felt sure that even if Mr. Ellingham did, he wouldn't mind. He was such a kind man and so full of fun.

Nothing could be safer.

That particular April day was strange and foggy, blurring spaces between the trees and blanketing all of Ellingham in a milky mist. Dottie decided that the weather lent itself to a mystery. Sherlock Holmes would be perfect. She'd read every Sherlock Holmes story, but rereading was one of her greatest pleasures, and this fog was just like the London fog in the stories.

She had learned which times were best to go to the little dome. It was a Monday afternoon—no one from the big house would be there. Mr. Ellingham had driven off that morning, and Mrs. Ellingham in the afternoon. Dottie took the collection of Sherlock Holmes stories from the school library and set out for her secret place.

The view from inside the little glass dome that day was like being inside of a cloud. Dottie stretched out on the floor, pulled the fur rug over her, and opened the book. Soon she was lost on the streets of London—the game was afoot!

Dottie got so lost in her reading that she was taken unawares by a noise directly below her. Someone was in the liquor room and was climbing up the stairs. Someone was *right there*. With no time to get away, Dottie pulled the heavy fur rug over herself and pressed herself as far against the wall as possible and tried to mix in with a pile of cushions. Just stay on the floor. Be a lump.

She heard the groan of the hatch being lifted, the *thunk* as it fell back against the stone. The person hoisted themselves into the dome and stood just a foot or so away from Dottie's face. She prayed they didn't step on her. She pulled herself in tighter.

The person moved away from her and set something down on the floor. Dottie took a chance and lifted the edge of the rug by just an inch and saw a gloved hand pulling items from a sack and setting them on the floor. She chanced another inch to get a better look. There was a flashlight, binoculars, a length of rope, and something that glinted.

The glinting thing was handcuffs, sort of like the ones her uncle the police officer had.

A flashlight, binoculars, rope, and handcuffs?

A flush of adrenaline ran through her body, skyrocketing her heart rate. Something was wrong here. She let the rug drop over her face and hunkered down tight, her face pressed into the floor, flattening the bridge of her nose. The person shuffled around the space for several minutes. Then, there was a sudden quiet. Had they gone? She would have heard someone leave down the hatch by her head.

Her breath came back hot against her face. She had no idea what was happening, but it made her head light. She began to count in her head. When she reached five hundred and there was still no noise, she made the decision to slowly lift the edge of the rug again. Just a finger width. Just a touch more.

No one was there in her line of sight. She inched it up a bit more. Nothing. She was about to lift it when . . .

"Hello," said a voice.

Dottie felt her heart pressing into the floor.

"Don't be afraid," the voice said. "You can come out."

There was no point in hiding now. Dottie crawled out from under the blanket, clutching her book. She looked at the visitor, and then at the objects on the floor.

"Those are for the game," the person said.

Game? Of course. The Ellinghams loved games. They were always playing them with guests—elaborate treasure hunts and puzzles. Mr. Ellingham had filled the student houses with board games like Monopoly and sometimes he even came down to play. Flashlight. Rope. Binoculars. Handcuffs. It could be a game. Monopoly had strange pieces too.

"What kind of game?" Dottie said.

"It's very complicated," the person said. "But it's going to be a lot of fun. I have to hide. You were hiding in here too?"

"To read," Dottie said. She held up the book and tried to keep her hands from shaking.

"Sherlock Holmes?" said the person. "I love Sherlock Holmes. Which story are you reading?"

"*A Study in Scarlet.*"

"That's a good one. Go ahead. Read. Don't let me stop you."

The visitor got out a cigarette and lit it, then smoked it while watching her.

Dottie had seen this person before. This was someone

who might very well have been playing one of the Ellinghams' elaborate games. But Dottie was also a New York girl who had seen enough to know when something was off. The look in the eye. The tone in the voice. Her uncle the cop always said to her, "Trust your instincts, Dottie. If you have a bad feeling about something or someone, you get out of there. You go and you get me."

Dottie's instincts told her to get out. But carefully. Act normal. She opened her book and tried to focus on the words in front of her. She always kept a bit of pencil up her sleeve for taking notes. When the visitor looked away and out the glass, she pushed the pencil down and into her palm, a move she had perfected over time, and roughly drew a line under a sentence on the page. It wasn't much, but it was a way of making a note that maybe someone would understand if . . .

No one would understand, and *if* was too terrifying to think of.

She shoved the pencil back into her sleeve. She couldn't pretend to read anymore. Her eyes couldn't track the words. Everything in her shook.

"I need to get this back to the library," she said. "I won't tell anyone you're here. I hate it when people tell on me."

The person smiled at her, but it was a strange smile. Not sincere. Pulled too far at the corners of the mouth.

Dottie became acutely aware that she was in a structure in the middle of a lake, halfway up a mountain. She ran all possible scenarios in her head and could see how the next few seconds were going to play out. Her heart slowed and the sound of its beating thudded in her head. Time was going very slowly. She had read many stories in which death was present as a character—a palpable force in the room. There was such a force in the room now, a silent visitor in the space.

"I have to go," she said, her voice thick. She started to move toward the hatch, and the person moved that way as well. They were like players on a chessboard, working things out to an inevitable end.

"You know I can't let you leave," the person said. "I wish I could."

"You can," Dottie said. "I'm good at keeping secrets." She clutched her Sherlock Holmes. Nothing bad could happen when she was holding Sherlock Holmes. Sherlock would save her.

"Please," she said.

"I'm so sorry," the visitor said with what sounded like genuine sadness.

There was exactly one move left in the game, and Dottie knew it was a bad one. But when you have no spaces left on the board you do what you have to do. She lunged for the hatch opening. There was no time to try to get onto the ladder—she dropped the book and leaped into the dark hole. She reached out blindly. Her fingers slipped along the rungs of the ladder but she couldn't get purchase. She was falling. The floor met her with a terrible finality.

She had a pulsing moment of consciousness when she landed. There was an ache that was almost sweet and something warm pooled around her. The person was coming down the ladder. She tried to move, to slide along the floor, but there was no use.

"I wish you hadn't come here," the visitor said. "I really do."

When the darkness came for Dottie, it was quick and it was total.

EXCERPT FROM *MURDERS ON THE MOUNTAIN: THE ELLINGHAM AFFAIR*

Ellingham Academy was located halfway up a mountain officially named Mount Morgan. No one called it Mount Morgan, though. It was always known locally as Mount Hatchet or "the Big Ax" because of the protuberance at the peak, which resembled the tools of the same names.

Unlike the mountains around it, which attracted skiers and vacationers, Mount Hatchet was largely undeveloped and wooded. Hikers liked it, and so did loners and bird-watchers and people who enjoyed mountain streams and getting lost in the woods. In 1928, when Albert Ellingham came upon it, people avoided the Big Ax. No roads, no matter how rough, went that way. The woods were too thick, the river too deep. There were too many falling rocks. It was too wild and strange.

According to the legend, Albert Ellingham had come to the place purely by mistake while trying to get to Burlington to the yacht club. How you accidentally found yourself up the side of an uninhabited mountain in 1928 is unclear, but he had done it, and proclaimed the spot perfect. He had long had a dream of establishing a school that employed his own principles and ideals—learning as a game, a blend of rich and poor students, everyone learning together at their own pace. The air here was clean, the birdsong pure. There was nothing to distract students from their purpose.

Ellingham purchased a massive plot at three times the asking price. It took a few years to dynamite enough flat space to build the school. Rough roads were cut. The telephone company ran wires and put in a few pay phones along the way. Slowly but surely, Mount Hatchet was connected to the world by a dirt track and a few wires and a stream of people and supplies.

Ellingham Academy, as it would be known, was not just going to be a school—the Ellinghams also built a home there, smack in the heart of the campus. And it wasn't just any home either. It was the grandest home in all of Vermont, as large as the largest buildings in Burlington or Montpelier.

Albert Ellingham wanted to live in his experiment, in his seat of learning. The grounds were full of statuary. The property was crisscrossed with pathways that made no real sense. The rumor was that Ellingham followed one of his cats and had a stone path made along any route it preferred to take because he felt "cats know best." The rumor wasn't true, but Ellingham enjoyed it so much that there was another rumor that he started the first rumor himself.

Then there were the tunnels, the fake windows, the doors to nowhere . . . all the little architectural jokes that amused Albert Ellingham to no end and made his parties infamously entertaining. It was said that even he didn't know the location of every tunnel or space, and that he had allowed the various architects to put a few in as pleasant surprises. It was, in short, idyllic and fantastical, and may have remained as such had it not been for that foggy night in April 1936 when Truly Devious struck.

Schools may be famous for many things: academics, graduates, sports teams.

They are not supposed to be famous for murders.

1

"THE MOOSE IS A LIE," STEVIE BELL SAID.

Her mother turned to her, looking like she often looked—a bit tired, forced to engage in whatever Stevie was about to say out of parental obligation.

"What?" she said.

Stevie pointed out the window of the coach.

"See that?" Stevie indicated a sign that simply read MOOSE. "We've passed five of those. That's a lot of promises. Not one moose."

"Stevie . . ."

"They also promised falling rocks. Where are my falling rocks?"

"Stevie . . ."

"I'm a strong believer in truth in advertising," Stevie said.

This resulted in a long pause. Stevie and her parents had had many conversations about the nature of truth and fact, and this might, on another day, have erupted into an argument. Not today. They seemed to decide, through some

15

mutual and unspoken agreement, that they would let the matter slide along.

It wasn't every day you moved away from home to go to boarding school, after all.

"I don't like that we're not allowed to drive up to the campus," her father said, for what was probably the eighth time that morning. Ellingham's information packet had been very clear on this point: DO NOT ATTEMPT TO DRIVE STUDENTS TO THE SCHOOL. YOU WILL BE FORCED TO LEAVE THEM AT THE ROADSIDE GATE. NO EXCEPTIONS WILL BE MADE.

There was nothing nefarious in this—the reason was well explained. The campus had not been designed for lots of cars. There was only a single road in, and there was no place to park. To get in or out, you rode in the Ellingham coach. Her parents had viewed this dimly, as if a place hard to reach by car was somehow inherently suspicious and impinged on their God-given American freedom to drive anywhere they wanted to.

Rules were rules, though, so the Bells were seated in this coach—a quality one with a dozen seats, tinted windows, and a video screen that did nothing but faintly mirror the window reflection back again. An older, silver-haired man was at the wheel. He had not spoken since he had picked them up at the rest stop fifteen minutes before, and even then all he said was, "Stephanie Bell?" and "Sit where you want. No one else in there." Stevie had heard about this famous Vermont reticence, and that they called outsiders flatlanders, but there was something spooky about his silence.

"Look," her mom said quietly, "if you change your mind . . ."

Stevie gripped the side of her seat. "I'm not going to change my mind. We're here. Almost."

"I'm just saying . . ." her mother said, and then she stopped saying it. This was another well-trod conversation. The morning was full of greatest hits and little new material.

Stevie looked back out as the view of the mystically blue Vermont skyline disappeared, eaten by the trees and the walls of sheer rock where the road cut through the mountains. Her ears popped from the slow increase in altitude as they drove along I-89, away from Burlington, Vermont, and deeper into the wild. Sensing that the conversation had come to its natural end, she put in her earbuds. Her mom touched her arm as she went to hit play on her podcast.

"Maybe this isn't the time to be listening to those creepy murder stories," she said.

"True crime," Stevie replied before she could stop herself. Making the correction made her sound pedantic. Also, no fighting. No fighting.

Stevie pulled out the earbud jack and coiled the cord.

"Have you heard from your friend?" her mom said. "Jazelle?"

"Janelle," Stevie corrected her. "She texted and said she was on her way to the airport."

"That's good," her mom said. "It will be good for you to have some friends."

17

Be nice, Stevie. Don't say you already have friends. You have lots of friends. It doesn't matter that a lot of them are people you know online from murder-mystery boards. Her parents had no idea that you could meet people outside of school and it wasn't freaky and the internet was the way of finding your people. And, of course, she had friends at school too, but never in the way she was supposed to, which apparently involved pajama parties and makeup and going to the mall.

That didn't matter now. The future was here, up in the misty mountains.

"So Janelle is interested in what again?" her mother asked.

"Engineering," Stevie said. "She makes things. Machines, devices."

A skeptical silence followed.

"And that Nate boy is a writer?" her mother said.

"The Nate boy is a writer," Stevie confirmed.

These were the two other first years known to live in Stevie's new dorm. They didn't tell you about the second years. Again, this was information that had circulated around the Bell kitchen table for weeks—Janelle Franklin was from Chicago. She was a National Student Spokesperson for GROWING STEMS, a program that encouraged young girls of color to enter the fields of science, technology, engineering, and mathematics. Stevie had gotten a lot of background: how Janelle had been caught (successfully) repairing the toaster oven when she was six years old. Stevie knew all of Janelle's likes: making machines and gadgets, soldering and welding, curating her Pinterest boards of organizational techniques, girls with glasses, YA novels, coffee, cats, and pretty much any television show.

Stevie and Janelle were already in regular text communication. So that was good. Friend one.

The other first year in Minerva was Nate Fisher. Nate said less and never replied to texts, but there was more to know about him. Nate published a book called *The Moonbright Cycles* when he was fourteen—seven hundred pages of epic fantasy written over the course of a few months, first published online and then in book form. Moonbright book two was supposedly in the works.

They were the kind of people Ellingham Academy accepted.

"They sound like very impressive people," her dad said. "And you are too. We're proud. You know that."

Stevie read the code in this sentence. *Much as we love you, we have no idea why you have been accepted into this school, strange child of ours.*

The entire summer had been like this, this weird mix of voiced pride and unvoiced doubt, underpinned by confusion about how this series of events had happened at all. When she had first done it, Stevie's parents didn't know she had applied to Ellingham at all. Ellingham Academy wasn't the kind of place people like the Bells went to. For almost a century, the school had been home to creative geniuses, radical thinkers, and innovators. Ellingham had no application, no list of requirements, no instructions other than, "If you would like to be considered for Ellingham Academy, please get in touch."

That was it.

One simple sentence that drove every high-flying student frantic. What did they want? What were they looking for? This was like a riddle from a fantasy story or fairy tale—something the wizard makes you do before you are allowed into the Cave of Secrets. Applications were supposed to be rigid lists of requirements and test scores and essays and recommendations and maybe a blood sample and a few bars from a popular musical. Not Ellingham. Just knock on the door. Just knock on the door in the special, correct way they would not describe. You just had to get in touch with *something*. They looked for a spark. If they saw such a spark in you, you could be one of the fifty students they took each year. The program was only two years long, just the junior and senior years of high school. There were no tuition fees. If you got in, it was free. You just had to get in.

The coach veered into the exit lane and pulled into another rest stop, where one other family stood in wait. A girl and her parents studied their phones. The girl was extremely petite, with dark, long hair.

"She has nice hair," Stevie's mom said.

Though she was talking about someone else, this was a reference to Stevie's hair, which Stevie had cut off herself in the bathroom in the early spring in a burst of self-renewal. Her mother had cried when she saw Stevie's blond hair in the sink and had taken her to a hairdresser to get it trimmed and shaped. The hair had been a major point of contention, so much so that at one point her parents said she would not be allowed to go to Ellingham as a punishment—but they backed down in the end. The threat had been made in high emotion. Her mother had been very attached to Stevie's hair, which on some level was why it had to go. Mostly, though, Stevie just thought that it would look better short.

It did. The pixie cut suited her, and it was easy to care for. There were problems when she dyed it pink, and blue, and pink and blue. But now it was back to normal, dusty blond and short.

The girl's bags were loaded into the bottom of the coach, and she and her family got in. The three of them were all dark haired and studious-looking, with large eyes framed by glasses. They looked like a family of owls. Polite, mumbled hellos were exchanged, and the girl and her family took their seats behind the Bells. Stevie recognized the girl from the first-year guide, but didn't remember her name.

Her mom gave her a nudge, which Stevie tried to ignore. The girl was again looking at her phone.

"Stevie."

Stevie took a long breath through her nose. This was going to require leaning over her mom and calling out to the girl, who was a row behind on the opposite side. Awkward. But she was going to have to do it.

"Hey," Stevie said.

The girl looked up.

"Hey?" she said.

"I'm Stevie Bell."

The girl blinked slowly, logging this information.

"Germaine Batt," she said.

Nothing else was offered. Stevie started to lean back, feeling like this had been a good effort all around, but her mom nudged her again.

"Make friends," she whispered.

Few words are more chilling when put together than *make friends*. The command to pair bond sent ice water through Stevie's veins. She wanted falling rocks. But she knew what would happen if she didn't do the talking—her parents would. And if her parents started, anything could happen.

"Did you come far?" Stevie asked.

"No," Germaine said, looking up from her phone.

"We came from Pittsburgh."

"Oh," Germaine said.

Stevie leaned back, looked at her mom, and shrugged. She couldn't *make* Germaine talk. Her mom gave her a *well, you tried* look. Points for effort.

The coach juddered as it turned off the highway, onto a rockier, smaller road dotted with stores and farms and signs for skiing, glassblowing, and maple syrup candy. Then there were fewer buildings and more stretches of farmland with nothing but old red trucks and the occasional horse.

Up and up into the woods.

Out of nowhere, the coach made a sharp turn into an opening in the trees, jerking Stevie to the side and almost tipping her out of her seat. Close to the ground, there was a small maroon sign with gold letters: the Ellingham Academy entrance. It was so inconspicuous that it seemed like the school was deliberately hiding.

The road they were now on was barely a road. It would be charitable to call it a path. What it was, in reality, was an artificial tear in the landscape—a meandering scar in the forest. At first, it went down, very fast, pitching toward one of the streams that bounded the property. At the base, there was a construction that you could laughingly refer to as a bridge that appeared to be made of wood, rope, and dreams. The sides were about a foot high and it looked like it would collapse if anything heavier than a steak dinner crossed it.

The coach barreled over it. The bridge shook violently, rumbling Stevie's seat.

Then they went up again, at a gradient usually reserved for ski lifts and airplane takeoffs. Nothing would stop the coach. The shade from the trees darkened the path completely. The branches scratched at the sides of the vehicle like dozens of fingernails. The coach made grinding noises and seemed to be fighting its way up the ever-narrowing path. Stevie knew there was nothing to be afraid of, but the coach seemed to be working against the forces of the universe itself to make its way up this driveway. It was unlikely that this would be the trip, this one with her and her parents, that the coach would give way and barrel backward the way it had come, running loose and wild, crashing blindly toward the river and sweet, cold, watery oblivion . . . but you never knew.

The ground started to level and trees gave way to a smoother path and an opening view of green lawns. The coach approached a gate guarded by two statues on pedestals, winged creatures with smiling faces and empty eyes, four paws, and tails.

"Those are strange angels," her mother said, craning to look.

"They're not angels," Stevie said. "They're sphinxes. They're mythical creatures that ask you riddles before you're allowed to enter a place. If you get it wrong, they eat you. Like from *Oedipus*. The Riddle of the Sphinx. That's a sphinx. Not to be confused with Spanx, which is a sidearm in the holster of the diet-industrial complex."

Her mother gave her that look again. *We kind of wanted the going-out, shopping, prom-going type, and we got this weird, creepy one, and we love it but what is it talking about, ever?*

Sometimes Stevie felt bad for her parents. Their idea of what constituted *interesting* was so limited. They were never going to have as much fun as she did.

Germaine peered over at Stevie with large, luminous eyes. Her expression was as unreadable as the sphinxes'.

In that moment, a blanket of doubt dropped over everything in Stevie's mind. She should not have been admitted. The letter came to the wrong house, the wrong Stevie. It was a trick, a joke, a cosmic mistake. None of this could be real.

But it was too late, even if all of those things were true, because they had arrived at Ellingham Academy.

2

THE FIRST THING STEVIE SAW WAS THE CIRCULAR GREEN WITH A FOUNtain in the middle, a statue of Neptune standing in greeting in the splashing water. A thick curtain of trees surrounded the green. Bits of buildings, flashes of brick and stone and glass peeped shyly in the gaps. At the very top of the green, the host of the whole affair, was a great mansion—the Great House, a mad Gothic manor, with dozens of cathedral windows, four arches around the door, and a multipeaked roof.

Stevie was rendered near speechless for a minute. She had seen hundreds of photographs of the Ellingham estate. She knew the maps and the angles and views. But being here in the fresh, thin air, hearing the splash from the Neptune fountain, feeling the sun on her face as she stood on the great lawn—being here gave her a head rush.

The driver unloaded Stevie's suitcases from the belly of the coach, along with the three bags of groceries her parents had insisted she bring. They were embarrassingly heavy, packed with jumbo plastic containers of peanut butter, powdered iced tea, and lots of shower gel and sanitary products and other things bought on sale.

"Are we supposed to tip him?" her mother said quietly, as all of this was unloaded from the coach.

"No," Stevie said, forcing confidence into her voice. She had no idea if you tipped the school coach driver or not. This had not come up in her research.

"You okay?" her dad asked.

"Yep," she said, steadying herself against her suitcase. "It's just . . . so beautiful."

"It's something," he said. "No denying that."

A large golf cart circled the drive and pulled up alongside them. Another man greeted them. He was younger than the driver, in his thirties maybe, rugged and muscular and dressed in well-worn cargo shorts and an Ellingham polo shirt. He was the kind of clean-cut person who made her parents relax, and therefore, Stevie relaxed.

"Stephanie Bell?" he asked.

"Stevie," she corrected him.

"I'm Mark Parsons," he said. "Head of grounds. You got Minerva. Nice house."

Stevie's things and the Bells themselves were loaded into the cart. Germaine and her family were put in another and sent off in the opposite direction.

"Everyone wants Minerva," Mark added when they were out of earshot. "It's the best house."

The property was full of smooth, twisting stone paths between copses of trees. They rode along under the heavy shade, and Stevie and her parents were cowed into impressed silence by the school buildings. There were some large, grand ones of stone and red brick, with Gothic arches connecting them and tiny turrets softening their corners. Some were bare and grand, while others were wrapped so tightly in ivy it looked like they were being presented as gifts to some forest god. This wasn't her local high school. This was clearly a Seat of Learning.

There were Greek and Roman statues of cold, white stone behind the trees, standing alone in the clearings.

"Someone's been to the garden center," her dad said.

"Oh, no," Mark replied, steering the cart past a chorus of heads, their eyes blank and empty but their expressions determined, looking very much like some committee in the middle of an important decision. "These are all the real thing. A fortune's worth of statues out in the open."

There were, to be fair, maybe too many statues. Someone should have had a talk with Albert Ellingham and told him to maybe relax with the statue buying. But if you're rich enough and famous enough, Stevie figured, you can do pretty much anything you want with your mountaintop lair.

The golf cart stopped in front of a low, dignified house built in alternating red and gold brick. It seemed to be in several parts—there was a large section on the right that looked like a normal house, then a long extension off to the side that ended in a turret. The entire structure was covered in a coat of Virginia creeper that obscured the bas-relief faces that peered from the roofline and from above the windows. The door was bright blue and hanging open, letting in the breeze and the flies.

Stevie and her parents stepped into what appeared to be some kind of common room, with a stone floor and a wide fireplace surrounded by rocking chairs. The room was cool and shaded and still smelled of wood and past fires. It was decorated in a slightly claustrophobic red flocked wallpaper and a mounted moose head that wore a crown of decorative lights. There was a hammock chair hanging by the fire, lots of floor cushions, a beat-up but exceedingly comfortable-looking purple sofa, and a massive farm table that took up most of the room. On the farm table was a tackle box and some small items that looked like craft supplies—beads, or the many mysterious things involved in the scrapbooking process. Right by the door, eight large pegs protruded from the wall. These were maybe nine or ten inches long—far too large for coats. Stevie touched one with the tip of her finger as a physical manifestation of the question: *What are you?*

"Hello!"

Stevie turned to see a woman coming out of the small kitchen area with a mug of coffee. She had a shaved head with just the smallest amount of peach fuzz and a petite but deeply muscled and tanned frame. Her arms were elegantly tattooed in sleeves of flowers. She was dressed in a loose T-shirt that read I DIG DIGS and cargo shorts, which showed off a pair of strong, hairy legs.

"Stephanie?" the woman asked.

"Stevie," she corrected again.

"Dr. Nell Pixwell," the woman said, extending a hand to each member of the family. "Call me Pix. I'm the Minerva faculty housemaster."

Stevie chanced a better look at the tiny objects by the tackle box. On closer examination, Stevie realized that these weren't crafting supplies—they were teeth. Lots and lots of loose teeth. Here. On the table. Whether they were real or fake, Stevie didn't know, and she wasn't sure it mattered. A table full of teeth is a table full of teeth.

"Did you have a good drive?" Pix asked, quickly sorting the remaining teeth into compartments.

(*Plink*, said a tooth, hitting the plastic. *Plink*.)

"Sorry, I was just sorting a few things out. You're definitely the earliest . . ."

(*Plink*, said a molar.)

"Can I get anyone a coffee?"

The group was herded into the tiny house kitchen, where cups of coffee were distributed and Pix could explain the eating situation to Stevie's parents. Breakfasts were provided in-house and all other meals were in the dining hall. Students could come in and make food whenever they wanted, and there was an online grocery-ordering system. As they came back into the common room, Stevie's mother decided to address the obvious.

"Are those teeth?" she asked.

"Yes," Pix said.

No other answer was immediately forthcoming, so Stevie jumped in.

"Dr. Pixwell is a specialist in bioarchaeology," she said. "She works on archaeological digs in Egypt."

"That's right," Pix said. "You read my faculty bio?"

"No," Stevie said. "The teeth, your shirt, you've got an Eye of Horus tattooed on your wrist, the chamomile tea in the kitchen has packaging written in Arabic, and you have a tan line on your forehead from a head covering. Just a guess."

"That's extremely impressive," Pix said, nodding. Everyone was quiet for a moment. A fly buzzed around Stevie's head.

"Stevie thinks she's Sherlock Holmes," her father said. He liked to make these kinds of remarks that sounded like jokes, and may have been well-intentioned on some level, but always had a hint of shade.

"Who doesn't want to be Sherlock Holmes?" Pix said, meeting his eye and smiling. "I read more Agatha Christie when I was younger, because she wrote about archaeology a lot. But everyone loves Sherlock. Let me show you around. . . ."

In that moment, with that one remark, Pix won Stevie's everlasting loyalty.

The six student rooms of Minerva House were all located on a single hallway to the left side of the common room: three rooms downstairs, three up. There was a group bathroom on the first floor with tiles that had to be original, because no one would make anything that color anymore.

If that shade required a name, Stevie would have to go with "queasy salmon."

At the end of the hall was the turret with a large door.

"This is a bit special," Pix said, opening it. "Minerva was used for the Ellinghams' guests before the school was open, so it has some features you don't find in the other dorms. . . ."

She opened the door and revealed a magnificent round room, a bathroom, with a high ceiling. The floor was tiled in a pearly silver-gray. A large claw-foot tub took center stage. There were long stained-glass windows depicting stylized flowers and vines that bathed the room in rainbows.

"This room is popular during exams," Pix said. "People like to study in the tub, especially when it's cold. It doesn't get a lot of use otherwise because there is a bit of a spider issue. Now let's show you your room."

Stevie decided to ignore what she just heard about spiders and moved on to her room, Minerva Two. Minerva Two smelled like it had been slowly baking for a few months, thick with the scents of closed space, new paint, and furniture polish. One of the two sash windows facing the front had been opened to try to air it, but the breeze was being lazy. Two flies had come in and were dancing around near the high ceiling. The walls were a soft cream color; a black fireplace stood out in stark contrast.

As they moved Stevie's things in, there was talk about where the bed should go, and could people get in that window, and what time was curfew? Pix handled these questions easily (the windows could be opened from the top and all had good locks, and curfew was ten on weeknights and eleven on weekends, all monitored electronically through student IDs and by Pix in person).

Her mother was about to unpack Stevie's bags herself when Pix intervened and dragged them off on a personal tour of the campus, leaving Stevie with a moment of stillness. The birds chirped outside and the breeze carried a few faraway voices. Minerva Two made a gentle creak as Stevie walked across its floor. She ran her hand along the walls, feeling their strange texture—they were thick with years of paint, one coat on top of another, covering up the previous inhabitant's marks. Stevie had recently seen a true-crime documentary on how layers of paint could be peeled back, revealing writing that had been hidden for decades. Since then, she had desperately wanted to steam and peel a wall, just to see if anything was there.

These walls probably had stories.

April 13, 1936, 6:45 p.m.

THE FOG HAD COME ON QUICKLY THAT DAY—THE MORNING HAD BLOS-
somed bright and clear, but just after four, a curtain of
blue-gray smoke fell over the land. That was the thing so
many people would remark about later, the fog. By twilight,
everything was wrapped in a pearly dark and it was difficult
to see more than a few feet ahead. The Rolls-Royce Phan-
tom moved through this fog slowly, up the treacherous drive
to the Ellingham estate. It pulled halfway up the circular
drive in front of the Great House. The car always stopped
halfway. Albert Ellingham liked to walk the drive when
he got out of the car to survey his mountain kingdom. He
stepped out of the back door before the car fully came to a
rest. His secretary, Robert Mackenzie, waited the extra few
seconds to make his exit.

"You need to go to Philadelphia," Robert said to the
back of his employer.

"No one *needs* to go to Philadelphia, Robert."

"You need to go to Philadelphia. We should also spend
at least two days at the New York office."

The last busload of men working on the final stages of construction pulled past them, heading back to Burlington and the various small towns along the way. It slowed so the passengers could raise their hands to their employer in greeting as they left.

"Good job today!" Albert Ellingham called to them. "See you fellows tomorrow!"

The butler opened the door on their approach, and the two men entered the magnificent entry hall of the house. Every time he entered, Ellingham was pleased with the effect of the place, the way light played around the space, bouncing from every bit of crystal, tinted by a well-spent fortune's worth of Scottish stained glass.

"Evening, Montgomery," said Ellingham. His booming voice echoed through the open atrium.

"Good evening, sir," said the butler, accepting the hats and coats. "Good evening, Mr. Mackenzie. I hope your trip was not too arduous in this fog."

"Took us forever," Ellingham said. "Robert was bending my ear about meetings the entire way."

"Please tell Mr. Ellingham that he has to go to Philadelphia," Robert said, passing over his hat.

"Mr. Mackenzie wishes me to inform you—"

"I'm starving, Montgomery," Ellingham said. "What's on for tonight?"

"Crème de céleri soup and filet of sole with a sauce amandine to start, sir, followed by roast lamb, minted peas, asparagus hollandaise, and potatoes lyonnaise, with a cold lemon soufflé to finish."

"That'll do. As soon as we can. I've worked up an appetite. How many hangers-on do we still have?"

"Miss Robinson and Mr. Nair are still with us, though they have been indisposed most of the day, so I believe it will just be Mrs. Ellingham, Mr. Mackenzie, and yourself, sir."

"Good. Get them. Let's eat."

"Mrs. Ellingham has not yet returned, sir. She and Miss Alice went out for a drive this afternoon."

"And they're not back yet?"

"I imagine the fog must have slowed her, sir."

"Have some men with lights wait at the end of the drive to help her on the path back. Tell her as soon as she gets back it's time to eat. Don't even let her take her coat off. March her right to the table."

"Very good, sir."

"Come along, Robert," Ellingham said, heading off. "We'll go to my office and have a game of Rook. And don't try to argue with me. There is nothing so serious as a game."

The secretary was professionally silent in response. Playing games with his employer was a nonnegotiable part of his job, and "there is nothing so serious as a game" was one of Ellingham's many mottoes. That was why the students always had access to games, and the new Monopoly game was mandatory for students, residents of the household, and staff. Everyone had to play at least once a week, and there were now monthly tournaments. This was life in the world of Albert Ellingham.

Robert picked the day's mail out of the tray and sifted through it with a practiced eye, tossing some letters immediately back in the tray and tucking others under his arm.

"Philadelphia," he said again. It was his job to make sure the great Albert Ellingham stayed on course. Robert was good at this.

"Fine, fine. Schedule it. Ah . . ." Ellingham plucked a Western Union slip from his desk. These tiny slips of paper were his favorite medium for writing short notes. "I started a new riddle this morning. Tell me what you think of it."

"Is the answer Philadelphia?"

"Robert," Ellingham said sternly. "My riddle. This is a good one, I think. Now listen. *What serves on either side, and if you wish to hide, may protect you from your foe, or show him where to go?* Well? What do you think?"

Robert sighed and paused his mail sorting to think.

"Serves on either side," he said. "Like a spy. A traitor. A duplicitous person."

Ellingham smiled and gestured that his secretary should keep thinking.

"But," Robert said, "it's not a who. It's a what. So it's an object that works from two directions . . ."

There was a knock at the door, and Ellingham hurried over himself to answer it.

"It's a door!" he said, throwing it open and revealing his ashen-faced butler. "A door!"

"Sir . . . ," Montgomery said.

"One moment. You see, Robert, the door can be used from either side . . ."

"And you can hide behind it, or it might show where you've gone," Robert said. "I see. Yes . . ."

"Sir!" Montgomery said. His urgent tone was entirely unfamiliar to the two men, and they looked at him in confusion.

"What is it, Montgomery?" Ellingham said.

"There is a telephone call, sir," Montgomery replied. "You must come at once, sir. On the household line. In the pantry. Please, sir, hurry."

This was so out of character for Montgomery that Ellingham complied without another word. He followed to the butler's pantry and took the phone that was held out for him.

"*I have your wife and daughter,*" a voice said.

3

STEVIE BELL HAD A SIMPLE DESIRE: SHE WANTED TO BE STANDING OVER a dead body.

She didn't want to kill people—far from it. She wanted to be the person who found out why the body was dead, that's all. She wanted bags marked EVIDENCE and a paper boiler suit like forensics wore. She wanted to be in the interrogation room. She wanted to get to the bottom of the case.

Which was all well and good and probably what a lot of people wanted, if only people would be more honest. But her old high school was not the kind of place where she felt like she could fully express this desire. Her old high school was a fine high school, if you liked high school. It wasn't bad or evil. It was just like it was supposed to be—miles of linoleum and humming lights, the warm funk of cafeteria stink too early in the morning, the flashes of inspiration that were quickly quashed by long stretches of tedium, and the perpetual desire to be somewhere else. And while Stevie had friends there, there was no one who fully understood her love of crime. So she had written a passionate essay, poured it all onto the screen, and sent it away almost as a joke. Ellingham would never take her.

Ellingham liked what they saw. They had given her this room.

The furniture was wooden and surprisingly big. There was a big dresser that wobbled when Stevie touched it; the polish couldn't cover the many nicks on its surface. Some were just scratches from use, but a few were clear words and initials. Stevie opened the drawers and found, to her surprise, that there were already some things in there: a plaid flannel blanket, a heavy purple fleece with the Ellingham Academy crest on the breast, some kind of military-grade flashlight with a new pack of batteries, a blue flannel robe, and some rackets with clamps on them. These Stevie had to remove and examine for a while before she determined that these must be the snowshoes, and the pegs she'd seen by the door were likely places to hang them.

Stevie had known that she was going to Vermont, and she knew Vermont could get cold, but these items suggested *survivalism*.

She started opening up her boxes and bags. She pulled out her old gray sheets, the striped comforter that she'd had since she was ten, two of the less-yellowed pillows from the closet. As she looked at these objects in the clear Vermont sunlight, they all seemed a bit—drab. She had a few new items, like the requisite bath caddy and flip-flops for trips to the bathroom, but these things didn't exactly liven up the room.

But it was fine. In her imagination, her dorm room was

going to look like Sherlock Holmes's residence on Baker Street—shabby, but genteel.

She put in her earbuds to finally continue listening to her podcast. This one was about H. H. Holmes, the Chicago serial killer: *". . . they would discover the many rooms of Holmes's murder castle: the rooms fitted with gas lines, the hanging chamber, the soundproof vault . . ."*

She'd marked one of her boxes with stars, and she opened this one now. This box contained the bare necessities of her life: her mystery novels. (At least, a carefully curated selection of a few dozen essentials.) These were lovingly arranged on the bookshelf in the order in which she needed to see them.

". . . the chute to the furnaces in the basement where the bodies could be . . ."

Sherlock Holmes on top with Wilkie Collins. Then Agatha Christie spread over two shelves, leading into Josephine Tey and Dorothy L. Sayers. She worked her way down to the modern era and ended with her books on forensics and criminal psychology. She stood back and examined the overall effect, then tweaked until the arrangement was just right. Where her books were, she was.

Get the books right and the rest will follow. Now she could address the rest of the room.

". . . acid, a collection of poisons, a stretching rack . . ."

Stevie was less concerned about the day-to-day items like her clothes. Stevie had very little interest in clothes and no money to buy them anyway, so her wardrobe tended to jeans and plain T-shirts. She coveted a heavy fisherman's sweater, because the detective in her favorite Nordic Noir wore one, and preferred a sensible cross-body bag like the one worn by her favorite English TV detective.

She did have one prized possession in terms of clothes—a vintage red vinyl raincoat, straight out of the 1970s, which she had found at the back of her grandmother's closet. It fit Stevie as if it had been made for her, and she decorated it with a selection of tiny lapel pins honoring her favorite bands, podcasts, and books. The coat had deep pockets and a thick belt, and when she was wearing it, Stevie felt powerful, prepared, and extremely waterproof. Even her mother, who disliked Stevie's taste in clothes, was on board for the red raincoat. ("Finally, some red.")

She was hanging the coat in her closet and had just closed the door when she turned and saw the zombie.

Stevie often read that actors look a little different from the general population because the camera distorts appearances. Someone who looks good on camera looks so good in person that reality starts to bend a bit. This was the case with the figure standing in Stevie's doorway. It was a guy dressed in a white linen shirt and a pair of bright-blue shorts, looking like a wandering J. Crew ad in search of a glossy spread.

His face was unmistakable. When she had seen it last,

it was grim, covered in dirt, frequently crying. Now it was smiling gently. His features were soft and rounded—happy cheeks, a small, playfully rounded nose, a dimpled chin. His brown hair was longish on the top and fell in easy waves. His brows had to be artificially shaped. No arch that arched existed in nature. He looked toned all over, but his calves were particularly so. His calves, in fact, had outgrown the rest of him. Beefy calves.

"Hey," he said.

His voice was deep and smooth and rich, like what gravy might sound like if gravy could talk. (Which, luckily, it cannot. Gravy might have a nice voice, but the conversation would probably be dull.)

"You're Hayes Major," Stevie said.

"Yeah." He chuckled in a soft, self-deprecating way that Stevie was pretty sure wasn't *truly* self-deprecating.

Hayes was a YouTube star. At the start of the summer, he had released a ten-part online show called *The End of It All* about a survivor of a zombie invasion. All of the videos were shot from a basement bunker, just Hayes to the camera, discussing his survival in something called the Hungry City, a beachside town that had a few pockets of human resistance. His show was one of those things that wasn't there one moment and was everywhere the next.

Stevie had known Hayes went to Ellingham and that she might see him at some point. She did not expect to see him standing in her doorway as she unpacked. She didn't know he would be in her house.

"Sorry, I was on the phone," he said. "I was talking to some people in LA."

He held up his phone, as if indicating the presence of tiny Los Angelenos inside of it. It wasn't clear to Stevie why he was apologizing or even explaining why he had been on the phone before she had seen him. But she nodded anyway, like this made sense. Maybe this was something celebrities—Hayes probably counted as an actual celebrity—did. They talked on the phone, and then they told you about talking on the phone.

"So, hey," he said. "Is there any chance you could give me a hand?"

Stevie blinked in confusion.

"With what?" she asked.

"My stuff."

"Oh," Stevie said, feeling the cold hand of panic on her neck. Already she sounded like a slack-jawed idiot. "Sure."

She followed him to the common room, where his bags and boxes (nicer than hers and more of them) were waiting. He gestured to a box.

"You have to be careful with that one," he said.

Stevie took this as a cue to pick that box up. It was a bit on the heavy side, full of some kind of equipment that was unevenly packed and slid around when she moved it.

"Yeah," he said, taking a smaller bag and heading back down the hall to the right circular stairs at the end. "It's been a weird summer. That's why I was on the phone."

"Oh," Stevie said, "yeah. Sure."

She tried to maneuver the box into the twisting space. The steps creaked loudly, and the box caught. Hayes moved ahead, but Stevie was stuck trying to pivot and angle without shaking the box too much. She paused for a moment, expecting Hayes to come back and give her a hand, but when he did not appear she took a deep breath and persevered, letting the box scrape along the wall.

Hayes's room was Minerva Six, at the very end. It was much like hers, but hotter and with an extra window.

"Oh, great," he said. "Set it anywhere. Thanks."

"Your show is good," she said. "I really liked it."

This wasn't entirely true. The show was okay at best.

In preparation for coming, Stevie had watched all the episodes. They weren't long, maybe ten minutes each, and they were fine. The story was pretty good. Hayes's acting, less so. Most of it was cheekbones and a low, sultry voice. Sometimes, that's all that was required. Stevie always tried to be truthful, but she didn't want to make her first acquaintance in her new house and say, "Your show was mediocre and overrated but I see why you are valued: for your looks and deep voice." People tended not to warm to that kind of thing.

"Thanks," he said, leaving the room in a way that suggested she was to come with him and get more stuff.

This was good. This was Hayes Major, internet star, talking to her. Also, this was Hayes Major, internet star, getting her to carry most of the heavy stuff, but still.

Another weird thing, Stevie thought, as she made her

way back down the twisting steps—she knew about Hayes's love life. Hayes had been involved in a publicized altercation over the summer at some convention when he got involved with another YouTuber named Beth Brave, star of a show called *Beth Isn't Here*. Beth had been dating Lars Jackson from a show called *These Guys*. Some kind of argument broke out when Hayes got together with Beth that had been widely recorded, and the three of them had a screaming fight in a hallway. There was online chatter after speculating that Beth would be involved in a second season of *The End of It All*.

This was the kind of life Hayes led. It was very different from Stevie's life.

"People in LA," he said unprovoked, as they picked up some more boxes. "There's been a lot of interest in the show for movies, so . . ."

He let that hang in the air until Stevie said, "Wow."

"Yeah," he said. "My agent wants me to make another series right away because there's a lot of interest right now."

Another trudge up the tight steps.

"More zombies?" Stevie asked as she caught her breath.

"I don't know. . . . You can just put that on the bed. . . . I mean, I did that already?"

"You turned into one at the end," Stevie said. "I think? It was kind of open-ended."

"Yeah . . . ," he said, and his tone indicated that he was no longer really warming to the conversation. "So, I just have to make a few more calls now that I'm here? Thanks a lot. I'll see you around?"

"Yep," Stevie said, wiping the sweat from her brow as she backed out of the room. "I'll see you . . . you know . . . here."

He was already dialing.

As she stepped out into the hall and went down the stairs, two things occurred to Stevie.

The first was that it was eight in the morning here, so five in the morning in LA. On a weekend. While they may keep strange hours in Hollywood, it seemed unlikely that Hayes was doing a bunch of important business at that time.

The second was that even though he lived in the same building as she did, Hayes Major had never asked her name.

April 13, 1936, 7:15 p.m.

"*WE HAVE YOUR WIFE AND DAUGHTER. DO EXACTLY AS WE SAY IF you want them to live. Do not call the police. We will know if you have. We have eyes on the police station. Take twenty-five thousand out of the safe. Come out to the lake yourself. Get into a boat with the money and come to the island. You have fifteen minutes.*"

The line went dead.

Three men stood in the butler's pantry: Albert Ellingham had the telephone. Robert Mackenzie and Montgomery, the butler, stood at the door. Albert Ellingham replaced the receiver on the hook and thick, frantic quiet followed.

"Montgomery," Ellingham said quietly, "have Miss Pelham secure the children at the school. Everyone back in their houses. Doors locked. Curtains drawn. Everyone is to go inside. Do this now. Robert, with me."

Robert Mackenzie again trailed his fast-moving employer to his office. Once inside, Ellingham shut and locked the door, then went to the French doors and looked outside. The dark had come down over the mountains. The dark had come down everywhere.

Ellingham marched to one of the bookcases in the windowless wall. He pulled down a book from a top shelf, but just halfway. There was a telltale *snick*, and the entire panel of wall gave. Ellingham swung back the bookcase, revealing a massive vault inside of the wall. He entered the combination and turned the lock. Robert, meanwhile, ran from window to window, pulling the curtains.

"We *have* to call the police," Robert said. "We have to call them *now*."

"Find a lamp and light it for me," Ellingham said, pulling out several bags of cash.

"There are still a few workmen on the property," Robert persisted, pulling the massive curtains that swept over the wall of French doors at the back of the room. "We could have them out in five minutes, surrounding the property and out on the roads. Some of them have shotguns. All of them are handy enough."

"Robert, *there is no time for this*. I am taking this money out to the lake. Light a lamp and then *help me count*."

Later, when asked about this moment, Robert Mackenzie would say that there really was no time to think. That was the genius of the demand—no time to think, no time to plan. He grabbed one of the oil lamps kept in every room of the house (power loss was frequent), lit it, and then dropped to his knees and started to count money. In the end, there was twenty-three thousand and a few extra twenties.

"It's not enough. We need more." For one of the first

times in his life, Albert Ellingham sounded desperate. "I only have five more minutes to get this outside. We need *something.*"

One of America's richest men raced around his office for a moment, pulling open drawers, looking for piles of cash he certainly didn't have, or anything that might be worth that much money.

"It will have to do," he said.

The bag of cash only weighed maybe twenty pounds. Ellingham hoisted it and opened the French doors.

Robert paused before handing him the oil lamp. "You know they can take you out there. It's probably you they want!"

"Then they'll have me."

"And then what?" Robert said. "This is *madness.* We need help."

Albert Ellingham took a crucial second's pause.

"Marsh," he said. "Call him at home. Don't say what's happened. Just get him up here on some pretense. No one else, do you understand? No one but Marsh."

Robert nodded. Albert Ellingham took the lamp and stepped out into the Vermont mountain fog carrying a bag of money. He walked the fifty or so yards to the lake edge, where there was a small dock. He set the money into one of the rowboats he had moored on the side facing the house and got inside carefully, then put the lamp on the empty bench seat. When he knocked the edge of land away with his oar, his entire body was shaking. Still, he reached the mound in a minute or two and threw the rope around the mooring post.

"I'm here," he called into the dark.

A flashlight shone down on him, blinding him for a moment.

"Get out," said a voice. "Bring the money."

"My wife and daughter—where are they?"

"Stop talking."

Ellingham threw the bag. It landed on the narrow strip of grass around the dome. He got out as well as he could, considering that he could barely see.

The person kept the light squarely on Ellingham's face, forcing him to look down and shield his eyes. He half crawled out of the boat onto the ground.

"Open the door," the voice said.

Ellingham pulled his keys from his pocket and opened the door on the side of the dome. This dome was his little thinking place—his island of peace. The person shoved him hard, pushing him into the dome, where he landed on the floor.

"Put the money in the hatch," the voice said. The person was speaking through a scarf, so it was muffled. There was an accent there, an accent he was trying to hide by pulling out the words in a strange way. His pupils were still constricted from the light, so Ellingham felt blindly along the floor, feeling for the hatch. He found it and opened it and pushed the sack into the hole. He heard it knocking some bottles off the shelves as it fell, and they shattered on the floor. He turned back to the stranger, but the light was shoved right back into his face, blinding him again.

Ellingham battled with himself for a moment. Should he lunge for this person? Just take him down now, beat his head into the side of the stone base of the observatory floor and demand with every blow where his family was? Fear and rage came in equal measure. But Ellingham had not gotten as far as he had in life by giving in to every impulse.

"It's everything I had in the safe," he said. "I was under two thousand short, but we gave you whatever we had. If I'd had more time . . . you can have whatever you want. Anything you want."

Something came down on his head, and then all faded to black.

4

AFTER MAKING SUCH A HUGE IMPRESSION ON HAYES MAJOR, STEVIE paced her room for a few moments and reviewed her introductory strategy. More confidence. That's what she needed. When she joined the FBI, she was going to need to walk up to people and shake their hands, look them in the eye, ask questions. Hayes had just caught her by surprise.

Her next chance was already here, kicking a laundry basket brimming with sketchbooks, pencils, oil crayons, and paints sitting by the door. A girl, the presumed owner of the foot, followed it in.

She wore a faded, shrunken yellow T-shirt from an auto repair shop and an old cheerleading skirt in deep blue with red internal pleats. Her legs were covered with little bruises and nicks—nothing serious-looking, more like the kind you would get by trying to climb trees or other objects. Her feet were just about covered in a pair of scruffy red cloth Mary Jane slippers held together with safety pins. Her hair was the real statement piece; it looked unwashed and matted, and it had been gathered in little bunches around her head and tied into bundles with what looked like baby socks. Down her left arm was a long tattoo, one massive line of elaborate script. Down her right arm were notes and sketches in different colors of pen.

"It is hot as *balls* in here," the girl said in greeting. "Balls. Seriously. When the hell are they going to get some AC?"

Stevie stepped forward, considered offering a hand for a handshake, and opted instead for a casual lean against one of the chairs.

"I'm Stevie," she said. "Stevie Bell."

"What's up," the girl said. "I'm Ellie."

There was no Ellie on the list of Ellingham students, but there was an Element Walker. And this person looked like an Element. Ellie, or Element, kicked a box that contained feather boas, a ukulele, a bowler hat, and a lot of plastic storage bags full of used makeup, and spilled glitter across the floor.

"Can I help?" Stevie said.

Ellie shrugged, but seemed happy enough with the offer.

Ellie's things were a lot scrappier than Hayes's or Stevie's—two old cardboard boxes, an oversized army duffel bag, a gold backpack, and a lumpen black laundry sack. It didn't take long to deposit these items in Minerva Three, which was down by the turreted bathroom.

"Pix," Ellie yelled as she dragged the last of her things into her room, then walked back to the common area. "Why is it hot as balls in here?"

(Note to self, Stevie thought, you could say *balls* to teachers here.)

"It's summer," Pix replied, coming into the common room. "Hey, Stevie. I left your parents out on the tour. They'll be back soon. And Ellie, the heat won't last long, and then you'll be freezing. So you can look forward to that."

"Why don't they get air-conditioning?" Ellie said, dropping heavily into the hammock chair. She spun around and turned herself upside down, letting her head hang off the bottom, dusting the floor with her hair bunches.

"Because this is an old building with old wiring," Pix replied. "Because fire. How was Paris?"

"Hot," Ellie said. "We went to Nice for a while. My mom has a new boyfriend and he has a place there."

Paris. Ellie had been in Paris. Obviously, Stevie knew that Paris was a real place that real people went to. Her school sponsored a French Club trip the last summer, and she knew three people who had gone on it. It was only a week long and the biggest story out of it was that Toby Davidson got hit by a bike and almost lost a finger. (*Almost Lost a Finger: The Toby Davidson Story.* Not a compelling read.)

There were shuffling noises by the door, and Stevie turned to see another person there. Though it was blazingly sunny, he had the look of someone caught in a rainstorm with a heavy backpack on. He wore a T-shirt that said IF YOU CAN READ THIS SHIRT, YOU ARE TOO CLOSE. His eyes were a strange pale gray. He had a shock of red-blond hair that had been cut by someone with more enthusiasm than skill.

"Nate!" she said. Out with the hand. Meet his eye. "I'm Stevie."

Nate looked at her outstretched hand, and then at Stevie's face, seemingly to check if this was a serious gesture. With a sigh that probably (probably?) wasn't supposed to be audible, he shook it once and let it go quickly.

Stevie decided to drop the handshake move.

Pix greeted Nate and got out his key, while Ellie examined him from her upside-down position.

"Nate's a writer," Stevie offered. "He wrote a book. *The Moonbright Chronicles*."

"Never read it," Ellie replied. "But that's cool. What about you?"

"I read it," Stevie said.

"No," Ellie said. "You. What do you do?"

"Oh, right," Stevie said, brushing away her mistake. She borrowed her technique from one of her current favorite TV detectives—Sam Weatherfeld of *Stormy Weather*. Sam never got stuck on moments like that; she always moved with the flow of conversation and didn't try to walk against the current. It was time to declare herself for what she was. She had considered many terms. It was too presumptuous and silly to say detective; she wasn't any kind of law officer or private investigator, and she had never really solved a case. Crime buff just sounded like a weird hobbyist with a high

55

gloss. Crime historian wasn't quite right and was definitely too dull. Her solution was not to give herself a title, but to state an activity.

"I study crime," she said.

"To do it or stop it?" Ellie said.

"To stop it," Stevie said, "but it probably works either way."

"So you came here because of the crimes?" Ellie said. "The murders?"

"Kind of," Stevie said.

"That's cool. Someone should. They're good murders, right?"

She did half a backward somersault out of the chair. Her skirt stuck up in the back, revealing her butt.

Ellie had simply accepted her, just like that. For a moment it was all endorphins and rainbows in Stevie's head. That was all it had taken—one nice, accepting word from another student and she realized it would all be okay.

And yes, they *were* good murders.

Then she caught something in her peripheral vision— her parents were coming down the path with another pair of parents, mostly likely Nate's. Nate's parents were very angular people, crisply dressed in near-matching polo shirts and long shorts. The colors were different, but the effect was the same. Stevie's dad was talking and gesticulating, and her mom was nodding. Nate's father was listening, and his mother was scanning the house and the middle distance.

The endorphins fled the scene and were replaced by cold

sweat. What were her parents saying? Were they talking about their views on the media? That the government was trying to control the lives of decent Americans? The myth of climate change? Or was it something more fun, like the price of bulk toilet paper? These were all favorite topics and all equal possibilities.

Stevie looked to Nate, who was staring at the door like he was watching an approaching cloud of locusts. He was also feeling the strain of parents meeting parents. Ellie was now scratching her exposed butt. (Well, not the butt-butt, but the upper-leg part where it meets the butt zone. Technically thigh, but butt for all legal intents and purposes.)

Stevie gripped the chair and braced for impact.

"Did you see a moose?" she said to Nate, in an attempt to make some kind of conversation.

"What?" he said. Which was fair enough.

All of the parents arrived at the door in a knot and trickled through into the common room.

". . . just avoiding the toll roads." Stevie heard her dad say. The conversation had been about the trip, most likely. That was probably very dull but safe. Then eight parental eyes turned to the exposed butt on the floor. Ellie rolled into a seated position, just a few seconds too late. Her matted, baby-socked hair stood on end for a moment.

Nate's parents showed no outward sign, but Stevie saw her parents take it in. Her father looked away. Her mom's mouth twisted into a small, confused grin.

"Let me show you what I did to my room," she said,

hooking one parent by each arm and hustling them down the hall.

"What in God's name was that girl wearing?" her mother asked, a little too loudly, as Stevie shut the door of her room behind them.

"I've never seen anything like that getup before," her dad added.

Stevie's parents labored under the belief that what a person was wearing had a direct correlation to their worth as a human being. There were normal clothes (good), and there were nice clothes (very good), and there was everything else. Ellie had just reset the limits on this last category.

"Did you like the campus?" Stevie said, smiling. "Isn't it amazing?"

That the campus was amazing was undeniable, and her parents made a clear effort not to dwell on Ellie and instead focus on this mountain paradise of mansions and fountains and art and natural beauty.

"We're going to have to head back soon," her dad said. "Are you . . . set?"

On that, Stevie had an entirely unexpected emotional pang. Her parents were about to leave, which was something she had known about and frankly wanted, but now in the moment, there was a hot rush of feeling. She gulped hard.

"Okay," her mother said. "You have your pills? Let's just put eyes on the pills."

Stevie's plastic bag of medications was produced and examined.

"You have a hundred and twenty Lexapro and thirty Ativan, but only take the Ativan if you need it."

"I know."

"But if you need it, make sure . . ."

"Mom, I know . . ."

"I know you know. And you call us every day."

"You be good," her dad said, hugging her hard. "You need us, you call. Doesn't matter the time."

Her father looked genuinely on the verge of tears. This was the worst. Bells did not cry. Bells did not show feeling. This had to stop.

"Remember," her mother said into her ear, "you can always come home. We'll come up and get you."

Her mother's final little squeeze said, *This isn't the kind of place you belong. You'll see. You'll be back.*

5

AFTER A FEW MOMENTS OF NOT CRYING (BUT A LOT OF BLINKING) AND staring at her medications before stashing them in a drawer, Stevie emerged from her room to find that Janelle Franklin had arrived, and Nate was nowhere to be seen. Janelle was shorter than Stevie had pictured. She wore a red floral romper and her braided hair was wrapped in a scarf of yellows and golds. She wore a light, summery perfume that trailed in the air behind her as she hurried over to wrap Stevie in a hug.

"We're here!" she said, clasping Stevie's arms. "We're here! Are your parents here?"

"They left a few minutes ago. Are yours . . . ?"

"No," Janelle said. "They're both on call today, so we did all my good-byes this week—family dinners and friends, we had a picnic . . ." Janelle happily chatted about the many events that had led up to her departure. She came from a big family in Chicago and around Illinois. She had three brothers, two in MIT and one at Stanford. Her parents were both doctors.

"Come see my room!" She grabbed Stevie by the wrist and led her next door, to a very similar room, but with everything flipped around. Their fireplaces were back to back.

"I'm probably going to need more space to build on," Janelle said, "but I think I can use that table in the common room. Pix said I could solder out there. Can you believe we're here?"

"I know," Stevie said. "I feel kind of dizzy."

"I think that might be altitude," Janelle said. "We're not super high. The highest point in Vermont is only forty-three hundred feet, and altitude should really become an issue at five thousand, but you may still need to compensate for the lower oxygen levels by drinking a little extra water. Here."

She opened her bag and removed a fresh bottle of water, which she pressed into Stevie's hand.

"I think I'm just nervous," Stevie said.

"Also possible. Water is still the answer. And deep, slow breathing. Drink."

Stevie opened the bottle and took a long sip, as instructed. Water never hurt.

"Is Nate here?" Janelle asked.

"He was. I guess he went upstairs."

"How is he in person?"

"Kind of like he seemed in his messages," Stevie said.

"Well, we're here in person now. Come on. Let's go see him."

Janelle had entirely changed the energy of the place. She was movement, she was action. Stevie found herself carried along in Janelle's wake as she hurried down the hall and up the tight circular stairs. Nate was in Minerva Four, the first one along the hall. The door was shut but he could be heard moving inside.

Janelle knocked. When there was no immediate answer, she texted.

A moment later, the door opened a bit and Nate's long face appeared. He didn't do anything for a moment, and then, with a barely audible sigh, he opened the door enough to let them in.

"Do you do hugs?" Janelle said.

"Not really," Nate replied, moving back.

"Then no hug it is," Janelle said.

"How about salutes?" Stevie said.

"Those are tolerable."

Stevie gave him a salute.

Nate's room was more or less identical to theirs, except it was already a mess. There was a rat's nest of cables on the floor, and a pile of books. He'd been organizing his books, just like Stevie had.

"The Wi-Fi here sucks," he said, by means of a greeting. "Cell signal too."

He kicked at the pile of cords with a Converse-clad foot.

"I haven't tried yet," Stevie said.

"Well, it sucks."

The box nearest to Stevie looked to be full of . . . parts. Just parts of things. Chair legs. Some kind of metal disk. Janelle went over and had a look at it.

"What's this?" she asked. "Do you build too?"

Nate swooped down on the box defensively.

"I go to . . . flea markets," he said, waving his hand as if this was just something that needed to be dealt with. "I collect things. I like clocks. And stuff."

He closed the box lid, and with it, any invitation for further comment.

Stevie enjoyed Janelle's brisk, confident positivity and she also liked Nate's grumpy demeanor. She had a little bit of both of these qualities, and she fit between them very comfortably.

"Tour's starting!" Pix called up the stairs. "They're waiting outside! Come on, you guys!"

Nate looked hesitant, but Janelle was not giving up.

"I think it's mandatory," she said.

Janelle, Nate, and Stevie made their way outside where a large group of people was milling around in wait. Hayes and Ellie, being second years, obviously did not have to go.

It looked like the group went from house to house collecting members, and Minerva may have been the last stop. Stevie looked at her fellow first years. She wasn't quite sure what she had expected—if she thought the students at Ellingham would all show up wearing lab coats, or they would all look like Ellie.

In general, they looked like any assortment of people from any high school. There were a few people with glossy, perfect hair who had already clumped together through that strange alchemy that joins all people with perfect, glossy

63

hair. There was one girl in a bright red-and-white-check vintage dress with cat-eye glasses, winged eyeliner, a red vintage purse, and a tiny red fascinator. She was the most dressed up, and her heels sank into the grass as they walked. There was another girl with green hair and a NASA T-shirt who handled the grassy terrain in her wheelchair with deftness. There was a girl with a sharply cut black bob, pale skin, and vibrant red lipstick who looked like some kind of silent movie star dressed in a formless but somehow unmistakably fashionable gray dress and thick black belt. There was a girl in a stunning floral hijab who took a lot of pictures of the campus on her phone. There was a guy who never took off his cat-ear headphones during the entire tour.

Their tour was led by a student named Kazim Bazir, who spoke quickly and excitedly. Kaz had bright, excited eyes and the upbeat tone of a salesman who really wanted to sell you your very own deranged mountain retreat.

"Ellingham Academy was built between 1928 and 1936 by Albert Xavier Ellingham and his wife, Iris Ellingham," Kaz said. "The right side of the campus, where our houses are, is known as wet campus, because the creek turns and borders the property. The fields and classrooms and most of the other buildings are on dry campus. Of course, it's all a dry campus . . ."

No laughs. Tough crowd.

Ellingham was splendid in the sunshine. That was the only word for it. The light fell like rain in droplets that hung in the air. A cloud of them surrounded the fountain that gushed merrily on the green, creating its own ecosystem of rainbows. The light found every nook and crook of the bright redbrick buildings. It made the gargoyles seem to smile. It deepened the green of the trees. It made the statues—well, it didn't do anything to the statues except reveal just how many of them there were.

"Do you think these get less creepy with time?" Nate asked as they passed yet another cluster of naked Greeks or Romans.

"I hope not," Stevie replied.

Kaz led the group around the pathways, pointing out all the buildings and their uses. Albert Ellingham had been a massive admirer of Greek and Roman culture. This was evident from the names of the buildings: Eunomia, Genius, Jupiter, Cybele, Dionysus, Asteria, and Demeter.

As they walked through the green, Stevie looked up at the Great House. Its name was simple and accurate. The Great House was a character in this tale—the first building erected on this spot, designed to meet the whims of the family who inhabited it, while serving as the center of a seat of learning. This was the home Iris and Alice Ellingham left that morning, down this very drive. Stevie counted the windows on the second floor.

"What's up there?" Janelle asked. "You're looking up there really intently."

"Right there," Stevie said, pointing at two of the windows on the left. "Those are the ones Flora Robinson said she was looking out of the night of the kidnapping."

65

"Who's Flora Robinson?"

"A friend of the Ellinghams'. Iris Ellingham's best friend. She was suspected for a long time because she gave a weird story that night. Her interview was really odd."

There was no time to linger on Flora and her story. The tour was moving toward the Ellingham library, a stone structure that looked a bit like a church, with a large rose window, a spire, and a rounded set of red double doors.

"It's designed this way on purpose," Kaz said. "Albert Ellingham said knowledge was his religion and libraries were his church, so he built a church."

Inside, the library was cool and still, with colored light streaming through the stained-glass windows. All of the buildings were impressive, but there was something majestic about this one. There was an overhang that filled about half the space, but once you got past this, much of the building was open, and you could see up three stories to the bookshelves that lined the structure. Elaborate spiral staircases made of wrought iron woven into patterns of twisting vines led up to the other levels. Out of all the buildings, this one should probably have been the quietest and the stillest, but this one seemed a bit . . . Stevie struggled to catch the right word. Wild? There was a loose wind spinning around and whistling near the ceiling. The iron vines seemed to genuinely crawl up the steps. The librarian, who seemed to have just run in, was out of breath. She wore a very professional-looking biking outfit, and her short black hair bore the imprint of a recent bike helmet.

"Hey!" she said, sounding a bit winded. "I'm Kyoko Obi. I'm your librarian. I also run a cycling club. We all do double duty around here. Sorry. One second . . ."

She took a long drink from an Ellingham-branded reusable water bottle.

"We have about half a million books on site," she said, "both here and in storage. We have access to millions more digitally. We're partnered with most of the Ivy League libraries, so we can get you more or less anything you require. It's my job to get you anything you need."

Stevie turned that over in her mind for a bit. One good thing about being from Pittsburgh was that the Carnegie Library was one of the best in the country. She had been able to get loads of books and materials there. But here there might be things related to the case, things not available anywhere else. Stevie wanted to stay, but Kazim was moving them on, all the way across the campus, to a large, circular tent structure that looked semipermanent.

"This is the study yurt," Kaz said, pushing back a heavy flap that served as the door. The floor of the inside was covered in a mix of beautiful woven rugs and piles of pillows and beanbags.

"A lot of people sleep in here," Kaz said. "It's for studying, but . . . it has all kinds of uses."

The girl with the bob laughed knowingly. A girl with short silver hair, a longer chunk of which poked straight up at the forehead, was lingering nearby. She wore round glasses, white overalls, and a short tank top underneath. She had been trailing Janelle, Stevie, and Nate for several minutes. The sun came out from behind a cloud, bathing all of them in strong, burning summer light. The girl tapped on her glasses and the lenses darkened.

"Magic," she said.

"Transition lenses," Janelle replied with a laugh. "Photochromic plastic."

"Vi Harper-Tomo," the girl said to Janelle, extending a hand. "And I *am* magic."

Something flashed between these two that was almost visible to the naked eye, which caused Stevie a second of panic. She had just met Janelle, Janelle was her best bet at a closest friend, and already someone else was coming into the frame.

Which was a crazy thought.

Stevie tried to push it out of her mind and focus on the prize of this tour—an inside look at the Ellingham Great House, the Ellinghams' former residence. She had studied the photos of the house for so long. Seen the floor plans. Knew the history. But instead, Kaz walked them right past it.

"Aren't we going in?" Stevie asked.

"End of the tour!" he said, walking them past the walled garden, and back into a clearing in the trees to a large, sprawling modern building of raw Vermont wood and stone. It had a high, peaked roof like a ski lodge.

"This is the art barn," Kaz said. "This is the only building that was added to the original campus, and it keeps getting bigger. They're adding to it now."

The ground around one side was dug up, and the construction looked new. Stevie couldn't help but note that the building bordered closely on the walled garden—the famous walled garden that held the lake where the Ellingham ransom drop had occurred.

The garden gate was open, and people wearing hard hats were passing through. Stevie craned her head to look, but the tour was moving on into the art barn. There would be time. She would get in.

"The art barn isn't just for art," Kaz said, while walking backward. "Everything kind of happens here. Yoga and dance, meetings, some classes."

Kaz was never so excited as when he was talking about the eco friendly construction of the art barn, the bamboo floors and the locations of composting toilets. Stevie began to twitch from anticipation. After what felt like an hour-long lecture on sewage, they left and walked back to the Great House.

When they stepped inside, Stevie stopped breathing for a moment. The house was built around a massive foyer, with balconies on the upper floors looking down over the space. Before her were the master stairs, sweeping up to the balcony of the second floor, and from there twisting elegantly up to the third. On the wall at the top of the first level of stairs was a massive painting, done by the famous painter and Ellingham family friend Leonard Holmes Nair. The setting was the lake and the observatory in the background, at night. Though that much was clear, the style was borderline hallucinatory. Iris and Albert loomed in the foreground of the picture—mythical figures in swipes of blue and yellow. Iris's short black hair seemed to spread from her head and weave into the branches of the trees. Albert Ellingham's face was merged with the full moon that hung over the observatory and spilled light onto the lake. They looked away from each other, their expressions stretched, their eyes pulling long, their mouths almost rectangular.

Stevie had seen many images of this painting. Online, it wasn't that impressive. But in person, it gripped her and held her attention. It was disturbing. There was something about it, something that seemed to haunt the shadows in the background, something that seemed to be behind the observatory. This was painted two years before the kidnapping, but it seemed to foretell the doom that was on the horizon, and that the observatory would be part of it.

The painting seemed to preside over everything.

"Meet Larry," Kaz said, indicating a man who sat at a large desk next to the front door. He was an older, uniformed man with salt-and-pepper hair clipped into a crew cut.

"I'm Security Larry," he said. "It's what people call me. It's what I answer to. I'm head of security for all of Ellingham. I already know all of your names. I get to know everyone before they arrive."

"Security Larry knows everyone!" Kaz said.

Security Larry didn't look excited by this interruption.

"We're very secure up here, but if you ever need us, you can hit the blue button on the alarms you'll see in the campus buildings and on some light poles. The rules here aren't hard, but you have to follow them. If you don't, I'll show up. I live just down the path at the gatehouse, so I'm always here. If something says Keep Out, that means Keep Out. It doesn't mean go in because someone dared you or because you heard about other people going in. Some of the original features of the property are no longer structurally sound. You may get in, but you may not get out. We've had people stuck for days, so they were starved and terrified before they were expelled. You've been warned."

"What does that mean?" Janelle said quietly as Kaz waved them toward one of the front rooms. "Original features aren't sound?"

"He means the tunnels," Stevie said. "And the hidden passages."

On the right side of the front door, opposite Larry's desk, was a dayroom with magnificent painted panels depicting twisting vines and pale roses, all decorated in delicate raised plaster patterns in silver. The furniture was upholstered in violet silk and the floors were covered in a massive decorative rug. This was an eighteenth-century room the Ellinghams had imported from Lyon, France—the furnishings, the rugs, the curtains, and wall decorations—all of it had been boxed up, shipped to America, and resized and assembled here.

The next room, the ballroom, had a set of glass double doors, the panes set in an elaborate art nouveau–style. The doors were partially open, so Stevie pushed them all the way and stepped into a massive room in front of them that stretched up two stories. The floor was patterned in black-and-white marble diamonds; the walls were slashed with floor-to-ceiling mirrors, sculpted and framed in delicate silver. The wall panels depicted scenes of costumed players in masks. The floor-to-ceiling rose-pink curtains were like theater curtains. The ceiling was painted in the light blue of early evening with the constellations and their representative figures all in gold. Most of America's high society danced in this ballroom in the 1930s.

"And this," said Kaz, leading them to a massive oak door, "was our founder's office."

The office had massive proportions—it was two stories high—but unlike the echoey main hall, this room was thickly carpeted from end to end in a lush, deep green, and over that there were Persian rugs. By the fireplace, there was a leopard rug, head and all, that was obviously and disturbingly real. Long windows stretched up to the ceiling and were covered in heavy satin drapes that blocked the sun. The second story of the room was entirely bookshelves, with just a walkway around for access.

The fireplace in this room was made of a rose-colored marble. Two massive desks filled one side of the room. One held six sleek black rotary telephones. There was a spinning globe that Stevie guessed contained the names of countries that had long ceased to exist, giant wooden file cabinets, and a strange piece of furniture with tubes coming out of it that Stevie recognized as being a Dictaphone—an early-twentieth-century recording device. Dictaphones were big in a lot of mystery stories.

This was where Albert Ellingham worked out the plan to try to save his family. They had counted the ransom money on this floor. She could have spent forever in this room.

But they were being ushered out again into the foyer. A man in a blue-and-white-striped seersucker suit with an Iron Man T-shirt underneath came bounding down the steps in a slow-motion run. His fine blond hair was swept to the side and bounced a bit as he came down each step.

"And now," Kaz said, "to welcome you all, the head of the school, Dr. Charles Scott!"

"Welcome, welcome!" he called. "I'm Dr. Scott. Call me Charles. Welcome, you all, to your new home. I say I'm the head of the school, but I like to think of myself as the Chief Learner . . ."

"Oh my God," Nate mumbled under his breath.

"As you're at the end of your tour," Charles said, we need to say a word about Alice. Alice Ellingham was the daughter of our founder, Albert Ellingham. Alice is technically the patron of our school, and we open each school year with a thank-you to her. So please join me in saying, *Thank you, Alice.*"

It took a moment and some gesturing for everyone to realize that this was serious, and literal. Eventually, there was a mumbled, "Thank you, Alice."

"That was cultlike," Nate said as they walked back to the green, where a picnic was being set up. "Why did we just thank a dead child?"

"It's all in the rules," Stevie said. "The school belongs to Alice Ellingham, if she ever turns up. We're all technically here on her dime, so we have to thank her. She's supporting us."

"But she's dead," Nate said.

"Almost definitely," Stevie replied. "She was kidnapped in 1936. But this place is hers . . . if she is alive and if she appears. She'd be old, but she could be alive, technically."

"That really is a thing?" Janelle said. "I thought that was a myth?"

"Really a thing," Stevie said.

"You said you know a lot about it?" Vi said. Vi had drifted out with them.

"Oh, Stevie knows it *all*," Janelle said. "Go on. Tell us."

Stevie had the strange feeling that she was being called on to perform, like a dog that knew how to use an iPad. At the same time, she now had an audience of people who wanted her to talk about the thing she loved, and that was a foreign and delightful feeling. The sun was warm and the grass was springy and all around her was the scene of murder.

They were heading toward the green, but the walled garden was just there, behind them. Stevie turned to have a look. The garden door was still open just a bit and there was no one around.

"Come on," she said. "I'll show you."

"Are we supposed to go in there?" Nate asked.

"It's open!" Vi said, stepping ahead.

The garden door was heavy and black, and passing through it had the quality of a dream. They stepped into a massive, lush garden surrounded by a high, perfectly spaced ring of trees. The grass was a brilliant, saturated green. The Great House stood at one end, with the low stone patio leading down to the lawn. There were small fountains and elaborate benches and planters. It was a regal garden, designed by people who took cues from the royal gardens of England and France. But there was one major thing that really stood out.

Most of it was a giant hole, covered in lush grass.

"What the hell?" Nate said.

"That," Stevie said, "was a lake. Iris Ellingham was a champion swimmer. This was her pool. Albert Ellingham rerouted a stream to fill it, and there used to be rowboats to go out to that."

She pointed to a knoll in the middle, where there was a round structure with a domed glass roof.

"That's the place the kidnappers had him go to drop off the money," she said. "After Iris and Alice were kidnapped, people used to contact Albert Ellingham with all kinds of theories. I think a psychic told him that Alice was in the lake, so he drained it. She wasn't there. But he never refilled it. It probably reminded him too much of what happened. He left it just like this."

"They call it the sunken garden on the map," Vi said. "I see why."

"Explain the dead child thing," Nate said.

"The deal is this," Stevie said. "The school and all the Ellingham fortune belong to Alice, but Ellingham kind of knew she was dead, even if he couldn't admit it to himself. When two years had passed, he reopened the school."

"And people came?" Vi said. "After the murders?"

"It was a one-off," Stevie replied. "And it was still the Depression. And this was one of the most famous places in America. Free school from one of the richest men in the country . . . that was a huge deal. And no one thought the kidnappers were coming back. They'd kind of taken everyone there was to take. So this school was supposed to be a beautiful thing for Alice to come back to. Albert Ellingham wanted the place to be lively. He was sort of . . . making sure there were people for Alice to play with."

"That's really grim," Janelle said. "Sweet, but . . . grim."

"So how many millions of people said they were Alice?" Nate said. "Before DNA testing, everybody must have claimed they were Alice."

"That was a thing," Stevie said, nodding. "But Ellingham had a plan. Alice's nanny was devoted to her and the family. She refused to give up any details about Alice. Ellingham had a secret file made of information about Alice, so that if anyone came forward, they would be able to check."

"What, like a birthmark or something?"

Stevie shrugged. "That's the point. No one knows except

the people in the trust, and they can't inherit. The people who run the trust are Alice's keepers. I mean, now they'd just use DNA, so the secret Alice file doesn't really matter as much."

"It's good to know we're going to the most morbid school in America," Nate said. "Now let's go. I'm hungry and I'm still pretty sure we weren't supposed to come in here."

"Again," Vi said, "gate was open."

"We probably should go," Janelle said. "But this is amazing."

And it was amazing. For so many reasons.

April 13, 1936, 8:00 p.m.

FLORA ROBINSON HAD A WELL-DEVELOPED SENSE OF IMPENDING trouble, a skill she had developed in her time working at a speakeasy. You had to be able to feel the ripple that went through the room when the police were approaching the door. You had to know a false alarm from the real thing. You had to develop the reflex to hit the alarm button at just the right moment—that button that tilted the shelves and opened the chute and sent hundreds, or sometimes thousands, of dollars' worth of booze and glass down into a hidden disposal area. Do it right, and you saved the club from closure and all the patrons from arrest. Do it wrong, and you simply ruined everything.

Flora could taste fear and anticipation in the air tonight. She turned and looked at the little silver clock on the side table. Iris and Alice had been gone for a long time. She'd seen them off at noon. Usually, when Iris took her drives, she was back in an hour or two. She'd been gone eight. No one had called Flora for dinner.

This break in routine made Flora extremely uneasy.

There was trouble around, somewhere in this quiet mansion tucked up in the mountains. She sat on her bed in her room, hugging her knees, listening and waiting. Her keenly tuned hearing and the acoustics of the house meant she heard the arrival at the front door. Iris was back. She slipped out of her bed at once and went to the edge of the balcony to see what had kept her friend.

Instead of Iris, the butler was ushering in a man. It was George Marsh, a close family friend and member of the intimate Ellingham circle.

Normally, George would have come in and made small talk with Montgomery as he handed over his hat and coat. Tonight, the hat and coat stayed on and the two of them walked briskly and silently toward Ellingham's private office.

George was a former New York police detective. Several years before, he had saved Albert's life when an anarchist placed a bomb in his car. Full of gratitude and impressed with his wits and courage, Albert called J. Edgar Hoover, the head of the FBI, and recommended that George be taken on as an agent. George tended to be wherever Ellingham and his circle were—if they were in New York, he worked out of the office there. If they were in Vermont, George would be moved up to Burlington to work on smuggling cases coming down from Canada via Lake Champlain.

George Marsh was Albert's de facto security man, and tonight, Flora could see he was here on business. Off duty, George was loose and gregarious. This was on-duty George, his step quick, his tone clipped. George and Montgomery were speaking in very low voices, but Flora could make out a few words.

". . . thirty-five minutes," George said. "Have you . . ."

"No, sir," Montgomery replied. "No police . . ."

Within a few seconds, he was ensconced in Albert's office along with Montgomery.

Police. Not a word Flora wanted to hear. She had to act.

She went down the servants' stairs to the floor below, and then made her way to Iris's dressing room by keeping close to the wall. She pulled a key from the pocket of her dress and unlocked the door to a large room—an oasis of comfort. The pearl-gray carpet was soft under her bare feet. The long silver satin curtains were still open and pale moonlight seeped in, causing the gold trim and threading on Iris's Louis XV furniture to take on a gentle glow.

Iris had so many things; Flora needed one object in particular. She started at the mirrored makeup table, where Iris's extensive collection of cosmetics were kept in rigorous order by her maid—lipsticks lined up like soldiers, French perfumes pleasingly arranged, silver hairbrushes and mirror tidily side by side. Flora tore into the drawers of powders, shadows, hairpins, creams, lotions . . . where was it? Not in here. She moved on to the chest of a dozen drawers that housed Iris's gloves, hat pins, cigarette cases, sunglasses, and any number of small accessories. Not in there. She worked the room, steady and fast, drawer by drawer, until every one was exhausted.

Flora heard knocking on the doors down the hall and

her name being called. The maid was looking for her. There wasn't much time. She had to think. Where had she seen it last?

An evening bag. The pink silk one they'd gotten that day in Paris when it rained so much they had to run barefoot down the street.

Flora ran to the closet, opened the baize door, and switched on the light. The closet was not a closet—it was another room full of racks and shelves of silk and satin, with beads and fur, with enough shoes to fill a store all lined up on shelves. The handbags took up an entire wall. Flora scanned them until she found the pink bag. She yanked it off the shelf, snapped it open, and removed a Schiaparelli makeup compact in the shape of a telephone dial.

The knocking was getting closer. Flora had to hurry. The maid was at the dressing room door, knocking and calling.

"Coming!" Flora said.

With only seconds to work, she shoved the compact down the front of her dress, wrapping her arms over her front to conceal any lump, and went to the door to admit the maid.

"You're needed downstairs," the maid said. "At once, miss."

"Why? What's going on?"

"I'm not sure, miss. Mrs. Ellingham and Miss Alice didn't come home and Mr. Marsh has come. That's all I know."

Flora pushed the compact down near her belted waist as she followed the maid downstairs; she would have to deal with its contents later. She was ushered into the office. She had only been in here once or twice before. It was the nexus of Albert's business, his private area. Tonight, the large room was strangely close, the long curtains drawn, the fire in the fireplace making a sweaty heat.

"Flora," Albert said. His voice had an urgency she had never heard before. "Did Iris tell you anything about where she was driving today?"

"No," Flora said. "Just that she was going for a drive."

"But she didn't say where? Was she going toward Waterbury? Burlington? Which way?"

"I don't know, Albert," Flora said. "What's happening?"

Albert turned toward the fire.

Flora looked to George. She and George knew each other very well. Normally, she could read his expression in a moment. He had a wide face, with a heavy jaw and big brown eyes—the kind of face that could take a blow, rattle a crook, or melt in infectious laughter. Tonight, he was a cypher.

"Please," she said. "What's wrong? Where's Iris? Where's Alice?"

"It's fine," George said. He was such a terrible liar, and what was the point of lying under these circumstances? "If you could just go back to your room . . ."

"I want to know what's happened to Iris," Flora said.

"Flora, please!" Albert cried.

The desperation in his voice made her physically cold. His secretary, Robert, shook his head, indicating to her not to press the question.

"Of course," Flora said. "I'll see myself upstairs, Montgomery."

The maid was out in the atrium, fluttering around. It was obvious to Flora she was trying to find some business near the office door so she could monitor what was happening inside.

"I'm in desperate need of a pot of coffee," Flora said to her. "Could you have one brought to my room?"

"Yes, miss," she said, and skittered off.

When the maid left to go to the kitchen, Flora turned quickly and silently to the ballroom, next to Albert's office. These rooms had intentionally been built side by side because they were rarely in use at the same time, and both benefited from high ceilings.

The lights in the ballroom were off and the curtains all drawn. The motley black-and-white floor still felt rough and dirty from the weekend's revels; the staff had not yet cleaned it. There, under the soft padding of her feet, were the paper streamers, the gravel from the drive tracked in on dancing shoes, the endless sticky patches of spilled champagne.

Iris had shown Flora a trick about these rooms: the mirrors in the room were interspersed with panels covered in wallpaper, in a pattern depicting the characters of the commedia dell'arte. On the last panel on the left side, there was a wall sconce in the form of a Venetian mask. Flora climbed quietly onto one of the gold chairs against the wall and stretched to reach it. She put her fingers through the eyeholes of the mask and pulled down sharply. The wall panel tilted, exposing a space behind. Flora pushed the panel, which swung open on a well-made hinge.

The ballroom and the office, while seemingly sharing a wall, actually shared a secret space, about two feet wide. The ballroom mirrors on this side were one way and could be used to watch goings-on in the ballroom. There were switches that could be used to make the lights dim and flicker, and tiny panels you could open to snatch a glass from a confused partygoer. The perhaps unintended second use was that it was a perfect place to listen to what was happening in Ellingham's office. Flora slipped along until she found the little door that led into Albert's office. The door was far enough away from the men and sufficiently hidden in the wall that she felt she could safely crack it open an inch without anyone noticing, exactly as Iris had shown her.

"Most of what I hear is very boring," Iris said when she showed Flora the passage and the door. "I wish he'd get a mistress and give me something better to listen to."

Flora had a feeling it would not be boring tonight.

". . . the one that came on Thursday," George was saying. "Do you still have it?"

"Of course." That was Robert Mackenzie. "Here." He handed George a paper.

"'Look, a riddle, time for fun,'" George read. "'Should we use a rope or gun? Knives are sharp and gleam so pretty. Poison's slow, which is a pity. Fire is festive, drowning's slow. Hanging's a ropy way to go. A broken head, a nasty fall. A car colliding with a wall. Bombs make a very jolly noise. Such ways to punish naughty boys! What shall we use? We can't decide. Just like you cannot run or hide. Ha ha. Truly, Devious.'"

"The envelope was postmarked Burlington," Robert added.

A phone rang, and it was snatched from the hook before the ring could even complete. Albert Ellingham said a breathless hello. The men gathered around the telephone on the desk and the responses were difficult for Flora to hear, until George's voice broke out of the cluster.

"We saw your man," a voice with a strange, unplacable accent said. "You called the cops."

"No," Albert replied. "George is a friend. He just came to visit."

"We know who he is," the voice replied. "You've made this worse on yourself. This is what you do now. You gather up all the jewelry, all the cash, anything you've got. You put them in pillowcases. You send your friend there alone, in his car. He drives east on interstate two and makes the left toward West Bolton. We'll take care of it from there and you'll get them back. Better move it. You have one hour from now."

The phone went silent. Albert said hello several times but no one replied. Flora chanced it and opened the door an inch wider to see what was happening. The men were standing around the desk, not moving and not speaking.

"I go alone," George finally said.

"No," Albert replied. "It's my wife and daughter . . ."

"You heard them, Albert," George replied. "They want me, so I go."

Robert Mackenzie had produced a map and opened it over the desk where the men were gathered.

"Here," he said. "They want you to go east on interstate highway two and take the left to go toward West Bolton. It's a dirt road. The drive looks like it would take a half hour, maybe more, depending on what happens once you turn."

"So we work fast," George said. "Get Montgomery to start gathering things. Jewelry, watches, anything you can get."

"Why you?" Robert asked. "You're in law enforcement. You're trained."

"I'm cheaper," George replied. "If Albert went and something happened to him—if they hurt him or killed him—that's international news. That's the president getting involved. That's the chair. An FBI agent no one's ever heard of? That's not such a big deal. It happens. They can't let anything happen to you, Albert."

"You're right," Robert said. "And they'd also get no more money, if that's how this goes."

"We have to move now," George replied. "We need to get the stuff they want. Where's the jewelry?"

"There are two safes upstairs, one in my dressing room and one in Iris's. The combinations to both are left five, right twenty-seven, left eighteen, right nineteen. Go, Robert. Get Montgomery to help you. Empty them."

Robert Mackenzie hurried off, leaving George and Albert alone with the map.

"I should go," Albert said again.

George's voice was quiet but it managed to fill the room and disturb the air. "You need to listen to me. You brought me here for a reason. It sounds like they're ready to give them up, so we just have to be cool-headed about it. We play by their rules, but we play smart. I'll go, and I'll bring them back to you. I know you feel like you have to go, but you have to put your feelings aside."

Albert leaned against the back of a chair and remained silent for a moment.

"If you do," he finally said, "you have my life."

"I'll be satisfied with a stiff drink," George said, grabbing his coat. As he did so, Flora saw his glance pass in the direction of where she was hiding, but he didn't seem to see the tiny opening in the wall panel. He simply picked up the coat and turned back. "Lock this place down. I don't want a mouse able to get in here. You have a revolver?"

"There's one in the desk," Robert said.

"You load it. You lock the school. You get the staff stationed at every door. And you two stay in here with that door locked and that revolver ready until I return. If I don't show up by, say, one in the morning, you call in the cavalry. This is how we have to do this. This is how we bring them home."

Crouching in the secret corridor, her head to the crack in the door, Flora felt her heart beat so fast that she grew faint. She slid down to the floor as silently as she could.

6

Back in Minerva, the two other residents were slouched cozily on the sofa, with Ellie's legs draped casually over Hayes's lap as she talked about Paris. Hayes didn't seem to be listening. He was working his phone. Pix was sitting at the table again but her tooth collection was gone, replaced by glossy Ellingham Academy folders and paperwork.

"You're back!" she said. "Okay. I need a few minutes to go through the basics. . . ."

"Don't you have to wait for David or something?" Ellie said with a groan.

"His plane from San Diego is late, and the sooner we start the sooner we're done. It's fast."

"But he's coming, right?"

"He's coming," Pix said.

Stevie, Nate, and Janelle took seats at the table. Ellie and Hayes remained in their huddle, and Hayes was still on his phone.

"Hayes," Pix said. "Just look up for five minutes."

Hayes tipped his chiseled face up and smiled easily,

setting the phone on the sofa.

"So," Pix said, consulting a list, "welcome, everyone, to Ellingham. ID cards. Each of you has been issued an ID card. That card is programmed to give you access to buildings you need to be in."

Ellie rolled dramatically off the sofa and onto the floor, where she landed facedown. Pix continued.

"Visitors from other buildings have to stay in the common areas, so they can be in this room or the kitchen, but that's it. You all got the official Ellingham rules of conduct, which includes information about consent and respecting other students. No means no here. Okay . . ."

Pix quickly scanned the list.

"Common sense stuff. No drinking, no illegal drugs. Any food in the kitchen needs to be in sealed containers and labeled for food allergies, but no one in here has a peanut allergy; I think we should be okay with that. No fires. Except for in this room when I'm present. Seriously, Ellie, no fires . . ."

Ellie groaned.

Janelle raised a hand. "Soldering?" she asked.

"Fine in the common room. No one has a microwave, okay . . . No unauthorized leaving of campus. We have shuttles to Burlington on the weekends leaving at ten in the morning and coming back at four. Alert me right away in case of a medical emergency in the house. There's a nurse living on campus, the doctor comes in three times a week, and security can respond to any medical emergency if you need immediate help. If you need to speak to anyone, you can speak to me in confidence, and we have two counselors on staff and you can make appointments online or in person. I think that's it. . . ."

She scanned the page again.

"Most of this you can read yourself. I said no fires already. Seriously, Ellie . . ."

"No fires," Ellie mumbled into the floor.

"Okay! Then that's it. Everybody take a folder."

Nate immediately grabbed a folder and scurried back to his room. Pix headed back up to her apartment. Ellie peeled herself off the floor and went to the table to lean in over Stevie and Janelle.

"Tub room," she said to Janelle and Stevie in a low voice. "Both of you. Fifteen minutes. Bring a mug."

It seemed like a command that should be obeyed.

Fifteen minutes later, mugs in hand, Janelle and Stevie knocked on the tub room door. Ellie was in the tub, dressed in what appeared to be nineteenth-century pantaloons and a corset. This alone would have caught Stevie's attention, but what held it was the fact that the water was bright pink.

"Shut the door," she said. "We needed to have a little cocktail party to celebrate your arrival."

She indicated a pile of wet, used towels on the floor next to her as if it was a comfortable divan.

Stevie wasn't sure where to start, really. The fact that they'd just been lectured about drinking. The fact that Ellie was in the tub, dressed in pantaloons, and dyeing herself pink.

Or the fact that there was a saxophone leaning against the tub. That too.

She decided to let the whole thing go and see where the conversation took them. That was a technique in criminal investigation when you wanted to get a sense of someone—let people talk, let them guide, and they'll take you to who they are.

"I'm just dyeing my outfit for tonight," Ellie said.

Both Janelle and Stevie decided to sidestep the fact that Ellie was also dyeing herself pink. No need to state the obvious.

"What's tonight?" Janelle asked.

"Tonight is the party!" Ellie said. "Here. Mugs. Here."

She reached around clumsily behind her and pulled out a champagne bottle.

"Mugs," Ellie said again, reaching out.

"But Pix just said . . . ," Janelle started.

"*Mugs.*"

Stevie passed over her mug, and after a moment, so did Janelle. Ellie poured some foamy champagne into each.

"It's warm," she said. "I only managed to bring a few bottles home from France, and it's cheap, but even the cheap stuff in Paris is better than most stuff here. Okay. I'm going to talk you through all of that. First . . ."

She raised her mug, and Stevie and Janelle got the hint that they were to clink.

"*Skål.*"

Ellie sipped heavily. Janelle looked into her mug. Stevie

hesitated for just a moment, and then decided to go for it. She had only drunk a few times in her life, but if there had ever been a time and a place, this was probably it. And they could probably ditch the mugs in time. Probably. The champagne was warm and had a hard, mineral taste and fizzed up her nose. It was not unpleasant.

"Drinking," Ellie said, draining her mug. "They know it happens. We're in the middle of nowhere so that kind of limits what goes on. This is a real no-one-can-hear-you-scream kind of place."

Janelle was still staring into her mug. She raised it to her lips a few times and was clearly pretending to drink.

"They don't really care as long as you don't get too messed up," Ellie went on, rolling to the side to adjust her wet clothing. "If Pix catches you, she just makes you dump everything out. My advice: buy cheap, buy often, put it in another container. Most people get stuff on the weekend coaches to Burlington. The only thing to watch for there is that Security Larry has a bunch of narcs in the liquor stores who'll call him if anyone from Ellingham shows up. They make things hard but not impossible. Plenty of people on the street will buy for you for five bucks. But don't get caught by Larry. He'll bust your ass. Okay! Next point."

She poured herself a little more.

"Curfews. This one is easy. You can handle it a few ways. One, you can have someone take your ID back to the house and fake tap you in for the night. Works sometimes, but if Pix is in the common room and sees it isn't you, that's bad.

Better solution, come back and go out the window. Again, Larry will bust your ass, but it's not as bad as drinking. The other security people, they vary. Depends on how hard Larry's been riding them. Having people in your room, not too hard. Pix doesn't really check very much. She's cool. She's also easily distracted. She's super smart but her mind is always elsewhere."

The way Ellie was holding her arms, Stevie got an eyeful of her tattoo. In fact, she was pretty sure that Ellie was holding her arm in the universal "ask me about my tattoo" position. It was composed of elegant script. The ink was very dark, and while there was no redness, there was just a bit of white scarring around it if you looked carefully. It was new, and it extended from the inside of her elbow to her wrist:

Mon coeur est un palais flétri par la cohue . . .

"It's Baudelaire," Ellie said when she saw that Stevie was fully engaged. "I got it over the summer in Paris. Do you speak French?" she asked.

"I do," Janelle said. "Well, some. I think it means . . . my heart is a palace . . . something . . . ?"

". . . debased by the crowd."

Stevie had no idea what the hell that meant, but she nodded.

"I was reading this poem one night in Paris over the summer," Ellie said, elegantly turning her arm, "and it just hit me, and I said to my mom, I've got to get it on my arm. My whole arm. And she agreed. We had some wine, and we went and found a place in the Canal Saint-Martin. My mom's new lover is a street artist down there and he knew a place."

Stevie reflected for just a moment on how she'd spent the summer. The majority of the time she was working at the Monroeville Mall in the knockoff Starbucks. When not working, she read. She listened to podcasts. She walked down to the ice cream place. She bought mysteries cheap from sale tables in front of the library. Doing everything she could to drown out the politics. Her life was the opposite of hanging around Paris with your mom and your mom's lover getting tattoos.

"Another thing," Ellie said. "The cell service up here sucks. The Wi-Fi goes out all the time."

"How do we watch TV?" Janelle asked.

Stevie had the feeling that Ellie was about to say she didn't watch TV.

"I don't watch TV," Ellie said.

Stevie gave herself a point on her mental scorecard.

"You don't watch *TV*?" Janelle said, in the same way you might ask, "You don't breathe *oxygen*?"

"I make art," she said.

"I make machines," Janelle replied. "And I keep the TV on while I build. I need TV. It's how I focus."

Janelle looked to Stevie in a kind of panic. Stevie knew from their summer conversations that Janelle was not joking. She seemed to know every show. Janelle was nature's finest multitasker, someone who could talk, build a robot, follow a show, all at the same time.

"Can't help you," Ellie said, proffering the bottle again. When Stevie and Janelle declined the refill, she topped up her mug. "I don't watch TV at all. Never have. We never had one growing up. My house was always about making art. I grew up in an art colony in Boston, then in a commune in Copenhagen, and then in New Mexico, and then we went to Paris for a while."

"Where did you go to school?" Janelle said.

"Wherever we were. The commune had a good school. If I could do anything—got rich or something—I'd start a commune. This place would make a good commune. So, tell me about your love lives."

Ellie punctuated this command by setting the bottle on the floor with a clunk. Stevie felt a queasy chill. This was not her favorite topic.

"I broke up with my girlfriend," Janelle said, staring into her mug. "That's when I reprogrammed the microwave."

"Creativity can come from things sucking," Ellie said. "I was in a rut last spring and I saw Roota in a pawnshop in Burlington. I had to have her. I didn't have the money at the time, but I found a way. I made a little art, I got a little cash, I got Roota. We've been together ever since."

She patted the saxophone.

"I'll tell you something else," Ellie said. "This place turns people into bunnies. It's the isolation. Trapped up here on the mountain, snowed in. When the power goes out, things get freaky. What about you?"

This was to Stevie.

The champagne bubbles reached Stevie's brain just then. Sitting in this high-ceilinged turret in the semi-dark, with her new friend Janelle and this strange but amusing artist dyeing herself pink . . . she was filled with warmth and a kind of slow relaxation. She would just be honest.

"I never met anyone who I was really . . . I don't know. I don't come from a very interesting place. Like, my parents are . . . do you know who Edward King is?" Stevie asked.

"The senator?" Janelle replied. "That asshole?"

"That's the one," Stevie said.

"Who?" Ellie said.

"Edward King is a jackass from Pennsylvania," Janelle said. "He'd like to roll everything back to the bad old days."

"My parents love him," Stevie said, leaning back against the radiator. "They work for him. His local office? Is our house."

"Oh my God," Janelle said. "You didn't tell me that."

"It's not the kind of thing you put in a message," Stevie replied. "But I did what I could to help. I went into the volunteer document the night before the last phone bank session and changed all the numbers. They made a lot of interesting calls. Krispy Kreme headquarters, the Canadian Embassy, Disney World, the Scientology Celebrity Centre, SeaWorld . . ."

"Beautiful," Ellie said, tipping back her head and laughing. "I love it."

Ellie had removed her ring and set it on the rounded edge of the tub. As she laughed, she swung out her arm and knocked it off the edge. It rolled under the tub.

"Oh shit," she said.

Stevie got down on the floor and reached around under the tub. As she pulled her hand back, something scraped against her skin.

"Be careful," Ellie said, putting the ring back on. "There are some old pipes or something under there. They'll cut you."

This seemed like something Ellie should have said before Stevie shoved her hand under the tub. Then again, Ellie did seem like the type who jumped before checking if there was a pool under her, and probably provided advice in the same style.

"So," Stevie said, "that's where I come from. And my parents are kind of obsessed with me partnering up with someone. To them, dating is one of the highest achievements of teenage life, so . . ."

"Understood," Ellie said. "Then do what you want up here."

"Definitely," Janelle said. "I mean, my parents are kind of the opposite. They're all about school. School now, girls later. And now I'm here, so . . ." Janelle let out a long exhale.

"We should get ready to go," Ellie said, standing up suddenly and bringing an end to the conversation just as Stevie had fully eased into it. Her clothes dripped heavy and pink.

"I'm coming for you in a few minutes. It's time for the party. Go get ready!"

In the warm darkness of the hall, Janelle and Stevie hunkered for a moment.

"What the hell was that?" Janelle said. "I mean, I like her? I think? But the stuff with the poem, the French stuff, living on the commune, the no TV thing. I don't know."

"Maybe this is what we came for?" Stevie said.

"Maybe," Janelle said. "Something about people who make a big deal out of not watching TV. I guess I never hung out with a lot of art people. Do you think this Wi-Fi thing is going to be a big deal? Seriously, I need my TV. I'm going to have to figure something out. There has to be a way to get a strong connection. Okay. I guess we get dressed. See you in a minute."

In her room, Stevie confronted her clothes, pawing through them quickly. She had not anticipated a party situation this early. She was never exactly party ready. When people at school looked online for party outfits and *looks*, she was genuinely confused. There were people who seemed not only to understand these things, but to accomplish them. A striped top, a wide-brimmed hat, shorts for that "special beach weekend." Lipsticks for fall, jeans that were perfect for a hayride, pendant earrings for that holiday party and snowball fight. Who lived these lives?

The party outfit was going to be black shorts and black tank top. Stevie owned no jewelry. Her concession to the occasion was a pair of red flip-flops.

Janelle appeared at her door dressed in a baby-blue dress covered in lemons, with matching lemon earrings, and a gentle lemony perfume. This was all acceptable from Janelle, because it made sense. If Janelle could build a machine, she could build an outfit.

Random, discordant bleating came from upstairs. Ellie was playing her saxophone, and one thing was clear—she did not know how to play.

"Oh," Janelle said, looking up. "That may get old, fast."

"Is this 'party' enough?" Stevie asked.

"You look great," Janelle said, and it sounded sincere. "I just, I got nervous. I wear my lemons when I'm nervous."

A moment later, Ellie, still pink, still drippy, came down the stairs, nudging a reluctant and unhappy Nate. She had saxophoned him out of hiding.

It was time to go to a party.

7

THE SLOW SUMMER TWILIGHT WAS FALLING AND THE FIREFLIES ROSE out of the grass and bobbed around as pockets of people made their way to the party, which was being held in the yurt. The Ellingham Great House windows caught the last of the dying sunlight, the windows glowing orange and gold. Ellie led the pack, blasting away on Roota in a series of off-kilter squawks that made the birds fly out of the trees as they passed.

"David needs to get here," she said. "You'll love him. He's the best."

As they went through one of the many wooded areas with statues, Ellie stopped for a moment in front of one of the statues, reached into her bag, and produced a small spray can. She painted the words THIS IS ART onto the torso in dripping blue letters, replaced the can, and kept skipping ahead and bleating on the sax.

"Someone has a case of the try-too-hards," Nate said in a low voice. The yurt was packed when they arrived. There was a hum of voices coming from within. Ellie peeled back the canvas opening and raised Roota high. A group of people on a small sofa in the back cheered, and she joined them. Within a minute, she was wrapped in a black boa that had materialized from somewhere. A first year was in this group, striking in black lipstick and a shaggy red dress. Her name, Stevie would pick up as the evening went on, was Maris Coombes, and she was an opera singer. Stevie learned this because she kept emitting high, clear snatches of arias.

An intense-looking guy with wild hair who wore a massively oversized dress shirt, like something a painter might drape over themselves, was gesturing with a vape. Hayes was there as well, sunk deep into the folds of the sofa. Maris was very close to him and they spoke face-to-face.

Janelle scanned the room and found Vi, who was sitting on a rug with three other people, playing a tile-based game.

"Let's sit there," she said to Nate and Stevie.

It was as good a place as any. Vi scooted over and made room for everyone, and introductions were made.

"This is Marco, DeShawn, and Millie," she said. "Do you like Castles of Arcadia? We were going to play."

"Sure!" Janelle said. "I don't know how but show me."

Stevie also didn't know how to play. Nate did, and this brought a bit of enthusiasm to his demeanor. He immediately started explaining the value of tiles with pictures of grain and bricks on them, the importance of the various green squares, why you needed to build by rivers and collect the tiny wooden sheep and cows and put them in fenced areas. Janelle remained focused, but Stevie couldn't help looking around the room, and soon she lost track of what the game was even supposed to be about.

A girl came in through the flap with a kind of queenly bearing. She had a crown of vibrant long red hair, thick and curly. Stevie had met people with long hair and people with curly hair and people with red hair, but this hair was like a force of nature. It wasn't fully curly—it was stretched out and full and golden. It was less like hair and more like a weather pattern. Someone called out the name "Gretchen" and Ellie hopped across the room to greet her. Stevie watched the girl stare down the group on the sofa, narrowing her focus on Hayes and Maris. She spoke to Ellie, then gave a massive hair flip and pointedly did not join the group on the sofa. Hayes just cocked his head for a moment, and then turned back to Maris.

Something going on there.

Germaine Batt, the girl from the coach, sat talking to Kaz, though she also appeared to be mostly looking around the room. She continued to work her phone with an intensity Stevie had rarely seen. "She does that show," Janelle said. "The Batt Report. She's some kind of journalist."

As the room grew louder and more crowded, it became clear that there would be no Castles of Arcadia, and Millie, Marco, and DeShawn split into their own group, and Vi and Janelle got to talking. Nate and Stevie remained together, with Nate sadly gripping a handful of wooden cows.

"This is fun," Nate said. "What are we supposed to be doing?"

"Meeting people," Stevie said.

Nate made a sound like a deflating balloon.

"You don't like meeting new people," Stevie surmised.

"No one likes meeting new people."

"I'm not so sure about that," Stevie said as she watched Janelle and Vi. Stevie found herself getting strangely nervous as Janelle and Vi talked, their heads getting a little closer together with each exchange, the laughs a little bigger. A bubble of jealousy rose in her and she clamped it down.

"It's true," Nate said. "Everyone pretends to. It's just one more thing we're supposed to pretend to like."

"I'm a new person you're meeting," Stevie said.

Nate didn't reply to that.

"So," she said, to make conversation, "are you working on the sequel to your book?"

"What?"

It was like a spotlight had come onto Nate and he was pinned to a brick wall, facing down the guards. He squeezed his cows.

"I started it," he said.

"How many chapters have you written?"

"It's not like that," he snapped. "Why are you asking me this?"

"What?"

"I mean . . ." Nate fidgeted. "You don't just write something and it's done. You don't just *do* it. You write parts and you rewrite and you have new ideas and you move stuff. I don't want to talk about the book."

"Okay," Stevie said. She pressed herself deeper into the futon, until the wooden frame was hard against the base of her spine.

Nate also shifted uncomfortably. "They let me in here because of the book," he said. "*That's why I am here*. Do you know how many pages I've written?"

"I thought you didn't . . ."

"Two thousand. *Two thousand*."

"That seems good?" Stevie said, unsure of what was happening.

"It's two thousand pages and *nothing happens*. It's all *terrible*. I wrote the first book and then I *forgot how to write*. It used to be that I would sit and write and I would go into some other world—I could see it all. I was totally in another place. But the second it became something I had to do, something in me broke. It's like I used to know the way to some magical land and I lost the map. I hate myself."

He leaned back against the pillows and exhaled.

"So, no, I don't want to talk about it."

Stevie nervously side-eyed Nate until it was clear he wasn't going to say any more. Then she turned her attention to the rest of the room.

Hayes was sidling up to Maris. Before long, they were in intense conversation again. Stevie wondered about Beth Brave—she probably wouldn't be happy that Hayes was sidling up to other people now that he was at school. Stevie also noticed she was not the only person paying attention to

Hayes and Maris. Germaine Batt was watching the two of them carefully, and at one point lifted her phone and took a photo. The girl with the red hair, Gretchen, also appeared to object to what she was seeing because she kept deliberately turning away.

Lots of strings attached to Hayes, pulling in all directions.

"It's David!" Ellie said, throwing up her arms and breaking Stevie's concentration on Hayes and his orbit. "David, David, David!"

As David David David came into the yurt, the strings of lights shook and a fragrant night breeze blew in. He raised his arms high, as if in triumph. Ellie sprang over and ensnared him in a boa-filled hug. He half lifted her and she wrapped her legs around his middle and stayed there, riding around.

Ellie directed the triple David over to the Minerva group. He was tall, with a shock of partially curly, partially wild dark hair that likely hadn't seen a pair of scissors in months. Many people in the yurt were casually dressed, but David was leaning a little more toward shabby—cargo shorts with visible wear and holes; a thin, dark-blue T-shirt with a logo that had faded into obscurity; broke-down-looking skate shoes.

In that first moment, Stevie had the feeling she had met David before. Something about him that just had a suggestion of . . . something she couldn't place. Something that made her brain itch.

"This is David," Ellie said from her position clinging to his torso. "He's the last member of House Minerva. Say hello, David."

Stevie had a strange thought that she really hoped he didn't say "hello, David" in reply, but that was exactly what happened. Another point on the scorecard. Maybe people at Ellingham were not so different after all.

David's eyes, which were deep brown and bright, went right to hers, as if he had clocked her disapproval. His peaked brows peaked a bit higher into his forehead, and he gave a long, thin smile. He set Ellie down on the back of the sofa and dropped between Stevie and Nate in a space not quite big enough for him to fit. Ellie did the introductions as she decorated David's hair with loose feathers from her boa.

David dug into a pocket and produced a battered deck of cards.

"Pick one," he said, presenting the pack to Stevie. As he leaned in, Stevie picked up a number of scents. There was something low and funky that she couldn't place, along with the stale air from a plane.

Stevie did not want to pick a card, but the pack was outstretched. So she pulled one out.

"Look at it," David said. "Don't show me."

Stevie eyed the jack of hearts in her palm.

"Okay," David said, tipping his head back, looking at the ceiling of the yurt. "Is it . . . the three of clubs?"

"No."

"Okay. The six of diamonds?"

"No."

"The ace of spades?"

"No."

David hmmed. Nate shifted in commiseration, but Janelle gave an obliging smile. Ellie draped herself over the back of the sofa.

"Seven of hearts?" he said.

"You should probably give up now," Stevie replied.

"No, no," he said, "I always get it within the first fifty-two guesses."

That got a little laugh from Janelle, but Stevie suspected it was simply politeness.

"Okay," David said, looking back down and taking a deep breath. "Last guess. Is it . . . the king of clubs?"

Stevie held up the jack of hearts.

"Yeah," he said. "I wasn't going to guess that. I was just naming cards."

He plucked the card from her hand and shoved it back in the deck. Stevie felt a burning rush of blood to her cheeks. Was this mockery? What the hell did it mean? Stevie could handle mockery. What she couldn't stand was *not understanding*. The yurt was close and the air thick.

Ellie gently whacked David on the head, sending feathers flying.

"You're so dumb, David," she said affectionately. She gave Stevie a reassuring smile over his head. "I was starting to worry you weren't coming."

"I almost didn't make it," he said. Then, to everyone, he

said, "I was a little distracted last year."

"He sat in his room and smoked weed and played video games," Ellie clarified.

"You make it sound like I was doing nothing," David replied. "It was all research."

"David makes video games," Ellie said. "Or he says he does."

"So," David said. "Who are you people?"

More introductions went around, thanks to Janelle. Nate was again singled out as the one who wrote that book that one time. And then they got to Stevie.

"She researches crime," Janelle said.

"Researches crime?" he repeated. "What does that mean?"

"What it sounds like," Stevie said.

"You . . . watch a lot of Discovery ID?" he said.

She did watch a lot of Discovery ID, as it happened. That was the all-murder channel. She did not say this, though.

"She does criminology and things like that," Janelle said, maybe a little defensively. "And she knows everything about the Ellingham case. That's why she's here."

"What, are you here to solve it?" he asked.

Stevie gulped in some air.

Yes, that was kind of the plan. But no one else was supposed to say it, and they really weren't supposed to say it like that. It was like he had just taken her dreams, which had been floating so gently and rising so high this whole day, and with one prick of a pin, popped them, exploded them. Rubbery dream pieces all over the yurt.

"You weren't going to say that, were you?" he said. His eyes were so bright, so piercing.

There was an awkward pause in their corner. To end it, Ellie tipped herself off the edge of the sofa into David's lap.

"I thought that was solved," she said to Stevie. "Wasn't it? Didn't someone confess?"

"Someone was found guilty," Stevie said. "He probably didn't do it. He confessed because . . ."

A burst of laughter from behind, and Ellie looked up to see what was going on. No one wanted to hear why Anton Vorachek, the local anarchist who was arrested and tried for the crime, confessed.

"He confessed because he was on the stand . . ." Stevie tried to continue.

Unlike before, when everyone was listening, now there was a dance breaking out and David was doing this weird smirk and Janelle, Vi, and Nate looked vaguely uncomfortable.

You know when your moment is over.

A flask appeared from somewhere. Ellie had some. David passed. It was waved in Janelle, Nate, and Stevie's direction, and they all shook their heads. Stevie thought drinking from containers other people drank from was gross. She embraced Locard's exchange principle: every contact leaves a trace, meaning in this case, backwash.

Ellie and David went away to talk to some other second years, leaving the first years on their own.

"He seems fun," Janelle said with forced brightness.

Nate was unable to bring himself to lie.

"I feel kind of better," he said to Stevie. "I think you're even more screwed than I am."

⚓

Nights always brought the worry. Night was hard.

It was three in the morning and Stevie was wide awake. If she was going to have a panic attack, it would likely be tonight. New school, new start, new friends, new home up here on the mountain when she'd never been away from home and her parents for more than a few days. The night brought cooler air, but still, the room felt a bit crowded. When she opened the window, a giant moth blew in. It beat a hasty path to the ceiling light and landed against it with a *thunk*.

"I know the feeling," Stevie said to it.

The panic attacks had started when she was twelve years old. No one knew why. Her parents tried to help but were largely confused by them. Medication took care of some of it, but Stevie had worked out the rest with some assistance from the school counselor and by reading more or less the entire internet.

It had been a year and three months since Stevie stopped having the panic attacks all the time, and at least six months since she'd had a big one. But the nights still worried her. She still paced before she slept, eyeing her bed, wondering if this was going to be one of the nights she was dragged out of sleep by a heart racing like a car with no driver and a board pressed up against the gas pedal.

She sat on the floor beneath the window, closed her eyes, and let the breeze play on the back of her neck. Breathe in. Breathe out. Count. One. Breathe in. Breathe out. Two. Just let the thoughts come and go.

You weren't going to say that, were you?

Let it go.

You can always come home.

Let it go, for real. Go full *Frozen*.

You're even more screwed than I am.

She opened her eyes and looked over at her bureau. She could take an Ativan and knock herself out, but she would be groggy tomorrow.

No. She was going to do this. It was going to be fine.

So she turned to her other medicine—her mysteries. Stevie had always loved mysteries from the time she was small. When the attacks hit, she found that mysteries were her salvation. If she was awake at night, she had her mystery novels, her true-crime books, her shows, her podcasts. Maybe most people wouldn't be soothed by reading about the acid bath murders, about Lizzy Borden or H. H. Holmes, about highway murders, about the quiet neighbor with the dark secret, about bodies in walls and latent fingerprints, about thirteen guests at dinner when you know they can't all live. . . . These things were problems for her mind to work on, and when her mind worked on the mystery, it couldn't panic.

So Stevie became a mystery machine, with true crime

playing in her ears between classes at school and while she filled bean containers at the coffee shop at the mall. She couldn't get enough. She got into the Websleuths world online. There, she found people like herself, people who spent their time looking into cold cases. It was there that she became transfixed by the Ellingham case.

Yes, the idea of her solving this case sounded improbable. She was a sixteen-year-old from Pittsburgh. This case was decades old. Everyone had tried to solve it. The FBI hadn't been able to do it. The scores of serious (and not serious) investigators had not been able to do it. Thousands of people obsessed over it all the time. Ellingham himself, a genius, had tried to find out what happened and the search had killed him.

You didn't just solve the Ellingham Affair.

She stared at the walls with their thick paint and their possible secrets.

She wasn't screwed. She was Stevie Bell, and she had gotten into Ellingham Academy on her own. They didn't exactly admit people by mistake.

Unless it *was* a mistake.

What if they'd made a mistake? What if they'd made the first mistake they'd ever made? Why had they done this to her?

Nope nope nope nope.

Stevie put on a podcast and pushed across the floor and opened up a still-sealed box. She pulled out several thick folders full of perfectly organized printouts and copies, a roll of heavy-duty tape and a pair of heavy-duty scissors. Once the box was empty, she set about breaking it down into flat pieces, trimming off the flaps to make the rectangles nice and even. She worked quickly, her mind split between the podcast and her task.

In police procedurals, there was always a case board—a place to store the images of victims and suspects, maps and diagrams. A visual reference when you needed to think it all through. The box would serve as a board.

At the top, she put three photos: Iris Ellingham, Alice Ellingham, and Dottie Epstein. Here were the floor plans of the Great House at the time of the kidnapping. The case board began to take shape as it filled.

In the center of her board, Stevie put the most notorious piece of evidence of all, the one people always talked about: the Truly Devious letter:

Look! A riddle! Time for fun!
Should we use a rope or gun?
Knives are sharp and gleam so pretty
Poison's slow, which is a pity
Fire is festive, drowning's slow
Hanging's a ropy way to go
A broken head, a nasty fall
A car colliding with a wall
Bombs make a very jolly noise

Such ways to punish naughty boys!
What shall we use? We can't decide.
Just like you cannot run or hide.
Ha ha.
Truly,
Devious

The physical letter was lost in the mess of the investigation, so it could never be tested or fingerprinted. Only a photo remained—a stark, terrifying communication that arrived at the Ellingham house a week before the kidnapping. It had been composed with words cut out of magazines and newspapers, that creepy, classic style of hiding your handwriting.

Of the many intriguing aspects of the Ellingham Affair, this was the one she always came back to—this strange declaration from an unknown person that said, "I am bad. I intend to do harm. I'm harming you now by inspiring fear. I am the knife. I am Truly Devious."

It was like trolling, kind of. Except so complicated. It took more effort to get under the skin of a famous person in the 1930s. They had to get a collection of magazines and newspapers, find the words they needed, clip them delicately and glue them with a crooked precision, then send it off in the mail, never knowing what effect it would cause.

Why announce yourself, Truly Devious? Why tell them you're coming?

Stevie added another photo to the board—Anton Vorachek. It was the Truly Devious letter that always convinced Stevie (and other people) that Vorachek was innocent. Vorachek could barely speak English—he probably wouldn't have written a *poem* in English, a poem modeled on the style of Dorothy Parker, no less. No one ever thought it made sense, but they found the marked bills on Vorachek, no one liked him, and he confessed on the stand.

Truly Devious hung over the case like a ghoul.

Over the next hour, Stevie assembled the images, organized the files. There were floor plans, copies of interviews, police reports. It had taken a very long time, a helpful librarian, and the assistance of other Websleuths to collect it all. She had run through two toner cartridges and a box of paper that belonged to the Edward King campaign (good) to print out this mass of information. And it *was* a mass. It was heavy. Stevie liked to hold the files and bundles of paper, to pore over it again and again until it all ran through her head like an ancient stream. Surely other people had come to Ellingham with an interest in the case. Some of those people came before the internet existed, so they wouldn't have had access to all Stevie did. And the others . . .

No. None had her passion. You know when you're the top fan—the one who knows the words and feels the gaps and senses the disruptions. You know when you are *the one who gets it*.

It was dawn when Stevie finished assembling her board

and putting all of her documents in order on her desk and in the bookcase. She went to the window and found a soft, friendly morning with a light, sweet breeze. She closed her eyes and took a deep breath.

The critical scene of the mystery is when the detective enters. The action shifts to Sherlock's sitting room. The little Belgian man with the waxed moustache appears in the lobby of the grand hotel. The gentle old woman with the bag of knitting comes to visit her niece when the poison pen letters start going around the village. The private detective comes back to the office after a night of drinking and finds the woman with the cigarette and the veiled hat. This is when things will change.

The detective had arrived at Ellingham Academy.

April 14, 1936, 4:00 a.m.

WHEN GEORGE MARSH PULLED UP TO THE FRONT GATES OF THE
Ellingham estate, two men in overalls holding shotguns
greeted him. They waved him along, and he steered his
Model B along the perilous Ellingham road for the second
time in only a few hours.

Albert Ellingham and Robert Mackenzie were waiting
for him on the drive. Mackenzie huddled in his coat, but
Ellingham didn't appear to feel the chill at all. He rushed to
the car door and was taken aback at the sight.

"What happened? Where are they? Your face! What
happened?"

He was referring to the trail of bruises along Marsh's jaw
and around to his eye, and to a gash in his left cheek. His left
eye was almost swollen shut.

"They weren't there," Marsh said, getting out of the car.

"What do you mean they weren't there? You didn't see
them?"

"When I made the turn toward West Bolton, I got about
a mile down before they blocked the road with a car. I got

out and they ambushed me. They want two hundred thousand more. There was no sign of Iris or Alice."

Robert let out a hissing sigh.

"You were right, Robert," Ellingham said. "They want more. So we will get them more. How long do we have?"

"Twenty-four hours," Marsh replied. "There'll be another phone call. They said to have someone wait by the phone box on Church Street at eleven p.m. tonight. They wanted you to deliver it, but I got them to accept me as the deliveryman."

"Surely now we call in the police and FBI," Robert said to Marsh. "We can have someone wake J. Edgar Hoover. We can't go on like this."

"They said the increase in ransom was because you involved the police," Marsh said. "Meaning, me."

"They don't want the police involved," Ellingham said. "I can give them whatever they want."

"This will go on," Robert replied, his voice cracking with urgency. "You are an endless source of funds. Don't you see?"

An owl cut across the sky with a screech.

"We should talk about this inside," Marsh said quietly. "Voices carry."

The Great House was quiet now, but it was not still. The electricity on the mountaintop was often erratic. The lights in the main hall flickered and dimmed. The house itself seemed to pulse. Two more men in overalls waited directly inside the door, guns at the ready. They looked confused, jumpy, and seeing Marsh's damaged face did not reassure

them. Montgomery, the butler, was still awake and attend-
ing.

"Should I bring water and bandages, sir?" he asked.

"What?" Ellingham said. Then, remembering Marsh's
injuries, he waved his hand. "Yes, yes. Bring them."

Inside the office, Ellingham walked restlessly to his
drinks table and poured some whiskeys with a shaking hand,
giving one to the detective and keeping one for himself.

"What have you told everyone in the house?" Marsh
asked. "They must have noticed that Mrs. Ellingham and
Alice have not returned."

"We said we had a threat of the usual type," Robert said.
"Anarchists. Mrs. Ellingham was told to spend the night in
Burlington with a friend until we sorted it out."

"Do you think they believe it?" Marsh asked.

"Unlikely."

The three descended into silence for several minutes.
Marsh lowered himself into a chair. Ellingham stood at the
fire, his hand gripping the mantle. Mackenzie sat and examined the letter again. Montgomery appeared with the water
and bandages. Marsh wiped the blood from his face.

"We'll get them back," Ellingham suddenly snapped.
"We'll give them whatever they want. Iris is strong and
resourceful. She will be able to handle herself and Alice."

"With respect," Robert said, "I must speak frankly in
this circumstance—Mrs. Ellingham is resourceful. She is
also strong-willed and athletic. She's a champion swimmer
and skier. Do you think she would allow herself and her

daughter to be taken without a fight? She will struggle. This has already gone wrong in several ways. Every moment we delay reaching out to the police at large is a moment she's in danger."

"They're already upset that someone else is involved. Look what they did to Marsh! We can do this. We can get them what they want without further attention."

"We may have no choice in that matter," Robert replied. "Even if we wanted to—do you think this is going to stay quiet? We have about twenty people in the house, we've got the school, and in a few hours, we're going to have a hundred men more show up for work. How does this stay out of the press?"

"Have work for this week canceled and arrange for the men to be paid anyway."

"That's not going to stop people from talking," Robert said. "This will be all over Burlington by dawn."

Ellingham looked to Marsh, who was sipping his whiskey carefully through swollen lips.

"Can you get that kind of money by tomorrow?" Marsh asked.

"The Burlington bank won't be able to handle a withdrawal of that size on no notice," Ellingham said. "Robert, wake someone up in New York and have them at the bank the moment it opens and you have it flown here. Get our contacts together. Money, pilots. I want people awake now. I'm going to make sure the property has been secured."

When Ellingham was gone, the policeman and the

secretary regarded each other by the light of the fire.

"I understand your disapproval, Mackenzie," Marsh said. "I don't like this either. But I think this is how we have to play it right now."

"That letter . . . should we use a rope or gun? Knives are sharp and gleam so pretty. Truly, Devious. The person who wrote that note is talking about *murder*, not kidnapping."

"We do it this way for twenty-four hours," Marsh said. "Whoever did this—they know this place well. Assume we have eyes on us. If this estate is flooded with FBI, they could panic and act rashly. We stay cool, we do as they say."

Ellingham reappeared at the doorway of the office.

"Word has just come that one of the students is missing— a girl named Dolores Epstein. We need to have the grounds searched. This has to be connected. She's a good girl. She wouldn't run off. My God, we need to protect the students. We can't give the game away. We'll need to get them all out of here on some excuse."

Robert Mackenzie wearily closed his eyes. He felt that he was watching a disaster in the making and could do nothing to stop it.

8

Stevie awoke with a jolt the next morning, in the unfamiliar bed. Her work of the night before was there on the floor. The faces of the Ellinghams stared up at her as she sorted her bath supplies into the blue plastic caddy she had so carefully chosen, shuffling the shampoo to one side, pushing over the shower gel, looking for the right place to stand the razor. She pulled on her pajama bottoms and a robe, put on her flip-flops, picked up the caddy, and stood in front of the closed door for a full two minutes working up the courage to go out into the hallway.

This was weird. Why was it so weird? She knew this was a dorm. She'd stayed over at friends' houses before. But this was different—these were the people she would be living with, and some of them were guys. Half of them were guys.

So what. She was wearing a robe and . . . so what?

She opened the door. No one was in the hall. Feeling victorious, she took measured, leisurely steps down to the bathroom. There was another bathroom upstairs; it was unlikely that everyone in the house would be crowded into this one. It wasn't very big, though, and it was already very steamy and the one shower stall was in use.

Stevie set her caddy on the windowsill and examined the frosted coating on the window to make sure it made it impossible to see inside. The shower curtain snapped back, and a dripping Ellie emerged. Technically, Ellie had a towel, but she was using it to dry her hair. The rest of Ellie was on show.

"Oh, hey," she said. "The water is kind of cold now. Sorry."

She continued walking past, leaving sopping-wet footprints along the way. As she reached the door, she looped the towel around herself, barely covering the major regions of her body, and headed out.

That, Stevie thought, is confidence.

Also, Ellie had bare feet. Stevie had the stupid flip-flops on. Her mother had convinced her that if she took them off for even a second, her feet would be attacked by terrible germs. The shower looked clean—but still.

Also, the water wasn't kind of cold. It was completely cold.

Still, a cold shower isn't the worst thing on a summer morning when you're already tired. This was pure mountain spring water. (It was likely some kind of municipal water or something, but it was important to tell yourself a good story when you were standing under ice-cold water.)

Janelle was already at the farm table, intently reading something on her tablet as she ate a bowl of cereal. Pix was settled in the hammock chair, knitting. No one else seemed to be up.

"Morning!" Pix said. "Breakfast things are in the kitchen."

Stevie shuffled into the kitchen and lunged for the coffee. She had a poke around the small kitchen, examining the contents of the cereal dispensers and the refrigerator.

Suddenly, a bowl materialized next to her, causing her to jump.

"It's free," David said. "Pix doesn't count the cereal and send you a bill."

Stevie wasn't sure if this was supposed to be some kind of jab about money and lack thereof. Who said things like that? People like David, who also snuck up behind you in the morning when you were still half asleep. Did he know her family had little money?

Did he want to play? Because she would play. No need to be nice, Stevie. Green light.

She assessed him. He was wearing the same clothes he had been in the night before, and there were still one or two wayward feathers stuck in his hair. Either he hadn't slept or slept in his clothes. She inhaled gently. Wine on his breath. Likely guess, he was up drinking with Ellie.

Interesting, but not enough. Look harder. In the daylight, she could get a better impression than she'd been able to in the dark of the yurt. His nose was long and fine. As he handed her the bowl, she took note of a band of wiry muscle that ran down his arm, and a beaten up but expensive-looking watch on his wrist. The crystal face was scarred, but refused to break fully, and the leather strap, while worn, was still holding strong. She got a look at the face. Rolex.

Now she was onto something. He had an unusual pattern of tan and burn on his arms. His one arm was bright red, the other just tan. Likewise, the one side of his face was much more red than the other. It was the kind of lopsided burn you got if you were half covered or turned the wrong way for too long.

"So," she said, gripping the bowl tightly. She stuck it firmly under the Froot Loops dispenser and poured herself a big bowl. "You're from California?"

"So I hear," he said, getting himself a mug.

She looked at the uneven tan again, the strips of healed sunburn, the pale patches. And his voice. It didn't have that slow, relaxed California tone.

"Recent?" she said.

"Recent what?" There was just a little edge in his voice. Good.

"You moved there recently?" she said, popping a few dry Froot Loops in her mouth.

"What makes you say that?"

He was smiling, but it was strained. His voice a bit crisp. The move was recent, and the circumstances weren't pleasant. Rich boy, recent move, the topic made him a little frosty, and clearly he was acting out and needed attention.

"Just something I picked up," she said.

"Do you pick things up a lot?" he asked. The smile was

full now, but thin. He leaned back against the refrigerator as the coffee machine hissed. He twisted the watch a bit on his wrist.

Stevie watched this motion for a moment. David stopped, seemed to realize what she was looking at, and put that hand in his pocket.

Something bad about that watch.

"Could you move?" she said. "I need the milk. I might as well get my money's worth."

He smiled even more broadly and stepped away from the fridge door.

"Of course," he said. "The girl detective needs her breakfast."

Stevie smiled right back as she poured the milk and replaced it.

"Daddy issues needs his therapist," she said.

He laughed out loud—a little cough of a laugh. She had found a mark. It was a wide and easy mark, but it had landed.

That little exchange should have been enough. It would have been perfect had it simply ended there. But, of course, there was no escape. He lived here too. He took a seat at the end of the table and stared down the length of it.

Nate joined them, creeping into the room with tousled hair. He seemed a bit more robust this morning and actually said hello to everyone.

"So," David said, a little too loudly. "What's everybody got today?"

"Adviser meetings," Janelle said. "What are they like? I have Dr. Hinkle."

"Do you like hearing people tell stories about getting lost inside the Large Hadron Collider?" David asked.

"Always," Janelle said.

"Then you'll be fine. Who do you have, Nate?"

"Dr. Quinn," Nate said.

"Oh." David shook his head. "Bind your wounds. She can smell blood."

"What?"

"And how about you, Stevie?" That thin smile was on her again.

"Dr. Scott," Stevie said.

"Captain Enthusiasm!" David replied. Stevie caught Pix give a little grin as she knit. "He's bouncy. Are you going to solve mysteries together?"

"David," Pix said.

"Only asking," David replied.

"What did you mean about the blood?" Nate pressed on. "Is she hard?"

"Just remember there's no shame in crying," David replied. "After, I mean. Like me after I lost my virginity."

"*David*," Pix said again. "Don't freak people out. Dr. Quinn is fine. You'll be fine, Nate."

Stevie was hanging back on the virginity thing. Was that a joke? Had to be a joke. What did it mean? Was that one of those things where you said something really vulnerable to make yourself seem above it all? Had he said virginity louder than any of the other words in that sentence? Was he talking about her virginity?

Oh, he was watching her now. He'd put it out there as a trip wire.

She shoveled Froot Loops in her mouth, but didn't savor them. The sugar scraped against her teeth.

"Is she going to ask me a lot about my book?" Nate asked.

"Like what?" David said. "Like, the plot? Best dragon?"

"Like, am I done, am I working?"

"Oh," David said. "Yeah. Probably that. What's your blood type, anyway? Just for reference."

"*David.*"

David held up his hands. "Kidding, kidding. He knows I'm kidding. You know I'm kidding, right, Nate?"

Nate did not look like he knew this. And Janelle, who had watched this silently, was now ready to step in.

"Come with me later on today, Stevie," Janelle said. "I'm going over to check out the workshop. I need to see where they keep the welding supplies. Can't wait to get my hands on my new blowtorch."

On the word blowtorch, Hayes appeared, wet from a shower. His golden hair was stuck to his head. Unlike David, he was pristinely dressed in white shorts and a blue shirt. Even in this early morning state he still looked unnaturally good. Except for his eyes. Those were completely bloodshot.

"What time did you get up?" David said, looking him over. "Four twenty?"

"Didn't sleep much last night," Hayes said with a roguish smile.

"No," David said. "Will we all be invited to the wedding? Beth too?"

Hayes shrugged and dropped into a chair.

"So," David said. "You're famous or something now?"

"Or something," Hayes said with a smile. "Yeah. Maybe."

"Zombie business is big business," David said. "People love the undead."

"That's my life," Stevie said. "I work at the Monroeville Mall."

No reply from Hayes.

"In Pittsburgh," Stevie said. "The Monroeville Mall."

Hayes cocked his head and smiled at Stevie, but it was a smile of *I have no idea what you are saying*. There was a definite echo of how her parents sometimes looked at her, and it made her cheeks burn.

Nate looked up from the milky depths of his cereal bowl, first to Hayes, then to Stevie.

"What made you want to write about zombies?" Janelle asked in what seemed to be an attempt to keep some normal conversation going.

Ellie stumbled into the room wearing a pair of ratty harem pants and a shirt that said ART HARDER. As a greeting, she sat down and casually put her bare foot on the table and examined it for a moment.

"I don't know," Hayes replied. "I went home to Florida last year, surfed for a few days, and it just came to me.

Sometimes, when you get away, get a chance to think, that's when you have an idea."

"You never know where you're going to get ideas," Ellie said. "In Paris, we'd all sit around, have some wine, let it come naturally."

"I'm kind of talking to P. G. Edderton about a movie," Hayes said.

"P. G. Edderton?" Nate said. "*Silver Moonlite Motel* P. G. Edderton?"

"We're just talking," Hayes said with a gentle smile. "But, yeah."

Even Ellie took notice of this. P. G. Edderton was the kind of director she would know. He made quirky, art house kind of movies about manic pixie everyones, movies that were turned into thousands of gifs, full of phrases everyone knew.

"Well," David said, "good luck with that."

Again, his meaning was unclear. It didn't sound like a good wish.

"You guys better get ready," Pix called from the steps up to her rooms. "You have meetings to get to."

Real life at Ellingham was calling.

9

Stevie walked in the clear sunshine of the Vermont morning, along the snaking paths and under the canopy of trees, to the Great House. She rang the bell by the massive front door. In Ellingham's day, the door would then have been answered by his butler, Montgomery. Montgomery came up a lot in books about the case. He was the head of the Ellingham staff, trained in England, had served royalty, and was stolen away from one of the finest houses in Newport to head up the Ellingham Great House. After the kidnappings, he remained in service but was broken, shaken, and died a few years after.

No butler now. Just a gentle buzz to signal the door was open. She stepped into the cavernous space. Security Larry sat in the shadows at his desk right by the front door.

"Dr. Scott, right?" he said.

Stevie nodded.

"Have a seat over there," he said, pointing to some chairs by the massive fireplace. A few people were already there, including Germaine Batt, who was doing something very intently on her phone. "When it's your time, go up the stairs and turn left along the corridor," he said, pointing to the balcony directly over his head. "He's the very last room at the front of the building."

"Iris Ellingham's old bedroom," Stevie said, looking up at the ceiling.

"That's right," Larry said, leaning back. "You're interested in the case? What's your favorite book on it?"

"*Murder on the Mountain* by Sanderson," Stevie said without hesitation. "His style is annoying, but I think he explores the case in the most depth."

"That's a good one," Larry said, nodding. "Did you read *The Ellingham Case Files*?"

"I think that jumps to a lot of conclusions," she said.

He nodded at that.

The air in the Great House was cool, and there was a faint smokiness to it despite the fact that it was very unlikely that anyone had smoked in there since the 1930s. She knew so much about this building. This main hall was made of rosewood imported from India. The eight-foot-high fireplace was constructed of pink marble from the Carrara region of Italy, where Michelangelo's marble was from. The fittings were all Austrian crystal, hand selected by one of the six architects who worked on the project. The stained glass in evidence everywhere was in the style of the Glasgow school (which meant something very fancy, Stevie wasn't sure what), including a sunroom with a roof made of interlocking flowers and hidden birds.

"Stevie? Stevie Bell?"

She looked up at the sound of her name. Call Me Charles was on the floor above, at the rail, looking down. He was wearing a Green Lantern T-shirt and chinos, his hair a floppy, schoolboyish mess.

"Come on up," Call Me Charles said. He met her at the top of the stairs and extended his hand for a shake.

A woman came out of a nearby door. The first thing Stevie noticed was her height, which was accentuated by a pair of black heels with a buttery, subtle sheen. As she turned, Stevie got a glimpse of the red undersides. She wasn't a fashion expert, but she knew that heels like that were expensive, as was the finely cut pencil skirt and the large, complicated blouse sweater, mysteriously flowing and folding. Her long hair was delicately colored in an array of auburns and golds. The woman was working her phone.

"Morning, Jenny," Charles called.

"Hey," she said, not looking up. She strutted on, never missing a beat of her typing. There was no missing the dismissive attitude. Stevie had never seen anything like it at her old school. Charles smiled and covered well.

"That's Dr. Quinn," Charles said. "She teaches a seminar in American history and culture to all the first years. Come on. Let's go to my office."

The creaking wooden floors had carpet runners to muffle the noise. Each door on this level was made of heavy, dark wood, with sharply cut crystal doorknobs that looked like they would be painful to touch.

The last door, Iris and Call Me Charles's, had a corkboard attached to the front. This was entirely covered in signs, small posters, and stickers: QUESTION EVERYTHING; STAND BACK, I'M GOING TO TRY SCIENCE!; I REJECT YOUR REALITY AND SUBSTITUTE MY OWN. The biggest sign was in the middle, and looked homemade. It read: CHALLENGE ME.

This was truly everything her parents feared, and it thrilled her as much as it repelled her.

Inside, the room had definitely been converted. The pale silver wallpaper was probably original, but now the room was crammed with bookcases, a few chairs, a desk, and a small sofa. There were books everywhere, filling the bookcases, stacked sideways on top of other books, piled on the floor, resting on the back of the sofa, stacked along the mantel. There were six different diplomas and certificates on the wall, all heavily framed—Harvard, Yale, Cambridge. There was a picture of a rowing team, a group photo from Cambridge . . . evidence everywhere of a long academic career of importance.

Charles waved Stevie into a chair. "So," he said, "I have to say, Stevie, yours was one of the most interesting applications I've ever read."

Stevie sucked in her breath. "Interesting" was one of those uncertain words.

"You're very enthusiastic about the history of this place, and in crime and criminal procedure. You have an interest in working for the FBI?"

Stevie nodded stiffly.

"That's excellent. Let's see what we've got here for you."

He consulted his laptop, taking a moment to put on a pair of glasses.

"So, based on your interests, this is what we came up with. You'll be taking anatomy and physiology, statistics, and Spanish . . . that covers your core and aligns with your interests. All very useful. Then we have you assigned to a tutor for readings in criminal justice and American legal history. You have yoga three times a week for your physical education. Everyone takes Dr. Quinn's literature and history seminar. Usually, students do a small project in the first year that leads into the major project in the second. Have you given any thought to this over the summer?"

Stevie swallowed hard. She'd said it out loud the night before, but now, facing Charles, facing the actual reality of the situation, could she say it again? She pushed the words past the lump in her throat.

"My project . . . is solving the case."

"Solving it?" Charles said, cocking his head. "Doing a report on it?"

"No," she said. "I mean . . . figuring out what happened."

Charles removed his glasses, folded them, and leaned back in his chair.

"That's a fairly tall order," he said. "Define that for me."

"I've read all the theories," she said, steadying herself in the chair. "I've read all the transcripts."

"There are a lot of those, I think."

"The main interviews are about eight thousand pages," Stevie said. "I think the answer is here. I think someone who was in the house that day was responsible."

"Hang on a moment," Charles said. He leaned back and considered her for a moment, pressing his fist against his chin. Each moment of his pause pulled Stevie down into her chair farther and farther.

"I have an idea," he said. "Follow me."

He grinned the grin of a presenter on some educational show with a cartoon dog, as if to say, "Come with me if you want to *learn*."

Stevie hopped up and followed him back down the hall, to the back set of stairs. They went up a floor to a door with a polite PRIVATE sign on it and a digital access pad. Stevie liked rooms marked PRIVATE with digital access pads. Stevie watched as Charles entered the access code on the pad. He made no effort to hide the number, which led Stevie to think he wanted her to see it.

"1936?" she asked.

"Not very creative," he replied with a smile. "But easy to remember."

The attic steps were narrow, plain, stained dark. Once they got to the top, everything opened up into a massive space that covered the footprint of the entire house. It was very dark; the windows were covered in light-blocking shades and curtains.

"Obviously," he said, tapping the digital buttons on a panel of lights, "the Ellinghams had a lot of stuff. The papers went to Yale, some to the Library of Congress. The really valuable things went to the Smithsonian or the Met or the Louvre or various art museums around the world. What we have here are the remnants of their lives. The furnishings. The dishes. The clothes. The household items."

Flick, flick, flick. The space came to light.

Everything was nooks and corners, every direction just racks of metal shelving that went from floor to ceiling. Archive boxes and books in one direction. Trunks in another. Lamps, vases, extra pieces of furniture—bedsteads stacked by a window, chairs clustered together in a tight communion, ottomans, dressers pushed back to back. There were rolls of old wallpaper, globes, boxes of crystal doorknobs.

Stevie felt like her brain had been replaced by a few dozen bees, bumping and swirling in her skull.

"This way," he said.

She followed without a word. Charles led her to the far wall, to a large lump, about four feet high and six feet wide, covered in a silver satin bedspread. He lifted the sheet carefully. It was the Great House in miniature. A perfect replica, in dollhouse form, right down to the flower boxes in the front, which were full of tiny flowers.

"Albert Ellingham had this made for Alice months after she disappeared," he said.

He reached over on the side and clicked a hidden button, then swung the dollhouse open on a hinge, like a giant book. There was the atrium, the giant staircase. Everything was perfect—the lamps and the tiny crystal doorknobs and the fireplaces. Even better, everything was arranged as it had been then.

"I read about this dollhouse," Stevie said. "I didn't know it was still here."

"You can go into the other rooms by opening the back and the side," Charles said. "It's beautiful, isn't it?"

Stevie moved closer and bent down to examine the little rooms. There was Alice's room, complete with teddy bears on the bed. Iris's dressing room had little silver hairbrushes and impossibly small cosmetics. The kitchen was full of china dishes the size of fingernails. And there was Albert Ellingham's office, with two desks, tiny telephones, pictures on the wall . . . a replica of the past.

"It's a masterpiece," Charles said. "It cost ten thousand dollars in 1936 money. We would have sent it to a museum, but all of Alice's things have to remain in the house, as part of the estate. Everything that's Alice's stays here."

Stevie helped him close the dollhouse, and the sheet was replaced.

"So," he said, "why do you think I showed you this?"

"Because it's awesome?" Stevie said.

"It is. But that's not why."

A dollhouse. The house in miniature. The world made small.

"It's simple," Charles said, cutting right to the answer. "A grieving man made a perfect toy for his daughter that she would never see. This is about real people, not figures from fiction. I know this crime is popular—that crime itself is popular. But crime has a human face. If you're going to study crime, you have to remember the people involved."

Stevie couldn't tell if this was a rebuke of some kind or just one of those one-to-grow-on lessons, but it was fair enough. At least he was taking her seriously.

"To that end," he said, "before you get caught up in trying to break the case open, I want you to get involved in a smaller project, something that restores a human face to this tragedy."

"What project?" Stevie asked.

"Oh, I don't do that. You do that. You come up with something."

"But is this a paper, or . . ."

Charles shook his head. "The rest is up to you. I've got to get to my next appointment. I'm excited to see what you're going to come up with."

As Stevie walked back downstairs, her head spun with all she had just seen. Germaine Batt came out of Dr. Quinn's door and hurried down the stairs, moving past Stevie. Her expression suggested someone who had just seen a document detailing how they died.

Nate was waiting below. He watched Germaine go, and then turned around to Stevie.

"Well?" he said.

"It was good," Stevie said. "He showed me the attic and

some stuff the family owned."

Nate nodded and folded his arms over his chest, looking around, not really paying attention.

"Did you notice something strange about what Hayes said this morning?" Stevie asked.

Nate turned back.

"You mean about Hayes not knowing anything about the Monroeville Mall, the setting of *Dawn of the Dead* and a super-famous zombie thing? Yeah."

Stevie was pleased at how quickly she and Nate seemed to link thoughts.

"What did you make of it?"

"I have no idea. The guy looks like he came out of a 3-D printer."

"Nathaniel," came a voice from above. Dr. Quinn looked over the rail. "You may come up."

"You'll be great," Stevie said, putting as positive a look on her face as she could.

"Yeah, don't do that," Nate said.

"Fine. It'll be horrible."

"Thanks," he said. "I guess I'll see you at lunch or something."

He settled his brown canvas backpack squarely on his shoulders and took the stairs like a man climbing up to the guillotine platform.

Larry watched this from his desk and stopped Stevie as she exited.

"Dr. Scott gave you a little tour?" he asked.

"Of the attic," Stevie said.

Larry tipped his chair back and picked up a pen, holding it like a dart.

"And what did you think of it?"

"I think it's the best place I've ever seen," she said.

Larry's expression never changed. His face was as stony and unmoving as the mountain they stood on.

"Good meeting otherwise?" he asked.

"I think there's a lot to do," Stevie said.

"You'll be all right. They work you hard here, but no one ever died of it."

"I guess if you do, you can just take the body out into the woods and bury it," Stevie said, smiling.

Larry did not smile. His eyes crinkled just a bit at the corners in an expression Stevie could not read.

This was maybe the kind of place where you didn't joke about the buried bodies.

April 14, 1936, 10:00 a.m.

LEONARD NAIR HOLMES WAS ACCUSTOMED TO GAPS IN THE CALEN-dar, days that simply went away. Once, in 1928, he misplaced all of June. And he had no solid proof that 1931 ever existed. People told him it did—they showed him newspapers and everything—but you can't believe everything you read.

So when Leo woke in his darkened room in Ellingham house that Tuesday morning, he went about his business after his nice, refreshing sleep. It was time to find breakfast. He scuffed out of his room in slippers and a tattered and overly long maroon silk robe that dragged behind, gathering dust. This was something, considering that Leo was well over six feet tall. He'd had the dressing gown made for a giant, all loose sleeves and big pockets and long drag. He made it as far as the landing before being scooped up by Flora Robinson, who pulled him to his room.

"Even if I wanted to, darling," he said to her, "I'm going to need a grapefruit, four eggs, and about three ounces of gin before . . ."

She clapped a hand over his mouth and shut the door.

"What's gotten into you?" he said, reaching his long-fingered hand into the dressing gown pocket to find his cigarette case.

"Leo! Iris and Alice have been *kidnapped*!"

Leo slowly raised his peaked black eyebrows and pulled a cigarette from the silver-and-jade case. He tapped it a few times on the side before putting it to his mouth. He patted his pockets. Finding nothing, Leo went to his bedstead and fumbled around for a moment, turning on the light and wincing. He dug through the pile of books and detritus, finally producing a battered box of matches to light his cigarette.

"They were taken when they went out for their drive yesterday, and there's been a ransom call," Flora said, keeping her voice low. "Albert brought George Marsh back. They're feeding the staff a bull story about how she spent the night in Burlington with a friend, and they're trying to keep the cops out of it for now. I know they did a drop last night that didn't go well. The kidnappers took the money but they didn't get Iris and Alice back. They asked for more money. Albert's getting it now."

Leo took a few long, lung-congesting draws to get his brain moving.

"Oh," he said.

"Oh? That's all you can say? They've been *kidnapped*."

Leo pulled hard on the cigarette, producing a burn audible from across the room, stroked the beard he had developed while he was sleeping with a blue-fingernailed hand. He examined the edges of nail varnish for a moment.

"Have you cleaned up?" he said.

"I did what I could," she replied. "For *her*. I went to her room as soon as I realized something was happening."

"For all of us, Flora. A rising tide sinks all boats."

"We need to do something," Flora said.

"Such as? I don't know where she is. I barely know where *I* am."

"We have to *think*. Who would do this? Maybe we should tell them everything. Maybe we have to."

"Flora," Leo said slowly, "I realize you have a conscience and that's what's talking now, but how will that help? It won't help us and it certainly won't help Iris or Alice."

"You don't know . . ."

"*Think*, Florie. Think. Have you noticed where we are? We are in the remote home of Albert Ellingham, tycoon. Anyone who likes money could have taken Iris and Alice, and everyone likes money. And anyone could do it because we are up on the side of a mountain. Albert will pay them."

Flora sank back against the wall.

"You, my dear, need something for your nerves," he said.

"No," Flora snapped. "I don't."

They were interrupted by a heavy rapping at the door. Leo motioned for Flora to open it.

"Morning, Albert," Flora said. "I was just getting Leo out of bed. Everything all right?"

"No," Albert said, all pretense gone. "It's not. Nair, I need you to make a batch of your invisible ink."

"I don't have my equipment."

"We have a fully equipped science lab here."

"Of course," Leo said. "Give me a few hours. . . ."

"No," Albert said. "Immediately. This moment. Make as much as you can as fast as you can. How long does it take?"

"An hour?" Nair said, looking at Flora uncertainly. "Maybe two. It depends on the quantity."

"Then you have an hour. You take whatever is necessary from anywhere, but you must be quick."

"Let me get dressed and I'll get to it."

When Albert was gone, Flora pressed the door closed.

"Ink?" Leo said.

"Ransom money," Flora replied. "He must be marking it. You get to it and I'll see what else I can find out."

Once Flora was gone, Leo locked the door and went to his closet. Inside, on a small table, was a small setup of scales and beakers and burners. There were delicate blue bottles that contained not an insignificant amount of chemicals of all sorts. Leo had always loved chemistry as a child. He mixed his own paints, which was why they had such an unusually vivid hue. He also made makeup, which was how he got blue nails and Iris and Flora got such remarkable eye shadows and blushes. It was why his own cheeks often sparkled faintly of silver.

This was not a paint set. Or a makeup set.

He didn't waste time. He put the bottles and beakers into his satchel, pulled a pair of trousers on over his night-clothes, and walked downstairs as if he didn't have a care in the world.

10

Stevie had great hopes for the boarding school dining hall. She knew better than to hope for floating candlesticks and ghosts, but long wooden tables didn't seem out of the question. Long tables were also featured in so many murder mysteries, when all the guests of the house were arranged, eyeing each other over their wineglasses, wondering who Lord Dudley was going to put into his will or who might have killed Ratchets with the golf club.

What she actually got was something that looked a bit like the buffet area in the conference hotel she stayed in with her high school forensics club when they did a tournament in Hershey, just a little more artisanal and maybe crossed with a bit of ski lodge. (Or what she understood ski lodges to look like. She had never been to one.) It had a high, peaked ceiling made of bright pine-and-stone walls, scattered with tables of varying shapes and sizes—round ones that could fit a large group, square ones for four, and quite a large number of small ones that could fit only one or two people. There were also some plaid sofas and beanbags along the wall farthest from the food, with a few low tables—clearly some kind of coffee shop area for people who were too far up a mountain to get to a Starbucks.

The chalkboard menu really seemed to emphasize that everything was local and that everything had maple syrup in it. The BBQ beef was in maple syrup BBQ sauce. The mac and cheese was made with smoked maple cheese. There was maple tofu and maple-syrup dressing for the salads.

"Did you forget you were in Vermont for a second?" Stevie said to Janelle as they took their trays. "Look down. You are standing in maple syrup."

"Yeah," Janelle replied, a bit dispiritedly, as she took some tofu and vegetables. "It's not my favorite."

Nate stared down the sneeze guard at the mapleized meats.

"I'll drink the living blood of trees," he said. "Hit me."

The drinks area had sparkling water on tap (fancy) and a cooler full of expensive natural sodas that were free to take, including one maple-lime-spruce-flavored one that Stevie examined out of intense curiosity. This was the kind of stuff she never saw and wouldn't have had the money to buy, and it was just sitting here. This, more than anything else, seemed to indicate what kind of place this was. Free fancy sodas full of maple.

She took one. She had to.

Since it was still warm and bright, there were tables set up outside. Ellie had commandeered a picnic table and began waving at them to come over. Hayes sat across from her.

Janelle and Stevie started for the open door but Nate hesitated.

"Eating outside is the worst," Nate said, waving away a fly from his plate, which seemed to be full of nothing but various meats.

"Vitamin D," Stevie said. "You need it."

"You don't know that," he said. "I want to eat my meat in my room with the lights off."

"As a writer, are those *really* the words you want to use?" Stevie asked.

"Yes," he replied.

"Let's just sit with the others for today?" Janelle said. "We'll sit inside next time."

Nate sighed and went along.

"So how was it?" Ellie asked as they sat down.

"It was great," Janelle said. "They're giving me access to the workshop and I'm getting space in the art barn to work on my Rube Goldberg machine for the Sendell Waxman competition. That's the high school version. There's even budget to get supplies. This place is amazing."

"Mine was okay, I guess?" Stevie said. "I'm supposed to come up with some project this week about putting a human face on crime."

Nate was quiet.

"Well?" Janelle said.

"She hates me," he said plainly.

"Come on," Janelle said, shaking her head. "Stop it. You can't be like this on the *first day*."

"Yeah, I'm not kidding."

"She *said* she hated you?" Janelle said.

"She never looked at me. She said something about how it's so easy for anyone to be published now and then read me a list of classes and told me to go."

"That doesn't mean she hates you."

"You had to be there," Nate said.

Stevie felt eyes on her back. Eyes to the side. She glanced around as subtly as she could and realized that no one was looking at her—people were looking toward Hayes. He was like a weak center of gravity.

"What the hell are you drinking?" Nate said, turning the soda bottle to look at the label.

"Natural soda," Stevie said. "It was there. I decided to try it."

"Why?"

"Because I want to know."

"It's going to be bad," Nate said. "What is there to know?"

"You don't know that."

"Oh my God." Janelle drew a hand over her face. "Seriously, Nate. You have to like something. You can't go around being miserable about everything."

Nate indicated that Stevie should drink and folded his arms. Stevie took a long swig. As soon as the drink hit the back of her throat, it attacked her palate with a woody, biting, cleaning-fluid type sensation that shot up the inside of her nose. She lurched forward, clasping her hand to her mouth just in time to avoid spraying Nate with a maple-lime-spruce fountain. She coughed so loudly that people at the adjoining tables stared.

"Yes," Nate said. "I see."

"Tell me more about your book," Stevie replied when she could speak again.

Nate returned to studying his plate of meats.

Janelle suddenly half stood and waved. "Vi!" she said. "Come sit here!"

Vi was back, with her tinted glasses, wearing an overall short set, a red tank, and striped knee socks. Her hair was perhaps a little spikier than the day before. She slid in beside Janelle.

Again, a tiny panic bubble glurped inside. What if Stevie was going to be completely friendless? What if Janelle didn't pair bond with her and Nate never talked and that was it? Maybe she had given up her life before and come up this mountain and no one would like her and she would have to go home an abject failure.

That was anxiety talking. Janelle did like her. All she did was ask Vi to sit with them, and that was because she wanted to flirt with Vi. And Nate, he was there. He was just a tough nut to crack.

Things righted themselves for a moment, until David came out of the dining hall, his unruly hair sticking up at odd angles. He still hadn't changed out of the clothes from the night before. Stevie had that same quiver of recognition, like he was someone she knew well. But there was no way they could have met before.

"Hello," he said much too loudly as he sat down. "You love looking at me. I get it. You didn't drink that, did you?"

He pointed at the bottle of soda in front of Stevie.

"I got it for you," Stevie said, pushing the bottle his way.

Ellie smiled and stretched out on the bench, putting her bare feet in David's lap.

"Bad news, Hayes," he said. "Someone was watching you last night."

He passed his phone down the table.

"Looks like we have our own personal TMZ," David said. "Someone named Germaine Batt?"

As he spoke, Stevie felt a ripple in the air around them. People had been looking, and now there was an undercurrent of chatter.

"Your girlfriend is going to be pissed," David observed.

Hayes looked at the screen but didn't seem disturbed by what he saw.

"Oh well," he said, passing it back to David.

"Guess that's what happens when you're famous," David said. "Eyes everywhere."

For no reason Stevie could determine, Ellie put her foot in David's face, and he bit it. She screamed with laughter. It just happened, out of the blue—something that weird and familiar. Stevie felt her insides flex and twist a bit, and a flush of anxiety run through her system.

Vi and Janelle exchanged looks. Nate stubbornly refused to look up. Hayes didn't feel like he was really part of the group at all, somehow.

Stevie felt very alone, except for a bee that had decided to linger by her ear and buzz furiously. Stevie was all right with being alone, generally, but this felt like she was being severed from the group bit by bit.

You can always come home . . .

When she got back to her room, Stevie sat on the floor for a bit, looking at her research board.

What if this place wasn't different? What if it was, as Ellie said, all bunnies on a hillside? She had come here because it was supposed to be different. What had she expected?

She drummed her fingers on the floor for a moment and stared at the faces of the Ellingham family. Then she pulled her computer out of her bag. She couldn't sit there entertaining these kinds of thoughts. If she could learn some more about the people around her, maybe that would help.

First, David. What was his deal? His last name, she knew from the student registry, was Eastman. David Eastman was a fairly common name, so there was a lot to sort through, dozens and dozens of search results. She added Ellingham. She added California. She looked up and down through every social media platform. An hour passed, and her butt grew numb as she sat in the same scrunched position, her computer pressed between her chest and her knees. The more she looked, the less David seemed to exist. No profiles anywhere.

"Where the hell are you?" she mumbled to herself.

There was a knock on her door and a gentle push. Janelle appeared in the space.

"Hey," she said. "Can I come in?"

"Sure." Stevie slapped the computer shut.

Janelle fluttered in. She had a delicate way of walking on the balls of her feet, lifting the hem of her long sundress from the ground. Unlike Stevie, who was once again in black shorts (there had been a three-for-two deal and she got three pairs, all black), Janelle looked like a summer picnic. A faint scent of orangey perfume wafted from her as she moved. Her braided hair was coiled precisely on the top of her head.

"I'm sorry," she said, coming and sitting on the floor opposite Stevie.

"For what?"

"I ignored you at lunch. I didn't mean to."

"It's okay," Stevie said. "You were . . ."

"Yeah," Janelle said, unable to contain a smile. She tucked her long floral dress around her knees and pulled the material taut. "You know I broke up with my girlfriend in the spring."

"You told me."

"And I didn't think . . . but Vi? I don't know. I just . . . I don't want to be that person who gets obsessed and ignores their friends."

Stevie felt a warm sensation all over, and something in

her released that she didn't know she'd been holding.

"You like her?"

"I like them," Janelle corrected her.

"Sorry. Well, they seem to like you too."

"I just have to take a breath," Janelle said, plucking a lip gloss from the side of her bra, blindly and perfectly applying a coat, and tucking it back in place. "We just got here. Maybe this is some kind of . . . I don't know. Gotta keep my head in the game. I have a machine to make, and this schedule I got this morning is nuts. I love math, but this scares me. Differential equations in the morning, calc in the afternoon, physics in the middle."

"That's nothing for you," Stevie said.

"I like your board," Janelle said.

"Everyone needs a conspiracy wall," Stevie said.

"No," Janelle said, pointing. "You came here to do this. I've heard you talk about this. You got me interested, and I don't care about this stuff. You and me, we have this. And no matter what, we're going to stick together this year. I'm going to make my machines and you're going to solve a crime."

When Janelle left, Stevie eased down onto her back and looked up at the ceiling.

She had Janelle. And yes, she would solve her case. But now she had another one. Who was David? There was something there. She could feel it under her skin.

Stevie had no fears of the dead. The living, however, sometimes gave her the creeps.

11

THE NEXT MORNING STEVIE SHUFFLED TO THE WINDOW, WIPING SLEEP out of her eyes, and peeled back the edge of the curtain to look out on a green sky. Had she believed in omens, she might well have taken this as a bad sign for the first morning of classes. But Stevie did not believe in omens. A green sky was a meteorological oddity, and maybe something for Instagram. Not a sign.

Stevie brought an umbrella.

Her first class, anatomy, was in the unsubtly named Genius Hall. There were only six people in the class. It helped that Pix was the teacher—at least something felt familiar.

"Welcome to Anatomy and Physiology," she said. "We are going to talk about the human body without any skin, about the body of muscle and bone and organs. Over here . . ."

She walked over to the skeleton hanging at the side of the whiteboard and picked up its hand.

". . . are the two hundred and six bones of the human body, fully articulated. One of the first questions I get about the skeleton is . . . is it real? Usually they're plastic, but this one is the real deal. It was a private donation to the academy, and every year, someone attempts to steal it. It is alarmed. Don't steal the skeleton. His name is Mr. Nelson. Be nice to Mr. Nelson. He's here to teach you about what's inside of you, inside of all of us."

Mr. Nelson, the real skeleton, grimaced at them with his big, empty eyes.

"The bones themselves have their own geography, peaks and valleys where they associate with muscle and tissue. You are going to learn the relationship of these things, all of these systems—skeletal to muscular, nervous and endocrine, digestive, reproductive, excretory, integumentary, cardio-vascular, respiratory. Once you learn what these things are, you will learn how they work."

There was talk of quizzes and tests (there were a lot), labs (twice a week), and dissections (far too many for Stevie's comfort). Teacher Pix was a lot more hardcore than house Pix.

As Stevie stepped onto the green, the rain began, and in a moment, she was in a hailstorm with chunks the size of marbles crashing around her. She put up the umbrella, but the battering was too severe. She ran. She made it as far as the cupola on the bottom end of the green, where she found herself stranded for a few minutes. When the hail got to the point where it was unlikely to pound her to death, she made a sprint for Eunomia, where she was to meet Dr. Velman for her one-on-one on criminology and sociology.

Dr. Velman looked to be about seventy and, after reading off the list of books he wanted Stevie to get—and finding she had read two of the major textbooks already—proceeded to spend half an hour talking about the art and craft of the hangman, and how the best of them knew how to tie a knot just at the right location so that the victim's neck was broken quickly instead of suffocating. The next half hour, he talked about the breeding of dachshunds.

After class, Stevie lingered for a moment outside the building, the rain drilling down on her umbrella. Her next class was in two hours. Ellingham ran like a college—you went to your classes and your time between them was yours to make of as you wanted. No moving along with the crush of a high school hallway. No study halls that stank of Doritos and the dishwasher steam from the cafeteria. This was like being an adult.

So she stood there in the rain like an idiot. Everyone else seemed to have some idea. She wondered if she should go eat or sit in her room or maybe just stand there forever. She took a deep breath of the moist mountain air. She had time. Where did she most want to go? What felt right?

She turned toward the library.

When she entered, no one was there except Kyoko, who sat alone at her massive desk, eating an apple.

"Hey!" she called to Stevie. "Come in! You're new, right?"

"Yeah," Stevie said. "My name is Stevie Bell. And there's something I'd like to see. . . ."

"You want to see Dolores's book," Kyoko said, balancing

her apple on her desk and wiping her hands.

Stevie had been about to ask if they had materials on the case, so the offer of Dottie's book stunned her into silence.

"I get a file on all the new students," Kyoko said. "It's the librarian's job to know what materials are needed. You're interested in the Ellingham case. Come on back."

She waved Stevie around the desk station to a deep brown wooden door with the words LIBRARY OFFICE painted in gold.

Behind the door was a large but cozy room. Everything here was original—wooden tables and desks, wooden cabinets. There were large tables with books that were in the process of being bound or covered.

"So you know the book was returned to us in 1993," Kyoko said. "We keep it out of circulation, because of its historical significance. Here."

She pulled a pair of blue nitrile gloves from a box and indicated that Stevie should put them on, which Stevie was only too happy to do. There was nothing she really wanted more than the satisfying snap of the examination gloves. It was a small thing, but it made the investigation just a touch more legitimate.

"Here we go," Kyoko said, putting on her own pair of gloves and opening up a glass-fronted banker's shelf and removing a thick volume. She set it on one of the tables and waved Stevie to it.

The book was well preserved from years in evidence and library storage. It had a pristine dust jacket with a picture of

Sherlock Holmes in a deerstalker with a meerschaum drawn in red on a white background.

The book made a faint crackling noise as Stevie opened it. The pages were faintly yellow and the type was very tight and dense. There was a slot for library cards that read ELLINGHAM ACADEMY LIBRARY, but there was no card inside. The book had been checked out, but never technically returned. Stevie turned the pages carefully, and as she got to the first story, *A Study in Scarlet*, she stopped.

There was a jagged pencil mark on one of the first pages, roughly underlining one line. It was a very famous line, one of the most famous in all the stories.

Sherlock said, "I consider that a man's brain originally is like a little empty attic, and you have to stock it with such furniture as you choose."

"Did Dottie do this?" Stevie asked.

"No idea. This particular book was checked out several times by students before her. Any one of them could have marked it up. But I noticed that as well."

Stevie glanced through the book, but there was nothing else in it. It was simply a book of Sherlock Holmes stories. But it was *the* book. That was what mattered.

"As it happens, we know a lot about Dolores's reading," Kyoko said. "This may also interest you."

She opened one of the wooden filing cabinets and removed an expanded file.

"The first Ellingham librarian, Diana Cloakes, was a remarkable person—one of the top research librarians at the New York Public Library. Albert Ellingham hired her to come work here. Everyone he hired was the best at what they did. She bought an incredible collection, and she took meticulous notes on everything."

Kyoko pulled a thick stack of typewritten sheets from the folder and paged through them, then carefully set a few piles down on one of the big book tables.

"When Albert Ellingham set up the school," she said, "it was the policy that any book a student wanted could be ordered, and we have all the records from that first year. This pile . . ."

She pointed at one of the stacks.

". . . shows all requests from the 1935–36 school year. Dolores alone put in requests for over five hundred books. The school ordered four hundred and eighty-seven of them. The remaining thirteen were at a library in a university in Turkey that refused to sell them. If it's one of Dolores's, it will have the letters *DE* after the title."

Stevie scanned down the list. Dolores had requested several works in Greek, a lot of novels Stevie had never heard of, some classics. There were all kinds of requests from other students, including a list of very intriguing titles.

"*Gun Molls Magazine*," Stevie read. "*Vice Squad Detective, Dime Detective, All True Fact Detective Stories . . .*"

"Oh, those," Kyoko said. "Yeah, I love those. All pulp magazines. Most libraries or librarians would never have ordered them, but Ellingham's policy was clear—whatever they asked for. I so wish we still had these, but I think the students took them and didn't give them back."

Stevie felt like she would have gotten along with those students.

⚜

Two days at Ellingham Academy passed by in a series of flashes. First, there was just the *weight* of everything. The readings. The thought. The writing. The expectation of knowledge. It was kind of an academic monster-truck rally. Everything went so fast. Session to session, reading to reading.

Meals developed more of a rhythm.

The overall groupings started to make sense—some sat by houses. Some were gamers. Some read. Some people took food away and never stayed. Germaine Batt tended to sit apart from everyone, watchful, always on a device. Gretchen with the astonishing head of red hair frequently held court over a long table inside. Hayes moved away from the Minerva table to start sitting with Maris and a very assorted group of artsy-looking people. Vi was a regular feature at the Minerva table. Nate started to talk a bit more. Ellie came and went, as did David, but they didn't come and go together. They didn't seem to be a couple—more just two people who were really comfortable in their skin and not very conscious of what made other people uncomfortable.

After lit class on Wednesday, Stevie was walking across the green when a larger pair of ratty-sneaker-clad feet fell in step beside her. Actually in step, deliberate and rhythmic. Stevie didn't need to look up, didn't want to, but her neck craned in that direction seemingly of its own accord, like a flower bending toward the sun, if the sun was an annoying person who lived upstairs. She managed to avoid conversation with David for the last few days. If he was at her table, he sat at the other end. In Minerva, he stuck to his room. But now he was here, smiling, his hair flopping and unruly, his navy blue T-shirt looking conspicuously worn. There were holes in his shorts large enough to lose a phone.

"Hey, Murder Girl," he said. "How's the case going? Got any perps? An unsub? How are your perps and unsubs? Am I doing it right? Perp? Unsub? Suspect?"

Stevie clenched her jaw. You could trip her. You could kick her in the shin. She could handle those things. But no one was allowed to go after her mysteries. That cut right into her.

"You know," Stevie said, "in a murder mystery, you'd end up dead."

He smiled wider and nodded. His body was . . . ropy. Like the word from the Truly Devious letter. He was long and thin and was probably strong. He seemed to be made of knots.

"What do you want?" she said, speeding up.

"I'm just walking this way," David said. "We live in the same place. What's the problem?"

"No problem."

"Oh, good."

They passed the cluster of statue heads on the way to Minerva. It was a weird landmark on the way home. Stevie was getting used to the statues, but this head-only grouping was still off-putting. It seemed like they were in the middle of a conversation and had stopped talking as strangers walked by.

"So Ellie was telling me about your conversation from the other day," he said.

"What conversation?" Stevie said. She'd had several conversations with Ellie, but none seemed worth recounting.

"About you," he said.

Stevie had to think about this for a moment. Was he talking about the conversation from the tub room? The one where Ellie had asked about their love lives and she explained she didn't have one?

"She said your parents work for Edward King," he said.

She exhaled. Right conversation, different topic.

"Yeah," she said, waving away a bee. "Some of us just get lucky, I guess."

"You a big fan too?"

"What do *you* think?" she said.

"Who knows?" he said. "Does anyone really know anyone else? You love some law and order."

There was no lower insult than this, and having to say she didn't like Edward King was even worse. Edward King was famously disgusting—rich, corrupt, vain. He was the root of a lot of the trouble in Stevie's life. In less than thirty seconds, David had made two successful digs in the softest parts of her psyche.

"I'm not a fan," she said in a low voice.

"Oh. I was going to say, it sounds like your parents—"

"I don't know why they like him," she snapped. "I try to work that one out all the time. I kind of want to get away from it here, so . . ."

"Sure," he said, loping along. "You can't control your parents. I mean, my mother is a beekeeper and my father invented the smorgasbord."

They had reached the blue door of Minerva. He tapped his ID to the panel to admit them.

"We have time to get to know each other," he said. "So much time. See you around."

He turned and went back the way they had come. He didn't even go inside. Stevie was left to wonder what the hell had just happened to her.

⊶

This would not be Stevie's only strange encounter that day. The next would come an hour or two later, in the form of Hayes Major leaning in her doorway as she was trying to read.

"Hey," he said. "Can I talk to you?"

He was wearing a tight white T-shirt. A fresh one. Possibly never worn before. (Stevie didn't buy white T-shirts. Their shelf life was too short.)

"Do you mind if I come in?" he asked.

"Sure?" she said.

He left the door wide open and came inside with his easy, comfortable way. She indicated that the floor was his, if he wanted to stay. He didn't sit; he squatted. It didn't look even remotely comfortable; it just showed off the tone of his leg muscles and the outline of his patellae. (Anatomy word! Kneecaps. She was already using her knowledge.)

"I had an idea," he said as he balanced on his little invisible stool. "You mentioned the other day that you needed a project. So do I. I was thinking, what if we worked together on something?"

Dust motes danced in the air between Hayes and Stevie. In the bright, late-afternoon light, his hair had an actual glow, like it was spun of golden thread. He could have been a statue model in Greece or Rome. The light was so rich that he seemed like a statue now, an otherworldly nature made of light and shade, with a southern accent and a formfitting shirt. Stevie wasn't sure if the wooziness she felt around him was attraction, or just numb confusion as her brain tried to work out his exact species. "Looks human," it was saying to itself, "but cannot be. Cheekbones not possible. Is simulation. Origin unknown."

"Together?" she said, pulling herself out of her mental wanderings.

"See, my *agent* . . ." He dug a neatly manicured fingernail coyly into the wooden floor as he said this word. ". . . thinks I should make another series. I've been thinking about what to do, and I thought . . . what about the stuff that happened here? The crimes. The kidnapping thing. You know about that."

"About?" Hayes was super distracting to talk to in close quarters, and now he was talking about making a series. None of this made sense.

"The crimes," he said again. "You know about the crimes, right? The crime here? Crimes?"

"Crimes," she repeated. "Yeah. I do. But . . . what?"

She was not coming off well.

"You'd be, like, the technical director. The expert. I even had an idea for a trailer. We could shoot it in that tunnel, the one under the sunken garden."

Everything came into sharp focus in a second.

"The tunnel?" she said. "You mean the one the kidnappers used?"

"Under the sunken garden," he repeated.

"That tunnel has been filled in since 1938," Stevie said.

"They dug it out in the spring," Hayes said, his smile widening. "For construction. They started at the end of last school year. I've already been in it."

"You were in the tunnel?" Stevie said. She was leaning forward and she made no effort to hide the urgency in her voice.

"Once," he said. "Last year, when they first excavated it."

The idea of the tunnel being open again had never occurred to Stevie. She really did not believe in fate, but the timing of this was incredible.

"I was just thinking how it would be a good place to make something. And you're here now, and you know all the stuff about the crimes. People would like that. We'd be the first ones to show what the tunnel looks like."

Stevie's heart was pounding hard.

"Are we allowed in there?"

"Well . . ." Hayes unfurled his smile slowly. "Technically, we don't know about it. They tried to hide the fact that they opened it up, but I was back there one day and we saw that they were taking out tons of dirt."

"And you actually went in?"

"Actually went in," Hayes said. "But it's just an idea. If you're too busy, I understand. . . ."

"I'll do it," Stevie said. "Write. Or, whatever. I'll do it."

"Great!" Hayes replied. "So, you'll get Nate. And you guys can write something over the weekend? By Monday?"

"Wait, what?"

"It doesn't have to be long," Hayes said. "Five pages or something. Ten. Just something about the crime, something that happens in the tunnel. Didn't some student die? Or the thing with the ransom? Wasn't there a thing with the ransom? With a boat or something? In the sunken garden?"

Stevie nodded.

"So that," Hayes said. "Do that. Write something with the tunnel and something about the ransom in the sunken garden. We can do that. This is going to be great."

Minutes later, he was gone, and Stevie wondered how

you made a script. It was a minor point. She was going into the tunnel. That was all that mattered.

⊕

Strange conversation three was instigated by Stevie.

"Think about it," Stevie said, sitting in Nate's desk chair later that evening. "I could give you all the facts. There are transcripts. There are files. It's practically written. You'd barely need to do anything."

"I don't know anything about writing scripts," Nate said.

"But you write!"

"Scripts are totally different," Nate said. "Scripts are . . . they're like an X-ray of a book. Just the bones. The words people say and the things they do. Books are . . . everything. What the characters see and feel and how everything is told."

"It sounds easier," Stevie pointed out.

"It's a different thing," Nate said. "I'm supposed to show Dr. Quinn outlines for the next three chapters of my book, plus all this reading . . ."

"Maybe," Stevie said, "if you wrote this, Dr. Quinn would let you have more time on the book. You could write *this* instead of *that* for a while? They love group projects here."

Much like Stevie had been lured in by the tunnel, Nate could not resist the offer of skipping out on his book.

"So I take this stuff and make it into some scripts," he said. "And you do what?"

"I advise on technical matters."

"Meaning?"

"I explain what happened," she said. "I help you. We could call it *Truly Devious*."

Nate exhaled long through his nose.

"Fine," he said. "Anything is better than doing what I'm supposed to be doing."

April 14, 1936, 3:00 p.m.

ROBERT MACKENZIE WAS SUPERVISING THE DELIVERY OF LARGE SUMS of cash from New York. Two hundred thousand dollars was piled on the floor throughout the day. As he and George Marsh sorted the money, Ellingham removed two small blue bottles from a cabinet, along with a fine brush.

"What's that?" Marsh asked.

"A solution that Nair brewed up that we use for our games," Ellingham said. "It dries completely clear. To see it, you need to use a solution and a special light. This stuff is so good that I've often suggested to Nair that he sell it to the government. If for some reason things don't go as they should tonight, I want to be able to track these bills."

The bills were marked down the side with a slash of the paint. Ellingham took the further measure of marking the bundle wrappers with his fingerprint. Fans were placed around the room to dry everything quickly, and then the money was packed into four bags.

"I got some people out watching street corners tonight," Marsh said. "Didn't tell them why or what for—just to mark down license plates and anything unusual. I gave them fifty cents each if they give me good info."

"Give them five dollars each," Ellingham said. "Give them whatever they want!"

"For five dollars," Marsh replied, "they'll know this is big and they might start coming up with stories. Fifty cents keeps them honest and the profile low."

Robert Mackenzie watched this all nervously.

⌖

The call with instructions came at 7:07 that evening. The instructions said to move the money into Burlington and wait by a selected telephone booth for a call. Ellingham himself drove the car, with Robert Mackenzie and George Marsh riding along. Each man brought a revolver. They arrived just before 8:00 p.m., when the phone rang. From there, they were instructed to drive toward Rock Point.

Rock Point is very much what it sounds like—a rocky point off the side of Burlington, jutting into Lake Champlain. The point was largely uninhabited and the terrain rough. Once they arrived, they found an arrow chalked on the ground, pointing to the narrow dirt-and-rock path toward the water.

"Robert," Ellingham said, "you stay here with the car."

Robert looked at the pitch-black path into the rocky wooded point.

"Mr. Ellingham, this is . . ."

"You heard me, Robert. Stay here. If you see or hear

nothing from us in an hour, turn around and drive back into town and get help."

Ellingham switched on his flashlight. His shoes slipped a bit against the slick rocks as he began the walk into the dark.

"There's a light ahead," he said.

The path was marked by a series of impromptu lanterns made out of tin cans that would later be traced back to a diner in town. The diner appeared to have nothing to do with the crime—they had simply put out their garbage the night before. The garbagemen on their route reported that their trash was empty in the morning. Someone had stolen the garbage.

Even with the tiny tin-can lights, the path was treacherous and blind, and it got more so as the lights spread out and led to the cliff face. Finally, at one rocky ledge, they found three cans and a coiled rope. Below, a lantern flashed.

"There's a boat down there," Marsh said, looking over carefully, his gun ready.

"Use the rope," called up a voice. "Lower the money."

"Not until you show us Mrs. Ellingham and Alice," Marsh called back.

"Look next to you."

Ellingham scrabbled around and called for his wife, but found on the ground a handbag and a child's shoe.

"We need a better sign," Marsh said. "Proof of life."

Ellingham dropped his bag to the ground and tied the end of the rope to the handles. Marsh sighed and helped him secure it.

"I'm putting the money on the rope," Ellingham yelled. "Please, get my wife and child to a safe place so we can collect them. We have no interest in you, only them."

The money went over the rock face, all four bags of it. Ellingham tossed the rope end over the side.

"That's everything!" Ellingham yelled.

Below, the lantern began to flicker in a strange pattern.

"What are they doing?" Ellingham said. "What is that? It's not Morse."

"I have no idea," Marsh said, cocking his revolver.

"Don't shoot at that boat! They could be in there!"

The lantern went out. For a solid minute, there was no sound but the gentle lapping of the water and the wind.

"What's happening?" Ellingham asked. For the first time that night, he sounded truly vulnerable and afraid.

"I don't know," Marsh said.

"Hello!" Ellingham yelled. "I gave you the money! What now? Where are they?"

The tiny boat sailed into oblivion, along with any chance of recovering Iris or Alice.

12

THE PROCESS OF WRITING *TRULY DEVIOUS*, THE VIDEO SERIES, WAS not as smooth as Stevie had promised.

On the first day, Nate greeted Stevie in the morning with a huge smile. "I drafted two chapters of the new book last night!" he said. "I mean, they're drafts. I was writing so fast, Stevie. I swear to you I wrote like fifteen thousand words last night."

"Is that . . . good?" she asked.

"I don't know!" he said. "But it turns out that making me write this screenplay made me want to write anything else, which meant I worked on my book!"

"Wait," Stevie said, "wait, does that mean you didn't write the script?"

Nate shook his head happily.

"Yep!" he said.

By dinner, the story had changed.

"Everything I wrote last night is terrible," he said. "And we have no script. Let's write this thing. Show me that stuff again."

174

This pattern repeated several times. Stevie would produce copied transcripts of the police interviews. These were all readily available online. Nate would go off to write. Nate would do something else. Finally, Stevie sat down with Nate at the farm table for five hours and side by side, passing the computer back and forth, they assembled ten pages of script.

The scene opened in the tunnel, with Hayes reading the Truly Devious letter. Then it went to the scene of the ransom drop, with Hayes playing Albert Ellingham. How Hayes was going to play Albert Ellingham, a man thirty years his senior, was not their problem. Nor was the fact that this scene involved Albert Ellingham rowing a boat across a lake that was no longer there. What mattered was that it all took place in the sunken garden, because maybe if they shot there, Stevie could get into the observatory.

Priorities.

All in all, she was pleased with what they had done. The result looked script-like, with people saying words and doing things.

On Monday evening, as it thundered outside, Stevie and Nate presented the script to a small team who assembled in the art barn. Along with her and Nate, there was Maris, who looked every inch the vixen in a tight, black, fuzzy sweater that was far too heavy for the weather. Her lips were a luminous poppy red. She had on semi-sheer black stockings with a seam running up the back, which she showed off by stretching her legs along the floor and rotating her feet, exposing her calves. She had a mug of smoky tea; its steam perfumed the space.

"I think you guys know Maris," Hayes said. "She's going to help with the filming and direction."

There was also someone Stevie had seen before—in the yurt that first night. His face was long, with a high forehead and a lantern jaw and premature worry wrinkles in his forehead. He wore a long black coat and a scarlet scarf swung over his shoulders.

"This is Dash," Hayes said. "He's going to be our stage manager. Dash is the best."

Hayes read out the script from his computer, with Maris filling in the set directions. It was rough in spots, and most of it was just verbatim from the various case documents, but Nate had given it enough of a shape. Stevie had chosen the best parts of the transcripts. And to his credit, Hayes did a good job of playing Albert Ellingham. Somehow, they had actually made something that felt like a show.

"This is amazing," Hayes said as he finished. "Hey, Maris, would you take a few pictures? Just to document the working process."

"Sure," she said, pulling out her phone and taking a few photos of Hayes studying his computer.

"I need more detail," Dash said. "What was it like that night?"

"It was foggy," Stevie said.

"We can do fog," Dash said, pulling out his phone. "You want fog? We can for sure do fog."

"Lots of fog," Hayes said.

"Ooh, yeah." Dash nodded. "I can rig a few T-90s all over the sunken garden. That chemical fog hangs low. We can make it look like the lake is full of fog."

"Great," Hayes said. "Fog."

"I'm going to need fog machines, some poles to rig lights. We can make this work."

<hr/>

The next steps involved making it all work, and Stevie and Nate were not off the hook yet. There were costumes to assemble and props to prepare.

For the costumes, Maris and Stevie went to the Ellingham Academy theater. It was a small, dedicated space that looked like a tiny Greek temple from the outside. The theater space had a long, low stage room for about a hundred people, and black walls. The costume area was accessed by climbing a ladder in the corner of the lobby, which led to an attic that was composed of two long rooms separated by a hallway only two feet wide.

The costume closet was on one side, with a sharply sloped roof Stevie kept hitting her head on. It was crammed completely with clothes racks overstuffed with random clothing items that seemed to be loosely grouped by type. There was a rack thickly packed with men's suiting of all kinds, a rack of coats, a rack of dresses from every era, racks of fuzzy things, plaster and plastic armor, amorphous items that probably made sense in some context like a giant foam French fry container and a brown sack covered in felt eyeballs.

The floor was a sea of shoes and boots, and the racks above were hats, helmets, purses, shields, feathers (just feathers? Just feathers. Why?) and items of no known nature or provenance. The whole thing smelled like a thrift shop that had been baked in a low oven and felt like a too-tight and too-long hug by a rejected Muppet.

Eventually, two suits were chosen, along with a hat and an overcoat. The prop closet, which was just as oppressive and even more loosely organized, produced a canvas bag and an oar for the fake boat.

Wednesday evening brought something unexpected—construction. The group gathered in the workshop, a barn structure off to the side of the maintenance area. It was open and cold and contained things that didn't feature much in Stevie's daily life: tables with circular saws, racks of tools, large industrial bins. This was where the students of Ellingham came to make things that required space and tools and fire. This didn't include too many people, but it did include Janelle, who had a welding mask over her face and was staring down two pieces of metal. She lifted the mask as Stevie came in, and waved.

"I need you to cut these into lengths," Dash said to Stevie, pointing at some wood. "Here are all the measurements."

He shoved a piece of paper at Stevie.

She looked blankly at a bunch of numbers. "What?" she said.

"Cut. The wood. Into lengths." Dash pointed at the wood, then the circular saw.

"You must be kidding," Stevie said.

"I'll do it," Maris said, her voice thick with a *can you believe this one doesn't even use a circular saw* vibe. She sauntered up to the saw in her fuzzy sweater and leaned over expertly.

The buzz saw cranked to life and Maris put a board on it and sliced it in two. The air filled with the scent of sawdust. Hayes came sauntering in while all of this work was going on, greeted everyone, and rested on the ground and studied his script.

"Hey," Janelle said as Dash scooped up some poles from an upright storage container in the corner. "What are you doing with those?"

"Making light rigs," Dash said.

"Oh no you are not. Those are *my poles.*"

"You can't need all these poles," Dash said.

"I do," Janelle said.

"We just need them for a few days."

"My poles are specially measured for my machine. These aren't just any poles," Janelle said.

"Look, there is no way you need all these poles. I'm taking some."

"Could we borrow a few?" Stevie said quietly. "I'll make sure you get them back."

"For you," Janelle said. "I would only give my poles to you."

Dash had the poles out of the bucket in a shot and hurried them out of the workshop.

Maris had stopped sawing for a bit and was looking in a large blue industrial bin on the side of the room.

"There's dry ice here," she called to Dash. "Lots of it."

"I have enough fog machines," he said. "The liquid is easier to work with."

Maris shrugged and shut the container.

After constructing their ramps and organizing their poles and all the things that would be needed to film in the sunken garden on Saturday, the plan was made for the excursion into the tunnel. It would be the next night, with everyone meeting behind the art barn at seven.

Still smelling of sawdust, Stevie walked home and dropped into bed. For a few minutes, she rested on her back, fully dressed, and felt the cool air from the window brush against her face. The late summer twilight fell into darkness. There were footsteps creaking above her. David was home. She could tell everyone in her house by their footsteps. She started to understand how Minerva settled and shifted almost musically. She reached up and felt the cool iron of the bedstead. She pulled her comforter over her, sealing herself in with the sawdust smell coming off her sweatpants. Janelle was behind one wall, Ellie the other. She was in the middle, and it felt utterly normal. The thought grabbed her. She had settled in. This was home, and she had almost completed a major project about the Ellingham case with her friends. Well, Nate was her friend, and probably Hayes and Maris and Dash. Her friend Janelle gave her supplies.

A pleasant wave of satisfaction swept over her, and it inspired her to lean over and grab her phone from the bedside stand. She had a note app on her phone that had carefully organized files of images and information about the Ellingham case. She clicked open the folder marked SOCIAL. This was her research on the life the Ellinghams had led up here before the tragedy, back when the house was just a weird and wonderful mountain showpiece, and famous friends would come to ski in the winter, watch the leaves in the fall, and drink all the time. Some of those people probably stayed in this building, in this room, back before the school was opened and Minerva was a guesthouse. Stevie flipped through, stopping on one of her favorites: an image of a guest list from a party in 1929. She had no idea who these people were, but she loved reading the names: Gus Swenson, the Billbody twins, Esther Neil and Buck Randolph, the Davis sisters (Greta and Flo), Bernard Hendish, Lady Isobella de Isla, Dr. Frank Dodds, Frankie Sullivan, the Van-Warners, "Telegraph" McMurray and Lorna Darvish . . .

The list went on and on. They had come to have their champagne here, to dance under the stars. Actors, writers, artists, socialites. And then, Dottie Epstein lived here. Stevie had read about Dottie—one of the brightest in her school. Strong-willed. Brilliant. A tough Lower East Side girl who could steal apples and quote Virgil. Stevie reached down for her phone to look at Dottie's picture for perhaps the thousandth time. She had a head of brown curls, apple cheeks, and a gap between her front teeth. She was the often-forgotten victim because she was not rich. She did not own a school. She was just a smart girl trying to make something of herself at Ellingham Academy. She read mysteries. She had gone to the observatory to read, leaving a book behind.

Stevie set her phone on her stomach and stared up at the ceiling for a long time. The case needed solving for all of them, but maybe Dottie most of all. Dottie, who loved mysteries. Tomorrow night, she would go into the tunnel that had been blocked since 1938. Truly, this was something no one else who looked into the case in recent decades had done. She was literally going to be on new ground. Dottie had passed through that tunnel. She had died in or near or because of it. The tunnel marked the place where Dottie crossed over from life to death.

Stevie fell asleep in this position, phone on her stomach, thinking about Dottie and the tunnel. A pulse of light brought her back to consciousness.

Stevie blinked, confused. Her brain tried to work out the source of the light for a split second. Car headlights?

No.

Still mostly asleep, she pushed herself up on one arm.

The light, or something made of light, was on the wall. It filled the space next to the fireplace. Blobs of color. Letters, words.

It was all a scramble in her brain until she realized the blobs were a message made of cutout letters:

RiddLE, RiddLE, oN ThE WaLL
MuRdER coMEs To PaY a caLL

a body in a lonely field
will its secrets be revealed?
or the lady in the lake?
will she give the
lucky break?
alice, alice, where are you?
won't you give
a single clue?
the detective's here.
it's time to play!
truly devious
lives another day.

In another flash, the message was gone.

13

STEVIE WAS OUT OF BED IN A SECOND, DROPPING ROUGHLY TO THE floor. Her eyes were throbbing slightly, reacting to the sudden wakefulness, the shift from dark to light.

The words were tumbling in her head as she crawled to the window. When she reached it, she huddled beneath it for a moment, her body shaking from the adrenaline. Was there someone there? Would she pop up and be face-to-face? The window was open about six inches. Would someone reach in?

Only one way to find out.

She pushed herself to her knees with one quick movement. Outside was dark and still. She clutched the window, unsure whether or not to slam it down or open it farther to look out. Her grip on the frame tightened.

Another idea: she pulled her heaviest book on criminology from the shelf, the one she had scored at a library sale for three dollars, the one that was her prize possession. She stuck it out the window and let it drop.

No one screamed. She heard the book land in the grass with a thud. She slid over to the closet and pulled out the tactical flashlight that the school had provided and switched it on and scanned the area. Nothing. Just darkness and more darkness and the slight rustling sounds of the night.

She closed and locked the window, pulled the curtains, and tucked her head into her knees. What had it said? *Riddle, riddle, on the wall, murder something something something* . . .

And then it hit.

Panic attacks are mean little freaks.

First came the speed. Then came clamping in the throat, the lightness in her head, the feeling of blind acceleration into confusion. Then comes the strange wind that blew into her mind, knocking everything over and turning everything into a mockery of reality. Every avenue was blocked off. Every option meant doom. Nothing made any sense. It felt like hands were around her neck. Stevie gulped hard, proving to herself that she could swallow, that her airway was open.

"It's fine," she said to herself. "Breathe one, two . . ."

But she couldn't breathe one, two because the universe was converging to a point. It would be a welcome feeling to pass out, except there was a terror that somehow the merry-go-round would just go on, even in an unconscious state.

People say depression lies. Anxiety is just stupid. It's unable to tell the difference between things that are actually scary (being buried alive, for example) and things that are not scary at all (being in bed under the covers). It hits all the same buttons. Stop. Go. Up. Down. It's all the same to anxiety. The curtains said fear and the floor said fear.

The dark said fear, and if she turned the light on, that too would likely say fear. She turned the light on anyway. The faces of the murdered Ellinghams looked at her accusingly from the case board. She hurried over to the dresser, pulling open the drawer with shaking hands. She knocked out one Ativan, then hurried back over to her nightstand and washed it down with a gulp of water from the bottle next to her bed.

It would take some time to work, and the universe was still howling in her ears.

She needed help.

She slipped into the hallway, bumping against the door frame as she went. She went to Janelle's door and knocked. After a moment, there was a sleepy, "Yeah?"

Stevie tried the door and found it was unlocked. She was too muddled to be embarrassed or feel bad for waking her.

"What?" Janelle said, sitting up. "Are you okay?"

"Panic attack," Stevie said. "Can I . . . can you . . ."

Janelle pushed herself out of bed, grabbed her robe, and put it over Stevie's shoulders. She guided Stevie to the bed and sat her down, putting an arm around her shoulders.

"Sorry," Stevie wheezed, "sorry."

"Here," Janelle said, taking her hand. "It's okay. We're going to do this. Hold my hand."

Holding Janelle's hand brought some semblance of reality back.

"Can I sit here for a minute?" Stevie said.

"You stay until it's over," Janelle said. "As long as it takes. Did something happen?"

Stevie couldn't bring herself to explain. Everything was wobbling. She leaned back against Janelle and the wall behind the bed and waited for everything to stop moving, for the words to stop running through her mind, for Truly Devious to leave.

⊞

The next morning, when Stevie emerged from her room, Janelle was in the common room, looking amazingly perky for someone who had been up half the night helping a friend. She was wearing a fleecy sweatshirt that said ASK ME ABOUT MY CAT and a pair of yoga pants, and her braids were coiled up under a cheerful red scarf. Stevie, on the other hand, was still wearing the sawdust-covered sweatpants. She had not consulted her hair. It could be doing anything. She had not bothered to wipe her face or crusty eyes or brush her teeth. She just needed to get up and shake off the night.

Stevie was embarrassed looking at her friend. She'd never really had an experience like that before, outside of her parents, where someone actually took care of you like that. Janelle had put her back into bed just before dawn, and Stevie had slept heavily for a few hours. Now she was groggy and heavy and slow.

"How are you doing?" Janelle asked in a low voice.

"I'm okay," Stevie said. "A little nauseous. Tired. But okay."

She couldn't bring herself to say "thanks to you" out loud, but she tried to convey it in her eyes, and then by generally being awkward. Janelle just shook her head in a *don't worry about it* kind of way.

Stevie went outside. The morning was fresh and bright—big blue skies and shaggy, happy clouds blowing over the mountains. It was the kind of morning that mocked the fear of the night before. This kind of pleasantness almost made it worse. How could she be anxious when everything was so cheerful?

Very easily, as it happens. Brain chemistry doesn't care about how pretty things are.

She stepped along the edge of Minerva, through the moist grass to retrieve her book from the ground outside her window. It was a bit damp, but on examination it showed no real damage.

What had happened? She had been reading case materials right up until the time she went to sleep. She was thinking about the kidnapping and the tunnel. She could have easily dreamed that note on the wall. But it was vivid, crisp. She had gotten out of bed. She'd thrown a book out her window trying to catch a stranger.

She watched the sky for a moment and held her wet book and tried to work out what was real, then she rubbed her burning, tired eyes. She still had to go to class. She dried the cover with her shirt and brought it back inside.

As she went to her room, she bumped into David coming downstairs.

It was nothing, really. He just kind of half smiled at her. He had that long mouth with the twisting edges. Just a smile.

But something about it made Stevie boil. She blocked him.

"Good night?" she said.

"It's so nice of you to ask," he replied, leaning against the wall. "Sure. How about you?"

His tone was neutral but his smile was expanding by just a few millimeters.

"Busy last night?" she asked.

"You have a lot of questions."

Still neutral, still half smiling. Something in his eyes, though. A flash. It was impossible to tell what was going on, but there was *something* there.

"This is fun and all," he said, "but can I go and get breakfast?"

Stevie stepped aside, but turned to watch him go. Could David have put that note on her wall?

⊲⊳

She was fairly unfocused during the discussion of *Leaves of Grass* that morning. She spent most of the discussion trying to remember the words she had seen.

Riddle, riddle . . . something murder, something lake, something Alice. Definitely Truly Devious in there somewhere. But the more she tried to remember, the more the words slipped away and didn't feel like words at all.

Walt Whitman was getting involved now:

*And the hints about old men and mothers, and the
    offspring taken
soon out of their laps.*

What do you think has become of the young and old men?
And what do you think has become of the women and
children?

They are alive and well somewhere . . .

Riddle, riddle. A woman in a lake, a girl in a hole . . .

She would be a girl in a hole later tonight, when she went into the tunnel.

She went in and out of the explanation of the functions of the axial and the appendicular skeleton in anatomy. Lunch brought her closer to the surface, and by the time she was in Spanish lab, the dread was burning away and she began to focus on going into the tunnel. She felt a flutter of excitement, which carried her through the afternoon.

Stevie hurried back to Minerva in the midafternoon to get her flashlight and gloves, then met Janelle for their first yoga class at five. Yoga was the class she picked from Ellingham's mandatory physical education selection. It sounded better than Running for Fitness and Clarity, Cooperative Boot Camp, or Perspectives on Movement. At Stevie's high school, they let you just go on the treadmill for half an hour and left you alone to listen to podcasts, which was literally the only thing she preferred about her old high school.

Janelle met her outside the art barn, a rolled mat tucked under her arm.

"Doing okay?" Janelle asked.

"Yeah," Stevie said. "I think so."

"Anxiety dreams are the worst," she said.

Stevie had, late last night, managed to explain to Janelle what she had seen. She must have made it sound like it was definitely a dream, and not some questionable occurrence that may or may not have been real.

"I guess . . . I guess I dreamed it?" Stevie said. "I don't know."

Janelle nodded, as if this was the only answer she had been expecting.

"But," Stevie said as they walked into the art barn, "let's just say for a second I didn't dream it. How hard is it to project something on the wall like that? I guess you'd need a projector?"

"Oh, that's easy," Janelle said. "You can make one out of cardboard and tape and a mirror. It's not impossible, but . . ."

"I mean," Stevie said. "I woke up. I was in bed, and I saw it on the wall. I threw my book out the window trying to catch whoever was out there. Like, tried to drop the book on their head."

"Did you catch anyone?" Janelle said. "See anyone?"

"No."

"If you're woken up in certain phases of sleep, reality and dreams, they blend together for a little bit. And being up here for the first time, it's probably going to cause some anxiety dreams. My anxiety dreams are all about how I just never go to class. And it's the end of the year and I've skipped everything. On a good night, I dream about advances in 3-D printing and Gina Torres dressed as

Wonder Woman. But here's the thing . . ."

She stopped Stevie before they entered the yoga room.

"I think we all come here because we have something in our heads we can't get out," Janelle said. "We're all kind of fixated on something. I want to make machines, and you want to solve mysteries, and Nate wants to write—or he doesn't want to write—and Ellie wants to live in her own art commune. Hayes, he makes shows. I guess David makes games. I see him doing coding, so I know he can. We're all kind of in our own world. It's that your world is a real place here. I think your brain is a little busy processing the information. You had an intense dream. Something woke you. You can carry through some of those states and see things and think you're awake and not really be completely out of a sleep state. Sleep is a funny thing."

Put like that, everything seemed to make sense.

"How are you so smart?" Stevie asked.

"I read a lot," Janelle said, smiling. She unzipped the front of her bag, shoved her pass inside and secured the lanyard to a clip, and zipped the bag back up again. Janelle did everything completely, even putting her pass away. "And I'm just amazing."

The class was in a small studio room. Everyone dropped their bags in the hall and crowded inside. Yoga was popular, and the mats were only inches apart. Stevie used one from the school supply; it was rubbery and purple and smelled a bit like bleach and feet.

The teacher, Daria, had a little accordion-piano thing

she played as she made everyone sit on some blankets at the start of class with their eyes closed. They were supposed to be focusing on their breath, but Stevie kept going back to that flickering moment where she had jerked out of sleep the night before and read the words on the wall. She played it back again and again. How awake had she been when her feet hit the floor, when she tried to memorize the words?

It was impossible to know. Sleep had its own mysteries, and Daria was telling them to get into downward facing dog. Stevie was still new at this yoga thing and Daria was soon standing over her and arranging her hands and hips and feet. Stevie had watched a few videos to prepare for this before coming, but in the moment, she was completely lost and whatever move she made was somehow wrong. She was two moves behind at all times, at best. Her knee was in the wrong spot, her arm not high enough, her twist not twisty. Daria hovered and, in a sweet, whispery voice, adjusted her positions again and again and eventually planted herself by Stevie as she guided the class. How did everyone else know how to do yoga?

The one advantage to all of this was that it cleared Stevie's mind of everything else. She heard exercise did that. Was this what they meant? You were so busy being confused and trying to stop your sweaty hands from slipping on a mat that you couldn't think anymore?

Stevie did approve of the fact that yoga ended by lying on the floor in corpse pose.

"You're doing your filming thing tonight, right?" Janelle said at the end of a class, as they went out into the hall to

193

retrieve their things. "Because Vi and I are going to . . ."

She was fishing hard in her bag, poking her hand into the bottom and the pockets.

"My pass," she said. "It's gone. I zipped it up. You saw me."

"I did," Stevie said. "Are you sure it's not there?"

Janelle yanked the front pouch open. No pass.

"How the hell did it get lost?" Janelle said. "Did someone take it? I need to find it. I get access to things, and if I lose that . . ."

"We'll look," Stevie said, already on the floor, digging around in the pile of other bags as people came out of class and took them away.

"They charge you a hundred and fifty bucks for a new one," Janelle said. "Crap. *Crap.*"

"It's okay," Stevie assured her. "Someone must have just screwed up."

"How? By going into my bag and taking it? I have to tell Pix. Who steals passes? Who went into my bag?"

Janelle was getting upset now. This kind of disorder agitated her. And she definitely had put her pass into her bag.

"Maybe it was a prank?"

"To steal my pass?"

Stevie almost said, "Or put a letter on my wall." But since the jury was out on whether or not that was real, she refrained. It was another weird occurrence in a short amount of time. A letter and a key. It had the feeling of a strange game, and one that filled Stevie with a low, simmering worry.

Games are not fun when you don't know you're playing.

14

It was a perfect night to go underground.

Autumn was different up here, Stevie noted, as she and Nate made their way down the path to the art barn at eight o'clock that night. It was more—wild. This was probably to be expected, but still, the experience caught her by surprise. There was more scurrying in the bushes, more drama in the dark treetops, more wind. The air was thick with the fecund smell of early dropping leaves and the fragrant decay of layers of undergrowth. Everything was alive or vocal in its demise. This smell, this feeling—*this* is why Albert Ellingham had insisted on the spot.

"My kingdom for a Starbucks or something," Nate said. "Are you feeling like we've been here forever too? When do we start eating each other or fighting for the conch?"

Stevie and Nate were both wearing dark clothes for this night mission. Nate was wearing baggy dark jeans and a slouchy black sweater that hung down to his fingers, making his long arms even longer. He looked about as excited as he normally did, but Stevie was used to this now. Nate was a rain cloud, but he was her friendly rain cloud, and the world needs some rain. Stevie was fully prepared for the venture with some black cargo pants and her black hoodie. Her wardrobe had not let her down. Both had the school-issued tactical flashlights in their bags.

"So this tunnel," Nate said as they rounded the path by the whispering statue heads. "What was it?"

"A supply tunnel for alcohol during Prohibition," Stevie said. "They used to have trucks come down from Canada. They kept the booze under the observatory in case of a raid, not that anyone would have raided Albert Ellingham."

"I mean the *tunnel*," Nate said. "Something about it being open again?"

"Because it was filled up for a while," Stevie said vaguely. She didn't want to say, "Since 1938, just unearthed, who even knows what's down there now."

"And we're allowed?"

"No one said not to," Stevie replied.

"But also we're not supposed to tell anyone."

"Act first, apologize later."

She felt Nate staring at her, but she turned the other way to look at one of the grimacing statue heads.

"I don't know if this is really going to count for three chapters," Nate said, digging his hands into his pockets. "We've only been doing this for a week."

"What did Dr. Quinn say?"

"That she would consider it when she saw it. But she

looks like she considers broken bottles to be part of your complete breakfast."

"I think you worry too much," Stevie said.

"Of course I *worry* too much," Nate said. "But I'm usually right. The people who worry are always right. That's how that works."

Stevie decided not to contradict him on that one.

Hayes, Maris, and Dash were already waiting by the far wing of the art barn, where the construction equipment and the Dumpsters were, out by the maintenance road. They were also dressed in black—Hayes in something formfitting, Dash in something artistically loose and flowing, and Maris in dark leggings and an oversized fuzzy sweater, with a tight black hat on her head. She even wore a musky, smoky perfume to match the occasion.

"Okay," Hayes said, switching on his flashlight. "Let's go."

They entered the woods—the ring of true wilderness that enveloped Ellingham Academy, the place where the trees were not orderly and no statues bloomed. At least, they entered the bit of it by the maintenance road. Stevie had a good sense of where the tunnel ran and where the opening should be, but the opening was going to be flush with the ground. Hayes seemed to have a very clear sense of where he was going.

"How did you find this?" Maris asked.

"The tunneling is the best part," Hayes said with a smile. "This one opened in the spring. They didn't want anyone to know."

"But you knew?"

"I saw," he said, grinning and shining his flashlight under his chin.

He led them about thirty yards from the road, into a tight cluster of trees. Then he stopped and started stomping at the ground. There was the heavy *thunk* of thick metal.

"Light," he said.

Maris shone a flashlight down as he scraped off an inch or so of loose dirt.

"They covered it up," he said, bending down. "And it looks like they put a lock on it. It wasn't locked before. That's going to be a problem."

"Let me see," Stevie said, kneeling on the ground beside him. The ground was spongy and cold beneath her knees.

"Just a standard padlock," she said, peering at the end. "Can you shine a light?"

Maris shone her flashlight down on the lock. Stevie went into her bag and fished around for a while until she found two paper clips at the bottom. She straightened them and inserted them into the lock. One she used as a tension wrench, and with the other, she manipulated the pins. It was all about slow, careful movement—feeling every millimeter. Locks are tiny, and their pins are tinier still, and the movement needed to lift one is barely a flinch.

Luckily, she had picked padlocks like this many times. It

was a good, cheap hobby to practice while watching mysteries, and it seemed like the kind of skill she should have.

It popped open.

"Whoa," Hayes said. "How the hell did you learn to do that?"

Stevie simply smiled, got up, and dusted off her hands.

"Nice one," Maris added approvingly. Finally, there was something Stevie could do that Maris could not.

Dash was texting, and Nate stood in stunned silence.

Hayes pulled open the doors, revealing a pitch-black hole in the ground. Stevie shone her flashlight down on a dozen or so bare concrete steps, leading into more darkness.

"That's not ominous-looking at all," Nate said.

Stevie made her way to the front and squatted down, shining her light into the hole. The space in front of her was a violent, velvety dark. Anything could have been there. A million spiders. Someone with a knife. Or worse—just a lot of dark tunnel.

She counted the steps and felt around with her foot to assure herself she had reached the last one before shining her light up. The million spiders, if present, were well hidden, and there was no one with a knife. The tunnel was made of brick and concrete and was in fairly good condition, aside from a few upsetting jags and cracks that were probably caused by years of snow and ice. There was an overwhelming smell of earth and age and stagnant air. The tunnel felt tighter than she thought it would be, snugly fitting two people across. It made sense, of course. It's not easy to build a secret underground tunnel. You needed it to be just big enough to get your boxes of booze, or sneak around with your friends while playing one of the Ellingham's famous games. The brick made it feel like they were inside a horizontal chimney.

Stevie got light-headed for a moment and ran her hand over the walls. They almost felt wet, and she traced the patterns of the mortar with her fingers. This was history, real history, opening up for her. It was almost too much to take in. She ignored the effort going on around her, as Dash pulled a tripod out of his bag and opened it up, and Maris and Hayes tipped their heads together to read the Truly Devious letter off his phone and work out where to stand.

Nate slid up alongside Stevie and broke into her reverie.

"Why do you know how to pick locks?" he asked.

"Because there are a lot of tutorials online."

"That's how," he said. "Why?"

"Who doesn't want to know how to pick a lock? It only took a few hours. Buy a lock for five bucks . . ."

"Still not why."

"Because they do it on TV," Stevie finally said. "It seems like a good thing to know. I like detectives, okay? We all have our hobbies."

"Remind me not to get on your bad side," Nate said.

Stevie stared into the dark. She shone her light into it, but there was no end in sight. Just more dark.

"Are they sure about the structural integrity?" Nate asked. "Should we really be in here? It feels like an elevator shaft on the *Titanic*."

"It's fine," Stevie said. Because it *probably* was. Most things are.

Stevie swept her light around, steering it away from a terrifying crack in the side, and then aimed it squarely forward.

"I'm going to the end," she said.

"Seriously?" Nate said.

"This is what I came here for. My dragons are down there."

"Stevie, I wouldn't . . ."

"You're not me," Stevie said. "If I die, avenge me."

She was joking, but not totally. She had to go, and it also felt like a possible mistake.

Some mistakes you have to make.

The distance, she knew, was about four hundred feet. Four hundred feet of dark tunnel may not sound like a lot of dark tunnel, but it is, in fact, a lot of dark tunnel. But she was going in, like people who crawled into pockets of pyramids sealed for thousands of years with no idea what was ahead of them went in. There were buried mysteries, and sometimes, you must go into the earth.

She wondered if she would panic. To her surprise, though, her heartbeat was slow, steady as she took each step into the velvety nothingness of the tunnel. Soon, there would be a door at the end. She reached her arm out in front of her to find it, and eventually she felt the heavy wood at her fingertips.

Her heart literally skipped a beat and sent a glug of confused blood popping.

The door was made of thick pieces of wood belted together with iron, that small, sliding window looking like something from a medieval jail. There was no knob on this door, no lock. Originally, this door would have been opened from the other side, so if it was locked on that side, that was the end of her exploring.

She pushed.

It opened.

She was going farther. She was going in. This was like a dream.

The room beyond was small. Three sides of the space were composed of shelving. This had been the liquor room. The deliveries would come in through the tunnel, then come into this room for storage. A metal ladder went up to a hatch in the ceiling. Stevie tested it for a moment with a shake. It seemed to be firmly secured to the wall and in perfect repair. Could she do this? Could she actually go to *the place where it happened*?

The others were nowhere behind her. She was doing this alone.

She tested the ladder again, then tucked her flashlight into her bag. She was going up into the dark. She proceeded slowly, trusting in the ladder and knowing that at some point her head would make contact with the hatch above. She would use that sensation as a guide.

Up, up, up into the dark, moving more slowly as she went. She felt the hatch against her hair, against her scalp. She backed down a rung and reached up to test it. It didn't give at first, but she pressed harder. There was an unholy squawk as the ancient springs were forced back into action, but the hatch popped open.

Some people want to go to see the Eiffel Tower or Big Ben. Some people dream of their proms or their someday weddings. Some people dream of going up in a hot-air balloon or scuba diving in clear Caribbean waters. Everyone has a dream place, and Stevie Bell was climbing into hers.

The domed observatory seemed smaller now that she was inside of it. The thick glass triangles that composed most of the structure were encrusted with dirt, so all was dark. She shone her light around the stone floor, the bench that ran around the side. There was nothing in here now but some dead leaves and dirt. It smelled like a shed.

Dottie had been here. This is where they found her Sherlock Holmes book. Albert Ellingham had come right through that stout door. He'd been struck and fallen to the floor. Here? On this spot? Had the money been counted here? Was this where it all started to go so very wrong?

She closed her eyes for a moment. Maybe, if she breathed this air and felt this space, maybe she could go back. . . .

"Hey!" Dash's voice cut through the silence as he yelled

from below. "Come on. We need you."

The moment was over.

⌖

The filming was very quick. All that was needed was for Hayes to recite the Truly Devious letter while walking down the tunnel length. He and Maris passed the camera back and forth to get some long shots, but it was dark and cold and hard to film, and time was not on their side. At eight thirty, they all crept back to the steps. A quick look outside showed that no one was waiting for them to pop out of the hole. The doors were closed.

"We can't all go together," Hayes said, holding the padlock in his hand. "If anyone sees us all coming from this direction, they might realize we were down here. Nate, Stevie, you guys go first. Dash, you should go the other way around. Maris, we can go last."

As Stevie and Nate walked back through the dark, Nate glanced over his shoulder.

"I think they're going to go back and bone in that tunnel," he said.

"Bone," Stevie repeated. "Did you have to say *bone*?"

"Tunnelboner," Nate said. "A new fragrance for men."

"They wouldn't," Stevie said. "They won't."

"Why not?"

"Because that's . . . the tunnel. You don't just *tunnelbone* in that tunnel."

"Sometimes a tunnel is just a tunnel," Nate said.

Stevie ground her jaw a bit and walked on, her hands

deep in her hoodie pockets. The magic of the tunnel and the observatory was still on her, and she wanted to hold it as long as possible.

She thought of the letter that she had seen on her wall. It really had been so vivid. Dreams had a way of blurring and fading the moment they were over. The edges were sharp on this, the colors bright. Her mind had taken a screenshot.

Had it been real?

It was possible; most things are *possible*. It wasn't *likely*, though. What was likely was that her anxious and excited brain, full of new stimuli, conjured up something bright and shiny for her, something so magical and odd that it stamped its impression on her brain cells for a little longer than normal. Thinking about it logically, who knew or cared enough about her to go to those kinds of lengths, and to what end?

It had been a dream, just as Janelle said. Janelle made sense.

Still, the feeling was there, and it felt like Truly Devious was calling out from the past. Truly Devious, the known ghoul, the laughing murderer.

But some things don't stay buried—not tunnels, not secrets. Truly Devious was not immune.

WHO IS TRULY DEVIOUS? 80 YEARS ON
Postdetective.com
April 13, 2016

On April 8, 1936, a letter arrived at the Burlington, Vermont, office of Albert Ellingham. Albert Ellingham was, at the time, one of the richest men in America. He constructed an estate and a school in the mountains outside of Burlington, and it was there he lived with his wife and his daughter, breathing the sweet, clean air. A Burlington office collected his personal and business mail, and every day, a car would take sacks of correspondence from Burlington to the house, well up on Mount Hatchet, where it would be sorted and processed by his secretary.

That day, in with the hundreds of letters, one stood out. The envelope was postmarked from Burlington. The address of the Ellingham estate was written on the front in dull pencil, in heavy, square strokes. Inside was a single piece of writing paper that contained the words:

Look! A riddle! Time for fun!
Should we use a rope or gun?
Knives are sharp and gleam so pretty
Poison's slow, which is a pity
Fire is festive, drowning's slow
Hanging's a ropy way to go

A broken head, a nasty fall
A car colliding with a wall
Bombs make a very jolly noise
Such ways to punish naughty boys!
What shall we use? We can't decide.
Just like you cannot run or hide.
Ha ha.
Truly,
Devious

Threats to Albert Ellingham and his family were not new—in fact, Albert Ellingham had barely survived a car bombing several years before. This was during a time in which industrialists were often under threat. What made this letter so different?

For a start, it was constructed of colorful words and letters that would later be determined to come from popular magazines. In bright, cheerful print, it spelled out a diabolical poem, one that listed the many ways that Albert Ellingham might die. The letter writer gave themselves a name: Truly Devious.

Five days later, while out on a drive, Albert Ellingham's wife, Iris, was kidnapped, along with their three-year-old daughter, Alice. Along with Iris and Alice, a young girl named Dolores Epstein, who was a student at Ellingham's new academy on the site, also vanished.

A ransom demand was called in that evening,

giving Albert Ellingham just a few minutes to bundle up the money in his safe and take it to a lake on his property. Ellingham was a bit short of cash, so the kidnappers beat up the person sent to collect Iris and Alice, and demanded more.

Robert Mackenzie, Ellingham's thirty-year-old private secretary, begged to call the police. But Ellingham was convinced that doing so would put his family in more danger. Instead, along with family friend George Marsh by his side, Ellingham took two hundred thousand dollars in marked bills to a remote point in Burlington and lowered the money down to a boat waiting below on Lake Champlain.

The boat sailed off. On May 16, 1936, Dolores Epstein's body was found in a field in Jericho, Vermont, in a shallow grave. She was discovered by a milk truck driver from a local dairy who had pulled off the road to relieve a call of nature. The cause of death was a massive blow to the head.

Three weeks later, on June 5, 1936, the body of Iris Ellingham washed up near South Hero, Vermont. Maude Loomis, the local resident who discovered the body, stated: "She was wrapped in an oilcloth and she was in bad shape, real bad shape. It looked like they tried to weigh her down." Iris's body was found to have three gunshot wounds.

Truly Devious seemed to be running down the list: there was a car involved, though it didn't go into the wall. (In fact, Iris Ellingham's cherry-red Mercedes was eventually found neatly parked deep on a country lane seven miles from the house, with no sign of a struggle.) There was a broken head, a gun, and a body found in water.

The FBI was called in three days after the kidnapping. Agents immediately took possession of the letter and started their examination. Specialists determined that the paper was of an ordinary stock, sold in thousands of stores. The only fingerprints on the letter were those of Albert Ellingham and Robert Mackenzie. The paste was basic white glue. The words and letters came from popular publications such as *Life* magazine, *Photoplay*, and *The Saturday Evening Post*. In short, there was nothing remarkable about the letter aside from its content.

Psychiatrists from all around the country had opinions on the identity of the letter writer. There were differing thoughts on the exact diagnosis, but all agreed that the writer was intelligent, highly verbal, and confident. Poets and literature professors examined the poem, with massively differing opinions. Some said the work was childish. Others said the poem was written by someone who knew poetry well, who was hiding their talent. One surrealist chillingly called it "the truest, greatest work of our time."

This presented a bit of a problem at the trial. While Anton Vorachek had some of the ransom money in his house and admitted to the crime, his English was extremely limited. Most experts involved in the case thought he was incapable of writing the letter, though one FBI specialist disagreed. Two years after Vorachek's death, a woman claimed that he had been with her on the day of the crime, but that she had been too frightened to come forward earlier. Her account was widely disputed.

Eighty years on, the questions linger.

With modern technology, we might be able to learn more about the Truly Devious letter—but there is a problem. It no longer exists. The letter was taken to the Burlington courthouse for the trial. A week after the trial concluded, there was a fire in the courthouse basement, most likely caused by a smoldering cigarette. A dozen boxes of evidence were destroyed before the fire was extinguished, including the box containing Truly Devious's work. So we are likely never to know Truly Devious's secrets.

Ha ha! as they might say.

15

"WANT TO HEAR SOMETHING WEIRD?" JANELLE SAID AS SHE STOOD IN Stevie's doorway. Stevie was still in bed, her phone alarm chirping, telling her that even though it was early Saturday morning, it was time to get up and shoot a video with Hayes. She wiped her eyes and looked at Janelle, who looked as perturbed as anyone can look while wearing baby-blue fleece pajamas covered in cat heads.

"This is what's weird," she said. She lifted up her arm, and hanging from her fist was an Ellingham lanyard with an ID dangling at the end. "Guess where it was?"

Stevie had no guess.

"Literally outside. On the path. Someone took my pass and then brought it back, but not even all the way to the building. They could have shoved it in the door or something. Instead they dropped it halfway up the path. *Who does that?*"

"Someone playing a prank?" Stevie said, rubbing at her short hair. "An asshole?"

"Definitely the last one," Janelle said. "At least I have it back. Crisis averted."

With that mystery resolved if not solved, Stevie got herself showered and dressed. The air was crisp, so Stevie put on her sweats and her Ellingham fleece. As she went into the common room, she was shocked to see David awake, in pajama bottoms and an old T-shirt from a surfing brand, sitting cross-legged on the purple sofa, hunkered over his computer.

"Are you working?" she said.

He looked up. His eyes were red, like he had not slept, and there was shade around his jawline. His curly hair stood on end. He looked *tumbled* and . . . attractive.

"I go here," he said. "Remember?"

"Do you?" Stevie said coolly, walking to the kitchen. Had she just thought David was attractive? Could he tell? It was acceptable to have the thought, but not for him to know, and somehow, he would know.

She filled her aluminum Ellingham bottle with coffee and left the house quickly, even before Nate came down.

It was an aggressively pretty morning, as if the season wanted to show off before everything went to pieces and the trees got naked and everything died. The sky was big and blue. Stevie had a real sense of purpose and lift as she made her way over to the sunken garden. This felt like going to school, she thought, as she looked around Ellingham. Up early on a fresh Saturday morning, coffee in hand, to make a project. The energy of the tunnel was still with her.

The door to the sunken garden was open, and Stevie stepped inside. There was no one there yet, so she took a moment to sit with her coffee and look.

Stevie was well aware that this man-made lake was large, but when you saw it in person, saw this massive crater in the earth, it brought home just what Albert Ellingham was willing to do to make his family happy. His wife loved to swim, so the ground was leveled, the rock blown away. When he got a tip suggesting that his wife and daughter or some evidence rested at the bottom, the lake was drained and dried and the earth scarred. And now, just the monuments remained—the statues that looked over the void, the observatory ridiculous on its little bump.

"Thanks for waiting," said Nate, coming in from behind her.

"Sorry," she said.

He was wearing cargo shorts, despite the fact that there was a little chill in the air, and a T-shirt that said MY OTHER CAR IS A DRAGON.

"You really love this stuff, don't you?" he said, sitting down next to her on the damp grass. "It's like you're at murder Disney World."

"Murder Disney World would be amazing."

"That's true," he said. "I'd go to that too."

"It's just . . ." Stevie looked for the words. "I've seen so many pictures of this place. I've read all this stuff. It was like everything I had in my head is . . ."

She waved her hands helplessly in front of her. Luckily, Nate seemed to understand.

"Yeah," Nate said. "I guess it would be like that if I could go somewhere in a book. I always wanted stories to be real, so I started writing my own. That seemed to make it more real. I'm kind of jealous you get to see your thing. Gandalf isn't coming for me."

"Never say never," Stevie said.

There was the modest sound of a golf cart coming, and Mark from maintenance drove in with their supplies, with Dash along for the ride. Hayes and Maris arrived last, and though they weren't holding hands, they walked close enough together and looked at each other in a way that made it clear that they had not parted ways right away last night.

There was a lot of moving things that day, lots of running and fetching. Janelle's beloved poles were set into stands on which lights were attached. The ramp was placed into the sunken garden to create a place from which Hayes could row his imaginary boat. There was a generator to power the lights and the fog machines, which required lots of position-ing and testing. Then the tripods were set, lights focused. It took hours, and it was boring. Nate and Stevie had little to do but obey commands to hold things and move things and get things. As Stevie and Nate went from the garden to the costume closet and back again, Stevie noted that Hayes didn't seem to be doing a lot of running or holding or mov-ing. He sat on a stone bench most of the time, looking at his computer. Stevie thought he was running his lines. The lines were all his—this was a monologue. The rest of the dialogue would be recorded separately and put on top as narration, so there was a lot to know. When she did a quick pass behind him, she saw he was looking at pictures and replying to messages.

While the ramp was being positioned for the fifth time, Stevie noticed that they had been joined by someone new. Germaine Batt had slipped in through the gate and was floating around and heading in Hayes's direction. Stevie wondered how this would play out, considering that Germaine had taken footage of Hayes the other night without his knowledge and posted it. But he seemed to welcome Germaine and even posed for some pictures. Stevie also noted that he made himself look very busy in those pictures.

There was a short lunch break, during which Hayes disappeared for a bit back to Minerva to put on his makeup. When everything was finally in place, hours later, he was nowhere to be found.

"Where the hell did he go?" Dash asked, looking around. "Stevie, can you find him?"

Stevie had been sitting on her bag, trying to get enough of a signal on her phone to download the latest episode of her new favorite true crime podcast, *Speaking of Murder*.

"Oh," she said, getting up, "yeah. Sure."

She wandered around the empty lake, around the edges of the garden. She heard voices coming from the folly by the back wall. She approached and heard a female voice, an angry one at that.

"You're so full of shit, Hayes," it said. "You *owe* me."

"And I'll give it to you," Hayes replied.

"That's what you said before."

"Because I will."

Stevie remained very still for a moment and listened.

"You think people don't know?" the unknown person said, her voice dripping with contempt.

"Know what, Gretchen?" Hayes said.

Gretchen. The girl with the hair. The queenly one.

"Oh, please. You're going to pretend with *me*?"

"Why do you even care?" he said.

"Well, first, I'm never getting paid back. Let's not pretend about that. You do this to everyone. To me. Probably to Beth. At least she knows now, thanks to that girl who did the video. What about these dumb SOBs who are out here doing your work right now?"

Dumb SOBs? Stevie was one of those dumb SOBs.

"Gretchen . . ." It came out as a long sigh.

"What if I tell that girl with the show all about it?"

"I guess you do what you need to do, Gretchen," he said. "Or you could take a Xanax and give me a week or two."

Before Stevie could move, Hayes came from around the back of the folly. It was clearly Hayes, but he was older. His hair was grayed and his face was full of lines and furrows. Maris had done a good job with the stage makeup.

"Hey, Stevie," he said, a little louder than necessary.

"Hey," she said. "It's time."

Hayes smiled a bit, and Stevie realized he thought she was providing him cover to get out of the conversation. Now that she had been labeled as a dumb SOB who was doing Hayes's work for him, Stevie regarded his expression with a lot more suspicion.

"Thanks," he said, his voice thickening and sweeting. Tupelo honey now.

Gretchen emerged as well. She saw Stevie, but, to paraphrase Sherlock Holmes, she did not observe. Stevie was a part of the landscape. She strode past without a word.

"Thanks," Hayes said, dropping a slow arm over Stevie's shoulders. "My ex. I mean, she broke up with me and she still seems mad about it. It's strange. But you know how these things are."

Stevie did not know how these things were, but she nodded.

"It's tough," she said.

Hayes nodded and slipped into a deeper, more comfortable smile. Hayes had a smile like a hammock—just get in, go to sleep, forget your troubles and cares.

⚡

A few things Stevie quickly learned that afternoon:

One, shooting the video involved a lot of not shooting the video, and standing around, and talking about doing things again, and then sometimes doing them again, and then running to the bathroom to find that things were just about where they were before.

Two, Hayes really could act. There was no denying him that.

Three, theatrical fog stank.

And four, it was possible for Stevie to tire of standing in the sunken garden and listen to the Ellingham kidnapping story being hashed over and over.

As the hours rolled on, she started to resent the fact that she had allowed Hayes to take Truly Devious as a subject. Sure, she had agreed, but there was something wrong about this, about making this weird little video. And though Hayes was doing a good enough job, and no matter how well the makeup was applied, he was still a seventeen-year-old guy playing a man in his late forties. This was Stevie's thing, and something about the whole filming process felt sideways and wrong in a way she could not quite place.

By six, Maris said they'd probably gotten what they needed and Dash called a dinner break.

"We'll eat and then we'll come back and clean up," he said.

"Tonight?" Nate replied. "Can't we do it tomorrow?"

Maris was helping Hayes wipe his face with a makeup remover cloth. When they were done, the group made their way out of the garden and to the dining hall. Stevie heard Nate's stomach grumbling out loud.

As they reached the green, Hayes took a step back.

"You guys go ahead," he said. "There's something I forgot."

"I'll come," Maris said.

"No, it's cool," he said, walking backward. "Go ahead and save me a place."

Stevie and Nate didn't have to be told twice.

⚜

It was strangely disconcerting to sit with a different group for dinner. Stevie worked her way through a plate of fried chicken and corn, watching across the room as some of her housemates reconfigured into groups. There was Janelle, taking a seat with some people from Vi's building. Ellie sat with people Stevie had barely seen before. David never showed up at all. Nor did Hayes.

"I wonder what's taking him so long?" Maris said, fidgeting in her seat. "He's not answering his texts."

"He's probably on the phone," Dash said, quickly eating some mashed potatoes.

Maris sat on her hands and glanced around the room, her gaze landing on Gretchen as she entered the dining hall. She ran her tongue over her teeth.

"I should go check," she said.

"Maris, he's coming," Dash said. "He's just doing something."

"We should go back and move the ramp anyway."

"Oh my God," Dash said. "Fine. Just let me finish eating for a second?"

Gretchen turned ever so casually toward them, her gaze passing like a cloud overhead.

What had she and Hayes been talking about earlier? What did Hayes owe Gretchen? And did being associated with Hayes cause this kind of turmoil? Maris was nervous, all of them were working on something that really benefited Hayes, Gretchen was literally seeking some kind of retribution.

How did some people lead these kinds of lives?

Dinner was finished quickly, much to Nate's chagrin, and the four of them—Maris, Dash, Stevie, and Nate—made their way back to the sunken garden.

It was now just coming on nightfall, the sky turning an electric blue with the trees standing out in stark relief. As they walked, Stevie heard someone approaching briskly, then turned to see Germaine Batt next to her.

"Where are you guys going?" she asked.

"To the sunken garden," Nate said. "To move a ramp. Or something. I don't know. I thought I just had to write."

"Can I come?"

"You want to move a ramp?" Stevie said.

"It's everyone's dream," Nate said, tugging his backpack higher on his shoulders. "Come to Ellingham Academy, move a ramp out of a hole in the dark."

"I just want to see what you're doing," Germaine said.

"More Hayes news?" Stevie said.

"I got fifty thousand views on that last one."

"That would be good on a tombstone," Stevie said. "*I got fifty thousand views on that last one.*"

"Say what you want," Germaine said, a frosty edge in her voice. "I honestly don't care."

When people say they honestly don't care, they care. Germaine hadn't done anything to Stevie. There was no reason to be spiky with her. Sure, it was a little unsavory what she was doing, but it didn't seem to be hurting Hayes any. If anything, he literally had a new girlfriend running after him right now, in front of them, in the gathering dark.

"Sorry," Stevie said. "Just kidding."

"It's fine," Germaine replied crisply. It did not seem fine.

The last lightning bugs of the season were dancing over the lawn as they entered through the gate. The hole in the ground looked a bit more ominous in the dark, and the dirty glass of the observatory caught the rising moon. There were piles of poles, and folded tarps, and the ramp.

"Hayes?" Maris called.

No reply. An unseen bird rustled in the treetops overhead.

"Where is he?" Maris said.

"Who knows?" Dash said. "He's probably on the phone somewhere and left us with this to clean up. Come on."

"He's got to be here somewhere," Maris said. "*Hayes!*"

Her bright, operatic voice rang from end to end of the garden.

"You'll figure this out fast," Dash said, picking up some poles. "Hayes is never around to do the dishes."

Maris shifted around, and for the first time, Stevie saw a first year like herself, someone who'd fallen for someone fast and was rapidly realizing things were not equal on both sides.

On their return home that evening, Nate went right to his room. Stevie decided to sit in the hammock chair in the common room and wait for Hayes to return. She could not fully explain why she did this. Maybe it was irritation. Maybe it had something to do with the tunnel. Had Hayes gone back there? Why had he turned like that and gone off on his own so deliberately?

Whatever the case, the hammock chair was a good place to sit and watch some episodes of *Stormy Weather*. She had earned them. The hours passed. Nine became ten, which was when Janelle returned, her face flushed.

"Hey," she said, dropping to the floor by Stevie's feet with a wide grin. "I was just doing some work with Vi. I saw you brought my poles back."

"I'll always have your pole," Stevie said. "And working with Vi?"

"Studying," said Janelle. "In the yurt."

"*Yurt studying?*"

Janelle smacked Stevie's shins playfully with the cord of her headphones.

"I'll get my stuff," Janelle said. "I'll sit with you."

Ten became ten thirty. Curfew was eleven, and there was no Hayes yet. Stevie began to think more about the tunnel. Hayes had clearly been in it before. Was it stable? It had been packed with dirt for many decades. It had been through all kinds of weather. It was locked. There were cracks. What if he'd gone down alone? What if it had gone down on his head?

No. Hayes was just being Hayes.

He wasn't with Maris, though. Maybe he was with Gretchen?

It didn't matter where he was. So why was she so anxious?

Because she had anxiety.

Pix also moved into the common room wearing a flowing pair of cotton pants and a black tank top showing off her muscular arms as she knitted away and watched a documentary on her computer. Ellie and David floated in at just before eleven, both grinning. They dropped onto the sofa together.

"So," David said to Stevie, "exciting Saturday night?"

"What's the matter?" Ellie said. "You look kind of freaked out."

Before Stevie could reply, Pix pulled off her headphones and looked at the group.

"Anyone know where Hayes is?" she asked. "He's about to be late."

Everyone else replied in the negative. Stevie decided to look blank and ignore the question.

Pix pulled out her phone and started texting.

Stevie felt the electric zing of anxiety shoot down her arms. He would come in at any second. He was just being stupid. Don't mention the tunnel. It would get everyone into trouble, probably, for no reason.

Eleven became eleven thirty.

"I hate calling Larry because people are late," she said.

"He's not answering my texts. He didn't tell anyone where he was?"

Stevie felt a vein beating in her forehead.

"Look," Stevie said, "I don't know where Hayes went—I don't—but a couple nights ago? We went in the tunnel."

David and Ellie jerked their heads up at this. Janelle had headphones on and did not hear.

"You need to be more specific," Pix said. "There are a lot of tunnels."

"The one under the sunken garden."

"That one is filled in," Pix said.

"Not anymore," Stevie said. "It was fine, but . . . I don't know. Maybe he went back there?"

"Are you kidding me?" Pix said. "Oh God."

Ten minutes later, Larry was at the door of Minerva.

"Mark is already on his way to the tunnel," he said to Pix. "Stevie, coat on. Come with me."

A few minutes later, Stevie was out in the cold alongside Larry, their breath puffing out in front of them, their flashlights making long, dancing dots on the ground.

"I knew someone would try to get in there," Larry said, gesturing for Stevie to get into the waiting golf cart. "I knew we should have welded it shut."

Stevie wrapped her arms tight around herself as the cart rumbled down the path.

"At least you had the sense to tell us," Larry said. "Jesus."

"It was fine," Stevie said, though her voice sounded small. "It seemed okay."

"That thing isn't sound," Larry said. "It probably wasn't sound when it was built and eighty years of burial couldn't have helped. I told them to seal it. If he's not in there, we're going to go around to everywhere else you've been working, because I am going to find him and talk to him. Jesus, that tunnel . . ."

Stevie's heart began to thud as they drove along. They met another other cart containing Mark and the nurse, Ms. Hix, as they drove alongside the garden wall, then around into the woods. They parked on the dirt maintenance road.

"Stay here," Larry said to Stevie.

Mark hopped out of his cart with a hard hat on. Ms. Hix was wearing a large puffer coat and had a fluorescent-orange emergency bag over her shoulder. The three moved into the woods. Stevie huddled inside of her coat.

"Hatch is unlocked," Larry said. It groaned as he pulled the door open. He started down the steps, shining his tactical flashlight into the space.

"Hayes?" he shouted. "Hayes, speak up if you're in there!"

No reply.

"I'm going in," he said to Mark. "Stand by."

The dark crowded around Stevie. Her fingers started to go numb from the tips down. Alone, in this cart under the thick dome of trees, Stevie felt a creeping dread, the kind that comes from cold, untamed spaces and uninterrupted dark and trouble that had no name. There would be trouble tonight. How did they punish people at Ellingham? Why was the night so wide? What the hell lived in the trees and undergrowth that made that much rustling? Did bats attack the heads of people in golf carts?

A shout pierced her devolving thoughts. It was Larry.

"Mary! Mark, call 911! Tell them we need the chopper!"

The words hit her like a bolt. Ms. Hix hurried into the tunnel. Mark stepped into a clearing to make the call. Stevie got out of the cart, taking every step deliberately, slowly, as though the ground itself might give way, and moved toward the opening in the ground. She heard muffled voices now. They were deep inside the tunnel, and something was very wrong.

She didn't have her big flashlight, but her phone was in her pocket, so she used that as a light. Carefully, with an ever-increasing pulse, she climbed down the steps. She could hear feverish conversation deep within—they were all the way down in the liquor room. Stevie stepped forward like she was walking into a dream, her tiny light guiding the way. She ignored everything Larry had said about the instability of the tunnel. Something was happening, and some force was pulling her in to face some grim unknown.

As she approached the door, she heard the nurse use the words *unresponsive*, *cold*, *cyanotic*. Larry turned and flashed his light on her as she approached.

"What happened?" Stevie heard herself ask.

Larry walked toward her. He did not run. You ran when you needed help. You walked when you had to start carefully containing the scene.

Larry's powerful flashlight was pointed down, focused on something on the ground. A mass, unmoving. It took a moment for Stevie to register that the thing was Hayes, his feet toward the door. He was in a semi-fetal position, one leg outstretched. His skin was a purple blue.

"Stevie," Larry said, blocking the door with his body.

But she had seen all she needed to. You know death when you see it.

16

Shock is a funny thing. Things get both sharp and fuzzy. Time stretches and distorts. Things come rushing into focus and seem larger than they are. Other things vanish to a single point.

"Come with me," Larry said, turning Stevie by the shoulders gently and leading her out of the tunnel and back to the cart.

"He's dead," Stevie said, looking up at the sky and taking a deep breath of cool air. "Hayes is dead."

Larry continued to lead her toward the cart for a moment before speaking. He settled her into the passenger's seat and looked her in the face.

"Are you okay?" he asked.

"Just tell me if I'm right."

Larry exhaled slowly.

"He's dead," he said.

"Why?" she asked. She sounded simple, like a child.

"I don't know," Larry said. "Do you? What was he doing down there tonight, Stevie? You need to tell me."

228

"I don't know," Stevie said. "Really. I don't know."

Larry studied her face for a moment then seemed to accept her answer. Stevie felt like she was gently hovering over the scene like in a recurring dream she had in which she floated from room to room of a neighbor's house, watching them do mundane things. A ghost in someone else's home.

"What are we going to do?" she asked.

Again, what a weird question. Inside Stevie could think. Outside Stevie was hugging herself and saying weird things.

"I'm going to take you back to Minerva," Larry said.

They said nothing as they drove back. Ellingham Academy rolled past her, looking like movie footage. Nothing was real. There was a far-off noise, a rupture in the air. Larry leaned forward and looked up as the lights of a helicopter appeared overhead and landed on the green. The ambulance had come, but the patient was gone.

She had wanted to see a dead body—but not this, not a real someone. Not sneakers upturned at the end of those legs, the legs that had been squatting so stupidly on Stevie's floor only days before. The kneecaps—the patellae—the real human who was now still and cold, and somewhere behind them in the dark.

When they arrived at Minerva, Larry told Stevie to wait a moment, so she waited. He spoke to Pix just outside the door. Stevie saw Pix put her hand over her mouth as she got the news, and then she came over to the cart and grabbed Stevie's hands.

"I'm okay," Stevie said.

"Stevie." Larry leaned in from the driver's side, his hand on the roof of the cart. "I'm going to ask you not to say anything to anyone else in the house right now, just for a little bit. Do you understand?"

"You don't want to cause panic and you need to keep the area clear to investigate what happened," Stevie said.

"That's right," Larry said. "That's real good, Stevie."

"Stevie," Pix said. "I'll take you up to my rooms. . . ."

"If you take me upstairs, the others will know," Stevie said. "I'll just go to my room. I'm okay. I can do this."

Larry nodded.

"She's doing good," he said. "You just go to your room and get into bed, Stevie. Just stay there and I'll be back for you in a while. We'll need you again."

Stevie tested the ground before she stepped out of the cart and found that her legs were steady. She resisted Pix's offer of an arm around her shoulders. Once inside, the common room now seemed very bright. The wall vibed red and the moose on the wall seemed grotesque. Janelle had gone but Ellie and David were still on the sofa, their feet facing each other, laughing at something. They stopped when Pix and Stevie came in.

"What's up?" Ellie said. "Is Hayes in trouble?"

"No," Pix said quietly.

David was looking at Stevie. She saw him peeling away her blank expression and attempting to go through her thoughts.

"I'm heading for bed," Stevie said, turning away.

David followed her with his eyes. Then she heard his phone chirp.

"Someone saw a helicopter," he said to Pix.

"I thought I heard something weird," Ellie said.

"Pix, is there a helicopter landing?" David asked.

"It's fine," Pix said.

Stevie hurried to her room and shut the door. She leaned against it, her head banging against the hook. A wave of nausea passed over her, and she moved to the trash can in preparation, but it passed. She climbed into bed fully dressed and pulled the comforter up around her.

Six had gone up the mountain, and then there were five.

Maybe she would go to sleep . . .

Shock. She was slipping into it. She sat up straight. Paper. She needed paper now. She went to her desk and snatched her anatomy notebook. She needed to write everything down, now, fresh. What had she seen? What did she know? Just write down everything, plain, without thinking about what any of it could have meant.

There was a knock at her door, and it creaked open before she could reply.

"Hey," David said. There was no humor in his face now. "What's going on?"

"I can't," Stevie said, bending over the notebook, her brow furrowed.

"What are you doing?"

"*Can't. Talk.*"

"What?" he said.

"It messes with your memory," she said impatiently.

"Something is going on," he said. "There are only a few reasons they send a helicopter. You also look like you just had three pints of blood removed. What the hell is happening?"

"I can't," she said. "I need to write it down now. Stories can change accidentally once you start to talk so I can't talk. Please, just shut the door."

There was a faint tremble in her hand. She balled it into a fist to steady it and jammed it under the covers. David backed away slowly, closing the door behind him.

Stevie pressed on her mind. Just list it. What did you see, Stevie? She let herself write. It started Thursday.

- Moved ramp and supplies to the garden
- Set up fog machines

More granular, Stevie. Put it in order.

- A few nights before, we went into the tunnel. We

No.

- ~~We~~ I broke the lock to get in

There was noise outside and in. She heard the drone of the helicopter as it flew away, the sound of voices from the common room. She put on headphones to muffle them.

The information was traveling and soon everything would be chaos. She had to get her thoughts together now. When she was sure she had recorded all she knew, she ripped out the page. Then she got up, removed her red coat from the closet, and put it on, taking refuge in the stiff vinyl. She put one Ativan in the left pocket and the folded list in the right. Then she sat on the edge of her bed, hands on her lap, until Larry came for her.

⚜

It was maybe an hour later. Stevie wasn't sure. Time was slippery now. Stevie passed through the common room like a ghost, not looking at the others. Outside, there seemed to be red and blue lights everywhere, winking through the trees, echoing into the sky and throwing strange shadows all around. The temperature felt like it had dropped about ten degrees. Nate was waiting outside with Pix. He looked blank and gray.

Larry drove Stevie and Nate to the Great House. He and Stevie sat side by side behind Larry in the cart, taking a bit of warmth from each other. A state-police cruiser was parked under the portico and the officer inside was entering information into the computer. There were more officers inside. Several faculty members were crowded on the balcony, looking down. Maris and Dash were already in the hall, sitting by the massive fireplace. Maris was sobbing and Dash was glazed over, staring at his phone.

"I think I may throw up," Nate said.

"Deep breaths," Stevie said, taking his hand. "With me."

She sat down with Nate on the bottom step of the grand staircase.

"The trick," Stevie said, "is to make the exhale longer than the inhale. So we're going to breathe in for four, hold for seven, out for eight. Do it with me. I'll count. One, two, three, four . . ."

Nate breathed with Stevie, slowing the response, slowing the fear.

This was the funny thing about Stevie's anxiety—when she encountered someone else who felt more anxious than she did, she leveled out. She'd first made this discovery a few years ago, when she got trapped on an elevator with another person in a hotel on one of the few Bell family vacations. The hotel was twenty stories high. Stevie and another woman got on at the eighteenth floor. The doors closed and the elevator went down, then the car dropped suddenly about a story, juddered, and stopped. Stevie's heart almost flew out of her mouth, but when she saw the woman cry out and sink into the corner of the elevator in panic, something new set in. The woman spent the next half hour sitting on the floor in the corner, half in tears, shaking. Stevie talked her through it, and when they were rescued, the woman had nothing but good things to say about Stevie and bought her a giant cupcake and a coffee from the café in the lobby.

This might be her future—talking to people who had just witnessed traumatic events. She would have to work with them, calm them, get them to a place where they could talk.

"Nate," Stevie said, taking his hand again, "what's your favorite book?"

"What?"

"Just tell me your favorite book. Don't think about it too hard. Just name a book you like."

"*The Hobbit.*"

"What do you like about it?" Stevie asked.

"I like the whole thing."

"But name one thing. Close your eyes and think about *The Hobbit* for one moment and tell me what you like."

Nate closed his eyes. His face smoothed just a bit.

"The round door," he said. "On Bilbo's house. I read it when I was little and I always thought about the door."

"That's great," Stevie said. "Keep that door in your mind. Keep Bilbo in there. Let's breathe again. Four in. Seven hold. Eight out."

After another moment, Stevie saw Nate settle a bit more. His shoulders relaxed a bit, and the strain of trying not to be sick let up. He exhaled one last time, opened his eyes, and looked at her.

"Okay," he said, nodding. "Okay. What's going to happen? What's happening? Stevie, what the hell is happening?"

"They'll ask us what we saw," Stevie said.

"I didn't see anything. I don't even know what's going on. They said Hayes is dead?"

"I mean how the day went," Stevie said. "They need to establish the facts."

"But what happened? How did Hayes die?"

"I don't know," Stevie said, though in her mind's eye, she was looking at the hatch door again. She felt it in her hand, the weight of it as she balanced on the thin-runged rail of the ladder. "But it's important we don't try to make anything up. Just be clear. Just say what you know."

"That's good advice." Larry was standing in front of them. He squatted down and looked Nate over, then looked to Stevie and nodded his approval. "This one here has a good head on her shoulders. The police need to go over the events."

One of the troopers called Nate's name and summoned him into the front parlor. Larry sat on the step next to Stevie.

"How you doing?" he said.

"I wrote some of it down," Stevie said, showing him the notes. "As fresh as I could."

Larry read the page carefully. Stevie followed his eyes as they went to each line.

"This is good," he said, passing it back. "You're handling this well."

"Do you know what happened?" Stevie asked.

Larry shook his head.

"Don't know?" Stevie said. "Or can't say?"

"They're ready for you," an officer said, stepping up to Stevie and guiding her into the security office.

Here she was, watching a case up close, giving a statement, experiencing all the things she so longed to experience.

All it took was for someone to die.

17

THE POLICE KEPT STEVIE ABOUT A HALF HOUR. THE QUESTIONS WERE exactly what Stevie expected. Run through the order of the day. Who went where and what time? What was Hayes doing in the tunnel?

The collection of information, she knew, needs to be clinical. Don't assume. Don't get friendly. Ask the questions. Establish the timeline. Record accurately and quickly. She tried to keep her answers clear, short, but complete. No embellishments. No editorializing on what it all meant.

When she was done, Larry was waiting with Nate so they could drive back to Minerva. As the three of them stepped outside, a crime scene processing van made its way onto the property. This caught Stevie short for a moment and gave her a quick surge of panic. She thought again of the hatch. But it was very likely that all death scenes where the cause wasn't immediately clear had to be processed.

The moon was thin like a hook, and the owls were calling. The smell of fall leaves blew on the wind and Hayes was dead.

They returned to a very wakeful Minerva. There was a kind of a suctioning sensation as she and Nate entered—like they vacuumed the conversation out of the air.

"Oh my God," Janelle said, hurrying to Stevie and hugging her. "Are you okay? Oh my God. Is he really dead? Stevie? What happened?"

Over Janelle's shoulder, Stevie looked at Ellie and David. They were hunched up together on the corner of the purple sofa. Ellie was largely in a ball—not crying, but vacant. David sat close to her, his arm dropped gently over her shoulder.

Nate started to giggle.

"What the hell are you laughing about?" Ellie snapped.

"I have no idea," Nate said.

"It's shock, El," Pix said. "Just laugh, Nate. You can't help how you react."

Nate started laughing harder, and then he started to hiccup.

Stevie felt the sleepiness descending hard now. She was utterly calm, just very tired.

"I'm going to bed," she said simply.

Back in her room, Stevie found that she was moving with very slow, precise motions. Most nights she just pulled off her clothes and threw them into her laundry sack. Tonight, she hung her coat carefully, pulled each arm delicately out of her shirt, removed her pants as if they were fragile. She rolled everything and dropped it carefully into the bag, then dug the warm, school-issued pajamas from the bottom of the dresser and put them on.

She climbed into bed, lights on, and stared straight ahead, gripping her phone as if waiting for it to ring. No one was going to call. It was just something to hold.

She had no idea how much time had gone by when there was a quiet knock on her door. At first she decided to ignore it, but then she pushed herself up and opened it.

Somehow she knew it would be David.

"Your light was on," he said quietly. "Can I come in?"

She blinked and rubbed her neck, then shrugged and left the door hanging open. He came in and shut it. Stevie sat on the floor against the foot of her bed. He leaned against the wall. His hair had been tamed a bit and his expression was unusually serious.

"Do you know what happened?" he asked.

"I know he's dead," she said. "That's it."

David drew his lips inward in thought and rubbed his hands together for a moment. He paced over to Stevie's bureau and drummed his fingers on the edge for a moment. He didn't seem to be focusing much on anything. He slid down to the floor. Stevie stared at the lower half of his sweatpants, which seemed like a safe place to stare. They were very old and may have once been deep navy blue. Now they were washed-out blue-gray with the word YALE on the leg in cracked white lettering.

"Why did you say that before, about not talking?" he finally asked.

"Because witnesses are unreliable," she replied.

"You think people will lie?"

"No," she said. "It's not that. It's that people don't know what they remember. It's not that people lie so much as people are just wrong about what they think they see. Humans are bad at estimating time, distance, and duration of events, especially when scared or stressed. And it's all a lot worse in the dark. But one of the worst things is when witnesses start talking to each other. As soon as you start talking to someone else, the story you have in your head changes. Human memory is rewritten like computer memory. You just get the most updated file. Which is why, if you see some kind of accident, you should record what you experienced right away, without speaking to anyone else. That's going to be your clearest account. You may still be off, but you won't start baking in mistakes."

The explanation ran smoothly from her lips, as if she had been waiting her entire life to deliver it to someone. It arrived fully formed. Now that she was talking about crime more hypothetically, her body warmed a bit and her senses returned.

"What?" David said.

Stevie looked around for a way to explain. The only objects she had to use for examples were pens and paper clips. They would do. She pulled off some caps.

"Say there's a robbery," she said, "and there's a getaway

car and a bunch of robbers with guns. Witness One may then recall three robbers, two with masks and one with a hat, and a black car."

She set down one black pen cap and two paper clips.

"Witness Two may remember four robbers, all with masks, and a blue car." She added two paper clips and replaced the black cap with a blue one. "And maybe they thought they saw a motorcycle."

She pushed a roll of tape past.

"Witness Three is sure it was three robbers," she went on, taking away a paper clip. "One wore a mask and a hat, and the car was green. I don't have a green cap, so . . . anyway. Witness Three is sure of what he saw. That's a big deal—people who think they have good memories are sometimes the least reliable but the most likely to sway others. And that witness then says that the motorcycle was with the green car."

"Is that the tape?" David asked. "And the green car is that blue cap?"

"The point is," Stevie said, "now that Witness One has talked to Witness Three, and Witness Three seems really sure about what they saw, Witness One may now think back and see three robbers in hats, not masks. Witness Two now questions the masks and thinks the car was green. And one robber was very tall. Witness Three claims they were all tall. And suddenly everyone starts to say that they were all tall, and that the motorcycle was with the green car."

David inched closer and examined the pile. He had gotten very close, actually.

"Okay," he said quietly. "But what actually happened?"

"What?"

"Was it three or four robbers?" he asked. "Was the car blue, black, or green? Was there a motorcycle involved?"

"The point is . . . ," Stevie repeated.

"And which witness was this?" he asked, reaching for a paper clip. He pressed it into her palm. His hand was warm.

Had she really just seen Hayes's body on the ground in that tunnel? She had seen the soles of a pair of shoes, his mottled skin . . .

Don't think about that. Don't make it real.

Something else was coming into her head instead. Well, not her head. Other parts of her. Her mind was quickly being stripped of rational thoughts. She and David were micropositioning themselves closer, an inch here, an inch there.

Was this really going to happen?

The last foot of space between them was rapidly closed up, and David pressed his lips to hers. She felt her body relax, and a warm ease fell over her. She let herself rest against the floor and David came over as well, supporting himself with an elbow. He was kissing her very gently, his lips pressing on her neck, tickling her ear, and she was kissing back harder, hungrily. He rested on the floor and she surprised herself by rolling on top of him.

Everything in her brain was saying *don't do this*—it would be a mess. It was David, and there was something about him that was so off, and he lived upstairs, and someone had just *died*. She'd seen a *body*.

242

But that was the thing that was also pushing her forward, probably. The thing that was filling her with some weird, urgent emotion and the need to do something, anything, anything at all. She kissed the strange crook of his nose, his high forehead, and back to his mouth. They changed positions, rolling forward to the fireplace. Stevie felt her back hit her case board and knew the cardboard was probably bending a little and she didn't care. She didn't care if the floor opened up and swallowed her or if she was sucked up the chimney. Her hands were in his hair and he was mumbling something that she couldn't quite make out.

"Hey."

That was a totally different voice, and it was coming from the doorway. The two of them stopped rolling. Neither moved for a moment.

Stevie realized she was sweating and David was out of breath, his heart pulsing above hers. Stevie tipped her head back and looked at the upside-down figure of Pix.

"I think maybe you should go back to your room," she said, not unkindly.

"Yup," David replied, rolling off Stevie gently and standing up, his back to Pix. "Yup. I'll do that now."

Pix stepped out into the hall and allowed David to pass.

"You should try to get some sleep," Pix said once David was gone. "Do you need anything?"

"Nope," Stevie said, her voice high and strange. "I'm good. Thanks, Pix."

"Okay. I'm just upstairs."

Stevie remained where she was for a moment, staring up at the ceiling where a moth was helplessly slamming itself into the light. Then, very slowly and very deliberately, she struck the back of her head against the wooden floor.

**FEDERAL BUREAU OF INVESTIGATION
INTERVIEW BETWEEN AGENT SAMUEL
ARNOLD AND FLORA ROBINSON
APRIL 17, 1936, 12:45 p.m.
LOCATION: ELLINGHAM PROPERTY**

*SA: I'd like to go over what happened on Monday. Is that
    all right?*

FR: Of course.

*SA: You've been here at the Ellingham house for two weeks
    now? Since April fourth?*

FR: Yes.

SA: You come to visit regularly?

FR: Yes.

*SA: And you live in New York City. That's how you know
    Mrs. Ellingham?*

FR: We met nine years ago.

SA: Where did you meet?

FR: At a social occasion.

SA: What sort of social occasion, Miss Robinson?

FR: At a literary salon.

SA: A literary salon?

FR: Yes.

SA: *Where was this literary salon?*

FR: *In New York City.*

SA: *Was this a drinking establishment, Miss Robinson?*

FR: *Why is that important?*

SA: *We just need to build a picture of Mrs. Ellingham's contacts. We want to know if she might have met someone somewhere who would want to hurt her. Alcohol isn't against the law anymore, and no one cares what happened nine years ago.*

FR: *I assure you, this establishment was full of the best people.*

SA: *Drinking establishments nine years ago were also full of criminals, Miss Robinson. By definition, they were run and supplied by criminals.*

FR: *Hardly the kind of criminal that . . . it was different.*

SA: *I understand. Let's talk about your relationship now. You're considered Mrs. Ellingham's closest friend, would you say? You spend a lot of time here with them in Vermont. The staff says you are here most of the time the Ellinghams are.*

FR: *I think that's fair to say, yes.*

SA: *There was a party at the house on Saturday the eleventh. Was that a small or a large party?*

FR: *A small party. The parties are very small now that the school has opened.*

SA: *Who was in attendance?*

FR: *I was, Leo was . . .*

SA: *Leonard Holmes Nair. The painter.*

FR: *Yes. Maxine Melville, the actress, and her husband, John Porter. One or two business associates of Albert's, but they didn't stay very long.*

SA: *It appears that most people left the house on Sunday. How long were you planning on staying?*

FR: *Until it felt like the right time to go. My invitations are open-ended.*

SA: *What did you do on Sunday?*

FR: *Albert was working, and it was raining, so we spent a good part of the day in the drawing room with Leo. He is working on a new painting.*

SA: *Anything else?*

FR: *We played with Alice for a bit. I took a long bath.*

SA: *And in the evening?*

FR: *I stayed up late talking to Iris and Leo. Maybe a bit too late. I didn't feel well in the morning.*

SA: *In the morning, Mrs. Ellingham called for you to ask you to come on her car ride, is that right?*

FR: *Yes. She came to my room at ten. I was still in bed. I had a terrible headache. I said . . .*

[Silence.]

SA: *Yes?*

FR: *I'm sorry.*

SA: *Take your time.*

FR: *I said I didn't feel well and she should go. If I'd gone . . .*

*SA: So you didn't go on the ride because you had a
headache.*

FR: I wish I'd gone. I wish I'd gone.

SA: What time did you get out of bed?

*FR: The maid brought me something to eat around noon. I
had her draw me a bath. I spent the rest of the day in
my room, reading.*

*SA: You went to Mrs. Ellingham's dressing room that
evening. Why?*

*FR: I heard something going on. I wanted to look out the
window. Iris's window faces the front garden.*

SA: So do several other windows.

*FR: Well, I know her room has a clear view. I just went in
to look. I was upset.*

*SA: Isn't it unusual to go into Mrs. Ellingham's personal
dressing room when she's not there?*

FR: I go to Iris's dressing room regularly.

SA: Even when she's not there?

FR: Yes. I am free to use her things.

*SA: Did Mrs. Ellingham let others have such open access to
her personal space?*

FR: I have no idea.

*SA: She sometimes didn't allow her personal maid into her
dressing room.*

FR: I'm not a maid.

SA: She typically locked the door, did she not?

FR: I have a key. Do you have a light for a cigarette?

SA: Sure.

[*Pause.*]

*SA: So you let yourself into Mrs. Ellingham's private
dressing room with your own key? How long have you
had a key?*

FR: Oh, I don't know. Some time.

*SA: It seems odd to me that you would take the time to go into
a locked room to look out of a window.*

FR: It may seem odd to you . . . but that's what happened.

SA: How long were you in the room?

FR: I don't know. I lost track of time.

SA: If you could guess.

FR: I don't know . . . fifteen minutes?

*SA: And then someone came and got you. The maid, Ruth.
She says she looked for you and found you at eight fifty.
She called for you but you did not reply.*

FR: I didn't hear her.

SA: She was out in the hall.

FR: I was very distracted.

*SA: Mrs. Ellingham keeps some very valuable things in that
room.*

*FR: Most of her things are valuable. Everything in this house
is valuable. It's not all locked up.*

*SA: That's a fair point, Miss Robinson. But there are some
things of unusual value in that room. Isn't that why it is
normally locked?*

FR: Of course.

SA: *You're not as wealthy as Mrs. Ellingham, are you, Miss*
    Robinson?

FR: *Few people are.*

SA: *You're not a wealthy woman, are you? That's what I'm*
    asking.

FR: *I resent this. My closest friend is . . .*

SA: *We're doing this because your closest friend is missing.*
    There's no shame in not being rich, Miss Robinson. I'm
    simply saying you are from different backgrounds.

FR: *She would give me anything. Anything. Iris is the most*
    generous person. Look at this school! They built a school
    that children could go to for free! They invite them into
    this house!

SA: *They are very generous. But let's keep to the subject.*
    What route did you use to get to Mrs. Ellingham's room?

FR: *What route?*

SA: *You didn't come down the main stairs.*

FR: *No, I took the side stairs.*

SA: *The servant stairs?*

FR: *Yes.*

SA: *Why not the more direct method, down the main stairs?*

FR: *I don't know.*

SA: *And you didn't hear anyone calling you?*

FR: *No.*

SA: *If anything, Miss Robinson, I would think you'd be more*
    attuned to someone calling your name at that moment.
    You spent all of that time looking out the window?

FR: *I was in a state.*

SA: *But you heard the maid knocking.*

FR: *Yes.*

SA: *She said it was several moments before you answered the door.*

FR: *I was in a state. I'd just heard my best friend was missing. It's just what I did. I don't know why.*

SA: *There are many valuable things in that room.*

FR: *Why do you keep mentioning how much her things are worth?*

SA: *Because she's missing and someone is asking for a lot of money for her return.*

FR: *My best friend is missing. Why are you doing this?*

SA: *I have to establish the facts.*

FR: *What facts?*

SA: *I need to know why you were in her room.*

FR: *I just told you. You should be out looking for them.*

SA: *Almost every police officer within a hundred miles is looking for them, and even more police beyond that, in every city on the East Coast. But what I need to know from you, right now, is what you were doing in Mrs. Ellingham's dressing room for those fifteen minutes.*

FR: *I told you . . .*

SA: *You were looking out the window.*

FR: *I was.*

SA: *Miss Robinson, let me be perfectly clear. This is no time to lie. Every second you waste by lying is a second Iris Ellingham and Alice Ellingham could be in danger. When you lie, you put them at risk and you put yourself at risk.*

FR: I'm not . . .

*SA: You could hear people in the hall calling for you. The
house was in chaos. There was nothing going on outside to
see. It was dark. It was foggy.*

FR: I'm aware.

SA: So you spent fifteen minutes looking at nothing?

FR: More or less, yes.

*SA: We know a bit about you, Miss Robinson. We know
you were a hostess at Carmine's, the speakeasy on
Twenty-Ninth Street. Carmine's was owned by Big Bill
Thompson, the mob boss. You worked directly for him.*
[REDACTED DUE TO ONGOING
INVESTIGATION. SEE FILE 248B-2.]

*FR: My job was to sing, to entertain, to talk to people. It
was a social job, and Iris and I got to be friendly because
we liked each other.*

*SA: One of the richest women in America and a speakeasy
hostess.*

*FR: I met a lot of important people at Carmine's. Half
of New York society passed through that door. Artists.
Writers. Actors and actresses. Politicians. Policemen. We
saw a lot of those in there.*

*SA: Big Bill Thompson is also associated with smuggling
operations that come down from Canada. His associates
have been known to be in this area. You may know that
from the fact that another FBI agent frequents this
house.*

FR: *You think George Marsh talks about his work? George Marsh is a brick wall about whatever he does for you. And I haven't spoken to Bill in years. I'm here because I'm visiting my friend Iris, and my friend is missing.*

SA: *It must be good to have rich friends.*

FR: *It's good to have friends, no matter what they're worth. Iris is my friend, and she'd be my friend if she was poor as anything. Let me tell you something about Iris. She makes me laugh.*

SA: *Makes you laugh?*

FR: *That's right. And that's hard to do. Iris and I are friends, real friends. I understand her. I would do anything for her. You don't know what it was like for her, coming here. She had such a good life in New York. Iris is an athlete. Did you know that? You should see her swim. She writes, did you know that? She wrote an entire novel. I've read it. It's good. She doesn't show anyone because she thinks they'll dismiss her as Albert Ellingham's wife and nothing more. But she is more. She should never have been up this godforsaken mountain, but she's also very loyal, so she supported this school because Albert had a dream. You don't know Iris. I do. She needs stimulation. . . .*

SA: *And how does she get that stimulation here?*

[*Silence.*]

SA: *Miss Robinson . . .*

FR: *I've told you everything I know. I have nothing more to say. I will do anything in my power to help my friend, but this is not helping. I'd go to the ends of the earth for that woman and for Alice. So why don't you get out there and find them? Because if you don't, so help me, I will get in a car and do it myself. Just try and stop me.*

[*Interview terminated 1:13 p.m.*]

18

THE EVIDENCE WAS ALL OVER THE FLOOR—THE PAPER CLIPS AND PEN caps. A sunbeam illuminated a dent she'd made in the case board.

The morning had come, and brought reality with it. And questions. Lots of questions, dancing around in her head in circles.

The questions, in no particular order:

What would the media make of this, another death at the infamous Ellingham Academy?

Wait, never mind the media—what would her parents make of this? *Fancy School Manages to Kill Student.* And the fact that she had *been* there?

Would the school close?

Maybe close for a few days. It couldn't close for the *year* because of this, could it?

Why was she thinking like this? Someone was *dead.* Hayes was *dead.*

Because that is what brains do. They think. Her brain attic was full of new and strange things she had not been able to classify and sort yet. Stevie couldn't feel guilty for her thoughts and she couldn't engage with all of her thoughts. That was something they taught you in anxiety therapy— the thoughts may come, but you don't have to chase them all. It was sort of the opposite of good detective work, in which you had to follow every lead.

She stuffed her face into her pillow for a while as her head throbbed gently. Her mouth still had a strange taste in it, the taste of . . .

Outside, she could hear strange voices and the occasional squawk of a radio. She managed to pull her face up and out of the safe, soft confines of the pillow and rubbed the gunk from her eyes.

Hayes. That had really happened. He had actually died. Hayes had died, and they had found his body. And, in response, she had come back and made out with David. It was all too real, too immediate, her feelings all coming together into one knot of terror and shakes and queasiness and embarrassment.

Focus.

Her brain floated around the facts for a bit. Hayes was on the ground, already dead. How could that have happened? She mentally looked around the little space at the end of the tunnel. She peered at the empty shelves on the wall. She scuffed at the stone floor with her shoe. She looked up the ladder, at the hatch that led to the observatory. . . .

About twelve feet up. If you fell from that distance onto the stone, you would be in bad shape. You could die.

Stevie saw it in her mind's eye. She had gone up there. She had closed that hatch behind her. Had Hayes gone up to look around? Maybe he stepped the wrong way in the dark and fell through the hole.

Why did he go back? Probably to film something. But Hayes would have brought someone for that, probably. It really looked like he wanted to go alone. She saw the way he did his backward walk, trying to slip back.

But he hadn't gone back to the garden. He'd gone all the way around, to the maintenance road, to the woods, to the tunnel. He'd gone back and died.

Riddle, riddle, on the wall . . .

She'd almost forgotten that, the terror that had woken her the other night. She had to have dreamed that. She was thinking about murder and death and tunnels and Truly Devious and her brain projected it all onto the wall.

Right?

Stevie rested flat on her back and practiced a few minutes of breathing exercises, making the exhales longer than the inhales, taking the air all the way down to her abdomen.

She could still smell some musky body wash or shampoo on her skin. David.

There was that as well. On any other day, this would have been the only story. Today, it barely made the cut.

"Okay," she said to herself. "Now. Okay. Now. Get up. Now."

She got up.

Shortly after, a showered Stevie, dressed in thin, loose sweatpants and her black hoodie, emerged into the common room. Janelle and Nate were at the table, both still in pajamas. Pix was on her phone in the kitchen. David sat on the sofa in rumpled jeans and a wrinkled maroon Henley shirt. His hair was wet, flattening some curls to his forehead. He looked at her when she came in—a direct, lingering look, but one without humor. He seemed to simply be taking her in, noting her presence.

There was little to say, some mumbled good-mornings, some nods. What do you say when your housemate dies, even if you don't know him that well? Even if what you did know you didn't like much?

You say very little.

Ellie appeared, wearing paint-stained, waffle-textured long underwear bottoms and a large, ripped-up T-shirt for a French band and long tube-sock tops on her arms. Her eyes were bright red and swollen. She dropped down on the sofa next to David, curled into a ball, and put her head on his lap. He absently set a hand on her mess of matted hair.

Stevie felt a swell of queasiness. Would they talk about what had happened? And if they did, what would they say? Maybe they would never talk about it. Maybe things that happened on nights like last night didn't count.

Something in her plunged at that thought, and she stared into her coffee. It tasted dank and bitter, but it was hot, and drinking it made her feel something other than weird. So she drank it.

"Stevie," Pix said, coming in. "That was Larry. They need to talk to you again, up at the Great House. He's coming for you."

Janelle looked at her fearfully. Nate went pale.

"That's normal," Stevie said. "The police do that. They need to ask the same questions several times to clarify the information."

"Everyone else has to stay here," Pix said.

"All day?" Ellie said, looking up from David's lap. Her voice had that thick tone that happens after someone has been crying a lot.

"For now," Pix said. "There are counselors coming if you need to talk."

David rolled his eyes to the ceiling.

⌗

There were two police cars from the Vermont state police under the portico of the Great House as Stevie and Larry approached it a short while later.

"Just say what you know," Larry said. "Just tell the truth."

"I know," Stevie said.

"How are you holding up?"

"I think I'm fine. Maybe it hasn't hit yet. Is that bad?"

"It's not bad or good. It just is. That's something you'll find out if you decide to go into this line of work. You have to take things as they are, not how you hear they're supposed to be."

That was one of the most sensible things an adult had ever said to Stevie.

Once inside, Stevie thought she'd be going to the security room, but instead Larry took her to the massive oak door that led to Albert Ellingham's office.

"In here?" she said.

"That's where the detective is speaking to people," he said. "Just answer her questions. You'll be all right."

A detective this time. Not a uniformed officer.

Two leather chairs sat by the massive rose-marble fireplace, the disturbing trophy rug spread between them. A petite woman in a gray suit sat in one of these chairs writing in a small notebook.

"Stephanie?" she said, consulting the book. "My name is Detective Agiter. Come sit down."

Stevie sat down in the opposite chair, one of Albert Ellingham's personal chairs. Even though it was very old, the leather was still in fine condition and it had an easy, comfortable give. This is where he sat, running his empire, thinking of his lost wife and daughter.

Detective Agiter was a carefully curated palette of neutrals. She had long, elegant hands. Her dark hair was swept tight across her head into a bun, not a single strand out of place. Stevie most admired her shoes, which were utterly nondescript black flats. There was a studied stillness to her face. Never give anything away. Stevie needed to master this look. This was what a detective looked like.

I'm just going to record this," she said, putting a digital recorder down on the small Art Deco table between them. "Interview between Stephanie Bell and Detective Fatima

Agiter, Sunday, September tenth, nine forty-five a.m. Now, Stephanie, or Stevie?"

"Stevie."

"Stevie, you were involved in the filming of video that was about the Ellingham kidnapping. Whose idea was the video?"

"Hayes's."

"How did you get involved?"

"He came and he asked me to help him make it."

"And why did he ask you?" the detective said.

"Because I know a lot about it."

"About the Ellingham kidnappings, you mean?" the detective clarified. Stevie nodded and admonished herself internally. You were supposed to be clear. *It* wasn't clear.

"I know a lot about the Ellingham case. It's what I came here to study. The crime . . . the history of it."

"So Hayes wanted to make a show about the Ellingham kidnappings, and he came to you because you know about it. And you asked Nathaniel because he's a writer?"

"Hayes asked me to ask him," Stevie said.

"So it sounds like Hayes was assembling a group of people, all with different areas of knowledge. There was also Maris Coombes, who has theater experience, and Patrick Dashell, who studies film. And together, the group of you put this project together."

"Correct," Stevie said.

"How did you access the tunnel?"

Stevie's heart lurched a bit.

"I opened the lock," she said.

"How did you open it?"

"I picked it," Stevie said.

The detective raised one of her well-groomed eyebrows, her only tell in this interview.

"You picked it?" she clarified.

"That's right," Stevie said. There was no denying it. She picked a lock. Good-bye, Ellingham. It was fun while it lasted.

"How do you know how to pick a lock?"

"YouTube," Stevie said, shrugging. The shrug was supposed to make it look like this was no big deal and just something that people did, but she wasn't sure how it came off.

"Any reason?"

"No? It's easy? No. People do it. It's a thing. Just a hobby."

This did not sound good. *Nothing to see here! I just pick locks for fun.*

"Larry told me your interest is in law enforcement," the detective said.

"Yes," Stevie said.

"We usually don't pick locks."

"No," Stevie said. "I know."

Detective Agiter scratched her ear for a moment, then moved on.

"When you were finished, did you all leave the tunnel together, or in groups?"

Strange. She didn't ask about the hatch opening at all. Stevie's heart skipped and her brain glitched for a second.

"We left together," she said. "Maris and Hayes . . . they stayed behind."

"Do you know what they were doing?"

"I can guess," Stevie said.

"What is it you would guess they were doing?" the detective said.

"Making out?" Stevie said. "Something like that?"

The detective half smiled and consulted her notebook.

"During the filming, there was theatrical fog. Do you know how this was created?"

"We had fog machines."

"Did you use anything else?" the detective asked.

This was a weird question.

"No," Stevie said.

"Just the three machines."

"Correct," Stevie said.

Seriously. Why was she asking about fog machines?

"I think that's about it, Stevie," she said. "Unless you can think of anything else that happened that was out of the ordinary?"

Stevie looked around her brain attic. There was, of course, the note on the wall. The note she probably imagined. You couldn't tell the police about stuff you thought you probably imagined.

Except, could you? People did that in murder mysteries all the time, and it was always important.

"Nothing," Stevie said.

"Okay. Interview complete at ten twenty."

She stopped the recording and Stevie pulled herself out of the deep chair.

"What happened to Hayes?" Stevie asked.

The detective looked up at her.

"We have to wait for the coroner's report," she replied.

"No," Stevie said, her face flushing. "Sure. Sorry."

She made her way to the door and had just put her hand on the sharply edged crystal knob when she had a thought.

"There was one thing," she said. "Janelle's ID."

Detective Agiter looked up from her notebook.

"What's that?"

"My friend Janelle," Stevie said. "Someone took her ID to Minerva. When we went to yoga class on Thursday, she had it. But when she went to leave, it wasn't in her bag. Then the next day, it was on the path in front of our building."

"Why do you say someone took it? Couldn't she have lost it?"

"It was clipped into the front pocket of her bag," Stevie said. "I saw it myself. She tapped us into yoga and put it back in the front pocket. When we left class, it was gone. And then it just showed up Friday morning outside."

"What's Janelle's last name?"

"Franklin," Stevie said.

The detective wrote this in her notebook.

"Thanks, Stevie," she said, dismissing her. "Why don't you head back to your house?"

There were two people from security in the main hall talking to police. Neither seemed to pay any attention to Stevie when she came out of the Ellingham office. Up on the landing, she saw Charles deep in conversation with Dr. Quinn and a few other faculty members. Stevie walked outside unaccompanied.

Outside, a cloud cover had come by fast. The campus was disturbingly quiet, as everyone was largely in their houses. There were many things to worry about at the moment, many things to feel and fear. But the thing that was currently at the forefront of Stevie's mind was fog. Why ask about the *fog*, of all things? Who the hell cared about the fog? There had to be a reason. She asked twice.

Stevie combed through anything she knew about the fog machines. They were rentals. They spat out fake fog. They stank, kind of.

There was a little echo in the back of her mind. Fog. It had come up in another context. Fog . . .

Dry ice. She had just been around dry ice. It was in the workshop, when Janelle and Dash got into it about the poles, and Dash looked into the container with the dry ice and said that the fog machines were easier to work with.

Stevie stopped halfway back to Minerva and pulled out her phone and Googled dry ice, paging through the various search results until she landed on one that also contained the words *safety hazard.*

Dry ice is solidified carbon dioxide . . . not normally

dangerous but caution should be used in handling . . .
sublimates into carbon dioxide . . . must be used in
ventilated spaces or else there is danger of hypercapnia,
as carbon dioxide displaces oxygen, especially in low-
lying structures such as basements, due to its weight.
This can lead to unconsciousness and death, which can be
rapid. . . .

Stevie swallowed hard.

The dry ice was in the workshop. Janelle's pass was taken. Janelle's pass opened the workshop.

She was supposed to go home. She'd already broken enough rules.

She should go back to Minerva.

So why was she turning away from Minerva and heading back toward the workshop area? Her pass wouldn't let her in. What did she even think she would find? Her every instinct pressed her on, though.

"I'll check the records," she heard Larry say.

He and Detective Agiter were coming up behind her. Stevie had just enough time to duck behind a golf cart.

"You have times in and out?" the detective asked.

"Yeah, the system records both. Hang on." Larry put his phone to his ear. "Jerry? I need you to pull up a record for me. The name is Janelle Franklin. I need to know the tags on her pass on Thursday evening."

Stevie trailed behind them at a distance as they walked

to the workshop. There was a pause as Larry got his own access card out and opened the door. Once they were inside, Stevie would lose track of this conversation, and losing track of this conversation seemed like a terrible idea.

That dreamlike feeling took over her again, and she found herself creeping low toward the door, catching it before it closed. She held it open with her finger to give them a chance to move farther into the room. She pushed it open a bit more and found that they were already on the other side of the room, looking at the blue dry-ice bin.

Was she doing this? She was doing this.

She pushed the door open farther and crept inside, moving behind a standing rack of yard implements.

"Jesus," she heard Larry say, "this thing was full. How the hell . . . yeah, Jerry. Okay. Here we go. Into the art barn at sixteen fifty. Then nothing until one twelve the next morning. Taps in here to the workshop. Yeah."

He tucked the phone away.

"So according to Stephanie Bell," the detective said, "Janelle Franklin's ID goes missing during a yoga class."

"I'll check that against her schedule, but they have yoga classes in the art barn. That checks out to me. So someone takes the pass . . ."

"And uses it to come in here at one in the morning. We'll need to take it and print it. This adding up to you? He comes in here, takes . . ."

This was when Stevie's phone started ringing.

266

Larry and the detective looked over at the same time.

There was no point in trying to stay concealed. Stevie stood up.

"Hey," she said.

She took a moment and glanced at the phone.

The screen read: PARENTS.

19

It was a slightly less kindly Larry who escorted Stevie away from the workshop.

"I know," she said, "I'm . . ."

"Listen, Stevie," he said. "You're a smart kid, and I like you. Let me just be clear. You need to do exactly what I say."

"I know. I just . . ."

"No. You know. Say you know."

"I know," Stevie said. "But Janelle . . ."

"So now you're going to stay here," he said. "In the security office. And you're not going to talk to anyone until I say so. Okay?"

Her phone started ringing again.

"Who is that?" he said.

She held it up. Again, it said: PARENTS. He indicated that she should answer and stared at her as she did so.

"Stevie!" Both her parents were on the line and it was impossible to tell who said her name first.

"The school just called us," her mom said. "We're coming to get you."

Stevie dragged a hand over her face.

"I'm fine," Stevie said.

"Stevie, someone *died*."

"Yeah, I know," Stevie said.

"So we're coming up and you're coming home," her dad said.

"Look," Stevie said, staring at the ground in panic. "It's horrible, but . . . it could have happened anywhere."

"No one died at your old school."

"That's not true," Stevie said. "There was a car accident in—"

"Look," her mom said. "Your dad and I are taking the day off and we're coming to get you. It's only been a few days. We can get you reregistered."

This shouldn't have been the moment Stevie started crying. She didn't want this to be the thing that did it. Hayes should have done it. But, as Larry explained earlier, things didn't happen the way you wanted. She brushed a tear away with the back of her hand and tried to keep the tremble out of her voice.

"Look," she said, "it was . . . Can we just talk about it when you're here?"

There was a grudging agreement on this. Stevie managed to get off the phone. Larry's expression had softened a bit from jagged rock to slightly less sharp and pointy rock.

There was a noise overhead, like the noise from the night before. Larry and Stevie looked up at the same time and saw a red and white helicopter.

"Press," he said. "It's out. They'll be at the gates."

He exhaled loudly and started walking fast.

"Come on," he said. "I've got to get you back to Minerva and then handle this."

"I lost my mind for a minute," she said. "I was scared for Janelle. But I won't. I promise I'll go right back and I won't stop on Go or collect two hundred dollars or anything. I'm sorry. You can do what you need to. You can trust me."

Larry regarded her for a moment.

"All right," he said. "But if I find out otherwise, you're burnt with me. And I can check."

She turned to walk off, to prove her word, but Larry called her back.

"Take care of yourself, Stevie," he said. "Go be with your friends. Even if you didn't like the guy, this is no time to be alone."

"Who said I didn't like the guy?" Stevie asked.

"Twenty years with the state police. I was a detective. You get a knack for these things."

"You were a detective?" Stevie said. "Seriously?"

"Fifteen years on homicide."

"Why did you stop?" Stevie asked.

"Because I opened too many doors and saw too many terrible things," he said quietly. "And some of those things never leave you. Every police detective has something they carry with them, something they see when they're trying to go to sleep at night. Twenty years is plenty. I know you are interested in being a detective, but don't play at being one, do you understand? No sneaking around behind the police."

"I know," she said.

"We understand each other?"

"Yeah," Stevie said. "I think we do."

⚡

Stevie returned to Minerva feeling numb. Her parents would definitely be a problem, and going home was a real possibility, if Ellingham didn't kick her out first. She looked at her building in a new light as she approached the big blue door. Maybe she was never meant to be here very long. Mistakes got made all the time. Fate had plans. . . .

No.

Stevie was not one of those people who thought fate decided for her. Fate was making choices. Fate was at least *trying*. The school hadn't kicked her out yet, and her parents hadn't taken her home yet. And something was going on. If Hayes had taken the pass, if Hayes had taken the dry ice . . . what the hell was he doing with it down in the tunnel?

She entered the common room still thinking about this. No one seemed to have moved from where she'd left them. Someone had built a fire in the fireplace, so the room was hot. The fire gave it a completely new character—the woodiness, the intimacy of it. It sounded like glass as it crackled.

"You okay?" Janelle asked. Nate turned as well.

"Yeah," Stevie said, pulling off her hoodie.

She looked around for where to sit. Ellie and David were still on the sofa, but there was space between them now. Ellie had a black notebook in her lap and was drawing. David had his computer, but again, he looked right at her.

Stevie caught his eye and looked away quickly. She sat at the table.

"Did they tell you what happened?" Nate said.

Stevie just shook her head.

"So are we going to be allowed out?" Nate asked.

"I guess so," Stevie said. "Soon. My parents called me. I guess the school let them know? So your parents will know soon. Everyone is going to know."

"Yeah," David said. His voice caused Stevie to start. She saw Janelle take this in, and look from Stevie to David curiously. "The word is out. So we're going to be knee deep in counselors soon."

He would not stop looking at her. And not just looking. It was a penetrating, unwavering look.

"I better call my parents first," Janelle said, grabbing her phone. "Can we do that? Do you think we can?"

Stevie shrugged.

"I'll wait," Janelle said, setting her phone down. "I'll ask Pix when she's out of the shower."

"*Après les déluge*," Ellie said, out of nowhere. "*Les parents*."

No one knew what to say to that.

"So we wait," Nate said.

"We wait," David said.

Stevie became very conscious of where David was in the room. Yes, it was just kissing last night, but it was a lot of kissing. It was a lot of rolling. What did you say to someone you'd rolled all over?

Ellie stood up suddenly and stomped off to her room. Then there were four, sitting in awkward silence until the knock at the door. It was Larry, with a uniformed officer.

"Janelle," Larry said. "Can you get your pass and come with us for a moment?"

Janelle's eyes went wide, but she got up instantly and went to her room for the pass, then stepped out the door.

"Why do they want Janelle's pass?" David asked Stevie.

"Because someone took it on Thursday," she said, watching the door.

"So?"

Stevie said no more. David got up and sat next to her at the table.

"You have no idea?" he said.

"I can't say anything," she replied.

"So you have some idea."

Nate observed this silently. Pix came downstairs.

"Was someone just at the door?" she asked.

"The police just took Janelle and her pass outside," David said. "For no reason Stevie can say."

"I'm not being a dick," Stevie said. "I just can't."

Pix hurried to the door and stepped outside.

The atmosphere in the room continued to thicken. Stevie looked at David's hand on the table. He had long fingers. Those fingers had run over her hair last night, and other places. His hands were strong, much stronger than they looked. She gave him a sideways glance. His eyebrows were thick and very expressive. They rose when he was playful, arched when he was being a jerk, and now were flat. He was watchful.

She had a strange desire to sit in his lap. To pull his face closer to hers. To kiss him again, right here, by the fire and in front of Nate and the moose head.

Where had that thought come from? It just shot through her brain like a rabbit across a road.

David pushed his chair back and went down the hall to Ellie's room, leaving Nate and Stevie.

"So," Nate said.

"Yeah," Stevie replied.

"Are you really okay?"

She nodded.

"Because you seem freaked out. It's okay to be freaked out. I was freaked out last night, and today I'm not as freaked out. So it's your turn, if you want."

"I always wanted to be around for a death," Stevie said. "You know I'm into this stuff. And now I am around death. I feel bad for saying I wanted that, but I'm . . ."

She shook her head.

"You're interested," he said. "I saw how you looked when Larry came and said the police wanted to talk to you."

"Is that bad?"

"No," he said. "This just happened. We were here when it happened."

He dug his nail into the grain of the wood.

"Thanks," she said.

"For what?"

"I just think you get me," she said.

"I do," he said, shrugging. "We have a limited emotional vocabulary. We're indoor kids."

The door opened again, and Janelle returned and sat next to Stevie, leaning her head into Stevie's shoulder.

"They're taking my pass," she said. "And they're going to go up to Hayes's room to look around. I don't know why they want my pass. I didn't do anything."

Stevie put her hand on her friend's head. It was an unfamiliar feeling, this warm head on her shoulder. Janelle just trusting her and leaning on her. Nate reaching out.

And David, the person she'd just been closest to, being meaningfully silent.

20

It seemed only natural that the vigil would take place in the yurt. There was no announcement, nothing formal. People just started going, taking up positions on the dusty floor cushions and the busted old sofas and futons. The atmosphere was confused, with an electric quality—everyone was talking, but quietly, all at once, in a low, constant sound. People brought food. There were bags of chips and candy and all varieties of snack circling the room.

Stevie walked over with Janelle and Nate. Vi was waiting for them to arrive by the door of the yurt, and threw her arms around Janelle's neck. They looked like a couple.

As soon as she walked in, Stevie realized she was the subject of a lot of attention. People turned to look at her in the way they looked at Hayes shortly before. People knew. She had been The One Who Was There.

Maris and Dash held court in a special area off to the back, on the largest sofa, with a small group sitting on cushions in front of them. Maris was all in black—tights, a formfitting sweater with a gold belt. She looked like she was dressed as Catwoman. Dash was in his oversized shirt again and was huddled, his knees pulled up near his chest. Maris was crying a slow, steady dribble. As Stevie came in, she looked up and put up her arms.

"Stevie!" she said. "Nate!"

Stevie walked over to them. When she was near enough, Maris clasped her hand.

Stevie looked at her captive hand. She couldn't tell if this was a real gesture, or a dramatic one, or a real dramatic gesture. She felt very tired and very awake at the same time, and a strange guilt followed her like a smell.

"Did you talk to the police again today?" Dash said. "We both did."

"Yeah," Stevie said.

"Did they tell you anything?"

"They kept asking about the fog machines," Stevie said.

"Yeah," Maris said. "Us too. And where we were. And what time we came home the night we were in the tunnel."

"What time did you leave him?" Stevie shrugged as if she asked out of an unspoken necessity. "I mean, he must have come home on time."

"Right before eleven," Maris said. "He went home. I went home."

Dash seemed genuinely thunderstruck.

"I'm sorry," Stevie said. "Did you guys do stuff together last year? Did you work on *The End of It All*?"

"No," Dash said. "That was totally something he did on

his own. He just produced that out of thin air over the summer. He was going to be a star, you know? I really think that. I think he was going to go to Hollywood and be in movies and be a big deal. He was just that kind of actor."

"That's what I said when I first saw him," Maris said. "Star. Star star star."

Stevie opted not to point out that Hayes already kind of was a star when Maris met him.

"He was honest," Maris said. "He was the most honest person I ever met. That's why his performances were so good."

"Honest?" Stevie said.

"Well, not honest," Maris said. "Pure. Well . . . *unencumbered*. I knew as soon as I met him that I had to be with him."

She paused for a moment and stared at her nails. Then she looked up suddenly. Stevie turned to see what she was staring at. Gretchen had come into the yurt.

"She," Maris said, "is a bitch."

"She was Hayes's ex, right?" Stevie said.

"She hurt him. Look at her."

Gretchen looked wrecked, actually. She was crying.

"The Beth thing was just something Hayes was doing for the show," Maris went on. "I know what people are going to say, but it was all for show."

All for show. That phrase struck something that Stevie had been thinking but hadn't been able to put into words. Something about this whole thing seemed—not staged, but . . . there was some kind of element of show about it. They had been making a show. And the way Hayes turned and didn't want Maris to come with him. The big, dramatic looks.

From across the room, Janelle waved Stevie over. She, Nate, and Vi were all hunkered over Nate's computer. David was there as well, having come to the yurt at some point.

"Germaine Batt again," Nate said, turning the computer around so Stevie could see.

Once again, the silent, all-seeing Germaine Batt had a report, and this one included the missing dry ice. The news spread around the room as people turned to their phones to watch.

"Dry ice?" Janelle said, her voice low. "Is that what happened? Is that what my pass was about? Is that how Hayes died?"

"How can you die from dry ice?" Nate said.

"You can die from carbon dioxide poisoning," Janelle said. "If you were trapped in a small space with enough dry ice it would displace the oxygen. Did Hayes take a bunch of dry ice?"

"It seems like that might be what happened," Stevie said. "I heard something about it when they took me up to the Great House."

Janelle's brow furrowed. "He must have taken a lot," she said. "And that stuff is heavy. Really heavy."

The group descended into thoughtful silence for a bit. Vi rubbed Janelle's hand.

"So what happens now?" Nate said.

"I don't think I'm going to be here much longer," Stevie replied.

"You think they'll kick you out?" Vi said.

"They won't," David said. He had come up behind them and crouched on the back of the sofa. "They don't kick anyone out. I've tried."

"My parents could take me out of here," she replied.

"Why would they do that?"

"Because they never wanted me to come."

"Why wouldn't your parents want you to come?" Vi said.

"Because," Stevie replied, "they like things that are normal. Ellingham is not normal. It's full of everything they worry about. *Other* people. They let me come because it's fancy and it's free, but they'd take any excuse to pull me back out. And I think someone dying counts as a pretty big excuse. So I am not long for this fancy, special world. It's back to the local Edward King headquarters for me so I can sit around and listen to people who believe in aliens but not climate change."

"Oh my God," Vi said. "Isn't there anything you can do?"

"I have no idea. Maybe if I suddenly became a prom-queen type. They like that."

"Maybe we'll all have to go," Nate said. "Maybe the school will close."

"You guys," Janelle said. "Come on. Hayes is dead."

"It doesn't mean we shouldn't talk about the school closing," Nate said.

Stevie heard someone repeat "the school is closing?" in the group next to them in a whisper. Life comes at you fast, and games of telephone, even faster.

The door to the yurt swung open, and Ellie strode inside.

She wavered, obviously drunk, and held Roota over her head.

"Hayes is dead!" she said. "Long live Hayes!"

She started squawking away.

This announcement did not go over well in the room. Unlike that first night in the yurt, no one was very receptive to Ellie's arting. David slipped off the back of the sofa and went over to her and whispered in her ear. She jerked away and played more aggressively. He hooked his arm through hers and tried to lead her out, but she pulled away again.

A few more art people got up from various corners and gathered around her. At first it appeared that they were trying to stop her, but then one of them started jumping up and down in a strange dance. Ellie did it too. Then another joined in. David shrugged and left the group, returning to his perch. Maris, who at first was staring at this in horror, got up and started dancing with all her might, her arms swinging furiously.

"Oh my God," Janelle said over the noise. "What's even happening right now?"

"The Bacchae," Nate said.

This little dancing group in the middle sucked all the rest of the air and energy from the room and continued until another group entered. This was a less festive group, consisting of Larry, Charles, Dr. Quinn, and two uniformed police officers. The room ground into quiet.

"Everyone," Larry said, holding up his hands.

Ellie bleated once on Roota.

"Element," Larry said. "If you wouldn't mind."

The saxophone was lowered.

"The police are going to need to speak to everyone for just a few minutes," Larry said. "It's nothing to worry about. We just have to get a baseline of information about what happened here. So I'm going to have everyone move back to your houses."

"Dinner will be brought around to your houses," Charles said. "And again, we have counselors on hand who can come to you. Anyone who needs help, just reply to the text I sent or speak to any faculty member."

Ellingham shuffled back to their houses, now more nervous.

"Everyone gets to talk to a cop," David said as the Minerva group walked home. "*You* get to talk to a cop, and *you* get to talk to a cop, and *you* . . ."

"I'm not going to," Ellie said.

"Good luck with that," David replied.

"I don't have to, and I don't want to," she replied. "This isn't a fascist state."

"I don't think that's what this is about," Nate said. "It sounds like they're trying to find out what happened."

"And you're drunk," David said. "Coffee before cops."

She laughed and pushed him in the chest, catching him off guard and knocking him backward to the ground.

"Could a drunk person do that?" she asked.

"Pretty sure that's a yes," he said, getting up and brushing himself off.

Ellie staggered ahead a few steps. She was drunker than

Stevie first realized. It was so hard to tell with Ellie.

"Come on," Janelle said to Stevie. "Get her other arm."

Janelle stepped ahead and expertly scooped Ellie by the crook of one arm and waited for Stevie to get the other.

"Let's go together," Janelle said. "Can we go together?"

"We can go together," Ellie said. "Why not? Together. Together!"

Holding Ellie upright was becoming a challenge.

"You know," she said to Stevie, breathing hot wine breath into her face, "he told me to get Roota. He got it. He *got* it."

"Okay," Stevie said.

"He got art. More than people knew."

"Okay."

David strode along, hands deep in his pockets. Having been knocked over, he seemed content now to let Stevie and Janelle handle Ellie.

"Hey, Nate," Ellie said. "You get it. You write. You get it."

"Sure?" Nate said.

"You do what you see in your *head*."

She tried to tap her head, but Janelle had a firm grip on her arm.

"Water," Janelle said. "We need some water! And then some coffee. And a bath! How about a bath!"

"A bath!" Ellie said. "You get it. You all get it! Except Stevie. Do you get it, Stevie?"

"I get it," Stevie said, having no idea what Ellie was talking about.

They managed to get Ellie inside without Pix seeing. Janelle ran a bath. Knowing that Ellie was not averse to bathing fully clothed, they put her in just as she was.

Ellie grew quiet in the tub, sipping her coffee dutifully. She was in reasonable enough shape when the police came by in the next few hours. Janelle, Nate, and Stevie had already been through it.

David was taken first. The questioning happened in his room and lasted about ten minutes.

"What did they ask?" Stevie said.

"Did I know anything about Hayes's plan? Did he say anything about the tunnel, about the dry ice. He didn't. I was here when Hayes was doing all of that, smoking a bowl with Ellie. I didn't say that, and I don't know if that's what she is going to say, but I guess we'll find out."

Ellie was sober enough not to say that. She said that she and David were at home working together.

The exhaustion of the day seemed to hit everyone at once after that. The Minerva residents slumped in the common room for a while, then, one by one, people peeled off to bed. Ellie went first, then Janelle, then Nate. David was in the hammock chair, rocking slowly back and forth.

"So," he said, "you really think your parents will make you leave?"

"I think someone will," she said. "If not them, the school."

David extended his legs, pulling the stretchy hammock material taut.

"They won't throw you out," he said. "They don't do that here. Believe me. I've tested the system."

"Did anyone *die* when you tested the system?"

"Nothing you did caused Hayes to die, right?"

"I don't think so. But . . ."

"You haven't done anything you regret, right?"

She looked up at him sharply. Was he talking about what they did? What kind of dark conversational game was this?

Not one she wanted to play.

"I'm going to bed," she said, getting up. "Good night, Westley. They'll most likely kill me in the morning."

"You might not want to make death jokes," he said as she went down the hall.

FEDERAL BUREAU OF INVESTIGATION
INTERVIEW BETWEEN AGENT SAMUEL
ARNOLD AND LEONARD HOLMES NAIR
APRIL 17, 1936, 3:30 P.M.
LOCATION: ELLINGHAM PROPERTY

SA: Mr. Nair. I need to ask you some more questions.

LHN: That's all we seem to do around here.

SA: We just need to establish the facts. I understand you once taught an art lesson to the students.

LHN: Please don't remind me.

SA: Why do you say that?

LHN: That was the longest afternoon of my life, trying

to explain Max Ernst to children. But that's one of
the prices you pay for knowing Albert. He believes his
children should learn from the best.

SA: *Did you meet a student named Dolores Epstein that day?*

LHN: *I have no idea. All children look the same to me.*

[*A photograph of Dolores Epstein is presented.*]

LHN: *Again, all children look the same to me.*

SA: *Dolores was a very gifted student. She was considered by
many of the teachers to be the brightest student here.*

[*Mr. Nair takes another look at the photograph.*]

LHN: *Now that you say it, there was one that seemed more
aware than the rest. She had a passable
knowledge of Greek and Roman art. This could have
been the one. She had curly hair like that. Yes, I think this
was the one. Is that the one that vanished?*

SA: *Dolores Epstein was last seen on the afternoon of the
thirteenth, when she checked a book out of the library.
Did you ever see her outside of your class?*

LHN: *You see them all, milling around. You know, Albert
opened this place and said he was going to fill it with
prodigies, but fully half of them are just his friends'
children and not the sharpest ones at that. The other half
are probably all right. If I'm being fair, there were one*

or two others that showed a bit of a spark. A boy and a
girl, I forget their names. The two of them seemed to be
a pair. The girl had hair like a raven and the boy looked
a bit like Byron. They were interested in poetry. They
had a little light behind the eyes. The girl asked me about
Dorothy Parker, which I took as a hopeful sign. I'm a
friend of Dorothy's.

[A silver lighter is placed on the table.]

SA: *Do you recognize this, Mr. Nair?*

LHN: *Oh! I've been looking for that!*

[Mr. Nair attempts to take the lighter. He is prevented.]

SA: *It's evidence, Mr. Nair. It has to stay with us.*

LHN: *It's Cartier, Agent Arnold. Where did you find it?*
     I've been looking for that for ages.

SA: *We found it in the observatory, along with Dolores's*
    library book and a pencil.

LHN: *I suppose I left it in there.*

SA: *We found Dolores's fingerprints on this lighter. Why*
    would Dolores have your lighter?

LHN: *She must have found it.*

SA: *You didn't give it to her?*

LHN: *Why would I give a child my Cartier lighter?*

SA: *I don't know, Mr. Nair.*

LHN: I lose things. I assume the girl found it and kept it because it's a lovely thing. She must have good taste. Do I get it back?

SA: When it's no longer needed, Mr. Nair. Let me ask you something else. Why might Miss Robinson go into Mrs. Ellingham's private, locked dressing room?

LHN: Any number of reasons, I suppose. Those two are thick as thieves.

SA: Specifically, this was on the evening of the thirteenth, when everyone in the house was looking for Miss Robinson. She did not respond to the many people calling for her and was found alone in the room, where she had been for approximately fifteen minutes. A strange thing to do during what was clearly a panic.

LHN: I can't say why Flora does what she does.

SA: You are friends with Miss Robinson?

LHN: Flora and I are friends, yes.

SA: Where did you meet?

LHN: Oh, some speakeasy. Years ago.

SA: So you are saying that Flora Robinson did not tell you what she was doing in Iris Ellingham's room on Monday evening at the time the alarm was raised?

LHN: She did not.

SA: She said nothing of the matter?

LHN: Flora doesn't tell me every time she goes in or out of a room.

SA: And when did you first learn of the kidnapping?

LHN: When Flora woke me on Tuesday morning, as you

*know, because I've gone through this ten times or more.
If you're suggesting that Flora had anything to do with
this, you couldn't be more wrong. Unlike me, Flora
has a heart. She loves Iris like a sister and Alice like
a daughter. Be careful with that lighter, would you? I
really do want it back.*

[*Interview terminated 3:56 p.m.*]

21

"So," Charles said. "Let's talk."

It was the next morning, and Stevie sat in front of Call Me Charles up in his office. The rain beat against the windows as classical music played very quietly from small white speakers. Stevie had been waiting for this call, and when it finally came, she felt like her body and soul were ready. She'd read about Marie Antoinette, waiting in a prison palace in Paris while they built guillotines outside.

"Let's talk about what happened," Charles said. "First of all, tell me how you're doing."

"You mean, how I feel?" Stevie said.

"However you want to answer the question."

Stevie was not someone who liked talking about feelings, but in this one instance, feelings were probably better than facts.

"I mean," Stevie said, "I'm okay. It's weird, but Hayes wasn't someone I knew well. So, it's horrible, but . . . we weren't close."

Charles gave a concerned nod.

"Can you talk to me about what happened? Whose idea was it to use the tunnel?"

"It was Hayes's," Stevie said. "I thought the tunnel was filled in."

"No," Charles said. "We dug it out in the spring. It's going to be demolished and filled in when we run the new water and sewer line for the art barn expansion. We thought we were keeping that fact under wraps, but . . ."

"I was the one who picked the lock," Stevie said.

It just felt important to say it to him. The police already knew. Best not to have the telltale heart beating under her until she lost her marbles.

"I know," he said.

Several long seconds passed. Charles didn't look so young and carefree today. No superhero T-shirts under his suit.

"Tunneling has been a feature of this school for a long time. We try to discourage it. And Hayes didn't—it wasn't the tunnel that hurt Hayes. What happened to Hayes was an extremely unfortunate accident. Extremely unfortunate. Should you have gone into that tunnel? No. But you didn't take Hayes in there that night."

Stevie looked at the pattern of the drops beating on the glass.

"Am I going to be expelled?" she asked.

"No," Charles said. "But there is something I'm going to have you do. Come with me."

Stevie followed him, almost in a trance, as he took her back to the attic entrance. She wasn't being kicked out—and she was being taken to the attic?

"We've decided after what happened with Hayes to double up on all security," he said, entering a new, longer security code into the panel. They made their way up the narrow stairs.

"When we spoke before," he said, turning on the lights, "I said I wanted you to find a project that put a human face on the crime that happened here, the loss. You found a project. No one could have predicted the terrible lesson on loss you learned. Now that you know about the tunnel being opened, there's something I can show you."

He took her down several aisles and turned down one full of archival storage boxes and three shelves of identical long, green leather books with dates on them.

"This row contains a lot of the records and personal effects from Albert Ellingham's office and the household management," he said.

At the end of the row, near the window, he knelt down to the floor and pulled a beaten metal box, about three feet in length and a foot or so high, off the bottom shelf. The box was clearly very old. It had been painted red, and parts of the paint remained, but much was worn or rusted away.

"When the crew first went in the tunnel, they found this packed into the dirt used to seal up the tunnel. It was locked when the crew found it. . . ." Charles carefully lifted the old latch. "Everyone was excited. A buried box in the tunnel . . . it could have been anything. So we opened it and . . ."

He lifted the lid, revealing two side-by-side piles of yellowed newspapers. The headline of the top one read: ELLINGHAM FAMILY KIDNAPPED. Stevie knelt next to Charles to have a better look. The newspapers were all different, different cities, different dates, but all featured the Ellingham Affair in the headline.

"Someone buried a box of newspapers in the tunnel?" she said.

"We don't know who put them there," Charles replied. "But I think it was probably Albert Ellingham. Maybe he was trying to bury the past, bury his pain."

"It must have been hard for a man who owned a newspaper to hide from the news," she said.

"A good point," Charles said, nodding. "But I think you understand, that tunnel was a sacred space. It's seen so much death. People are going to sensationalize this."

Stevie took this as a bit of an admonishment.

"So here is what you are going to do," he said. "These rows . . ."

He took her back out and to another row, labeled *38*.

"Thirty-eight through forty-five are full of household items. Things were gathered up in boxes but not well sorted. I want you to sort and catalog these seven rows of materials."

"Is this my punishment?" she said.

"We don't do punishments," Charles replied. "We do projects. This is your project. Sort, organize, catalog."

Stevie looked down the row. It looked like it contained bins of doorknobs, stacks of old magazines, bags of junk.

"You can start now," he said, "if you feel up to it."

"Sure," she said.

"Then I'll leave you to it. Just let security know when you're done. You may need to do this over a few days, so I'll arrange it that someone can take you up here."

He left her alone with all of the treasures. As punishments went, this was about as good as it got. She wandered the aisles, taking in the view passively. She allowed the patterns to sink into her mind—clothes here, furniture there. Globes, books, dishes . . . It was her and the Ellingham items, and they became familiar with this repetition.

She spent some time standing in front of a massive cabinet with horizontally glass-fronted shelves before working up the courage to open it up and pull out a delicate soup bowl—white, with a pattern of pink flowers and tender green vines, edged in gold. At the bottom of the dish, the letters AIE were also painted in gold. There was a stack of books near the china.

She returned to the first row he had taken her to and looked at the long green ledgers. Some contained orders of groceries and household supplies. These people went through a lot of food on the weekends—endless lemons and oranges and eggs and mint for drinks. Massive orders of cigarettes to be put in cigarette dispensers. Notes of dozens of smashed champagne glasses and orders of fresh ones. Floor wax for the scuffs in the ballroom.

One book just contained household menus. Stevie paged through until she found April 13, 1936. It was written in a neat, precise hand:

MAIN TABLE:
Crème de céleri soup
Filet of sole with sauce amandine
Roast lamb
Minted peas
Asparagus hollandaise
Potatoes lyonnaise
Cold lemon soufflé

April 14 was not as elaborate:

No main table service. Tray taken to office.
Sandwiches of cold chicken and ham salad
Sliced celery and stuffed olives
Lemon cake
Coffee

Guest, Miss Flora Robinson, tray service: clear
*   soup, tea with milk, tomato juice, sandwiches of*
*   cold chicken salad, sliced celery, junket*
Guest, Mr. Leonard Nair, tray service: scrambled
*   eggs, coffee*

Insignificant though this may have seemed, it gave a sense of the day and the change in the household. Everything had been going along as normal on the thirteenth. On the fourteenth, it was a different place. The tray of cold sandwiches, thrown together because they had to eat to keep going. The weird addition of just some sliced celery that had probably been around from the day before and some olives (eat anything, anything, whatever is there), some cake that was probably already made. The coffee to keep them going.

Flora Robinson and Leo Holmes Nair seemed to have eaten in their rooms, simple foods, foods you ate when you were sick or hungover. Scrambled eggs. Broth. And more coffee and tea. Just stay awake. The whole house, crackling with nervous energy, waiting for the phone to ring. And still, the butler recorded it, this desperate meal, because that was how things were done. The kitchen staff had probably been questioned as well, so they didn't have as much time to prepare food.

She worked her way along the row, pulling out boxes of old office supplies—three telephones, rolled maps, wax tubes, telephone directories. One large, velvet-lined box held a number of items that seemed unique—a crystal ink pot, a fine pen, pushpins, paper clips, a stack of business cards, an invitation to a dinner party on October 31, 1938.

That was a meaningful date. These were the things that must have been on his desk when he died. She shuffled through them, the notepad with some circles and numbers drawn on it, with drips of ink on the page. A bit of ripped newspaper with information about the stock exchange. A Western Union telegraph slip with the words:

10/30/38

Where do you look for someone who's never really there?

Always on a staircase but never on a stair

His last riddle, with no solution given. On the thirtieth of October, 1938, Albert Ellingham told his secretary that he was going for a sail. He seemed strangely bright that day. He took George Marsh, his loyal friend, with him. They sailed out of Burlington Yacht Club. Later that evening, residents of South Hero heard a boom and saw a flash on the water. Ellingham's boat had exploded. The wreckage revealed a bomb had been placed on board. The anarchists who had long dogged him, who had been blamed for the murder of his wife and the disappearance of his child, seemed to have gotten him in the end.

Last things were so strange. Most people had no control over or concept of what their last acts would be. She wondered for a moment if Hayes had realized what was happening to him, that he was going to die while filming a video at school.

For a moment, she remembered the letter on the wall, her vision. It had seemed *so real*, but there was no way it could be. It made no sense. It had simply been a vivid dream caused by a racing mind. Stevie did not believe in psychics, in precognition. She didn't think she had seen Hayes's death coming. The word *murder* had appeared in her dream, but that was because murders happened here. There was nothing spooky about it. She dreamed of a murder, there was a murder. Albert Ellingham wrote a riddle, as he did many times, and then he died.

She stared at the little telegram slip for a long time, examining the words, the ink, the old but well-preserved paper. This must have been Ellingham's last riddle, something he was working on the day he died. A little bit of nonsense, a return to his old way of being. And then fate interrupted. Had anyone noticed this before, this little bit of detritus from his desk? Or did no one care about his little games in the wake of his death, when the great empire had to be managed? Who cares about a little riddle when one of the richest men in the world dies?

Stevie carefully put the slip of paper back in the box, like she was setting a flower on his grave. Her eyes teared up a bit and her throat grew rough.

She wiped her eyes with the back of her hand and went over to one of the windows and looked out over the expanse of the campus and the view beyond. Death had come to Ellingham again. Death loved this place. But if Stevie was going to cope with being here, cope with the job she wanted to do, she had to look death in the eye. She could not be afraid, or cry whenever she saw a sad memento. She had to be tough. That's what the dead deserved.

But, Stevie wondered, what was the solution to the riddle? What was always on a staircase but never on a stair?

FEDERAL BUREAU OF INVESTIGATION
INTERVIEW BETWEEN AGENT SAMUEL ARNOLD AND GEORGE MARSH
APRIL 17, 1936, 5:45 P.M.
LOCATION: ELLINGHAM PROPERTY

SA: Thank you for taking the time to speak to me again.

GM: Whatever you need me for.

SA: This has been a difficult few days.

GM: I haven't slept in two nights. Doesn't matter. Iris and Alice are still out there. Can I have one of your cigarettes?

SA: Of course. Can I just go over your relationship to Albert Ellingham and the safety concerns in the past? You were with the New York police department when you met?

GM: That's right. I was a detective. We'd been working an anarchist gang that was causing trouble. We found out that they were planning to bomb an important industrialist. We found out it was Albert Ellingham, and luckily I got there in time.

SA: You personally saved his life moments before the car exploded.

GM: I did my job. After that, Mr. Ellingham was kind enough to recommend me for the FBI. I worked out of the New York office. You ever work out of New York?

SA: No. Only Washington. Director Hoover sent me up here to work this case.

GM: *Mr. Ellingham asked me to come up to Vermont when he built this place. I do field work for the bureau and I consult for him.*

SA: *But you don't live here in the house.*

GM: *No. I live in Burlington. I come here whenever Mr. Ellingham needs me. I usually come up when important guests are here. I was here for the party that weekend, mostly because Maxine Melville, the film star, was here. He wants to sign her for his studio, so he had her come up for a visit. The weekend party was mostly to entertain her. I watch the place, watch for press, make sure the staff don't get too nosy. They're pretty good, but people get strange around famous people.*

SA: *What's your thought on the missing student?*

GM: *Wrong place, wrong time, most likely. I've looked through her school files. Good kid. Real smart. One of the brightest here. But she liked to find places to hide and read. I heard you found a book of hers in the observatory?*

SA: *That's right. We did.*

GM: *Damn. Poor kid.*

SA: *What was your assessment of the letter that came in on April eighth? The one that we've been calling the Truly Devious letter.*

GM: *Mackenzie handles all the correspondence. He shows me the ones he thinks are trouble.*

SA: *But he didn't show you this letter until after the kidnapping?*

GM: *It was a busy weekend. I think there wasn't time. By*

the time I saw that letter, the thing was under way.
Mackenzie's always on top of things. It's just too bad he
didn't tell me. Not that it would have changed anything.

SA: *What do you mean?*

GM: *I mean that it's hard to get Albert Ellingham to change*
his plans. Like this place, for example. You see exactly
what I see. The advantage and disadvantage of this
place is its location. On one hand, it's hard to get to, so
it's not going to be the target of spontaneous crime. You
have to really make an effort to come here, and then you
have to make a bigger effort to get away. But, as we've
found out, the disadvantage is that there are many places
to ambush and many ways to escape.

SA: *Surely, as someone who foiled a bomb plot on Albert*
Ellingham once before, this occurred to you?

GM: *It worried me to death. I talked about it with Albert.*
I suggested getting more men up here to guard the place.
He said no.

SA: *Why?*

GM: *His words, "It's not conducive to playful learning." His*
words.

SA: *So he went without the necessary security?*

GM: *Listen. There's something you need to understand*
about Albert Ellingham. He's a great man. No one I
admire more, aside from J. Edgar Hoover himself. But
he thinks he's invincible. He thinks he can do anything.
Because in his experience, he can. He made all of his own
money. Everything he has—his newspapers and movie

studio and the rest—he built from nothing. *The guy was a newsie as a kid, lived on the street, didn't have two pennies to rub together. Man's a genius. But he thinks nothing can touch him. I don't think he keeps me around because he thinks I actually help—I think he sees me like a lucky rabbit's foot. I saved him from that bomb, but he saw it as luck and he took me along. I'm grateful. But he believes his will is enough. Something like this was always bound to happen. I knew it. You can see it. It was always bound to happen.*

[*Interview terminated* 6:10 *p.m.*]

302

22

THE ELLINGHAM COACH SYSTEM WAS BACK IN EFFECT THE NEXT DAY on a special schedule to allow students and parents to meet.

There were two stops—the rest stop and Burlington. Stevie had arranged to meet her parents at the rest stop. She waited for the coach with a number of other people. To settle herself, she had her earbuds in and her podcasts on.

And she was settled, until David sidled up next to her. He was not dressed in his normal David gear of wrecked jeans and some old T-shirt. He had on a crisp blue fitted dress shirt, one that tapered elegantly down to a pair of well-cut black pants. He even wore black dress shoes. Everything about his appearance was crisp and tailored and showed off his slender, muscular frame. All of this was capped off by a slim-fitting black coat.

Stevie had limited experience with guys in dress clothes. (Suited detectives on TV didn't count.) David was showing his plumage, and it stirred feelings in Stevie that were physically agitating.

"I hope you get the job," Stevie said, looking away from

him. "I think they really need you up in corporate account-ing."

"Is that a deduction?" he said. "Get it? Accounting joke and detective joke."

"Where are you meeting your parents?"

"I'm not," he said, pushing his hands deep in the pockets of his long black coat. "They are safely far away. I'm just getting the hell out of Dodge."

"So why the . . ."

"I like to look nice when I go to see His Majesty, the Burger King. And where will you be going?"

"To eat. And hopefully coming back to school if my parents don't think this place is full of deranged liberals that let people get murdered, which is sort of what they are currently thinking."

The coach pulled up and Stevie and David got in. Stevie sat by the window, and David plopped down next to her.

"So," he said, "you want to talk?"

"About what?"

"About the other night?"

Most of the other people in the coach—not that there were many—were talking or listening to something already. But this was still public. Stevie felt herself break into a cold sweat.

"Is there a reason you're doing this?" she asked.

"I just want to know. I like learning. That's why I'm an Ellingham student. Learning is fun. Learning is a game."

"How serious are they about the policy regarding using

violent language with another student?" she asked.

Her palms were starting to sweat. And her forehead. And her feet? What the hell was that? Why was the human body such a jerk? Why did it flood you with hormones and sexy feelings and also *flop sweat*?

"Deadly," he said sternly.

"Look," she said, "I have enough to worry about. My parents are probably going to pull me out of school tonight, so . . ."

"Life finds a way," he said. "Didn't you learn anything from *Jurassic Park*?"

He rested his head back and put a large set of over-ear headphones on and left Stevie to think that one over.

⊷

The coach made its way back on the path past the farmyards and the maple-candy stores and the glassblowers and the Ben & Jerry's signs, back to I-89, and all the way to the rest stop where Stevie's parents waited now, next to their maroon minivan, bundled tight.

David stood to let her go by, and then he continued right off the coach. She thought he was just taking extreme steps to make room for her, but he remained off the coach and followed her right to her parents.

"I'm David," he said, extending his hand. "David Eastman."

Why was David introducing himself to her parents?

"Nice to meet you, David," her mother said. "Are you meeting your family here?"

"No. Stevie said I could maybe ride into Burlington with you? If that's no trouble. If it is, I can just catch the coach when it comes by again."

Stevie saw the light come on in her parents' eyes. They looked from David to Stevie and back to David again, and they liked what they saw. Stevie felt the ground moving away from her feet.

"Of course not!" her mom said. "You'll come with us."

"We're going to get something to eat," her father said. "If you'd like to come."

Stevie couldn't move. Her body had gone rigid. David, don't, David, it's not a joke, David . . .

"Sure," he said with a smile. "If it's not a bother?"

"Oh, it's no bother," her dad said.

She saw David take in the EDWARD KING sticker on the back of the minivan. He gave her a sideways look, then went to the back door of her family's car and opened it.

"After you," he said.

"I will kill you," she said in a low voice.

"I'm telling you they are serious about that policy."

She walked around to the other side.

All four of them were off together in the Bell family minivan, down I-89, as the dark fell over the land. The ride into Burlington was quick. They rode through the university section, got stuck on the waterfront road along Lake Champlain, and turned back onto one of the many small and charming streets.

The entire order of the world was now thrown. There

should be no David here, with her parents, in this place. Though the volume was turned low, Stevie could hear the familiar mumble of her parents' favorite talk radio show— the one that always talked about how "those people" were trouble, the one that proselytized about Edward King. They switched it off, which was something.

There were many fine restaurants in Burlington, and fine restaurants tend to be expensive. Stevie had looked up a place off Church Street, the main shopping and social area, that looked like it had good sandwiches and salads and didn't cost too much. There were free places to park as well. The restaurant was the kind of place where you ordered at the counter and paid and took a number back to any table you liked.

Stevie's mom and David ordered first. Stevie's dad took longer to examine the menu, and Stevie considered impaling herself on the potato chip display rack.

"Vegetarian roast beef sandwich," her father said. "I wonder how that works."

"They use a substitute," Stevie said in a low voice.

"Then it's not roast beef, is it?"

Stevie's eyes fluttered closed for a moment.

"Don't make that face," he said. "I'm just making a joke. Can't I make a joke?"

Don't make that face, Stevie. Don't be smart, Stevie. You think you know so much, Stevie, but wait until you get into the world you'll see things don't work that way. . . .

"We came up to see you. Can't we make this a good visit?

We can always take you right back home."

Don't react. Don't give in. Just get through this, go back.

The moment settled.

"I like him," her father said. "Very polite. Opened the door for you."

"He's a treasure," Stevie said.

At the end of the line, down where you picked up your order, David appeared to be entertaining her mother to no end and . . . oh no. He was getting out his wallet. He was insisting, clearly *insisting* that he pay. There was the credit card. Another joke. She was laughing away, charmed half to death.

Stevie distinctly felt part of her soul die. She hoped it wasn't an important part.

They took a table by the window. The cold air penetrated the glass, and Stevie invited the chill. It suited her mood. She examined her overstuffed chicken sandwich, found it was too heavily stuffed to ever pick up and eat, and so tipped it to the side and ate the component pieces with a plastic fork while her parents quizzed David.

David, for his part, was all dark hair and eyes and waggling eyebrows on the other side of the table. He managed to get his massive sandwich in his mouth and conduct a conversation at the same time. His speaking voice was clearer, she noticed, like he was putting on a show.

He was messing with her head.

"So what do your parents do?" Stevie's father asked.

"My mom is a pilot," he said between bites.

Stevie looked up. David calmly ate a fry and then stacked the remainder into a Jenga pile.

"A pilot?" her father repeated. "That's very impressive. Must be hard to have a family when you do that kind of job. What does your father do?"

"Well," David said, breaking a fry in half and examining the fluffy insides. "He runs a fertilizer plant."

Stevie looked up at him sharply. Was he making fun of her parents? A pilot and someone who ran a crap plant? Stevie felt a wall of rage building inside of her. She may not have agreed with her parents on things, but they were *her* parents, not for anyone else to taunt.

"Very impressive," her dad said.

Her face was burning. She put her cup on her cheek for a second to cool her skin.

"So," her mother said, "we need to talk about what happened. This is a pretty serious conversation we need to have with Stevie, David."

"Sure," David said. "I had it with my parents too."

"And what did they say?"

He leaned back in his chair with that ease that only guys are supposed to possess and that Stevie intended to master.

"It's horrible," he said. "But accidents happen."

"How did the school let this happen?" her mom said. "That stuff should have been under lock and key."

"It was," Stevie said. "He broke in."

"Couldn't have been that well locked up, then," her dad said.

"Some people go to a lot of effort to get into locked places," David said with a long, steady look at Stevie. "He stole someone's pass."

"He was famous," her mom said. "The news is making him out to be a nice kid."

"That doesn't mean anything," David said. "The news can't tell you what people are really like."

"That's the truth," Stevie's dad said.

Stevie tensed. *Please don't start.*

"Stevie and I don't see eye to eye on some things," her dad went on. "But the media . . ."

She felt her resolve slipping. Her eyes were going to roll back into her head and she was going to exit via the window and escape. She could live in the mountains and eat rocks.

". . . tells us what we want to hear, generally," David said.

Stevie felt her heart stop for a moment. Also, now her father was going to go for him, which would be something to see.

"Interesting," Stevie's father said, nodding. "You've got a smart one here, Stevie."

It was like she'd been punched in the gut. Stevie said stuff like that *all the time* and was told she was wrong. David said it once and he got a nod and a compliment.

Oh, the magic of dudes. If only they bottled it.

"We got a call, Stevie," her dad said, picking a bit of tomato out of his sandwich. "Edward King called us. Well, his office. His people."

"Edward King is our senator," her mom explained to

David. "He's a great man. But Stevie is not a fan."

Stevie clasped her hands together into a knot and pressed them into her solar plexus.

"We've been asked to become the volunteer coordinators for the entire state," her dad said. "I know you won't like this, Stevie . . ."

Turn to stone, Stevie. Become a mountain.

"That's amazing," David said, slapping on a huge smile. "Congratulations."

Her parents were both looking at her. This was the test of fire. She could explode. That was her instinct. That mountain she had become was really a volcano. But . . . if she could swallow it—if she could handle this—she would appear to be changed in a way they liked. And if she could do that, then maybe the door was not shut. Maybe, just maybe . . .

It hurt. It genuinely hurt. The muscles of her face resisted. Her throat wanted to close.

But she pushed. She forced herself into—if not a smile, then something that sort of resembled one. She pushed the air out of her lungs, up her throat, and out of her mouth.

"That's great," she said.

Two words. *That's great.* The worst two words she had ever uttered. Her parents looked at her. They looked at David in his dress shirt. This whole strange little drama had an effect. And she knew at that moment that they would let her stay.

So why did it feel like she'd just lost the game?

23

THERE WERE ONLY TWO SEATS LEFT ON THE RETURN COACH WHEN they reached it, so it was David and Stevie together again. Stevie felt the tightness in her chest and realized that she was balling her fists so hard in her pockets that her nails were cutting into her palms.

"They seemed to like me," he said.

"What the hell was that about?" Stevie said.

"You're welcome," he said.

Stevie got out her phone and stuck in her earbuds. David pulled one out.

"What? You get to stay. Why are you so mad?"

"Because," Stevie said. "I don't get to stay because of me. I get to stay because of *you*. Because they think we're dating. Because they probably think I've landed some rich, preppy boyfriend. I get to stay because there's a guy."

"I know," he said, his brows angling in annoyance. "That's why I did this. You said they thought that was important. That's why I came along. If you want me to learn my valuable lesson, you have to spell it out."

"Dating," she said coolly, "is what my parents think girls do. They date. So I have now achieved all they expect from me. Also, the Edward King thing? Yeah. I had to sit there and swallow that whole."

"Seems to have worked out," David said. "Again, not seeing why you're mad. You're here, they're far away."

"Because again, it's not me. It's Edward King, the guy who represents literally everything I hate. The guy is racist, fascist scum and now my parents run his goon army for the state, and I had to smile."

"I just want you to know, you didn't smile . . ."

Stevie was too enraged for a moment to speak. She breathed heavily until she found her voice again.

"Also, your mom isn't a pilot, you lying freak," she added.

"How do you know? She might be."

"And your dad runs a fertilizer farm?" she asked.

"That one is true," David said.

"Near the beach in San Diego?"

"Never swim there," David said, gravely shaking his head.

"I know one thing that is full of shit," she said. "And it's you."

He shrugged as if to say, *Fair enough*.

"What the hell is wrong with you?" she asked.

"Lots of things," he said.

"You're a liar," she said.

"Maybe we both are a little sensitive about our parents. I just wanted to help you solve your problem. Problem solved.

You want to be mad, be mad. Here."

He picked the dangling earbud back up, and she reinserted it. But she didn't turn anything on. She looked out the window, and at his pale reflection in the glass. She found herself annoyingly transfixed by the line of his jaw. At first, it had looked so sharp to her, like his face was coming to a point. It wasn't that sharp after all. He must have been tense before, jutting it out.

He was looking at his phone now, paying her no attention.

Except he had made his hand into a little spider and was dancing it along his thigh. She watched it, as she was surely supposed to, and it crept closer to her leg . . .

. . . then backed off.

. . . then it approached again, with one tentative spider-leg finger hanging over hers but not touching, not touching . . .

. . . just the very tip touched; *was* it even touching?

Her entire body was static, anticipatory.

The coach made the violent turn into the drive, jolting them and washing the spider away.

Stevie walked ahead of David when they got out on the drive. When she was halfway to Minerva, she slowed, expecting his footsteps behind hers. He was nowhere in sight. She entered the common room a ball of frustration.

"How was it?" Janelle said when Stevie passed her room. Janelle was in the middle of a pile of math books and wires and an open computer playing a TV show.

"Good," Stevie said, taking as casual a stance as she could. "Good. I think it's okay. I'm staying, for now."

Janelle made an excited squeaking noise.

"Come sit," she said.

"I'm just going to . . ." Stevie tilted her head toward her room. "I just need a few minutes."

Inside her room, she paced around with her coat on. She looked at herself in the mirror. Her cheeks were bright red from the cold. Her short hair was pressed flat against her head from the pressure of her knit hat.

It was time to ask herself something she had never seriously considered—was she attractive? What was attractive? What did other people like? She knew what she liked—the short hair. She liked the way she looked when she narrowed her eyes, because it was sharp and penetrating without being too squinty. She liked the fullness of her mouth, because she was not afraid to speak up. She felt solid in the fullness of her hips.

Was this what pretty was?

Who knew. This was what a Stevie was, anyway.

She grabbed the top edge of the bureau and stretched her arms out, looking down at the floor. Stevie knew about panic. What she didn't understand as much was this new hormonal cocktail her body had on the menu and what it meant for her plans. She wanted to go upstairs. She wanted . . . David.

She *wanted* him. David, who had just made her madder than anyone else aside from her family. David, who she had to see every damn day. Someone who came in from a run

315

smelling rank and appeared again in the common room all spicy and clean and . . .

Why him? Out of anyone, why did the hormone gods pick *him*?

She heard him come in. Heard him come into the hall. Was he going to stop?

No. There was the loud creak of the steps.

She had to go and talk to him, maybe. She wasn't sure what about. She slipped out of her coat, paced the length of her room, and found herself leaving and heading upstairs.

Once at his door, she stood there uncertainly. She didn't come up to this floor that often. The guys had to come down, but this place was optional. It was darker up here. The wind made more noise. She raised her hand to knock and held it in place for a full minute before bringing it timidly down on the wood.

When David opened the door, he did not look cocky. The heat collected up here, so it was extremely warm. The only light on inside was a small bedside lamp.

"You want something?" he said.

"I want . . ." What did she want? ". . . to understand."

"What? Life? The universe?"

"I want to know what your deal is," she said.

"My *deal*? What's a *deal*?"

"There's something you're not saying," she said. "There's something . . ."

"There's something you're not saying either," he replied.

"Why won't you mention that we made out?"

"What am I supposed to say about it?" she said, her face flushing.

"Wow, you've got real blushing issues. You gotta work on that."

She tipped her head up angrily.

"What is it we are supposed to talk about?" she said. "Technique?"

"We could. I thought yours was good. You really like to explore with that tongue. Every part of you is a detective, I guess . . ."

"Okay," she said, turning to the door. "Good-bye."

"I annoy people," he said. "Believe me. I'm aware. It's an effective way to communicate if you don't have any other options. If you can't get in through the door, throw a rock through the window. And I think maybe you're the same way."

This grounded her for a moment. It made sense, and she was always willing to grant when someone else made sense. He left the door open and moved away from it. She went toward it hesitantly, pushed it open a bit more, and stepped inside. He was sitting on his bed.

"She comes in," he said.

Stevie tapped the doorframe nervously.

"I think maybe I'm embarrassing you by talking about what we did the other night," he said. "I actually don't want to embarrass you. That's not my goal. Maybe I'm more comfortable talking about that stuff. I guess there are some things I just don't give a shit about, for the right reasons. I can tell you I liked what we did."

Her wrists were throbbing. Her pulse was going to make her hands balloon up, maybe explode from the pressure.

"The fact is," he said, "I liked you from the first moment I saw you, when you looked like you wanted to punch me in the face for just being alive. That probably says something dark about me. And I think you like me because I annoy you. Both of us have real problems, but maybe we should make our weird personalities work for us."

Stevie had often wondered how these conversations worked, when people talked about *feelings* and *touching* and all of the stuff she thought was meant to be kept carefully bottled inside her own personal apothecary. Now someone wanted in, to take the lids off the vials, to peer at the contents. Stevie was unaware that people were even allowed to talk about emotions this frankly. This was not how things happened at home.

She shut the door. Her hand shook as she did it, but that didn't matter. She took the few, nervous steps to the bed and sat gingerly on the edge. Sitting on his bed. This was new, dangerous territory.

He didn't move.

"So?" she said. "What do we do?"

"What do you want to do?"

Her eyes were going in and out of focus. She moved over toward him and reached around, putting her hand on the back of his head and pulling him closer. She wondered if he would strain against her hand, if this was all wrong, but his head moved forward. She pressed her lips to his.

This time, the kissing was slow as they delicately balanced on the very knife edge of the bed. Their lips met and they would be together for a minute, then they would both stop and stay where they were for another few seconds, faces together, before doing it again. There was no pressure, no anxiety. It was like they were talking easily through the kisses. Her hand slid down his chest and she felt his heart beating hard. He was stroking her hair, running his fingers up the short strands. He leaned back against the bed, and Stevie rested on top of him gently.

And then, a knock.

"David?" Pix called.

Everything stopped dead. Reality came down with an audible thump. This could not happen again.

"Closet," David whispered.

Stevie found her legs were wobbly when she went to stand. She stumbled over to the closet and climbed in with a pile of shoes and bags and ski equipment, all jumbled and smelling (not overpoweringly, but still) of use, pants and shirts crowding her head. She shut the door, closing herself in. David greeted Pix.

"You need to go over to the Great House," she heard Pix say. "Nothing's wrong, Charles just needs to talk to you about—"

"It's fine," he said. "Sure. I'll come now. My coat's downstairs."

Quiet. They seemed to have gone.

Stevie crouched in the closet, her heart thumping, rumpled and a bit overheated, her breath coming fast. She slowed it down, turned on her phone for light, and shone it around the closet space. She looked at his shoes, picking them up, giving them the once-over. All had relatively unworn soles. Stevie had sneakers that had worn straight through the bottoms, and most of her shoes had scuffing to the toes, to the sides, little imperfections she either tried to hide or just accepted. These were new shoes. Replaced regularly. And all name brands. There were dress shoes in here, made of soft leather, with the name inside: ELLIS, OF LONDON. Tennis gear. Skis. Everything confirmed the diagnosis of well off, and not the son of a pilot and the manager of a fertilizer plant, probably. When she heard nothing outside the door, she crawled out of the closet and went to the door. No noise.

She was just in David's room. Alone.

There is a principle often discussed in murder mysteries. Agatha Christie even wrote a book with the title: *Murder Is Easy*. The idea is that the first time is the hardest, but once you transgress that barrier, once you take a life and get away with it, it becomes progressively easier each time. Stevie had yet to see anything in her reading that showed that this was necessarily true in real life, though it certainly seemed true that people may commit additional murders in a state of panic. Still, it logically held up. Murder is easy. And going through rooms is easy, especially if the owner of said room is someone who let you in and left you alone there.

And she had so many questions. Who was David, the David with no social media? The guy who kept telling weird lies about his family. The desire to know was like hunger, really—it rumbled, it demanded information.

Maybe she could just have a little look around? Just eyeball the place. There would be time. To walk over to the Great House, meet with Charles, come back—that was a minimum of twenty minutes, even if Charles said very little. And it was probably best she wait in here a minute or two anyway, just to make sure Pix was gone.

Just a little look around.

He had a video game system, lots of computer gear. Good speakers—Stevie had seen the brand advertised. Good headphones. Good everything. His books were haphazardly piled. Subjects: philosophy, game theory, lots of literature, books on how to write (interesting), graphic novels. There was an e-reader on the stand next to the bed. She flipped through the library contents: more graphic novels, lots of sci-fi (David liked a space opera, clearly), books about history. David was a reader. An avid one.

She put the e-reader back on the page it had been on when she picked it up and replaced it. She had a look at his bedside light: an Italian brand, another quality piece. Everything in his room was just a little bit better, from the weight and smoothness of his sheets (she sat down on the bed and gave them a feel; they smelled of him) to the heavy down comforter.

She allowed herself to rest back on the bed for a moment.

What else was in plain view? Police could look at things in plain view when they came inside with no warrant. The room was clean. Not *tidy*, but generally clean. An effort had been made to keep things in the right place. There was one old Led Zeppelin poster, but Stevie got the impression that it had just been put up as a kind of non-decorating. Get the first object you see, stick it up. The vast majority of the room was a blank canvas, without photos or decorations.

She leaned back and her hand struck something hard. She reached into the sheets and pulled out his laptop.

His laptop, just sitting there.

She looked it over for a moment. No stickers, no markings. She put her hands on the edge of the computer.

To open or . . .

The thing about looking just a little bit means it's really easy to look a little bit more. Once you've touched it, well, you've touched it, and if you have the computer in your lap and you open it and a screen comes up, there you are.

Maybe this was what Pandora felt like when she got her famous box. Open it and the light pours out . . .

"What the hell are you doing?"

Everything stopped for a moment. How he had come upstairs without her hearing him was unknown. She must have been too into what she was doing—of course, what she was doing was going through his computer.

Answering his question would have been self-incriminating, so Stevie sat there, still and silent. Still things can sometimes appear invisible.

"What," David said again, "are you doing?"

"I was just . . ."

He came over and put his hands out for the computer. She passed it over.

"I . . . didn't even look."

"It seems like you did," he said.

Well, yeah. It did. He was right. Stevie felt her defenses snap back into place.

"What's the big secret?" she snapped back. "You've met my family. You just got in the car and came along. You've had a look at me."

"And you wanted a look," he said. "Did it ever occur to you there's a reason I don't want to talk about my family?"

"We all have reasons," she said. "You're not special in having a weird time with your parents."

"My parents are dead," he said. "Does that count as special?"

One time, when she was little, Stevie was outside playing on a cold day. She caught some speed on a patch of ice and went, full speed, into a wall. As her abdomen made contact, she remembered the feeling of all the air being violently forced out of her body, scraping her throat as it exited.

It sort of felt like that now. The angles had come back into David's features, and something else.

Hurt.

"Just get out," he said.

"I . . ."

"Get out," he said quietly.

FEDERAL BUREAU OF INVESTIGATION INTERVIEW BETWEEN AGENT SAMUEL ARNOLD AND ROBERT MACKENZIE APRIL 17, 1936, 7:10 P.M. LOCATION: ELLINGHAM PROPERTY

SA: *Just a few more questions, Mr. Mackenzie. We have to go through these things several times.*

RM: *I understand.*

SA: *When did you start working for Albert Ellingham?*

RM: *When I left Princeton, eight years ago.*

SA: *And you are his personal assistant in business matters?*

RM: *Correct. I am his personal business secretary.*

SA: *So you see quite a number of Mr. Ellingham's transactions.*

RM: *I see nearly all of them, if not all.*

SA: *Do you find it odd, running the business from up here in this mountain location?*

RM: *I don't think any of us expected to be here this long.*

SA: *What do you mean?*

RM: *The school was just another project. Mr. Ellingham has a lot of projects. It seemed like he was planning for this to be a retreat, maybe to be used a few weeks in the summer. But he's been here since September. We all seemed to be waiting for him to say, "All right! Back to New York." But it never happened. We were here all winter. Do you have any idea what winters are like up here?*

SA: *Cold, I'd imagine.*

RM: *Half the time you can't leave the house for all the snow. The locals don't seem to mind, but everyone else had wild cabin fever. Mrs. Ellingham . . .*

[*Pause.*]

SA: *What about her?*

RM: *Mrs. Ellingham is lively. She likes society and athletics. She did some skiing, but that wasn't enough. You could see it wearing on her.*

SA: *Did this cause friction between Mr. and Mrs. Ellingham?*

[*Silence.*]

SA: *I know you feel a sense of loyalty, but there are things we have to know.*

RM: *I realize that. Yes, maybe a bit. They are very different people. A loving couple, of course, but very different people. I think being up here has been hard on her at times. She has Miss Robinson to keep her company. That seems to help.*

SA: *They're close?*

RM: *Like sisters.*

SA: *And what is Mr. Nair like?*

RM: *Mr. Nair is a brilliant artist and an inebriate.*

SA: *A frequent drinker?*

RM: *Often and in high quantities. I once watched him drink an entire case of champagne by himself. I was surprised he didn't die.*

SA: *Is he aggressive in that condition?*

RM: *On the contrary, he usually just paints or talks and eventually we find him somewhere on the grounds, asleep. The students once pulled him out of the fountain. If you're asking if he's capable of arranging a kidnapping, I don't think Leonard Holmes Nair is capable of arranging breakfast. This was organized.*

SA: *You're an organized man.*

RM: *Which is why I know organization when I see it. I'm professionally dull, Agent Arnold. It's why I was hired. I'm a foil to Mr. Ellingham's exuberance.*

SA: *It sounds like you're sensible. On the night of the thirteenth, you advocated calling the police.*

RM: *And I regret I didn't do it, even though I was told not to.*

SA: *You obeyed orders.*

RM: *I obeyed orders.*

SA: *Can you tell me about the letter that was received on April eighth, the Truly Devious letter? What did you make of it?*

RM: *We get, on average, two or three threats a day in with the regular correspondence. The vast majority of it is nonsense and a lot of it from the same people. At first, this one struck me as a bit of a joke.*

SA: *Why a joke?*

RM: *The cutout letters. The poem. But then I noticed a few things. I noticed it was postmarked from Burlington. And then I noticed the address. You see, Mr. Ellingham has business correspondence from all around the country. As I'm sure you can imagine, mail delivery here is difficult. So we have all business correspondence directed to an office in Burlington, and we have it delivered by car every day, weather providing. If the weather is too bad, we have a secretary there who can read it to me over the telephone. What was unusual was that the letter didn't come to any of the business addresses—that's where most of the abusive mail goes to. It was addressed here, to this house. This one seemed much more personal.*

SA: *But you didn't show it to George Marsh.*

RM: *I was going to. But there was a great deal going on over the weekend. I was going to show him the next time he came by.*

SA: *So there was a party over the weekend?*

RM: *For Maxine Melville, yes.*

SA: *Did you attend?*

RM: *Only in the sense that I was in the house. I was very busy finalizing the paperwork on an important deal Mr. Ellingham has been working on. He's purchasing a newspaper in Philadelphia.*

SA: *Was there anything out of the ordinary about the weekend or Monday morning?*

RM: *Absolutely nothing. We went to Burlington on Monday morning to do some business and send some cables. We* came back in the evening.

SA: *Let's talk about this house and the school. Did you feel this location was insecure?*

RM: *Absolutely, considering the threats and the attempted bombing.*

SA: *Did you speak to your employer about this?*

RM: *I tried.*

SA: *You seem like a smart man, Mr. Mackenzie. Your instincts were always to reach out to law enforcement. You have your eyes open. Where do you feel Iris and Alice Ellingham and Dolores Epstein might be?*

RM: *Nowhere good. To be honest with you, I think . . .*

SA: *Yes?*

RM: *I hate to say the words, Agent Arnold. I think that letter was from the kidnappers and Truly Devious meant every word on that page. I think they're dead. God help me, I think they're all dead.*

[*Interview terminated 7:32 p.m.*]

24

ONCE UPON A TIME, A YOUNG GIRL NAMED DOTTIE FROM NEW YORK City came to Ellingham Academy and ended up dead from a knock on the head.

Once upon another time, an actor from Florida came to Ellingham Academy and found out dry ice was not so nice.

Third time's the charm. A girl from Pittsburgh came to Ellingham Academy and she wanted to see a dead body.

She got her wish.

That same girl snatched victory from the jaws of defeat and got to stay at Ellingham Academy, but then, worried that defeat might be hungry, promptly fed the victory right back to its gaping jaws. That girl had a taste of something she didn't know that she wanted or needed, and she had messed it all up.

And life went on.

Ellingham mourned and was counseled. There was an informal memorial in the cupola on the green, where people left candles and pictures and a small zombie doll. There were letters and phone calls from Charles and the other members of the board. Security tightened. Everyone's passes were checked and upgraded. Curfew became a real thing, and rooms were checked and grounds patrolled. It wasn't that anyone forgot about Hayes's death—the subject was constantly talked about—it was just something that had happened. It was part of reality.

Though the investigation was not yet formally closed, information was made available to reassure everyone. Hayes seemed to have died in an accident of his own making. Hayes, a person known to make videos in dark corners, took something that didn't belong to him. His fingerprints were on Janelle's ID and the golf cart used to move the dry ice, and a hand truck. This was, it was pretty clear to everyone, a case of Hayes really messing up. And he had stolen property as well. He had gone to great lengths to break rules, so his parents could hardly sue.

The common wisdom was that Hayes had gone into the tunnel to film something new for *The End of It All*. Hence going back alone. Hence the secret. He'd seen the dry ice, looked in the tunnel, and had an idea that put it all together. He just put it together very badly.

It was back to piles of books and anatomy labs and essays. Something called the Silent Party was scheduled—a dance with no sound or something. It was going to be in the Great House. That would pass as entertainment. Back to school. Because that was what Ellingham was, a school. Stevie tried to do this, but found her concentration was broken. She couldn't finish her reading, couldn't write her essays.

The weather turned resolutely gray. Mountains are not kind when the season turns. The leaves on the trees started to turn gold and red at the tips and a few overachievers made the trip to the ground.

David did not talk to her.

He was over Stevie's head, literally. She heard his steps, but that was about all she heard from him. He made himself scarce from the common room and the kitchen, and if he and Stevie crossed paths, he looked away.

She would open books, stare at a page, and realize she hadn't taken anything in. Then she would read it again, the words slipping in the front door and out the back. There were essays to write that never got past the note stage. There was some leeway in all of this because of recent events, but the leeway was not going to go on forever.

None of this escaped the attention of Janelle, who finally hooked Stevie by the arm and pulled her into her room and sat her on the bed.

"Are you going to tell me what the hell happened with the two of you?" Janelle said.

"What?"

"You and David," Janelle said.

Stevie blinked.

"Do you think we don't know?" Janelle said. "Everyone knows. There is nothing in the world as obvious as the two of you. So what happened?"

"We made out," Stevie said.

"Yeah, I got that. And then what?"

Shame is a terrible thing. Janelle would never go through Vi's room. Sure, Vi wasn't a lying weirdo, but even if she was, Janelle wouldn't do that. Janelle had standards. Janelle was loyal. Whereas Stevie was a cretinous person who had no principles.

Janelle waited for a reply, and when she realized none was forthcoming, Stevie saw a light go out in her eyes.

This left Nate and Ellie.

Ellie's reaction to Hayes's death was to go maximum Ellie. Minerva was woken in the morning by the terrifying cries of Roota. When painted makeup appeared on the Minerva gargoyles and some of the statues, it was fairly obvious who the culprit was. There was more drinking and bathing and French poetry.

Which left Nate, and Nate had retreated to the misty mountains in his mind. He was always reading now, turning away from every conversation, frequently eating alone. Stevie found him in the dining hall at one of the small, high-top tables, his face buried in a copy of *The Earthsea Trilogy* and his fork working a plate of turkey meatballs and pasta.

Stevie pulled up a chair and slid over her tray of lasagna and salad with maple dressing, because she had given up fighting the maple syrup.

"Hey," she said.

Nate peered out of his book.

"Hey," he said.

She waited for him to put the book down. It took him a moment to get the hint. He put a napkin carefully between the pages as a bookmark. Nate didn't press books facedown and ruin their spines.

"Talk to me about writing," Stevie said.

"Why do you hate me?" he replied.

"Seriously. Tell me about it."

"Tell you what?" he said. "You write. That's it."

"But how do you do it?" she said. "Do you just sit down and write? Do you have to plan first? Do you just write whatever comes into your head?"

"Is someone paying you to do this to me?"

"It's just . . . remember that first day when we were talking about zombies? And Hayes had no idea what the Monroeville Mall was?"

"Yeah?"

"That was weird," she said.

He waited for her to explain what she was saying, but she had no explanation. Nate returned to his book and meatballs.

"It's like Truly Devious," she said after a moment.

Nate looked up with tired eyes, but he still looked up.

"What about it?"

"The person they arrested for the Ellingham murders," she said. "Anton Vorachek. He could never have written that letter. His English was too rough. Anyway, who announces they're going to commit a murder?"

"Pretty much every serial killer," Nate said.

"Very few serial killers do that," Stevie corrected him. "The Zodiac was one of the only . . ."

"In movies," he said. "In books."

"Here's another thing," Stevie said, warming to the topic. "There's an old mystery riddle. A man is found hanging in an empty room, locked from the inside. There is no chair, nothing for him to stand on. How did it happen?"

"Stood on a block of ice," Nate said. "Everyone knows that one."

"Right," Stevie said. "It's just like the one about someone being found stabbed to death in a locked room and there's no weapon. The weapon was an icicle. It's so well known that no one can use that device in mystery stories. It's like saying the butler did it, but worse. It can never be ice."

"Yeah, well, this isn't a mystery story."

"Don't you wonder what Hayes was doing in the tunnel?"

"We know what he was doing," Nate said. "He was making a video or something."

"That's what everyone thinks he was doing."

"What else would he have been doing there? No one else was down there with him, and even if they were, you don't bring a few hundred pounds of dry ice along to make out. I'm not up to date on my kinks but I don't think that's one."

Stevie sat back and picked at her lasagna. She looked around the dining hall. She saw Gretchen coming in—rather, she saw Gretchen's hair, but Gretchen was with her hair.

Of all the people here, Gretchen possibly knew Hayes the best. She had been with him last year, definitely longer than Maris. And out of everyone at the school, she looked the most consistently shell-shocked. Maris was getting the sympathy, but Gretchen genuinely looked caved in. Stevie watched her at the counter getting a salad in a to-go box.

"Writing is a lot of sitting down," Nate said, finally answering the question. "It's a lot of trying things out and screwing up. You saw it when we worked on the script."

"But we used things that existed," Stevie said. "What if you're totally making it up?"

"It's either amazing or it's the worst thing in the world," he said. "Sometimes it goes well, and it's all you think about, and then, it's gone. It's like you're taking a ride down a river really fast, and then all of a sudden, there's no water. You're just sitting in a raft, trying to push it along in the mud. And then you've become me."

"But you seem to be writing now," she said.

"Yeah, and if I talk about it, it will all go away."

He had finished talking, leaving Stevie with her thoughts. Her thoughts would not settle. The more she was alone with them, the more they whistled and spun.

There was no point in trying to eat. Stevie composted the remains of her dinner and went back outside, loosely trailing Gretchen. She headed back to the art barn, and Stevie followed. Once inside, she lost track of Gretchen, but a few moments later she heard thunderous piano playing coming from one of the rooms. Stevie peered along the hall until she saw Gretchen at one of the pianos. She played wildly, percussing against the elements themselves. She wore tight athletic clothing to play, sort of like something dancers might wear—black tights, ballet-style slippers, a tunic top that tied at the waist.

Stevie knocked at the window and Gretchen stopped playing abruptly. Stevie stepped into the practice room. She hadn't planned what to say. Luckily, Gretchen spoke first.

"You were with Hayes the other night," she said. "You're Stevie, right?"

"Yeah," Stevie said. "Sorry. I heard you playing and . . . could I talk to you?"

"Weren't you the one who found him?" Gretchen said.

"I didn't find him. I was just there when they did."

Gretchen nodded absently and looked at her salad container on the floor. She hadn't touched it.

"The other day," Stevie said, "I walked in on you guys talking . . ."

"Yeah," Gretchen said. "Not a great last conversation to have. I was pissed."

"I know you dated him," Stevie said. "And I know you broke up. But I'm sorry."

"Sorry?" Gretchen said. "Yeah. It's weird, being the ex-girlfriend of the guy who dies. You're actually the first person who's said sorry."

"Can I ask you about Hayes?" Stevie said, sliding in and sitting on the floor.

"What about Hayes?" Gretchen said.

"I just . . . I'm confused after what happened, and I feel like maybe if I knew more about him, I wouldn't be."

Gretchen considered this for a moment.

"You know what I am?" she said. "I'm pissed. I'm pissed

that I can't be pissed at him. It's like he's done it again."

"Done what again?" Stevie said.

"Played me," she said, shaking her head. "I feel stupid. And if I ever say anything bad about him, I'll be a monster. And I don't know what to do with that."

"I don't think it makes you a monster to tell the truth about someone."

"It does if that person dies in a weird, tragic accident."

"What was it he took from you that he wasn't giving back?" Stevie asked. "That thing I walked in on?"

"Oh," she said. "He borrowed five hundred dollars from me in the spring. That five hundred was money I got from teaching piano at a summer camp. It was pretty much all the cash I had. I wanted it back when we got back to school this year. I know he made money off that show. He's been promising to pay it back, but I don't think that was ever going to happen. You know, like . . ."

She shook her head and wiped away a tear quickly.

"God," she said. "Why am I crying? I'm so mad."

Stevie looked away as Gretchen settled herself.

"Hayes was one of those people who seemed like he had it all together," Gretchen said, wiping her face. "He could act; that's how he got in. But inside? There was no *there* there. People did things for him because he was handsome, and he has—had—that voice. You'd do him favors. You know when you like someone. You do dumb stuff. You do stuff you know makes no sense."

Up until very recently, Stevie would not have known

that. But now she had a pretty good sense of it. Maybe you go through their stuff, for instance.

"I was just *so* into him," Gretchen said. "But last year . . . he used me. Like, really used me. First, he asked for a little help with his paper on Jonathan Swift. He asked me to read it, maybe make some edits. So I did that. Then he was doing a production of *The Glass Menagerie* and he was busy, and he said he didn't have time to write an essay on Dryden, and would I help him out by just finishing a little of it? Then I was doing some of his French units so it looked like he was working on that. Then, one day, he asked me to write his ten-page midterm on Alexander Pope, and I realized just how much of Hayes's work I had done.

"When I said no to that, he was annoyed at first, but then he was all apologies. He said he knew he'd asked too much. Everything went back to normal. Later, when we had broken up, I found out I wasn't the only one doing his work. He met people online, other people around school. There were probably four or five of us doing everything for Hayes. Four or five of us."

Gretchen sniffed for a moment.

"There was a week or two in there I thought I loved him," she said. "When Hayes turned it on, it was *on*. But then things got bad. One night, we were all sneaking off campus to go to some party in Burlington. Ellie Walker had a few of her burlesque friends drive up along the back road with their lights off. We slipped out and were meeting them. There's a spot where the cameras don't work that well and if you time it right, you can get out. But it happened that some grounds guy was working out there that night because there was a report of a bear. He had a car on the road and was keeping watch and he caught us. The guy said he was going to report us. Hayes said to him, 'Wouldn't it be terrible if they found pot in your car? What if you got busted for dealing to students?' The guy looked terrified, and Hayes smiled and said, 'Just kidding.'"

"Seriously?" Stevie said. That was a side of Hayes she had not seen.

"Seriously. That was when I should have been done. I should have turned and gone back to my house. Ellie was so mad at him for that. She smacked him on the back of the head on the way to Burlington and yelled at him, told him that was no way to treat people. Hayes said sorry. Hayes always said sorry. He said it was a joke, but . . . you don't get to say that, you know? You don't get to frighten people and threaten them and say you're only kidding. Because you're not."

A picture was developing, and it was not a pretty one.

"That guy, the security guy?" Gretchen said. "He left, maybe three weeks later. I don't know why. I always wondered. That was it for me. I broke up with Hayes. It was on April first, so I think he thought I was kidding. I wasn't. He took it really well. A little too well. He said he understood. Everything was good for a day or two, and then he texted me and said he wanted to talk for a minute, nothing serious. Could I meet him in the art barn? So I did. Once

I was there, he suddenly goes into this whole *performance*. He starts saying how much he loved me and how he can't believe I cheated. I mean, it was Oscar-worthy and it came out of nowhere. I didn't cheat on him. He kept saying all this stuff I'd supposedly done, all made up. And there were lots of people in the room next door, so everyone heard it. When he was done, he nodded to the wall and smiled at me and wiped his fake tears. He was trying to get me back by making me look like a villain. He already had someone else lined up, by the way. Beth. That girl he hooked up with in Chicago? That was already going on."

She stopped for a moment and shook her head.

"This is why I can't talk about it," she said. "No one wants to hear this about a guy who died."

Stevie let this statement linger for a moment. A new idea popped into her head—suddenly she had the words for something that had been eating at her thoughts.

"Do you think he wrote his show?" she said.

Gretchen looked over in confusion.

"What, the zombie thing?" she said. "Definitely not."

Stevie didn't expect such a firm answer to a question that had just come into her head.

"I told you," Gretchen said. "He didn't do his own work."

"He told me he wrote it," Stevie said.

Gretchen gave her a *what did I say* face.

"Sorry to bother you," Stevie said, getting off the floor.

"Are you with David Eastman?" Gretchen asked as Stevie was about to leave.

Stevie gulped.

"No," she said after a moment.

"Oh. I thought you were. I was going to say, good luck with *that*."

Stevie wanted to ask what this meant, but Gretchen had turned back to the piano and began playing again. It was passionate and powerful, the music drumming out of her furious hands.

25

STEVIE'S HEAD WAS THRUMMING AS SHE MADE HER WAY BACK TO Minerva. That was what was bothering her. What if Hayes hadn't written *The End of It All*? What did that mean?

Well, for a start, that movie he was talking about—that could have gotten kind of complicated.

When she arrived home, she found Pix opening a number of boxes in the common room.

"What are those for?" she asked.

"Hayes's things," Pix said quietly. "His parents have asked me to box up his room so they wouldn't have to do it. It's the least I can do."

There was a key on the table with a cardboard tag hanging off it that said *6*. The key to Hayes's room.

"Are you doing that tonight?" Stevie said.

"Tonight, tomorrow," Pix said. "I have a meeting in half an hour and I'll probably start afterward. Are you okay?"

"Yeah," Stevie said. "Fine."

Back in her room, Stevie considered this development. Hayes's things would be gone soon. Which meant information would be gone. Not that she needed information. It's just that something . . . something . . . something was wrong. And the answers to what was wrong might be up in his room. For example, maybe there was an answer about *The End of It All?*

What would that give her, though?

Stevie paced. She walked around the room, staring at the edge of her case board peering out from under her bed. No good had come of her looking in rooms upstairs, but . . .

Stevie returned to the common room.

"You know," she said to Pix, "I feel like I need to help. Can I put together these boxes?"

"Sure," Pix said. "Sure. That would be great, Stevie."

Stevie smiled the smile of the lying and took Pix's seat at the table. The key to Minerva Six was next to her.

"I'll head off," Pix said, grabbing her field jacket from the hook by the door and covering her peach-fuzz head with a woolen hat. "You're sure you're okay?"

"I'm fine," Stevie said. "It's just good to have a project."

"I get that," Pix said. "Back soon."

As soon as she was gone, Stevie took the key.

❧

Hayes's room was dark when Stevie let herself in. The curtain was drawn. There was a towel hanging on the back of the door. She set this by the crack at the bottom of the door to keep light from escaping, in case anyone came by. She slipped her shoes off to lessen the sound of her steps on the floor, then stepped gently across the room to Hayes's desk, turned on the desk light, swiveled Hayes's chair toward the center of the room, and sat down.

Yes, she was going through another room. But her reasons were good, and that was what mattered. She was here because something about Hayes's death was bothering her, and Hayes couldn't do anything to help himself.

That sounded like a good excuse.

The first step was to take in the scene—not looking for anything in particular. Just to take it in, as it was. She allowed herself to gently spin in the chair, getting a panoramic view.

This was how Hayes left things in his life. He had come to his room to prepare for the show. His bed appeared to have been made, but then disturbed. The top blanket was twisted and pulled up. Hayes's desk was a dumping ground for all kinds of things—computer, hair products, cables, camera, microphone, piles of fan mail and fan art. There was a bag from a bookstore sitting on the desk shelf. Stevie picked this up and pulled out the contents. Four books on acting, all apparently unread, a receipt sticking out of the top of one of them. The books had been purchased at a store in New York on August 26, just a few days before Hayes went back to school. There was another bag of books on the floor. These were all plays: David Mamet. Sam Shepard. Tony Kushner. Tom Stoppard. Arthur Miller. Shakespeare.

"What a dudely selection," she said to herself. She ran a finger along the spines for cracking or signs of use. There were none.

Into the desk drawers. The first one contained sticky notes, packs of good-quality pens, three Moleskine note-books. With the exception of one notebook and one pack of pens, all were still wrapped, and only one pen had been removed. The next drawer, a bigger one, contained mostly cables. The last drawer was empty.

She made her way around the room clockwise. The bureau was piled with bath and styling products, all in dis-array. She had a brief look in the drawers. She examined a drawer of colorful boxers. She pushed these to the side, looked for anything underneath. Nothing remarkable. The same went for a drawer of T-shirts, another of socks. Around to the closet, which was already partially open. His clothes all looked fairly new, all normal labels like J. Crew and Aber-crombie & Fitch. Mall brands, but the more expensive ones.

On the mantel were several containers of Ben Nye stage makeup—most still open, with powder spilled onto the black surface. There was silver-gray hair liquid, buff powder, spirit gum, bone wax, latex, pancake base, pencils of various colors, blood capsules, used sponges and brushes, and weird little pieces of fake skin. A comb was stained silver from the hair treatment. There was a kit on the floor that looked like a tackle box that had even more makeup inside. It was all messy, but it was professional.

The fan art—that was the main feature of the room. It took up two walls. Stevie examined it all under the tiny glow of her phone flashlight. Most of it was drawings of Hayes as Logan. So many drawings. Some in black-and-white pencil, some in color. Some were rough and amateur, but some were of a very high quality. There were also letters, poems, photos of Hayes with fans, hearts, cards . . . every variety of paper communication was there. The larger objects were on the floor or the fireplace—stuffed animals, cross-stitch, a model of the *End of It All* set with a tiny Hayes in clay.

Hayes's room was, in short, a tribute to Hayes. Riddle, riddle, on the wall, who's most famous of them all?

She took pictures of it all, starting in one corner of the room and working section by section. It took about half an hour to do it all. By the end, she had a fairly clear picture of someone who was interested in the business of being Hayes.

Stevie turned her attention to Hayes's computer. The top had a thick patina of stickers—again, mostly for Hayes's show, but a few for online channels and skiing. There was a scrape down the front as well. Hayes hadn't been too careful with the laptop, clearly. There were very few files on the computer. One was marked IDEAS. She opened up a text document that simply read:

> Summer camp that trains killers
> Camp that trains spies
> Spies who
> Camp?
> A world where you can

The list ended here.

"I think Hayes was out of ideas," she said to herself.

She did a search on his computer for files related to *The End of It All*. There were loads of emails, but only a few video files—one long one and lots of short ones of similar size, as if the long one had been cut up. The main one was dated June 4, and the others June 9–14.

A quick Web search revealed that *The End of It All* had been released twice a week, starting on June 20. There were ten episodes in total. June 20, June 23, June 27, June 30, July 4, July 7, July 11, July 14, July 18, July 21. A quick check of last year's schedule showed that Ellingham's move-out day was June 6.

The main file had been made on June 4.

It was made here.

I went home to Florida last year, surfed for a few days, and it just came to me . . .

"No, it didn't," Stevie said aloud.

So why say it was? Why lie about *where* you made it?

There was a voice outside. Stevie froze in position. It wasn't outside, though. It was coming through the wall, and it sounded angry.

David's voice. She couldn't make out what he was saying, so she set the computer aside and crept over to the wall. She could still only make out a mumble, and then one shouted word: "Allison!"

"Who is Allison?" Stevie whispered to herself.

She felt an anxiety rumble. Allison. A girlfriend? A real one? Not some idiot at school. Allison instantly developed a face, an entire profile. She had long hair and a surfboard.

347

She looked good in shorts. She got waxings. She laughed in her sleep.

Stevie slapped herself gently on the forehead to make it stop and continued to try to listen, but all had gone silent on the other side of the wall. Now it was just her and her thudding heart in Hayes's room.

Pix would be back soon. Stevie shut off Hayes's computer and tucked it back where she'd found it. She turned off the light, picked up her shoes, and returned the towel to the door. Then, after making sure there was no noise in the hall or coming from David's room, she cracked open the door.

The hall was empty.

She slipped out, shutting the door quietly behind her. She got all the way to the steps when she heard a door open behind her. She turned to see David looking at her.

"Hey," she said.

He didn't reply. Nor did he seem to know that she had just come from Hayes's room.

"Come on," she said. "Say something. You can't not talk to me forever. We live together."

"Something," he said. But there was no humor in his voice.

"How about this," she said. "Can you listen? You don't have to talk. I'll keep it short. Will that work?"

David considered this for a moment, then shrugged.

"Can I come in for two seconds?" she said.

He indicated his door was open, and then went back

inside. Stevie steadied herself, then followed.

David did not sit down. He stood in the middle of his room, his arms folded.

"What?" he said.

"I want to say I'm sorry."

"Fine," he said.

Then, nothing.

"I'm sorry," she said again.

"Fine. If that's it, you can go."

"Seriously?" she said. The anger was building up again. All the feeling she had been pressing down for a few days shot up unexpectedly. "Come on. You won't tell me anything about yourself. You lied at dinner."

"I made a joke at dinner because I didn't feel like talking about my dead parents."

"I'm the worst. I know I am. But I'm also sorry. You don't know how sorry."

"Why are you holding your shoes?" he said.

Stevie had forgotten about the shoes.

"I just took them off," she said.

He tilted his head to the side and looked at her for a long minute. She had an idea, which was probably a terrible idea. But lacking any other ideas, it was the one to go with. Radical honesty. Just tell him. Open up.

"I was in Hayes's room," she said.

He burst out laughing, but again, there was no humor in it.

349

"I know how that sounds," she said, talking over him, "but I had a key. Listen to me. I had to go. Pix was about to box it up and everything would be gone."

"And you just needed a few more minutes with his memory?"

"Something weird is going on," she said. "I can't put my finger on what it is. . . ."

"I think I can," he said. "There's someone in this house who keeps going through other people's stuff. Someone should do something about it."

That hurt. She felt her eyes sting.

"So why did you have to go in there?" he asked. "Do you have to get into every room in this hall? Is that your thing?"

"Hayes didn't write *The End of It All*," she said.

"Says who?"

"Says common sense. I worked on a show with him. He never did anything. And someone else did all of his school-work last year. And there is nothing on his computer that shows he did any of it or that he had any ability to write something new. And his ex-girlfriend thinks . . ."

"Gretchen," David said, rolling his eyes.

"Gretchen," Stevie replied.

"Gretchen was pissed at him. She broke up with him. It was a whole drama last year."

"Hayes played everyone," Stevie said. "Hayes used everyone. Hayes did none of his own work but took the benefits. And then Hayes dies doing the project that would have allowed him to go off to LA and reap the benefits of everyone else's labor. Doesn't it sound unlikely that Hayes would have gone to all that effort to do something that *doesn't even make any sense?*"

"So what are you saying?" he asked. "Are you saying someone did it on purpose? That someone *murdered* Hayes?"

The words were surreal said out loud. Hayes. Murdered.

"No," she said, staggered by the idea. "No . . . like, an accident. Some kind of plan to screw up the filming."

Now that the word had been introduced, it bounced around the hallways in Stevie's head. Murder requires motive, and there was plenty of motive. For a start, all the people Hayes was dating and screwing over and using, the fact that he didn't write his show, but he was about to get credit for it and make a whole lot of money. That was all very solid motive.

Murder? Was that what she really thought this was? Was this the reason she felt so restless?

"You know what's weird?" David said as Stevie was lost in thought. "What's weird is making a hobby out of the death of your classmate. You know what's also weird? Going through people's rooms, including the room of your dead classmate. Because you seem crazy."

People might be dismissive of someone obsessed with mystery stories, as if the line between fiction and reality was so distinct. They didn't know, perhaps, that Sherlock Holmes was based on a real man, Dr. Joseph Bell, and that the methods Arthur Conan Doyle created for his fictional detective inspired generations of real-world detectives. Did they know that Arthur Conan Doyle went on to investigate mysteries in his real life and even absolved a man of a crime for which he had been convicted? Did they know how Agatha Christie brilliantly staged her own disappearance in order to exact an elegant revenge on a cheating husband?

They probably did not.

And no one was going to discount Stevie Bell, who had gotten into this school on the wings of her interest in the Ellingham case, and who had been a bystander at a death that was now looking more and more suspicious.

She was not crazy. And Hayes's key was in her pocket and Pix was on her way back.

Stevie turned away and left David's room without saying anything else. Because she was also not going to let him see her cry.

THE BATT REPORT
Internet Star Dies in School Accident

Hayes Major, star of the summer's viral internet sensation *The End of It All*, died on Saturday night. Major, a student at the Ellingham Academy, was filming a video about the Ellingham kidnapping and murder case. He was found unresponsive in a disused tunnel that had recently been unearthed. The cause of his death was not immediately evident, but sources close to The Batt Report say that he died of asphyxia in what was likely an accident. Police have determined that Major removed a quantity of dry ice from the school's workshop and maintenance area using a pass stolen from another student, most likely to produce a fog effect for the video. Left overnight, the dry ice melted in the contained underground space, filling the room with a lethal level of carbon dioxide.

The head of Ellingham Academy, Dr. Charles Scott, released a statement on Tuesday morning: "All of us at Ellingham Academy are heartbroken by the loss of Hayes Major, a promising actor and creator, and a beloved friend. Our hearts go out to his family, his friends, and his many fans. His loss is profound."

26

"MY NAME IS LOGAN BANFIELD," HAYES SAID. "AND I DON'T KNOW where I am. I don't know if anyone can hear me. I don't know what happened. I don't know if I'm alone. I don't even know if I'm dead or alive."

Stevie sat cross-legged on the floor of the Great House attic watching *The End of It All* and counting doorknobs. Two days had passed since Hayes's things had gone away, since she had confronted David. For those two days, she was supposed to have resumed working, resumed studying. The pile of books next to her bed didn't read themselves, and the essay she was supposed to hand in tomorrow remained unwritten, despite the number of times she opened up her computer and stared blankly at the screen before watching *The End of It All* again.

Each episode of *The End of It All* was about ten minutes in length. She started from the beginning, from the very first moments when Hayes's character woke up, confused as to what was happening. All of it was filmed in the same location, some kind of bunker, except for the very last minutes.

A lot of the show was rambling, reacting, listening. In some episodes, Logan got memories back of the zombie attack. In others, he found communications from possible survivors. It was all standard zombie apocalypse stuff. What made it popular, Stevie guessed, was just that Hayes was so intense. And good-looking. He was a good-looking guy hiding from zombies and slowly losing his grip on reality. In the last episode, Logan left his bunker. Was he being saved, or was he giving up?

Over and over she watched. And now she watched from row 39 of the Great House attic, which contained small household items, antiquated light fittings, boxes of hammers, cans of screws. And these doorknobs. This house had a lot of spare doorknobs.

Just a girl and her doorknobs and zombies.

Stevie had spent most of these last two days tuning out everything to the exclusion of these things. And now, as evening came and her stomach rumbled, she pulled out her earbuds. She couldn't watch it again.

She got up and looked through the box of Albert Ellingham's desk contents again, until she got to the Western Union slip with the last riddle.

Where do you look for someone who's never really there?
Always on a staircase but never on a stair

She leaned against the metal racks for a moment and stared at the slip under the green fluorescent glow. Someone who's never really there was sort of how Gretchen had described Hayes. *There was no* there *there.*

Always on a staircase but never on a stair could mean a lot of things. A rail. Something on the wall. The cracks between the stairs.

Albert Ellingham wasn't coming back to tell her the answer to this riddle.

That musk of aged things was present, but the atmosphere had climate and humidity control, so instead of being stale and hard, there was a sweetness to the attic. The rich even decayed well.

Stevie set the little slip of paper on the ground and looked up at the shelves around her.

What the hell did it all mean? So what if he didn't write it? What the hell was she doing, avoiding work and people and life to sit in an attic, staring at Hayes, counting dates and sorting doorknobs? She could work on that essay that was due, oh, tomorrow. She could . . .

What? Try to talk to David again? That had gone well.

She put the doorknobs back in their box. As she pushed the box back into position, she scraped her hand on the shelf above it. A thin trickle of blood came from the cut.

"You're an idiot," she said to herself. Once finished, she trudged down the steps of the Great House, her backpack hanging low. Larry sat at his station by the door, carefully going through something in a binder. She was going to walk right past without saying anything, but as she made the door, he called out to her.

"Not even a hello?" he said.

"Sorry," she said. "I was distracted."

"I see that. About what?"

She shook her head. He tipped back his chair and considered her for a moment.

"How's it been going?" he asked.

"It's going," she said.

"You don't seem too enthused."

"No," she said. "I'm not."

"Well, come sit down, then."

Even though she didn't feel like it, an order from Larry was still an order from Larry. She went to the chair in front of his desk and sat in it, perched on the edge so her backpack could fit and so she could get up quickly.

"Any new thoughts on the Ellingham case?"

"I haven't had much of a chance to think about it," she said.

"Well, if you want to solve a cold case, that's what you've got to do. You don't avoid the work. Cold cases get solved because someone goes to the trouble of doing everything. They read every file. They listen to every tape. They talk to every witness. They track down every scrap of evidence. And then they do it all again; they do it until something clicks, until it gets warm again. You do the work. And sometimes, you get lucky."

"How much of it is luck?" Stevie said.

"Luck always plays a role. Something is eating at you."

"Just school," she said.

"No," he said. "I don't think it's just school. I think it has something to do with Hayes Major. Something is eating at you and it's not grief. Something else."

"You don't know that."

"Twenty years as a detective. I do know that."

Stevie pushed back into the chair a bit and squared off to Larry.

"Can you just tell me what you know about his death and what happened?" she said.

"You mean, details?"

"Yeah."

"I can't give you all of them," he said. "I can give you a few. There was a lot of dry ice taken. There were ten units in that container, ten inches square in there, and seven of them were gone. Each one of those squares weighed over fifty pounds. We found Hayes's fingerprints on Janelle's ID and on a golf cart. Janelle's ID tapped into the art barn at 1:12 a.m. We found the container the dry ice was moved in. We know Hayes went into the art barn when you were in your yoga class. We know from testing that the dry ice was in that space for about eighteen hours and that the level of carbon dioxide in the room was extremely high. It's lucky we weren't killed when we went in there. The door was open, so the room aired out a bit. Had Hayes been able to shut the door behind him, and then if one of us had gone in there after, we could have died as well."

"So Hayes walked into the room that he'd left the dry ice in," she said. "And died right away?"

"Probably almost immediately, or at least, he probably lost consciousness almost immediately. Death would have come quick. It was a death trap in there. It's not a pleasant thing, but that's what happened."

"And you're sure?"

Larry let the chair fall forward and leaned into the desk, folding his hands.

"What makes you say that?" he said. "Is there something more you know?"

Oh, just a dream I had about murder right before, when a ghostly note appeared on my wall. . . .

"No," she said. "Just a weird feeling."

He considered her for a moment, then he opened the top drawer of his desk and pulled out a Band-Aid.

"For your hand," he said. "Look, you've been brave . . ."

Brave.

There was someone else she could talk to.

"Thanks, Larry," she said, sticking the Band-Aid on. "Good talk."

Beth Brave was sitting in her set in her apartment, wall of fan art on display in the background. Hers was more carefully curated than Hayes's was, with framed prints sitting on white floating shelves.

Beth was a striking blonde, with stick-straight, shiny hair and giant eyelashes that Stevie assumed were fake. Her long nails, which Beth had constantly been examining during their conversation (seemed like a nervous habit) were grand examples of nail art, with the four houses of Hogwarts represented on the fingers of both hands, and the thumbs painted with a very tiny replica of Harry's face. It was not the kind of thing you did yourself; it was the kind of thing you spent hundreds of dollars and several hours having someone else do.

Contacting Beth had not been as hard as Stevie thought. She had over a million followers, but all it took was Stevie sending a message and explaining how she had been at Ellingham Academy with Hayes, and how she worked on the show, and—and this part was where the fib came in— how they wanted to make a tribute and feature her. A reply popped up less than an hour later, and fifteen minutes after that, Beth and Stevie were looking at each other through Skype windows.

"Thanks for reaching out," Beth said. She had blindingly white teeth, big as the doors of kitchen cabinets. "It's been rough. I'm sure for you guys as well."

"Definitely," Stevie said.

"It's nice that you're making a video," Beth said. "He would have liked that."

Behind the Skype screen, Stevie could see the top of an unfinished (well, *unstarted*, really) essay peeping up, saying *yoo-hooo!* That was due tomorrow. It would get done. It would. She just had to talk to Beth for a minute.

"There's something kind of . . . ," Stevie said, ". . . there's something . . . I just . . . I wish I could make you feel better but I'm just so afraid . . ."

"What?" Beth said.

"I just feel like someone should tell you because it's going to come out," Stevie said. "I mean, you saw that video . . ."

"You mean that girl?" Beth said.

"Yeah," Stevie said. "That girl, Maris . . ."

"Oh, I know about that," Beth said.

"And you're okay with it?"

"The thing is," Beth said, "and this isn't for the video, right? You're not recording?"

"No," Stevie said. (She never had been.)

"Of course he was dating someone at school. I date someone else too. It's not like either one of us is supposed to be single. We're going to get together . . . we were going to get together when he got to LA. But we discussed that it was okay to see other people when we were apart. But that's not for the fans. They'd be upset. We knew how to be apart from each other."

"Did he mention," Stevie said carefully, "the video? Doing an effect with dry ice?"

"No," she said. "Nothing. I wish he had. I mean, I talked to him the night he took that stuff."

Stevie felt a tingle on the back of her neck.

"Wait," Stevie said, "you spoke to him on Thursday night?"

"Yeah, we usually Skyped before bed. I was probably the last person he talked to that night," she said.

"You talked to him late?"

"Oh yeah," Beth said.

"Do you know when?"

"I don't know . . . late."

"The thing is," Stevie said, "it would be so amazing if . . . if you talked to him late that night and it was . . . like the romantic high point of this tribute. I mean, do you have the time on Skype?"

"Let me look." Stevie got a close-up of Beth's nose as she leaned in to read. "Here it is. It was . . . ten twenty."

That made no sense. Hayes had been with Maris then.

No, stupid, Beth was in California. That was 1:20 in the morning.

But Janelle's ID had been used at 1:12 in the morning. There was no way Hayes could have used it and gotten back to his room by 1:20.

Either Hayes went into the workshop or he was speaking to Beth at 1:20 a.m., but he wasn't doing both. And the one he was most likely doing was the one someone *saw* him do.

Which meant someone else put that dry ice in the tunnel but made it look like Hayes did it.

Which sounded a lot like murder.

27

THAT NIGHT, IT RAINED. IT WAS NOT A GENTLE RAIN, THE KIND THAT lulled Stevie to sleep. It was a sideways, angry rain that threw itself haphazardly at the walls and windows and roof. It was a rain that made Hayes's empty room feel even more vacant.

It was a rain that pounded Stevie Bell into alertness.

What you lack in any investigation is time. With every passing hour, evidence slips away. Crime scenes are compromised by people and the elements. Things are moved, altered, smeared, shifted. Organisms rot. Winds blow dust and contaminants. Memories change and fade. As you move away from the event, you move away from the solution.

This is why no one found Dottie and Iris until it was too late. The days dragged on. If someone had called the police that night. Maybe it would have all been different for the Ellinghams. But they didn't.

Stevie had information now—real information. She could take it to Larry, but Larry had already warned her off playing detective. She could go to him when she knew

something, when she understood what she knew. So she
started making lists.

Facts:

Someone took Janelle's ID from the art barn when we were in
yoga.

Someone used that ID to get into the workshop at 1:12 the
next morning. At the same time, seven pieces of dry ice
were removed from the storage unit.

Hayes's fingerprints were on the ID.

Hayes was Skyping with Beth at that time.

Hayes lied about *The End of It All*.

Strong possibilities:

Hayes did not write *The End of It All,* at least not alone.

Conclusions:

Hayes had that ID at some point, but he was not the one who
went into the workshop.

Question:

Why did Hayes turn around and go into the tunnel?

Did he know the dry ice was there?

Did he ask someone to get it for him?

That morning, she sat in anatomy lab in her oldest T-shirt
and hoodie, glassily staring as Pix worked the skeleton.
She was entering the too-awake stage. The head of a femur

looked like a strange mushroom. Stevie turned it around in her mind, working her way around the bone. The greater trochanter. The lesser trochanter. The head that articulates with the acetabulum and that thing in the pelvis, the tuberosity of ischium . . .

She was drooling a bit. She slapped her hand to her chin and looked down at her notebook and the names of bones she had scrawled there as they were written on the board. It was all gibberish. She thought of Hayes, his knees, seeing his feet on the floor.

In Lit, she nodded off, only to be jerked awake to answer questions about the poem "The Love Song of J. Alfred Prufrock." ("And what do you think it means, Stevie, when Eliot writes that *the evening is spread out against the sky like a patient etherized upon a table*?" Answer: "He's . . . tired?")

She ate lunch alone and listened to people discussing the Silent Party that would be held that evening.

She continued stumbling through the day, trying to process everything her brain had accumulated. By the time she got to yoga, she was straining to keep herself awake. She took her slightly smelly purple mat from the stack in the corner and left a spot next to her for Janelle, but someone else took it. Janelle came in, saw that Stevie had set up without her, and quietly made a space for herself on the other side of the room.

She left class before Stevie could catch her.

That night, Stevie skipped dinner and went over her facts again. Her stomach growled as the rain beat on her window.

Janelle and Ellie had gone over to the Great House for the dance. What David and Nate were doing, she had no idea.

Think, Stevie. *Think.*

But her thoughts had gone stagnant. She had gotten this far, but nothing more was coming up. She put her earbuds in and turned up some music, loud, trying to get her head somewhere else, somewhere she could see the pattern. So she didn't hear the knocking and was surprised to see Nate standing next to her in a pair of loose corduroys and a plaid shirt and a tie. He was speaking, but Stevie couldn't hear him with her earbuds in and her hoodie over her head. She jerked the buds out and the hood off.

"Huh?" she said.

"You," he said. "Are coming with me."

"I am? Where?"

"To the dance."

"Dance?"

"Yes, dance," he said. "There's this dance tonight. And you are going with me. Not *with me*, with me. But we are both going."

"I have no idea what you're talking about," she said.

"Dance. Thing. At the Great House. Everyone. Over there. So come on."

"I can't," she said.

Nate came into the room and kicked the door half closed behind him. "Here's the thing. You've gone kind of psycho. I have never willingly gone to a dance in my life. But I am doing this because you are my friend, okay? And something is wrong with you. I don't want to go to this, obviously. And you don't want to go to this. I'm doing this for you, for your own good. This is the one and only time I'm offering to do something like this. Sometimes you have to leave the fucking Shire, Frodo. If we're friends, get up, and come with me now. And you should take that seriously, because you are kind of losing friends all over the place."

He extended his hand to her.

"You're serious."

"I'm serious."

She looked down at her lists and up at Nate.

"You're wearing a tie," she said.

"I know."

"Is that a dance thing?"

"How would I know? Do I look like I go to a lot of dances?"

Stevie felt like she was made of concrete and attached to the floor. But seeing Nate there, seeing the effort he was going to, she felt her moorings coming loose. She got off the floor. Her hoodie was dusty. She wasn't wearing makeup. She had sneakers on.

"Like this?" she said.

"You look good to me. Not that I'm saying you look good. I'm saying come on before I lose the nerve to go to this."

⊕

It was a strange walk over to the Great House. Stevie could see gently pulsing lights coming from the long windows of the ballroom.

367

"So what are you doing that's making you so weird?" Nate asked.

"Solving Hayes's murder," she said, stuffing her hands deeper in her hoodie pockets.

"Say that again?" he said.

"I'm solving Hayes's murder," she repeated.

"You're shitting me."

"Nope."

"Are you drunk?"

"Nope," she said. "Hayes didn't put that dry ice in the tunnel, and I can prove it."

"How?"

Stevie sat Nate down under the portico of the Great House and explained all that she had discovered.

"Okay," he said. "So this is why you've been weird."

"Mostly," she said, looking up at something flying past the cupola. A bat, probably. Ellingham was full of bats. Nate saw it too, and got right to his feet.

"So, you're going to tell Larry, or someone, all of this?" Nate said after a silent moment.

"I think I need to wait," Stevie said.

"Why? For what?"

"If I do this wrong, if I'm wrong, the whole school could be shut down," she said. "If it's an accident and Hayes did it, we're okay. If there's someone out there, we're all in trouble."

"But something has happened. You have proof that Hayes didn't do this himself. So you want to find this person yourself because you don't want to go home?"

"I want to find this person because I want to find this person," she said. "And because I don't want to go home. But I guess now I'm going to dance. With my friend."

She reached over and squeezed him by the arm.

"You did this for me," she said.

"Yeah, I did this for you, but don't make it a thing. And how do we go into a dance after what you just said?"

"We go in," she said. "Because you brought me here, and because the answer may be here."

"Are you really serious about all of this?" he said quietly. "You're not messing with me?"

"I'm not messing with you," she said.

"Do you think they knew it was lethal? Not an accident?"

"That," Stevie said, meeting his gaze and feeling herself break out in a sweat, "I don't know."

"So we could be dancing with a murderer?"

"We might be," Stevie said.

"And you really think this should wait?"

"Give me tonight, at least," Stevie said. "To look around. I promise you, I'll talk to Larry soon."

Nate took a heavy breath.

"Okay," he said. "If you say so. This is probably only the second stupidest thing I've done since I got here."

August 13, 1937

THE BUTCHER FIGURED IT OUT FIRST. HE WAS THE ONE WHO NOTICED that the local anarchist, Anton Vorachek, was suddenly buying some better cuts of meat. He usually bought remnants and offal—whatever was going cheap—and not much of it. One day, he came in and bought some cube steak.

Or maybe it was the waitress at the diner. She said that Vorachek came in for his weekly single scrambled egg—he always did this on Sundays to try to talk to people at the counter and recruit. That Sunday, he ordered two eggs, hash-browned potatoes, a side of bacon, and toast. He even had coffee. And he tipped her a quarter on a thirty-five-cent check because "the worker deserves a greater share of the profits."

Or maybe it was the bus driver, because Vorachek suddenly had money for the bus.

All of Burlington reported a man who, if not vying with the Rockefellers for wealth, was more flush than he previously had been.

He was not liked by many. He started strikes and handed

out anarchist literature. He shouted "Death to tyrants!" when Ellingham's name was mentioned. Albert Ellingham was much beloved in the area. He provided money for the police and the schools and the fire department and the hospital and any other cause that came his way, and had touched many thousands of lives in Burlington. This was a man who provided free ice cream for poor children. And now he had opened a school of his own.

So people took offense to calls for his death.

Officially, the police searched his house because a witness came forward and said he saw Vorachek scouting out telephone booths. Then someone else came forward and said that they definitely saw Vorachek place a call at 7:07 on the night of April 14. Seven separate witnesses from the night of April 14 who received fifty cents for their reports said they saw Vorachek heading for Rock Point. It didn't seem to bother many people that it took a few months for these people to realize they had seen these things, or that the witness accounts didn't match. Two of the people writing reports claimed that Vorachek went to Rock Point in a black car. Two said on foot. One said in a cab. One said on a bicycle. One could not explain the means of transport.

In any case, the Burlington police had enough to go and have a look in his house, where they found a pile of cash painted with Leonard Holmes Nair's glowing paint, and even a cash bundle with Ellingham's invisible fingerprint. More troubling, they also found a child's shoe, the match to the one left on Rock Point.

Vorachek was arrested and charged with the kidnapping of Iris and Alice Ellingham and the murders of Iris and Dottie Epstein.

"I did it," he said when handcuffed. "All tyrants will fall. This is only the beginning!"

The wheels of justice began to grind. All that fall and winter the evidence was examined, experts brought in. A famous attorney came in to represent Vorachek. In the spring, everything seemed ready to start, but then there were delays. The anarchists came to town to protest Vorachek's arrest. There was talk of moving the trial, but that was quashed.

Finally, everything was set to start on July 15, during a devastating heat wave. Burlington was almost broken from the weight of it all. There were no hotel rooms, so Albert Ellingham simply bought a house near the court. The press lived on the lawn and cracked the sidewalk from their pacing. The case was front page, every day, everywhere. There were reporters from every paper in America, all over the world. There were so many telegraph wires outside the court that when Robert looked up, sometimes he couldn't see the sky. Then there were the onlookers, the people who simply came to watch. You couldn't walk down Church Street. The restaurants ran out of food daily. Boatloads of people came across Lake Champlain just to be in Burlington, to see Anton Vorachek stand trial. Vendors set up out in front of the court and sold cold beer and popcorn and lemonade. It was like being at a baseball game.

Every day during that brutal month, Robert Mackenzie sat in the stifling courtroom next to Albert Ellingham and watched the presentation of evidence. He took notes that weren't really necessary, but he was the right hand, and the right hand needed to do something. He saw the police show the photos of the money they found under the floorboards, the notes they had painted with Leo's special paint. They saw the one paper wrap that Albert Ellingham had marked with his fingerprint in the invisible paint, proving without a doubt where those bills had come from. Leo testified about making the paint and the process by which it was revealed.

Vorachek used the courtroom like a pulpit to rage against the industrialists of the world. This was revenge, he said. Soon, all people like Albert Ellingham would pay. The anarchists cheered and were taken from the court. The crowd gasped and cried and ate their popcorn.

Albert Ellingham sat expressionless through it all. Sometimes he didn't even sweat. He was gray and unmoving. His focus never waved. Every day he said to Robert, "Maybe today he will say where Alice is."

Vorachek was found guilty on all counts.

On the night before sentencing, Albert Ellingham came into Robert's room at the house.

"We're going to the court," he said simply. "I'm going to talk to him."

Robert grabbed his hat and followed. They surprised the journalists, many of whom were off having dinner or eating sandwiches on the grass. They walked down Church Street, a gang of people on their heels, barking questions.

Because of the interest in and the sheer magnitude of the event, Anton Vorachek could not be housed in the normal jail. A cell had been built in the basement of the imposing custom house and post office next to the court, in a space usually reserved for storage. George Marsh met them there.

"He's this way," he said, beckoning them down the darkened hallway to the stairs.

Robert and Ellingham were escorted inside, down through the sorting rooms and the sacks of mail, into the empty depths. There, behind a specially constructed barred door, sat the man convicted of it all. He was small, with a sharply pointed beard and bright eyes. He was dressed in the rough brown coveralls he had been given to wear in his cell. Robert could tell they had not been washed in some time. There was a smell even a few feet away. The cell Anton Vorachek occupied had a cot and a wooden bench; buckets had been provided for bodily necessities. There was no window, and the light came from outside the cell, so he was mostly in darkness.

"They keep you safe down here," Ellingham said in greeting.

Anton Vorachek blinked and took a seat on his bench, hunching his knees close to his chest. A guard brought a wooden chair for Albert Ellingham, and he put it directly in front of the bars so he could look deep inside the cell.

"Tell me where she is," Ellingham said. "Tell me who helped you. There's no way you did this alone."

Anton Vorachek said nothing. For an hour he sat in silence and Ellingham watched him. Robert smoked with George Marsh and the guards. They stood, and shifted on occasion, but no one broke the spell.

"They're going to put you in the electric chair, you know," Albert Ellingham finally said, leaning back.

Anton Vorachek finally left his seat and came to the bars and gripped them tightly.

"Why does it matter who I am?" he said. "Your kind destroys mine every day."

Why does it matter who I am? Robert thought. What a strange thing to say.

"This is your last chance," Ellingham said.

"What does it matter?" Vorachek said.

"What does it matter?" Albert Ellingham almost quaked from the force of his speaking. "If you tell us where Alice is, I will speak to the judge. I'll go to his house. I'll plead on your behalf. You can keep your life. Even if you tell us where her body is . . ."

There was just the tiniest quiver at the word *body*.

Anton Vorachek stared at Ellingham for a long moment, and the look he'd had on the stand vanished. The mask was dropped and a human sat in front of them. A human who looked . . . sympathetic?

"Go home, old man," Vorachek finally said. "I have nothing for you."

"Then I will watch you die," Ellingham replied.

He stood and pushed back the chair. On the way back

375

upstairs, George Marsh put a hand on his back.

"He was never going to crack, Albert," he said. "Tomorrow, it will end."

"It never ends," Ellingham said. "Don't you understand? Tomorrow, it *begins*."

Robert Mackenzie slept poorly that night, even worse than he had in the last brutal weeks. Usually he could beat through the horror and heat to get a few scattered hours, but this time he turned and twisted the entire night through.

He went to the window and looked at the moon hanging over the city and Lake Champlain. It was almost ridiculous to say something felt wrong in a situation where everything was wrong, but something bad was coming.

He dressed at dawn, splashing himself with cold water. He found his employer ready as well. They arrived at the courthouse early and stood in the hall, waiting for Vorachek to be brought around for this final day.

On that last day, something changed. Instead of bringing Vorachek in through the back, as they had every day before, the police walked him around the front. Vorachek held his head high as he walked to meet his fate. The press crushed in and the crowd erupted in shouted questions and small explosions from the camera flashes.

Robert would later remember that he didn't hear the noise at all, that it blended in completely with the shouting and the flashes. Vorachek crumpled, possibly tripped. The crowd seethed, and suddenly someone started yelling, "Down! Everyone down!"

George Marsh grabbed Albert Ellingham and pulled him into the vestibule of the courthouse. Robert Mackenzie was caught in a general wave of people and police lunging for the door. He heard cries of "shot" and "gun." Everyone was screaming and running.

Vorachek was dragged into the courthouse lobby, his shirt thick with blood, blood on his hands, smeared on his face. Leonard Holmes Nair, who was there that day, would later paint the scene, lashing red paint over the small form on the ground.

The police pushed everyone back and a doctor came forward, but it was clear that there was nothing to be done. In his final moments, Vorachek attempted to speak. Mostly, blood and foamy spittle came from his mouth, but Robert was close enough to hear him say, "Did not . . ."

Then Anton Vorachek died.

28

Stevie stood at the threshold of the ballroom, her sneakers touching the chessboard of the black-and-white floor. The lights were dimmed—only a few of the gold sconces were turned on at half brightness, and beat in time with some unheard song. Around her, the rest of Ellingham was gyrating with glowing pink-and-green headsets on their heads, to music Stevie could not hear.

"I feel like I'm walking into a metaphor," Stevie said.

"Hey!" Kaz danced over to them. He was wearing a black suit jacket with a red flower in the pocket. "Glad you guys could make it! Here."

Stevie and Nate were each presented with a pair of glowing headphones.

"Just turn them on and dance!" Kaz said.

With their headphones on, Stevie and Nate entered the ballroom. Stevie couldn't help but be amazed again at the way this room played with light, bouncing it across and back with the mirrors. The faces of the masks on the walls grinned blindly at them.

Stevie switched off the music, so she just heard everything in a slightly muffled way. Nate was looking around nervously and doing a jerky, faint bending-at-the-knee-in-time move. Stevie bounced along for a moment in a show of solidarity. It really did move her that Nate had done this.

She glanced around and saw Janelle and Vi over on the side, their arms draped over each other's shoulders, swaying together. Maris was nearby, in a shaggy dress, doing some complicated, slow move with Dash. They had both bounced back.

There was Gretchen, the jilted ex, discreetly in a corner with some other second years. And there, on the far side of the room, were David and Ellie. Ellie was wearing something black and shiny that, on closer examination, looked to be a bunch of trash bags bound together to make a goofy skirt, with a camisole on top. She was dancing a crazed, loopy dance with lots of swinging arms. David was not dancing, but was leaning against the wall, watching. Like Stevie, he was not dressed up. He wore his same rumpled jeans and a ragged green T-shirt.

When Nate and Stevie entered the room, he pulled himself away from the wall and crossed over to them, taking off his headphones.

"Nice tie," he said to Nate.

"Don't be a dick to Nate," Stevie said.

"I wasn't," David said. "Nate. It's a nice tie. And you're dressed up. Are you Banksy or the Unabomber?"

"I'm a pretty, pretty girl," Stevie said. "Who likes to be comfortable."

Vi had also noticed Stevie's presence, and was dragging Janelle across the room. Vi was properly dressed up in a dress shirt and yellow tie with white dots. Janelle had on a yellow skirt and a white blouse. Matching outfits to a dance. It was beyond anything Stevie could understand, but it was so right for them.

"Hey!" Vi said with a bit of forced cheerfulness. "Everyone's here!"

Janelle looked down at the floor for a moment.

"Yeah," Stevie said. "I wanted to hang out. *We* wanted to hang out."

"I live to dance," Nate said.

"So, let's dance," Vi said.

Stevie did not actually know how to dance. This seemed like information other people were born with, something that was as natural as walking. It was very puzzling to her how people managed to just pick it up. But Janelle wanted her to dance, and Nate had brought her to this dance, and right now she had to observe at a dance . . . so that meant she was going to dance. She tried the knee-bending thing first, but even Nate looked at her with pity. So she tried employing her arms instead, windmilling them like Ellie across the room.

How this looked to David, who was standing there watching, was unclear. It didn't matter. There was nothing left to lose.

Janelle burst into uncontrollable laughter and had to lean

on Vi for support. Then she wrapped her arms around Stevie's neck.

"You are ridiculous," she said.

"I know," Stevie said.

Janelle and Vi swung back into each other's arms and started dancing more slowly. Stevie looked at David, but he had already turned and made his way back to the wall. She ignored the ache this caused.

At the end of so many Agatha Christie books, Poirot would gather the suspects to look at them. If Ellingham was gathered in one room tonight, then she could examine everyone at once. Look for someone who would have reason to put that dry ice in that tunnel and never come forward. Look for the reason Hayes turned around.

She rotated, taking in this room decorated in honor of masks and mischief. Commedia players on the wallpaper and masks supporting the lights. Everything was a trick with mirrors, making the room repeat.

Where do you look for someone who's never really there....

Albert Ellingham wanted her to think.

Was it Gretchen? Gretchen, who openly confessed to doing Hayes's work for him, to being furious? Gretchen who was owed five hundred dollars?

"Come on!"

Janelle had come up behind her and taken her hand. She started to dance with Stevie again. Stevie tried to keep up, moving as best she could. It was good to see Janelle smiling at her, at least, and Vi gave a little nod of, *It'll be okay.*

Maybe this was enough. Just to be with her friends. Be a normal girl. Stop thinking you found a murder. Close your eyes and dance.

Janelle squeezed Stevie's hand gently, putting just a little pressure on the scratch she'd gotten earlier.

Something shot through Stevie's brain.

Her hand. Something about her hand. A pain in her hand. A scratch. She put her attention there, on the back of her hand, focusing it like a soft spotlight. The hand would speak to her. The hand would tell its story if she let it.

Her hand cycled through its memories. The cold that rubbed the skin dry. The warmth of the inside of her fleece pockets. The feeling of David's skin . . .

"Be right back," she said. "I have to . . . go to the bathroom."

The music changed and everyone began to move more frantically. Stevie knocked the headphones off her ears and craned her neck to look around. There was one person she needed to see, one person who was always there whether you noticed her or not. And she was there, of course, sitting on one of the low benches by the windows, working her phone. Stevie made her way over.

"I need to see your pictures from the day in the garden," she said.

Germaine peered at her curiously.

"Why?"

"Because I do, Germaine," she said. "Please. I'll owe you. Please."

"I like I'll owe you," Germaine said. She flicked through her phone for a moment and then held it toward Stevie. Stevie swiped until she found what she hoped was there—a clear shot of Hayes sitting and acting like he was working on his laptop. She zoomed in.

Her heart thudded.

"Hey," Nate said, coming up behind her.

"Wait," Stevie said. "Wait a second."

The three of them stood in their puddle of silence as everyone gyrated around them.

Stevie pulled up her own pictures of Hayes's room. The fan-art wall, the bureau, the desk, the computer . . .

She swore under her breath in a continuous stream.

In Germaine's pictures from Saturday, Hayes's computer was scratch free. But when it appeared again in Stevie's photos from her room search after his death, there were three clear marks down the front, like the claw marks of a cat. They were three marks she had seen before on her own hand, when she reached under the tub on that first day.

"What's happening?" Germaine said, watching Stevie's face closely.

Someone had taken Hayes's computer and hidden it under the tub.

Why would you do that?

Think, Stevie.

If you needed to look for something, maybe evidence that you had written a show that Hayes was taking credit for, a show that was going to be a movie. Maybe you did

383

something to mess with him. Maybe you killed him by accident. And then maybe you had to cover your tracks afterward. Make sure there was nothing on his computer identifying you as the true author.

Janelle and Nate could be eliminated. They were not at Ellingham last year. That left Ellie and David.

It had come down to this.

Ellie, who loved art and went to Paris and got tattoos. Ellie who was funny and careless and maybe tried much too hard. David, who lied. David, whose parents were dead. David, who held everything in. David, who messed with people.

The lights in the room flashed pink and pulsed, like rose-colored fingers reaching for the ceiling. The eyes of the masks glowed.

Either one of them was capable of getting out at night. As for Hayes's fingerprints on the ID? Simple. You just gave it to him to hold.

Intent. Planning. Maybe the goal was just to get him kicked out and everything went wrong.

Of the two, David should have known better. He studied more math and science. David would likely have had a better sense of what that much carbon dioxide might do. Ellie, on the other hand, might have liked the idea of the artful cloud of fog.

Could it really all come down to a few scrapes on a computer?

"What is going on?" Nate said.

"I'm still working that out," Stevie said.

"Let's just talk to Larry right now," he said. "Let him get the police."

"The police didn't get this far," she said. "I got this far. And I can get the rest of the way."

"Don't say things like that," Nate replied. "It makes me feel like you're about to get us both killed or something."

"No," she said. "We just have to go home."

The dance ended at midnight. Stevie watched to make sure all her Minerva people were in sight. Janelle and Nate were by her side. Ellie and David walked ahead of them. David occasionally turned around to look at Stevie curiously.

Could she have kissed a killer? What did a killer kiss like? Could a killer be as warm as David had been? Was that what made him so attractive to her? Was that the thing she had recognized in him from the very first moment she saw him, when something about his face reminded her so strongly of something she knew, something she wanted to fight?

Or Ellie, skipping along now in her trash bags like a deranged ballerina? Could she have playfully led Hayes into that tunnel with a bottle of wine? Told him to just go ahead?

Germaine Batt followed them for a bit. She said nothing, but was always just a few footsteps behind. Stevie could practically feel her listening for hints as to what was going on. She would have followed them all the way to Minerva if she could, but at the juncture with the collection of statue heads, a group of her housemates turned in the direction of Juno and Stevie loudly wished her goodnight. Germaine squinted a bit in frustration, but she left with the others.

"You guys are being really quiet," Janelle said.

"Just feeling all excited," Nate said stiffly. "From dancing."

"Have either of you *ever* been to a dance before?"

"Nope," they answered in unison.

The night had a theatrical quality to it. The moon was obligingly low and yellow. A huge harvest moon, furiously bright in the clear, dark sky. Like a spotlight.

"Do you have some kind of idea what you're doing?" Nate asked Stevie quietly.

"Some kind of idea," she said. "But you won't like it."

29

Once inside, Pix dutifully checked them all in and went up to bed. It looked like Ellie and David were about to go to their rooms when Stevie said, "Who wants to play a game?"

Nate threw her a confused look.

"What game?" Ellie said.

"I never," Stevie replied.

"I like that game," Ellie replied. "David, come play. I'll get us some wine. We can't play it without wine."

"Then we should play in someone's room," he said.

"Let's go to my room," Ellie said.

Nate gave Stevie a look, a concerned look, but Stevie nudged him on.

Ellie's room, while technically the same size and shape as Stevie's, was a kind of different world. The walls were covered in sketches and flyers written in French. There was a ratty rug on the floor that was embedded with a thick smell of incense. There were loads of mugs and cups and bowls from the kitchen, all dirty and some collecting mold. Pens and paper were all over the floor, and dried candle wax spilled on the edges of the furniture.

"You've all played, right?" Ellie said, settling herself on a cushion on the floor and pulling a bottle of wine out from between her bedside stand and bed. "You start by saying *I never*, and then you give an action. If you've never done it, you don't drink. But if you have, you confess by drinking. It's simple. I'll show you. I've never made out with anyone in this room."

She smiled broadly and looked over at David. David side-eyed her.

Neither Stevie nor David moved at first, then Stevie reached for the bottle and took a very tiny sip, just enough that the wine touched her lips and the scent flooded her nose. She set the bottle down, and David slowly reached for it.

Ellie laughed.

"And that's how it's done," Ellie said. "Now you, Nate."

"Okay," he said. "I've never been to a dance before tonight."

"You said that earlier," Janelle said.

"Nothing in the rules about established facts," he replied.

Janelle sighed deeply and took a short sip, then Ellie, then David.

Janelle was next. "I've never started a fire," she said.

Only Ellie drank, and she took a long sip. Now it was David's turn. He leaned back against Ellie's bed and stroked his chin for a moment.

"I've never gone through someone else's room," he said.

Stevie paused, and then drank. This caused everyone to

look at her, but no one said a word. It was Stevie's turn now.

"I've never taken something that didn't belong to me," she said.

Janelle and Stevie didn't drink. Nate did—at least he lifted the bottle.

"Pretend I drank," he said.

"Oh, no," Ellie said. "You have to drink. What did you take?"

"Who hasn't taken something?" Nate said. "Everyone does that. How can you go through life without taking something that doesn't belong to you, even by accident?"

"That's true," Janelle said, reaching for the bottle. "This game is kind of intense, and I don't really drink, so . . . I may be out."

"Then I'll have to play," Ellie said, reaching behind her to get Roota. The saxophone was resting next to her bureau.

Roota.

What had Ellie said about Roota? *I had to have her. I didn't have the money at the time, but I found a way. I made a little art, I got a little cash, I got Roota.*

"How much was Roota?" Stevie said as Ellie went to put the mouthpiece in her mouth. "I was thinking about maybe getting an instrument."

This got disbelieving looks from most present.

"About five hundred bucks," Ellie said. "But worth it. She's been a true friend."

Five hundred dollars.

"And when did you get her? In the spring?"

"Yeah," Ellie said, looking a touch more uncomfortable.

"You said you earned the money by making art. What did you do?"

Now Ellie was shifting in her seat a bit.

"Sold some drawings and stuff," she said.

"Five hundred dollars' worth of drawings," Stevie said. "That's really good. How many other times have you sold drawings?"

"A few," Ellie said. "Look, if we're not going to play and we're not going to drink, everyone can leave."

Nate looked at Stevie. He knew. He understood. Janelle started to get up, but Stevie motioned for her to stay.

"Why don't we talk about Hayes for a second," Stevie said. "It seems like we should, you know, take a moment."

"Yeah," Ellie said. "I'm not feeling that."

"What are you doing, Stevie?" David asked. He was smirking but there was real concern in his voice.

"The thing about Hayes," Stevie said, "he kind of took stuff that wasn't his. He would have had to drink just then. He had other people do his work. Like me. Like Nate. Like Gretchen. Ever do any work for Hayes, Ellie?"

Ellie's eyes were locked on Stevie now. They were such a light brown that they were almost a gold color.

"What are you even talking about?" Ellie said.

"Yeah, Stevie," David said. "What *are* you talking about?"

"Weird thing," Stevie said. "Hayes himself told me that he made *The End of It All* in Florida at the start of last summer. He lied. He made it on June fourth, and Ellingham closed for the summer on the sixth."

"What?" Ellie said. "I . . ."

"I know this because I went through his room," Stevie cut in. "I go through rooms. I'm the worst. I get curious when things don't make sense. But I found some things out. I found out Hayes lied. He made the show here, and he didn't make it alone. And last spring, he borrowed five hundred dollars from Gretchen, his ex-girlfriend, that he never paid back. And you paid five hundred dollars for making some art last spring and bought Roota."

"You're being a freak, Stevie," Ellie said, but there was a tremble in her voice. "Get the hell out of my room. Everyone get the hell out of my room."

"Something else," Stevie said. "Sometime between the time Hayes died and the time I went into his room, someone had taken his computer. That person shoved it under the tub. It left three scratches down the front. Those scratches weren't there before. There's proof."

"Stevie . . . ," Janelle said, her voice fearful. "What's going on?"

But Stevie had gone down the road now, and there was no going back. There was a thick atmosphere in the dark room, with the stink of old patchouli and paint. There was no coming back from this night, this sudden drilling into Ellie's background and Hayes's life and death. If she was wrong about this, she would have to pack up and go. She felt like someone walking out onto the branch of a tree, feeling it bounce and give under each step.

And she loved the feeling.

"One more thing. Beth Brave. She was Skyping with Hayes at the time Hayes was supposed to have been removing the dry ice from the workshop. Did he know about the dry ice? Was it his idea?"

Ellie's face had taken on the cast of one of the masks on the wall of the ballroom—features wide, long, stretched in emotion.

"Get out of my room," Ellie said. "Everyone get out of my room."

David had shifted and was now half squatting. Janelle was moving back toward the wall. Nate, however, was like a rock, watching all of this with folded arms.

"Stevie," David said slowly, "you know this thing that you're saying is kind of intense?"

"I know," she said.

"So you'd have to be pretty sure . . ."

"I am."

"So I helped him with his show," Ellie said. "God! I helped him with his show."

The first piece slid into place.

"The movie," Stevie said. "He was going to go to Hollywood and work with P. G. Edderton and take all the credit."

"So? Do you think I wanted people to know I helped make a zombie show? I just needed money for Roota."

"So why did you take his computer?" Stevie said. "The police were here. You had to see if there was evidence on there about your involvement because you knew . . ."

"I knew it didn't look good. Hayes . . . Hayes said all kinds of dumb shit. Hayes did dumb things and he died and I'm sad about it and now you all need to *get out*."

When no one moved, she got up herself, snatching her bag from the floor.

"Ellie," David said, getting up and following her, "where are you going?"

He reached out for her, but she yanked away her arm. She hurried down the hall to the common room and was at the door in a moment.

Stevie scrambled to her feet and followed. Ellie threw open the door and hurried outside . . .

. . . right into Larry.

"I texted him about fifteen minutes ago," Nate said, coming up behind Stevie. "I kind of didn't want you to get us all killed."

"Fair," Stevie said, slumping against the wall. "That's fair."

The residents of Minerva were taken as a group to the Great House, where everyone was loaded into Albert Ellingham's office. The night closed in around the house, and Larry drew the heavy curtains.

Charles looked like he'd been woken up and was dressed in a pair of jeans and a cashmere sweater. Dr. Quinn was also present, wearing a stark black dress and looking like she had been called back from some other affair. Pix came down with them and oversaw the proceedings in an oversized sweater and army pants.

Ellie compacted herself into one of Albert Ellingham's leather chairs, tucking her head into her knees. The events of the evening were recounted. When Stevie was finished, the room was silent for several moments.

"Element," Charles said, finally speaking, "did you help Hayes write the show?"

"Sure," Ellie said. "Fine. I helped him with his show. Who cares?"

"Didn't that show make a lot of money?" Larry said.

"I have no idea," she said. "I don't care about money. I grew up on a *commune*. This isn't about money. Not for me."

"What's *this* mean?" Charles asked.

"Just . . . this. Whatever."

"Did you take Hayes's computer?" Larry asked.

"I don't want to talk about this. This is bullshit."

"Element," Larry said. "Did you take his computer? It's a simple question."

"I *looked* at it," she said.

"Why?"

No answer.

"Did you put the dry ice in the tunnel?" Larry asked.

"No," Ellie mumbled from her knees.

"There's something here you aren't saying," Larry said. "You need to explain to us what's going on. This is serious."

Ellie pulled herself upright suddenly. Her eyes were full and tears were starting to run down her face.

"God, he was so dumb. Why did I pay attention to him?"

"What do you mean?" Larry pressed.

"This whole place," she said, shaking her head and smiling grimly. "This whole place. Hayes and his stupid ideas. That's what got him killed, his stupid ideas."

"I have real concerns about going on with this," Dr. Quinn said, raising a hand. "Ellie, I think you should stop speaking until we get you representation. And everyone else, let's get you out of here."

"I agree," Charles said. "I'm going to call our general counsel and have them come here to consult with you. Larry, if you could take the others back to Minerva . . ."

Larry went over to say something quietly just to Charles and Dr. Quinn.

"Okay," Charles said. "Dr. Pixwell, if you could take everyone to the teachers' lounge. They can use the guest rooms if anyone needs to go to sleep."

"We can't go home?" Nate said.

"Let's just keep everyone here for a while," Dr. Quinn said. "Until we sort this out."

"What, am I under arrest?" Ellie said. "Is *Larry* arresting me?"

"No," Larry said. "And I agree. Let's wait for the lawyer, Element. You wait in here, all right? Just sit tight."

The change was a stark one—from a group of students recounting a dorm room conversation to the school administration, to full names and calling for a lawyer. Ellie suddenly looked very small and a bit wild, her eyes red and bright.

"I'm leaving," she said, standing up.

"Element," Larry said in a warning tone.

"You can't keep me here."

"Ellie," Charles said, stepping in. His voice was calming. "I know this is frightening. But we're getting you help. The very best thing you can do is be calm and sit. If you stay and talk to the lawyer, things will be better, but if you leave now . . ."

"There's nowhere to go," Dr. Quinn said. "We're on a mountain and it's the middle of the night. Ellie, sit."

Ellie sat.

"We'll get you something to drink, something to eat," Charles said. "How about that? You could use it. Pix, could you . . ."

There was some awkward shuffling getting out of the room, as it wasn't really clear what condition Ellie was in. The Great House creaked and groaned a bit in the fall wind. Ellie was left in Ellingham's office. Once everyone else was outside the door, Larry turned the key in the lock.

"You're locking her in?" Charles said.

"You're damn right I am. And the French doors are secured from the outside."

"She's not a prisoner," Charles said.

"No, but she may have killed someone. She's safe in there."

"Well, I'm getting her some food and water," Charles said.

"Whatever you want," Larry replied.

He gestured for a security officer to stand in front of the door.

"You," he said to Stevie. "With me."

He took her into the security office and shut the door.

"Sit," he said.

He called for a police cruiser to be sent at once. When he got off the phone, he looked at Stevie gravely.

"You should have come to me," he said.

"With what?" Stevie said.

"When you knew Hayes was on the phone when he was supposed to have been in the workshop."

"Sorry," Stevie said. "It didn't seem like enough."

"Enough for what? This was not your call. Do you realize what could happen here? It's clear Element is hiding something. It's possible she killed Hayes. More than possible. You don't play with that."

"I know," she said.

Larry rubbed under his eyes.

"So you'll wait here until the police come and we'll sort it out."

He got up and left, leaving Stevie in the chair to look at the security screens that showed nothing but darkness and the forms of trees and the occasional glowing pair of animal eyes. She went into a kind of trance for a moment.

The letter she had seen on her wall re-formed itself in her mind. It had body now. The words began to return. *Riddle, riddle, on the wall . . .*

. . . murder comes to pay a call.

That's what it said. Maybe it was real. Maybe Ellie had done it? Maybe it was an art thing. Because there would be no reason to say you were going to murder someone, right?

There was yelling outside the door. Stevie sprang up and looked out. The door to the office was open, and Charles stood by it, holding a water and some fruit. The other security officers ran to the door.

"What do you mean?" Larry was saying. "Goddammit, she could get killed out there if she goes too far . . ."

"How did it happen?" Dr. Quinn said.

"She must have popped the panel," Larry said. "How the hell did she know about the panel? Dennis, get to the basement. The passage leads to the basement. Lauren, Benny, get outside, check all the windows. . . ."

The panel. Stevie had read about this. There was supposed to be some kind of passage between Ellingham's office and the ballroom, mostly used for jokes and games. It led to the basement. But apparently it was worked cleverly into the wall, not easy to see.

Ellie was gone.

October 30, 1938

THIS PARTICULAR MORNING WAS STUNNINGLY BRIGHT AND BLUE, A PER-
fect fall day, not a cloud in the sky. The trees were holding
on to the remains of their golden crowns.

Robert Mackenzie sat at his desk, listening to the tick-
ing clock on the mantelpiece. This was more or less the only
sound he heard, aside from Montgomery or one of the other
staff walking past the door, or the occasional voices of the
students moving from building to building. But even they
were subdued. When he watched them from the window
they always turned away when they saw someone in the
Great House looking back.

Mackenzie now had far more space than he needed,
since he'd been moved out of Albert Ellingham's office and
into one of the front sunrooms after the trial was over.

"You might as well use the space," his employer had said.
"It's not being used for anything else."

But he knew that the real reason was that his employer
wanted to be alone. Alone in that office all day, the doors
shut. Meals were taken on occasion. Visitors were rare. The

curtains were closed to the world. But there was always the possibility of Alice.

The possibility of Alice. Never found. The question, always hanging. Was she . . . ? Was she . . . ?

Ellingham spoke of Alice in the present tense, always. The household always prepared for her return. Three times a year, Ellingham had a buyer in New York send back a full wardrobe of that season's children's clothing, each time in the approximate size Alice should be. Piles of dresses and pinafores, tiny sweaters and stockings in every color, pajamas, coats, hats, gloves, fur mufflers, patent leather shoes . . . all of it would be unboxed by Iris's personal maid, who was still on staff, and arranged in Alice's closets. The previous, unused set would be given to charity. She received birthday and Christmas presents—a magnificent Stewart Warner radio, a rocking horse from London, a library of classics, a porcelain miniature tea set from Paris, and a stunning dollhouse replica of the Ellingham Great House.

These tasks were so depressing that the staff frequently cried while performing them, but never in front of Mr. Ellingham. In front of him, they always spoke of Miss Alice positively. "Miss Alice will love her new spring dresses, sir." "Wonderful radio for Miss Alice, sir. She'll be thrilled."

It was the possibility of Alice that led to the draining of the lake last June. An anonymous tip suggested that Alice's body might be on the bottom. Despite the fact that this was unlikely, Ellingham ordered the lake to be drained. Robert felt that this was almost an act of revenge against the lake for its unwitting role on that horrible night. Now the lake was a pit, a constant reminder of loss.

This was the airless atmosphere in the Great House that morning when the buzzer went off on Robert Mackenzie's desk. He picked up his notebook and pencil and went into Albert Ellingham's office. This morning, the curtains were open. The wall of French doors revealed that still-surreal view of the empty lake. Robert would never quite get used to seeing the gaping wound in the ground.

"I am going to the yacht club," Ellingham said. "The weather is fine and clear. I've asked Marsh to come with me. We could both use some time in the air. We've been in dark places too long."

"That's a very good idea," Robert said. "Would you like me to arrange a picnic basket for the trip?"

Albert Ellingham shook his head.

"No need, no need. Here. I wrote a riddle this morning. What do you think?"

He passed Robert a Western Union slip. Albert Ellingham hadn't written a riddle in some time, so Robert took it eagerly.

"Where do you look for someone who's never really there?" Robert read. "Always on a staircase but never on a stair."

He looked up at his employer. There was a strange intensity in his eyes.

"It may be the best riddle I've ever written," Ellingham said. "It's my Riddle of the Sphinx. Those who solve it pass.

Those who don't . . ."

The thought trailed off. He plucked the paper back and set it on his desk.

"I have something very important for you to do today, Robert," he said, putting a paperweight on the riddle. "Get out in the air. Enjoy yourself. That's an order."

"I'm going to. I have about ten pounds' worth of correspondence to get through first."

"I mean it, Robert," Ellingham said more sternly. "The winter will be here soon and you'll wish you took advantage of days like this."

The remark was so thick with meaning that Robert had no reply.

"You're a good man, Robert," Ellingham said. "I wish you had the happiness in your life that I've had in mine. Remember to play. Remember the game. Always remember the game."

He would remember later that Albert Ellingham didn't look morose as he said these words. There was more vigor in him, suggesting, perhaps, that he was making a marble monument of his grief. Maybe it was time to resume life. It had been a year since the trial. Maybe it was time.

Robert ignored the order to go out and had a productive afternoon at his desk. He handled calls from New York and the new movie division in Los Angeles. He caught up on correspondence. He barely noticed the passing hours and the creeping dark. His mind felt lighter than it had in some time. Perhaps, he thought, everything might turn around a bit. Perhaps Albert Ellingham would begin to heal. He wasn't old. He was rich. He was vital. He might marry again, have another family. Perhaps the terrible curse on this place would be dispelled. Perhaps something would be made right again.

At seven thirty, Robert stopped, satisfied at all he had done. There was a tidy stack of completed paperwork. His correspondence tray was empty. It was fully dark and the wind had kicked up. It whistled around the corners of the room and snaked down the chimney.

Robert lit a fire and called for his supper. The cook was always happy to make food for someone who would actually eat, so soon he had a heaping plate of chops and creamed spinach and potatoes. He switched on the radio and settled down at his office table. He was looking forward to the Mercury Theatre program. They had done some very good shows recently, productions of Sherlock Holmes and *Around the World in 80 Days*. The program was one of the highlights of Robert's week.

Just as the music played and the announcer said, "*We take you now to Grover's Mills, New Jersey . . .*" the telephone rang. Robert put down his napkin, turned down the radio volume, and answered it.

"Robert Mackenzie," he said, wiping a touch of creamed spinach from the corner of his mouth.

"This is Sergeant Arnold." His voice was breathless and almost breaking. "Can you confirm, Albert Ellingham, his

403

boat . . . he took the boat out."

"Yes, hours ago," Robert replied. "With George Marsh."

"He hasn't returned yet?"

"No," Robert said. "He said he would likely stay in Burlington. What's going on?"

"There were reports of a boat going down off South Hero . . . ," the sergeant said. "An explosion . . ."

There was a hollow sound in Robert's ear, a feeling of falling, of many things converging to a point as he listened to the following words and low drum of the radio and the sound of his own heart echoing through the halls of his body. He would later say that he felt like he was floating up to the ceiling, looking down on the room for a moment.

He would always remember the strange conversation he'd had with Albert Ellingham that day. His Riddle of the Sphinx. The command to enjoy.

It was like Ellingham knew that that was his day to die.

The riddle would run through Robert's head for the rest of his life, but he never did figure out the solution.

30

It had been a long night.

The residents of Minerva had to stay out of the house while the police went through it. There were some rooms in the Great House reserved for when faculty or guests were snowed in. Janelle and Nate took these. David was in the faculty lounge on the sofa. Stevie sat awake, watchful on the massive staircase for hours and hours, her brain echoing with facts and riddles.

Always on a staircase but never on a stair. But she was always on a stair. All night on a stair.

She watched police and security come in and out, and Charles and Dr. Quinn and the school lawyer. A search was made of the property, but little could be done in the dark. The woods were dark and deep. There was talk of bears but not of moose.

Still, no moose.

A window was found propped open in the basement and a pile of boxes beneath it. Gone, gone, gone. Up the mountain. Down the mountain. Around the mountain. Who knew?

So Stevie sat in the throbbing heart of the Great House, once again the scene of a search in the night. In the wobbling version of reality playing in her tired and overextended brain, Stevie ran through the events of the last few weeks, finally settling on the message she had seen on her wall a few nights before Hayes died. *Riddle, riddle, on the wall . . .*

So many riddles.

She rubbed her hands over her face and covered it for a while. She nodded off like that for an unknown period of time, until she was awoken by a cup of coffee being held out to her.

"Not sure if you want to sleep like that," Larry said. "There's a cot in the security office and more sofas upstairs."

"I don't want to sleep."

"Sometimes it's not about what you want."

Stevie shook her head. "Did you find her?" she asked.

"It's getting light now. The chopper is coming in."

"Can I go outside? Get some air?"

Larry rocked back on his heels.

"Just stay right out where I can see you from the front," he said.

So Stevie took her coffee and sat on the wet grass of the green and stared at the Great House and stopped thinking for a while. Dawn broke over Ellingham Academy in a swirl of rose pink going into a bloodless blue. Stevie watched the newly risen sun come up over the Great House like a celestial game of peekaboo. She wasn't out there that long before she saw someone else come out the front door.

David made his way over in his easy, loping walk, his hands jammed into his pockets. He dropped down next to her and said nothing.

There is something about early mornings that changes your perceptions subtly. The light is new; no one has put on the defenses of the day. All is reset and not quite real yet.

Whatever had happened between David and Stevie didn't exist at this moment. Everything was dew and Larry's instant coffee and the gentle, buttery morning sun.

"Well," David finally said, "I guess the school's fucked."

Stevie took a long sip of the coffee. It was too strong and full of clots of powdered creamer, but it was wakeful.

"One student dead," David said, looking up at the faint sound of chopping from above. "One student missing, presumed to have murdered him, I guess. This one is going to be hard to spin."

"Yup," Stevie said, taking another sip.

The wind was cutting sharply through the mountains like an audible gasp from nature. A helicopter was nearing.

"I guess they're doing an air search," David said.

"Yup."

"You have a lot to say for someone who just busted open her first case. Aren't you excited? Don't you get a sheriff's star?"

Stevie put the coffee cup on the grass. She watched it for a moment to see if it was going to tip over and scald her. It did not.

"Let me just ask you," Stevie said. "The night that the

407

dry ice went into the tunnel, you said you were with Ellie. You were, right?"

"Until midnight or something," he said. "But I did lie to you. We weren't smoking a bowl. We were just talking."

"So you added that . . ."

"Just for fun," David said.

The helicopter was now visible, circling back over the woods.

"I still can't believe this," he said. "Ellie's not malicious. I get that something is happening here I don't understand, but she's not . . . she doesn't hurt people. Not on purpose, anyway. I don't know. Maybe I don't know anything."

"Do you have any idea what she was saying at the end?" she asked. "About how Hayes knew things? When she kept saying *this whole place* and Hayes's idea?"

"No clue."

Stevie rubbed the grass between her fingers until she stained her fingertips green. Maybe it was just the lack of sleep. She'd put it together. Ellie had admitted to writing the show. Ellie had bolted. Why run if you haven't done anything?

She thought of Hercule Poirot, and how he would hesitate when he lined up the facts and found that something did not tally. He always talked about the psychology of the crime. Things here were not clean. They were not clear.

Just like Vorachek. He had had the money in his possession. Vorachek even admitted to the crime. But there was no way it was Vorachek.

Two police officers came out of the trees from the direction of Minerva. One carried a box.

"It looks like they've gone through her stuff," David said. "I guess we can go back."

The both got up, stiff and tired, with wet-grass impressions on the backs of their clothes.

⚒

Minerva was silently creaky in the morning, filled with pale light and cool ghosts of old smoke. The moose had a more genial expression, and even the red wallpaper looked a bit less aggressive. The house felt hollow. It was empty of people at the moment, and at least two people were never coming back. Maybe no one was coming back.

Down the hall, Ellie's door hung a bit open. Stevie stood there for a moment, looking in through the space. David was close behind her. She could feel the heat coming off his body.

"You're going in, right?" he said. "That's your thing."

She didn't answer.

"I'm not arguing this time," he said, reaching over and pushing the door open wider.

The scene of their game hours before had been much disturbed. The police had pulled Ellie's bed away from the wall and left it slightly crooked toward the middle of the room. The covers had been pulled straight. Books were tipped down or taken from the shelves and stacked in neat piles. The drawers were all closed, which meant they'd gone through them all—last night most of Ellie's drawers were cocked or ajar with something sticking out of them.

"It actually looks cleaner in here after the cops went through it," David said.

He poked around the edge of the bed before sitting down. Stevie looked over at him. In the morning light, his face looked gentle. There was something a little—angelic about David. His large eyes and the light curl to his hair.

She remembered her mother commenting on the way in to the property that the statues were strange angels, and she had said no, those are sphinxes. Angels or sphinxes?

She really needed sleep.

She sat next to David on the bed and stared at Ellie's things. Her canvas backpack. The pile of dirty clothes in the corner. The scatter of pens on the floor. The little phrases she'd written on the walls. There was a framed picture next to her bed, one with dozens of people in it. That had to be the commune she had spoken of. Roota leaned against Ellie's bureau, glinting in the sun and looking lonely.

"I'm sorry," Stevie said, sort of to Roota and mostly to David.

"Sorry?"

"About going through your stuff. I've felt bad since the second I did it. I just . . . I don't know. I just wanted to know. About you. And you were being weird . . ."

"This is a great apology."

"Fine." She started again. "I was wrong."

The helicopter sounded like it was hanging overhead, beating the air. Ellingham would wake up and Ellie would be gone and there would be chaos again.

"Yeah," he said after a long moment.

"Yeah?"

He shrugged.

"If this whole place closes down, I guess we shouldn't be mad at each other."

"Probably not," she said.

The silence was long. Then David picked up her hand and, with one finger, he traced a small circle in her palm. Stevie was almost staggered by the flood of feeling. Could you kiss in the cool light of morning, when everything was visible? On the bed of your vanished classmate? Who probably killed someone?

He was leaning in a little, and in response, she leaned back just a bit. As she did so, her hand landed on something hard hiding in the bedding.

She pushed the quilt aside and revealed a small box. It was red metal, about eight by eight inches, with rounded corners. Age had taken a bit of a toll on it—it was dented and rusted, but still the artwork was fairly clear. It was marked OLD ENGLISH TEA BAGS and had a picture of a steaming cup of tea on the front. Some weird old junk.

There was something thrumming now.

Really thrumming.

Actually, that was the helicopter hovering very, very low. It was now impossible to ignore. David squinted at the window, then released Stevie's hand and got up to have a look.

Stevie took a deep breath and steadied herself. She examined the strange box, prying off the lid and pouring the contents onto the bed. There was what looked like the remains of a white feather, a torn piece of cloth with some beading on it, a gold lipstick tube. There was a square rhinestone clip and a miniature red enameled shoe that turned out to be a very tiny pillbox. Stevie opened and closed this a few times, peering into the dulled bronze interior.

"This is weird," she said. "Come look at this."

"Hang on," he said.

Stevie continued looking. Pressed on one side of the box was a piece of lined, folded paper and a dozen or so old black-and-white photographs, rough and unevenly sized. Stevie looked at the paper first. It was fragile along the sharp lines of the folds, but only a bit yellowed. Written in a neat but loose handwriting was the following:

The Ballad of Frankie and Edward
April 2, 1936

Frankie and Edward had the silver
Frankie and Edward had the gold
But both saw the game for what it was
And both wanted the truth to be told

Frankie and Edward bowed to no king
They lived for art and love
~~They unseated the man who ruled over the land~~
They took

The king was a joker who lived on a hill
And he wanted to rule the game
So Frankie and Edward played a hand
And things were never the same

The photographs pictured two teenagers, one male and one female, in a variety of poses that were both familiar to Stevie and utterly baffling at the same time. The guy wore a suit and hat with a loosened tie. The girl, a tight sweater and skirt set with a cocked beret. They posed in front of a car in one photo. In another, the girl had a cigar. In another, they were face-to-face, the girl holding the guy back at arm's length. Stevie flipped the photos over. On the back of one was written *11/4/35*.

Stevie stared at the photos for a long moment before it clicked. These people were posing like Bonnie and Clyde, the famous 1930s outlaw couple. They were *cosplaying*.

One of the photos was different; it was a touch thicker, heavier. Stevie examined this one more carefully and found that it was actually two photos stuck together. She ignored the sound of the landing helicopter out on the green. This—whatever this weird collection of photos and items was—was extremely important. She tried to pull the photos apart delicately, and when that failed, pulled with more force. They started to give way. There was something stuck between them. It looked like . . .

A word? From a magazine?

It was the clipped out word *US* in bright red letters on a yellow background. Tiny. Maybe a quarter of an inch.

Stevie's hand began to shake.

A letter cut from a magazine in a box of things that were dated from 1935–36. Photos of two people her age cosplaying Bonnie and Clyde. And part of a poem—a poem not unlike the Truly Devious letter, written only days before the Truly Devious letter arrived. A rough, short poem about playing some kind of game with the king who lived on the hill.

This was Truly Devious. Whoever wrote this poem, whoever Frankie and Edward were. Stevie ran through her mind attic feverishly, tearing open boxes, looking in drawers. She was far away from this strange morning and David and Ellie's room. There. She had it. She was looking at a page of a witness statement taken from Leonard Holmes Nair about a boy and a girl he thought showed some spark. They were a pair. She had hair like a raven and he looked like Lord Byron, and the girl asked him about Dorothy Parker. Two students from the first class at Ellingham Academy.

Students had written the letter. She had proof of that in her hand.

Had students murdered Iris Ellingham? Was Dottie's murder committed by people who knew her well? Was this about *Dottie*? Stevie's mind was whirring.

"David . . . ," Stevie said. There was a tremble in her voice.

In response, David left the room. He was walking with some speed. His departure was so abrupt that Stevie couldn't quite make the mental leap for a moment. She blinked, and then, still clutching the photos, she followed him. He was already out the door, walking toward the green. The helicopter was there, its rotors slowing. There were some people out now. Ellingham was awake.

It wasn't a police helicopter. The lettering was dark bronze, faintly reflective. It said . . .

King?

David had stopped abruptly at the top of the path leading to the green and was staring at the helicopter.

"What the hell is happening?" Stevie said, catching up to him. "Is that what it looks like?"

David did not answer, but he didn't need to. The helicopter door opened and someone stepped out.

In life, Edward King was smaller than he appeared on television, his expression more hassled, his hair blowing strangely in all directions. He ineffectively tried to smooth it down.

David still hadn't moved. It was as if he had turned into one of Ellingham's many statues, a stone replica of himself.

In myths, Medusa turned you to stone if you looked directly at her.

"How is this happening?" Stevie said. "Why is it happening? What is happening? David?"

David did not reply.

And then, the convergence. All the facts in Stevie's brain attic assembled themselves in the necessary order. She did a number of tiny calculations, working out the proportions of his face. Her mind flashed back to that first moment she saw him in the yurt, that weird dislike, the thing that scratched-scratched at her mind. The angle of the nose, the bearing of the shoulders . . .

She couldn't place it then. There was no way she could have. It was all so impossible.

Edward King was making his way across the grass in their general direction.

Now it was a torrent of calculations. David's avoidance, his lack of social media, his lack of photographs, the move to California, the beaten Rolex . . .

"David," she said quietly.

He did not look at her.

"David?" she said one last time.

He glanced sideways at her. He looked helpless, trapped.

"Remember when your parents got that position?" David finally said. "With him? Well. I told you I was trying to help."

Stevie's grip on the photos tightened, though she had forgotten she was holding them.

"Tell me what you mean," she said.

David started to smile, but it was like the smile Stevie pasted on her face that night at dinner with her parents. With every second, her hope slipped a bit further, until she was scrabbling at the edge of hope, trying to gain a hold. And then she felt herself lose contact.

"Meet my dead dad," he replied.

To be continued . . .

ACKNOWLEDGMENTS

I HAVE MANY PEOPLE TO THANK.

First and foremost, thank you to Katherine Tegen. There would be no *Truly Devious* without her.

Thank you to the many people who shepherded this book through the editorial process—my editor, Beth Dunfey; Mabel Hsu; and all of the staff at Katherine Tegen Books. Thank you to Anica Rissi, who first brought me into the Katherine Tegen fold.

My agent, Kate Schafer Testerman, keeps me alive. She assisted in this effort by my assistant, Felicity Disco (or Kate Welsh, as she is *sometimes known*). Without them, who knows? I dare not speculate.

I can honestly say that without the help of my friend Robin Wasserman, this book would not exist. And it is impossible to overstate the support and help I've gotten from Cassandra Clare, Holly Black, and Sarah Rees Brennan.

Thank you to Daniel Sinker, who insisted I come along with him and make something called the *Says Who?* podcast. This has contributed greatly to my sanity, such as it is.

Thank you to Dr. Jason Sutula and Erin Wert, RN, for the scientific and medical help.

Thank you to Oscar and Zelda. I love you.

Thanks to my mom for nursing me through a long-term illness while I wrote.

And there are countless people who improve my life on a day-to-day basis. If you've read to the bottom of the acknowledgments page, you are probably one of them. This one is for YOU. Yes, YOU.

Read on for a sneak peek of THE VANISHING STAIR

Book Two of the TRULY DEVIOUS trilogy

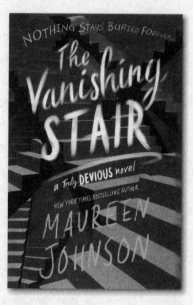

OUT OF EVERYTHING IN HER PITTSBURGH NEIGHBORHOOD, THE Funky Munkee coffee shop was the thing that reminded Stevie Bell most of Ellingham Academy, though there was nothing about the place that was actually similar. It was a 1990s relic, with a sign written in a kooky festival font. It had walls painted in bright, primary colors, each wall a different shade. It played an obligatory coffeehouse soundtrack of mid-tempo guitar music. There were blown-up pictures of coffee beans, and plants and wobbly tables to sit at, and oversized mugs. None of which were features of her previous school.

The part she liked, and the part that was like Ellingham, was that it wasn't her house, and when she was here, no one bothered her.

Every day this week she had come and ordered the smallest, cheapest coffee. She would take this to the back of the shop, to a stuffy, small alcove room with red walls. The room was dark and dingy, the tables unbalanced and always a bit sticky. Everyone else avoided it, which is why Stevie liked it. This was her office now, where she did her most important work. If she had tried to do this at home, her parents might walk in. Here, she was in public, but no one actually cared what she was doing or even noticed her.

She put her headphones on but played no music—she needed some muffled silence. She put her backpack on the table, zipper facing her, and opened it. First, she removed a pair of nitrile gloves. These she had purchased at CVS the day she returned. It was probably an unnecessary precaution at this stage, but still, it could not hurt. She snapped them on. It was a very satisfying feeling. Using both hands, she reached down to the bottom of her bag and removed a small, battered tea tin.

The tin was too valuable to leave at home. When you find something of historical importance, you keep it close. It stayed with Stevie wherever she went—locked in her locker during the day, tucked in her bag at home. Out of sight. She periodically reached around to touch the lump on her backpack where it rested inside to make sure it was secure.

The tin was square and red, dented in several places, with rust along the lip. It read OLD ENGLISH TEA BAGS. She opened the lid. It stuck a bit, so it required a gentle wiggle. From inside she produced: a bit of white feather, a bit of beaded cloth, a tarnished, gold-colored lipstick tube with the mummified remains of a red lipstick, a tiny enameled pillbox in the shape of a shoe, and some pieces of notebook paper and black-and-white photographs, and the unfinished draft of a poem.

These humble objects were the first pieces of real evidence in the Ellingham case in over eighty years. And the moment Stevie uncovered them was the moment her Ellingham dreams fell apart.

Ellingham. Her former school. Ellingham, the place she had dreamed of going. The place she had made it to for a short time. And Ellingham, the place that was now behind her.

No one in Pittsburgh really understood what happened at Ellingham. They only knew that Stevie had left to go to some famous school, and then that YouTube guy died in an accident there, and Stevie came back a few weeks later.

As to why Stevie was back in Ellingham? Well, there was the death of Hayes Major. That was the start of it. But the person who was responsible for Stevie Bell's parents hauling her out of Ellingham Academy was named Germaine Batt, and she did it entirely by accident.

Everyone at Ellingham Academy had a *thing*, and

Germaine Batt's thing was reporting. Before Hayes's death, she had a modest site and a small following. But death is good business if you are in the news. "If it bleeds, it leads," as they say. (*They* being . . . Stevie wasn't sure. People said it. It meant that bloody, gray, horrible stories always go to the top, which is why the news is always bad. People don't care when things go well. News equals bad.)

The piece that did Stevie in came out the day after Stevie confronted Element Walker about creating the show *The End of It All*. She knew that Ellie had taken Hayes's computer and stashed it under the bathtub in Minerva. Stevie also knew that Hayes could not have been the person who used the pass to get the dry ice that would kill him.

So, Hayes did not get the thing that killed him.

Also, Hayes did not write the show that made him famous, the one that was about to get him a movie deal. Ellie did that.

That was all Stevie was trying to tell everyone on the night in question. Ellie had been confronted, first in Minerva, and then in the Great House after Nate called for help. And Ellie had vanished from a locked room, specifically from Albert Ellingham's office. Just like that. *Poof.* She had gone into the walls of Albert Ellingham's office, through a hidden passage, and from there . . . out. Away. Somewhere.

The school did not release that information. Ellie wasn't officially guilty of anything. She was a student who ran away from her boarding school. Except Stevie's parents had a Google alert for all things Ellingham after Hayes's death, and that's how they saw the Batt Report blog post about how Stevie had been investigating Hayes's death, and now there was a potential killer on the loose. Two hours after Germaine's story appeared, Stevie's phone rang, and ten hours after that, her parents were roaring up the drive to Ellingham, despite the school rules about no outside vehicles. The night had been tearful; Stevie cried all the way back to Pittsburgh, silently and without pause, staring out the car window until she fell asleep. The next Monday, she was back in her old school, hastily inserted into some classes.

The trick was not to think about Ellingham too much—the buildings, the smell of the air, the freedom, the adventure, the people . . .

Especially not the people.

She could send messages to her friends Janelle and Nate. Mostly Janelle. And mostly it was Janelle sending them to her, dozens a day, checking in on how she was. Stevie could only reply to every third or fourth one, because replying meant thinking about how she missed seeing Janelle in the hall, in the common room, across the table. How she missed knowing her friend was on the other side of the wall as she slept—Janelle, who smelled of lemons or orange blossom, who wrapped her hair in one of her dozens of colorful scarves to keep it safe while she worked with industrial equipment. Janelle was a maker, a builder of small robotics and other devices, who was currently preparing a Rube Goldberg machine for the Sendel Waxman competition. Her texts indicated she had been spending a lot more time in the maintenance shed building since Stevie had been gone, and that she was getting much more serious with Vi Harper-Tomo. Janelle's life was full, and she wanted Stevie to be in it, and Stevie felt far and cold and none of that made sense here, at the shopping center with the Subway and the beer and cigarette place, in the Funky Munkee.

But she had the tin, and as long as she had the tin, she had the Ellingham case.

She'd found the tin in Ellie's room shortly before she left. She had dated it using online images. It was from somewhere between 1925 and 1940, and the tea was popular and widely sold. The feather was about four inches long and looked like it may have been attached to a piece of clothing. The cloth was two inches square and was a luminous blue, with silver, blue, and black beads, and had torn edges. Another piece of detritus. The lipstick had the word KISSPROOF on the side. It had been used, but not entirely. The pillbox was the only thing that looked like it might have value. It was just over two inches in length. It was empty.

These four items Stevie thought of as a group. They were personal, they concerned jewelry or clothing. The feather and the torn cloth were junk, so the reason for saving them was mysterious. The lipstick and the pill case could have had value. All of these items likely belonged to a woman. They were intimate. They *meant* something to whoever put them in this tin.

The other two items probably had a lot more significance.

They were a set of photographs of two people pretending to be Bonnie and Clyde. Stevie stared at them until her sight went blurry. The girl had dark hair cut in a sharp bob. Stevie had Googled some pictures of Lord Byron, the poet, and found he did have a resemblance to the boy in the photos. They had written a poem about themselves. But who *were* they? The trouble was, there were no online records of all the names of the early Ellingham students. Their names had never mattered—they were never part of the case. So they weren't printed anywhere. Stevie had searched the internet, read down every thread on every message board she frequented on the case. At the time or in the following years, a few students had come forward and given statements or spoken to the press. The one who appeared the most was a Gertrude van Coevorden, a New York City debutante who claimed to have been Dottie Epstein's best friend. She gave tearful interviews for weeks after the kidnappings. That was not helpful.

Then, there was the poem. It wasn't a good poem. It wasn't even a whole poem.

The Ballad of Frankie and Edward
April 2, 1936

Frankie and Edward had the silver
Frankie and Edward had the gold
But both saw the game for what it was
And both wanted the truth to be told

Frankie and Edward bowed to no king
They lived for art and love
~~*They unseated the man who ruled over the land*~~
They took

The king was a joker who lived on a hill
And he wanted to rule the game
So Frankie and Edward played a hand
And things were never the same

Stevie didn't know a lot about poetry, but she knew about true crime. Bonnie Parker, the famous 1930s outlaw who Frankie was modeling herself after in the pictures, wrote poetry as well, including a famous one called "The Story of Suicide Sal," which was all about a woman in love with a gangster. This poem looked like it was modeled on hers.

And there were several things in the poem that seemed to be about Albert Ellingham—the mention of games, the king who was a joker who lived on a hill. And in the poem Frankie and Edward did *something*, but what, the poem never says.

There was only one thing she could find that might explain anything about Edward and Frankie. Stevie had read the police interviews with the various suspects many times; they were collected in an ebook she kept on her phone. She had flagged a section in which Leonard Holmes Nair, the famous painter who was staying with the Ellinghams at the time of the kidnapping, described some of the students:

LHN: You see them all, milling around. You know, Albert opened this place and said he was going to fill it with prodigies, but fully half of them are just his friends' children and not the sharpest ones at that. The other half are probably all right. If I'm being fair, there were one or two others that showed a bit of a spark. A boy and a girl, I forget their names. The two of them seemed to be a pair. The girl had hair like a raven and the boy looked a bit like Byron. They were interested in poetry. They had a little light behind the eyes. The girl asked me about Dorothy Parker, which I took as a hopeful sign. I'm a friend of Dorothy's.

There was no question in Stevie's mind that these two students described by Leonard Holmes Nair were the same two students in these photographs.

Anyway, the critical clue was actually contained in the photographs—or rather, between them.

Her phone buzzed. There was a text message from her mom: WHERE ARE YOU?

Stevie sighed.

WALKING HOME.

GET A MOVE ON, she replied.

It was only four o'clock. At Ellingham, Stevie's time was her own. When she ate, what she ate, when and where she studied, what she did between classes . . . all of that was up to her. There was no one looking over her shoulder.

She drained her coffee and returned the items to the tin, packing them as carefully as she had found them. Head-phones back on her head, she started the rest of the walk home. It was the lead-up to Halloween, and every business and home had a pumpkin or an autumnal banner. There was still a little late-summer lift in the air before the cold snapped down and killed everything right to ground level.

Winter would be unbearable here.

Her phone rang. The only calls Stevie got were from her parents and from Janelle. She was surprised to see Nate's number appear. Nate was not a caller.

"Let me guess," Stevie said, on answering. "You're writing."

Nate Fisher was a writer. At least, he was supposed to be.

When he was fourteen, he wrote a book called *The Moonbeam Chronicles*. It started out as a hobby. Then, as he published parts of it online, it grew more and more popular until it had a robust fandom and Nate wound up as a published author. He had even gone on a book tour and appeared on some morning shows. He had gotten into Ellingham on the back of this achievement. Stevie got the impression that he liked it there because it was remote and people left him alone. At home, he was that writer kid. He didn't like publicity. His social anxiety made every event a nightmare. Ellingham was a retreat in the mountains where he could be among people who also did weird things. The only problem was, he was supposed to be writing book two, and book two did not want to be written. Nate's entire existence was avoiding the writing of book two of the Moonbeam Chronicles.

Which is why, Stevie surmised, Nate was calling her.

"Not going well?" she asked.

"You don't know my life."

"It's that bad?"

"Do books have to have a middle?" he said.

"I think whatever happens in the middle is probably the middle," Stevie said.

"What if there's just a beginning where I tell you everything that happened in book one in a series of contrivances, like found scrolls and speeches and drunk bards at the tavern who tell the story to some traveler and then it's like two hundred pages of question marks and then I explain where the dragon is?"

"Is there kissing?" she asked.

"I hate you."

"You can't write *anything*?"

"Let's just say that I needed to have Moonbeam fight something and the only thing I could come up with was called the Pulsating Norb. It's like a wall that jiggles. The best thing I came up with this week is a wall that jiggles called the Pulsating Norb. I need you to come back here and kill me."

"Wish I could," Stevie said, hitting the button to cross the intersection. "I'd like to meet a Pulsating Norb."

"How is it there?" he said.

"The same, squared. It's my house. My parents are still my parents. School is still school. I didn't realize how much the place stinks like cafeteria and hot dishwater before. Ellingham is all . . . woody."

When she called up the sense memory, Stevie felt a pain run through her. Like a punch in the gut.

"So how's everyone else?" she said quickly.

"Uh . . . Janelle is all in love and power tools. And David, I guess . . ."

And David, he guessed. Nate paused long enough for Stevie to know that there was a *there* there. Only Janelle knew most of the facts—that Stevie and David Eastman were some kind of thing. David was an annoying rich boy, scruffy and difficult. Whatever ability he had—and apparently he had considerable ability in computer programming—he hid from the school and others. His likes were video games, not going to class, not talking about his past . . .

And Stevie.

Janelle knew that David and Stevie had made out several times. Nate likely guessed; he did not want to know details, but it would have been evident. There was something neither of them knew about David. Something Stevie was holding on to. Something that could not be said.

"David what?" Stevie said, trying not to sound too interested.

"Nothing. I should go, I guess. . . ."

Stevie suspected that Nate wasn't going because he was going to write; he was going because this was probably the longest phone conversation he had ever had, at least voluntarily.

"My parents have a sign hanging in the bathroom that I think sums it up," Stevie said. "It says: 'Believe in yourself.'

Do you want me to send you a pic? Do you want me to send you a whole bunch of inspirational quotes?"

"Good-bye," he said. "You're the worst."

Stevie smiled.

It always hurt, but now it hurt a tiny bit less. She picked up her chin and took firm, decisive steps. She'd read somewhere that the way you move could influence your inner state—take on the shape of the thing you wanted to be. FBI agents walked decisively. Detectives kept their heads up, their eyes moving around. She fastened her hands on her backpack straps to pull herself to a straighter stance. She would not be broken. She quickened her steps and almost bounded up the crumbling concrete path to her front door, turning away, as she always did, from the weathered KING FOR SENATE sign that was still on their lawn a year after the election was over.

"Hey," she said, knocking the headphones down to her neck and pulling off her coat. "I decided to walk. . . ."

It seemed they had a visitor.

New York Times bestselling author
MAUREEN JOHNSON
returns with the thrilling Truly Devious series!

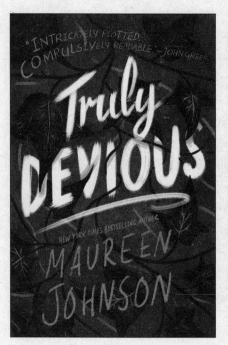 

A riddle. A disappearance. A murder.
Can you solve the mystery?